THE

WHISPERING

DARK

THE WHISPERING DARK

KELLY ANDREW

SCHOLASTIC PRESS/NEW YORK

Library of Congress Cataloging-in-Publication Data available

ISBN 978-1-338-80947-3

10 9 8 7 6 5 4 3 2 1   22 23 24 25 26

Printed in the U.S.A.   37

First edition, October 2022

Book design by Maeve Norton

FOR ANYONE WHO KNOWS WHAT IT IS TO
FEEL ALONE IN A CROWD, OR TO DRAW
SOLACE FROM DAYDREAMS

PART ONE

THE RESURRECTION
OF COLTON PRICE

The gates of hell are open night and day;
Smooth the descent, and easy is the way:
But to return, and view the cheerful skies,
In this the task and mighty labor lies.

Virgil, *The Aeneid*

1

Delaney Meyers-Petrov wasn't made of glass, but sometimes she felt as though she might be. The early-September morning was bright and warm, the wide green square of Howe's tree-lined quad banded in thin sapling shadows. Overhead, the bluebird sky was laced in pale, pretty clouds, and it wasn't so much that she felt close to breaking, but rather that her parents were watching her as if she would.

Her parents, who she'd asked repeatedly to stay home. Her parents, who were terrible at listening, for two people whose ears worked perfectly well. Her parents, who had vehemently ignored her requests and had shown up on her first day of class—woefully out of place among the climber ivy and the baked-red brick and the buildings hewn from old money—with a sign on which they'd written her name.

WE LOVE YOU, LANEY!

The inscription was done in fat black letters. The poster paper was bubble-gum pink. The entire experience was, as far as experiences went, extraordinarily humiliating. More than one student on the quad was pointing. Perched under the slender branches of a fledgling elm, her mother didn't appear to notice the attention she attracted. At her side, Delaney's father looked positively out of place, his arms inked in grayscale sleeves, his hair slicked back, his beard threaded silver. His expression was a mug shot capture, and though the other students on the walkway gave him and his scowl as wide a berth as physically possible, Delaney could tell that the tight line of her father's mouth was only there because he was doing his very best not to cry.

Shouldering her briefcase bag and swallowing her pride, she wriggled her fingers in as inconspicuous a goodbye as she could manage. And then off she went, careful to keep to the sunniest of spaces, stepping over shadows the same way small children skipped over clefts in the sidewalk—*Don't step on the crack or you'll break your mother's back.* Every step she took—the children's rhyme looping between her ears, her parents cheering for her like spectators at Fenway, the shadows cool and leering—she felt less and less like an incoming college student and more like a child toddling to her first day of preschool, lunch box in hand.

It was, she supposed, sidestepping an elongated branch of dark, hard to fault her parents. Brittle of bone and prone to catching cold, she'd cut her teeth on the edge of death well before she could read. She'd slipped away in a hospital bed, lights winking and machinery humming, and resurfaced from the cataleptic dark to find her ears no longer worked. She was left with silence whispering in her head and shadows whispering at her feet and the very distinct feeling that she'd been somehow fractured on the inside.

Every silent day since then, she'd been handled with care.

A glass girl, in a glass menagerie, all the world a whispered hush.

If she was honest with herself, Delaney Meyers-Petrov had never really expected to go to college. Her parents made modest incomes— the kind that kept the lights on, not the kind that paid tuition. Free spirits, they spent their evenings booking spoken-word gigs at local indie venues, their days driving Delaney out to Walden Pond to skip stones across the water. They didn't put much stock in things like capitalism and folded laundry and formal academia.

Little breakable Delaney hadn't just fallen far from the tree. Her apple had been picked up by a grazing deer, carried over meadow and hummock, and discarded miles away. While her parents eschewed the notion of higher education—*"It's just an expensive piece of paper, Laney; it doesn't define you"*—she wanted nothing more. She wanted the regimen, the freedom, the promise of opportunity.

She wanted the chance to prove she was made of tougher stuff than glass.

She *wanted* to be defined. Not by the silence between her ears or her fear of the dark, but by the sum of her achievements. Not by what she couldn't do, but by what she could.

That was why, the minute she was of age, she'd gone online and registered for the placement scholarship. The applicant exam was an intensive labor, spanning the course of a week. It assessed mental and physical health, personal aptitudes, and, the forms ominously noted, *etcetera*. Her results, once factored, would determine her placement in a field that most closely matched her individual skill set.

The needs-based fellowship came with a single caveat: They'd pay her tuition in full, so long as she agreed to go wherever she was placed.

Her parents had been visibly hesitant, but their abhorrence of discipline meant they wouldn't ever force her hand. *"Lane,"* they'd said, *"if it's a degree you want, there are plenty of online programs with manageable tuitions. Not only that, but they'll be far more accommodating to your needs. There's no bar here. You don't have anything to prove."*

But Delaney did.

Not to other people, but to herself. She'd been handled with white gloves all her life, kept high on a shelf, and it wouldn't do to sit up there forever, collecting dust. Glass, she'd learned, was terribly easy to crack, but the pressure it could weather was immense. She wanted to parse out her limits, even if doing so earned her a few nicks. She wanted the chance to melt herself down and shape herself into something new.

Someone capable of conquering the world all on her own.

Someone who wasn't eighteen years old and still afraid of the dark.

The first day of the exam, she and three hundred other hopefuls spent the morning locked in the echoing chamber of a public high school gymnasium. She'd felt, as she often did in wide, empty spaces, the soft tiptoe of unease down her spine, the unsettled ruffle of shadows along her periphery.

It was a bad habit—her tendency to personify the dark. To imagine it restless, the way she had when she'd been little and lonely and looking for a friend. To fear the way it drew her eye, the way it pulled at her like a tide. As the proctor rattled off rules she couldn't hear, she'd busied herself with setting her pencils into a neatly sharpened line and done her best not to stare into the gymnasium's murky corners.

The second day of testing, the aspirants had been called one by one into a little wan room by a little wan man, made to sit in a polypropylene chair with the legs gone loose. There, the darkness had pressed cool and close. It fell across her lap in shallow pools of blue. It coiled against her like a happy cat.

Hello, she imagined it said. *Hello, hello.*

Across from her, the interviewer watched her much too closely, firing off a series of seemingly unrelated questions. Delaney fidgeted on the edge of her seat and did her best to read his lips beneath the wiry fringe of his mustache. She kicked herself for imagining the way the shadows purred.

On the third day, Delaney was swapping out the dull lead of one pencil for the pin-sharp nib of another when the proctor summoned her by name. *"Delaney Meyers-Petrov?"* Several curious heads picked up. *"I'd like to see you in the hall."* Ears burning, she followed the thin slip of a woman out of the gym and into the menthol-green colonnade of lockers. The slam of the fire doors rattled her teeth.

"Pack your bag, Ms. Meyers-Petrov," the proctor said, without pre-amble. *"You're done here."*

The elimination hit like a sucker punch. Delaney wanted to push back. She wanted to resist. But she hadn't been built to cross lines, and so she thanked the proctor and slunk back inside to pack up her things. That afternoon, she'd lain in bed and thought of all the things she might have done wrong. When dusk settled, she'd felt the dark of her room *tsk* reproachfully at her, and a bubble of shame beaded deep inside her chest.

Maybe she'd answered a question wrong.

Maybe they didn't want an applicant who couldn't hear.

Maybe they thought she was a little bit odd, this girl who side-eyed the dark.

And then. *And then.* One day, on a very unremarkable Tuesday morning, she received a letter in the mail. It was late April, the days wet and insipid. She'd huddled by the mailbox, fingers numb, and torn into the seal of the Grants and Scholarships Committee, all hard wax and insignia. The header was embossed in glimmering silver, the paper fine cream-colored card stock.

Ms. Delaney Meyers-Petrov,

Congratulations on a job well done. You are a recipient of our needs-based placement fellowship. Due to your decidedly unique capabilities, the placement committee has determined that your talents would be best utilized in a neo-anthropological field. As such, you have been assigned to Howe University's Godbole School of Neo-Anthropological Studies. The scholarship will be sent directly to the college, indicating that it can be used for tuition, fees, or books.

Your presence is expected at the Godbole building, auditorium B, on the morning of September 1st. More information pertaining to your placement can be accessed on the global student portal. Please see the attached documents for your login information. If you have any questions, feel free to call the student resources department at the number listed below.

At the bottom, the signature of a board member was signed in a looping scrawl. She'd stood there for a long time afterward, rain needling her skin. She'd heard of Godbole. Everyone had. It was a highly prestigious yet controversial program, a magnet for those who dabbled in the occult.

It's all smoke and mirrors, she'd seen someone comment, when a leaked video purported to show a Godbole student slipping between worlds. *Anyone with a laptop can doctor footage. These students are paying into a sham.*

The video looked like something out of *The Twilight Zone*. One instant, the student stood perfectly still and stared behind the camera, waiting for a cue. Then, with a nod, he took a single step. The sky swallowed him up. The air rippled like water in his wake. He didn't reappear.

Unique capabilities, her letter said.

People had used plenty of adjectives to define Delaney Meyers-Petrov in her eighteen silent turns around the sun. Tragic Delaney, who'd fallen too sick too young. Fearful Delaney, who still slept with the lights on. Fragile Delaney, who needed constant coddling.

But capable Delaney—that was something new.

She liked the fit of it, like an unwashed sweater.

And so, on a bluebird day in September, she packed up her things and she went. To conquer the world, and maybe some others. To prove that she could.

She took a breath and she took a step.

And the shadows followed.

Howe University looked like everything Septembers were meant to embody—like bricks and books and new beginnings. It smelled like it, too. Fresh-cut grass and petrichor, coffee grounds and vanillin and the faint, autumnal smack of sour apples.

At the far side of the quad sat the Godbole building. An imposing glass monolith, it sparked like a diamond in the light, a structural incongruity among the neat rows of ivy-clad brick.

The irony didn't escape her. A glass girl, bound for a glass palace.

The chilly cling of early autumn faded away the moment Delaney stepped inside. The foyer was minimalist in design and built for aesthetic. At the room's crux, a colorless floral arrangement of dripping hyacinths sat atop a sleek marble plinth. At the windows, the sun fell and fell. Each slap of her combat boots across linoleum cracked through the space in a startling eddy of thunder, and she was unsure— as ever—if the sound was magnified only by her cochlear implant, or to everyone in the vicinity.

Fortunately, there appeared to be no one else in the vicinity, only Delaney Meyers-Petrov and endless dazzling white. She wasn't sure if she liked it. The rest of the campus looked like old money and old books, all brick and ivy and nostalgia. But Godbole—Godbole looked like the future. It looked like Januarys, bleak and severe.

She rounded a corner, tailed by the warped slip of her reflection in the glass—high pigtails deepening to a pale periwinkle, black blouse framed by a white baby-doll collar, all punk and pastels. *Loud*, a woman on the T called her outfit once. Loud, to make up for the unassailable quiet. Amid the sterile white of Godbole, she stuck out like a sore thumb.

And she was alone, which meant she was likely late. She hated being late.

Up ahead sat a pair of elevators, one set of doors steadily trundling shut. She caught diminishing sight of a figure within—gray sweater and burgundy tie, the neat gloss of chestnut curls. A single striking eye met hers through the thinning gap.

"Hey," she called out, breaking into a run. "Could you hold the—"

The doors clicked shut just as she skidded to a stop, her nose inches from the crack.

"Asshole," she said into the metal panel, and jabbed the button with her thumb. Once, twice, three times for good measure. She stepped back to wait for the other elevator to make its way down from the fifth floor, conscious of the steady trickle of seconds passing her by.

To her horror, the first elevator ground back open. Inside stood the stranger. He lounged against the wall, hands braced on the rail, the round face of his watch winking in the light. His hooded eyes were the color of coffee, his straight nose framed by pale, prominent cheek-bones. His mouth was a dagger, unsmiling. The shadows pressed against him in a way that felt hungry—like they had teeth, and he was something sweet. Like everything about him beckoned the dark.

The stranger's brows drew together at the sight of her. He looked, she thought, surprised.

"Lane," he said.

❦ 2 ❧

The day Colton Price came back from the dead, he'd opened his eyes to find a little girl peering down at him. The sky was a mid-March blue, whipped in white and fringed with trees. She bowed over him, sunlight streaming around her braids. A flat stone was clenched in her mittened hand, primed for skipping.

He'd gasped for air, exhaling in cold, murky breaths. The sucking mud pulled at his clothes. Pond water lapped against his skin. *Hush*, it said. *Hush. Hush. Hush.* He didn't understand. When he'd died, the pond had been frozen. Winter thick, but not dense enough to bear the weight of two young boys on skates.

He'd felt it crack beneath him seconds before he fell through. Like a bone cleaving in two. Like the tectonic shift of plates. He'd listed to the side, his skates going akimbo, and met his brother's wide-eyed stare. "*Liam*," he'd cried. And then he'd gone under. His teeth cracked together against the broken shelf. His gloves scrabbled for purchase. It was no use. The water swallowed him whole.

Lying on the shore, feeling slow-crept back into his limbs. His jaw ached. It was a dull, heartbeat pain that pricked when the wind blew. He'd been dead. He'd been *dead*. At nine years old, he'd known little of death, but he recognized it when it came for him. His heart had slowed to a stop. He'd watched his vision go black.

But there was his heartbeat, hammering beneath his bones.

And there was the little girl, a study in rainbows. Rainbow stockings. Rainbow mittens. Rainbow bows. He was alive, alive, alive, and the girl was watching him out of an owl-eyed stare, stark and suspicious.

"Are you a boy," she whispered, "or are you a shadow?"

His chest heaved in reply. The water in his lungs tasted like dirt. He rolled onto his side, coughing, coughing. Water needled his face. Mud squelched, and he glanced up to find the little girl crouched down, pond water lapping at her pink rubber boots. The fringe of one braid tickled his jaw.

"The water's too cold for swimming," she said, as if he were flailing in the muck of his own volition. "You need to get up."

Something cracked in the woods. A car door slamming shut. Startled, a magpie took flight. It careened through the air with a rasping *kureeek*. A woman's voice carried through the balsam trees. "Lane? Laney, don't wander off."

Then a man: "She's gone ahead to the water. I don't think she can hear you."

The girl reached out and touched a mitten to Colton's chin. The wool came away red. She held it up between them for inspection. "You're bleeding."

Colton was distinctly aware of the wrongness of his circumstance. The sky was the same. The trees were the same. The pond was the same. But the air—the air was several degrees too warm. This was not, he thought wildly, the same day that he'd fallen through the ice.

"Lane!"

The girl's head whipped around. "Mama," she called. "Mama, I found a boy in the water!"

The realization that Liam was missing snapped something deep in Colton's chest. He flopped onto his stomach, army crawling through the muck. Seconds ago, his brother had been there. Skating out onto the ice after him. He was sure of it.

Liam, pulsed his thoughts as he dug through silt and scum. *Liam, Liam, Liam.*

"Wait!" The girl splashed after him. "What are you doing? You'll drown."

She seized his arm, drawing him back. He snatched at her, choking, afraid. He'd meant to shove her off him, but his hand only closed on the purple cuff of her jacket sleeve. A tether. A handhold. He couldn't bring himself to let go. He could feel something tugging him, like a thread wound around his ribs.

He didn't want it to take him again.

The water, dark and cold.

The strange pulsing in his skin.

The feeling, odd as it was, that some small piece of him had been scooped clean out of his chest.

The little girl looked down at him, frowning. Her leggings were striped with red, orange, yellow, and green. Drowning had been cold and dark, but every part of her was bright, bright, bright. Her tiny mitten cuffed his wrist. The stitching was lumpy, done by hand.

"Don't let go," he pleaded. "Don't let go of me."

"Okay," she said, so unafraid.

He meant to speak again, but when he opened his mouth, there was the dirt in his lungs. There was that buzzing in his empty chest, the tight spool along his bones. His arms ached, as if he'd dragged himself some unfathomable distance. Somewhere nearby, he heard the sound of running feet. He burbled, choking and fading and so, so very afraid, and the world shut up silent as a tomb.

She was standing in front of him.

Lane. His Lane. It was Monday, and there she was. It was 10:40 in the morning, and there she was. It was impossible.

And there she was.

She was four feet away from him, and for the second time that day, the elevator doors were about to slam shut in her face. He leaned over and jabbed a button, halting their advance. She watched him with a razor-sharp acuity. She didn't move. Her cheeks were pinked, her wide-eyed stare fringed by dark lashes. With slow-budding alarm, he realized he'd spoken her name right out loud.

Lane.

As if he knew her. As if the years hadn't rendered them strangers.

He was an idiot. This shouldn't have come as a surprise. He'd known she'd be here today. Lane. His Lane. In his school. In his personal space. In his immediate orbit. He'd been briefed of her imminent arrival well in advance. Warned, really.

"It's happened. The Meyers-Petrov girl has been accepted to the program. She's to start in September. You'll keep away from her, Price, do you understand?"

He jabbed the button again. The doors rattled on their track like ponies at the gate. Because he had to say something, he said, "Are you planning to get into the elevator at some point today?"

He'd meant it to come out cordial. Instead, the strain of his surprise robbed him of tact. His delivery was bladed. She blinked and pushed past him in a huff, the pert tip of her nose rising into the air. With more force than Colton felt the situation merited, she propped herself against the adjacent wall.

It's for the best, he thought, a little bit miserably.

She'd grown, over the years. It shouldn't have surprised him, but standing so close like this, it felt like a shock. That was what people did. The earth turned and the years turned and so had she. The sight of her now sat at odds with his memory. For so long she'd existed singularly in his head. Frozen the way he remembered her. A small, cherubic point of light. Her nose pinched red by the cold, her tiny mitten scuffing his wrist.

"Are you a boy, or are you a shadow?"

There was nothing cherubic about her now. Everything on her was bold and dark. Her skirt was gray pleated gingham. The white scalloped collar of her shirt buttoned in the triangle of her throat. Everything else was black, down to the dark matte of her lips. She wore her hair in two high pigtails. Like she was going to a comic book convention and not to class. Like this was Ivy League cosplay and she was Wednesday Addams. The white-blond spill deepened to a pale violet coil at the ends.

The color reminded him of the coat she'd worn.

The one he'd clutched in his fist as he swallowed water.

"Another fantastic insult is 'bunch-backed toad,'" he said, because she'd caught him staring. The elevator lurched into motion. "In lieu of 'asshole,' I mean. It's got a lot going for it. It's Shakespearean. It's unique. Classy, but still rude."

He wasn't supposed to talk to her.

He knew it, and yet he couldn't keep the words from carving out of him anyway.

"Personally, I'm partial to 'lump of foul deformity.'"

She pinned him in a withering stare. "I think I'll stick with 'asshole.'"

Instantly, something in his chest deflated. The elevator was tight and mirrored on all sides, and Lane stared dead ahead, making a terrific show of not paying him any attention. It was a ruse. From where he stood, he could very clearly see her studying the profile of his reflection.

The elevator climbed between floors, pulleys groaning. Colton checked his watch. The time was 10:42. The morning's seminar was meant to begin at promptly 10:45, which meant he was going to be late. He hated to be late. Exhaling a sigh, he tipped his head back against the glass. As he did, he found an endless, darkening train of Lanes silently scrutinizing him. Color crept into her ivory complexion. Her gaze dropped to her boots. The elevator ground to an infuriating stop, and Colton fought the growing urge to loosen his tie.

In front of them, the doors rumbled open to reveal a familiar face. A lump solidified in Colton's throat as Eric Hayes pushed over the threshold, ramming his substantial height into the already small space. The look he shot Colton's way made him feel as if he'd been caught with his hands down his pants, and a hot well of resentment rose in his chest.

"Price," Hayes said, leaning in for a greeting that was half hand-shake, half hug. He was broad-shouldered and black-skinned and built like an athlete, the disarming curve of his smile solely for Lane's benefit. "I like your tie. It's such a relief to know a summer away hasn't made you look like less of a douche. Who's your friend?"

"It's unclear," Colton lied, because he wasn't supposed to know her, and both of them knew it.

"I'm Lane," she said. She spoke to Hayes, but she looked at him. It felt as though she was daring him to say it again.

"Love the purple." Hayes grinned over at her. "It's very edgy."

"Ignore him," said Colton, but she didn't. She smiled up at Hayes with a small, hesitant smile that made Colton's chest draw tight. He still couldn't believe she was here. Little rainbow Lane who'd held his hand. Feeling him staring, she let her gaze slip back to his. This time, he didn't bother looking away.

It felt like an eternity before the elevator finally jolted to a stop. They'd reached their floor, and not a moment too soon. He was positive the oxygen supply was rapidly diminishing. He checked his watch again. It was 10:45. He should have already been inside the lecture hall. He should have never said her name. Everything about this morning was throwing him off.

She was throwing him off.

The seventh floor of Godbole was as flat and as open as the first. The tile was lacquered to a sheen. The white dais at the room's crux supported a wide urn of some dripping floral arrangement. He gave in and tugged at his tie.

Up ahead, Lane was being borne away on the conversational tide that was Hayes, her black boots stomping in a noisy *click-clack-click*.

"Wednesday," he called out, unprompted.

He wouldn't say her name again. Lane. Lane. Lane. In the hall, Hayes and Lane stared back at him. Light from the theater spilled around them in falls of gold. It dawned on him that he hadn't thought of anything to say. He'd only wanted to stop her leaving.

"He means you," Hayes put in. He was still sporting his trademark easy grin, though there was something steeled off in his gaze.

A warning. A reminder. There'd been a singular expectation set in place at the start of this year: *Don't make friends with the Meyers-Petrov girl.* He knew it. Hayes knew it.

Delaney Meyers-Petrov was off-limits.

Colton's thoughts spun out, scrambling for something intelligent to say. Falling woefully short, he landed only on, "You're late."

Next to Lane, some of the tension went out of Hayes's shoulders. The sight of his relief rankled Colton beyond measure. He wasn't a child. He didn't need a keeper.

Sliding his hands into his pockets, he said, "I'm sure you've read the syllabus, but four counts of tardiness equal a failing grade. This is your first. Not a good look. If I were you, I wouldn't let it happen again."

❦ 3 ❧

D elaney recognized Colton Price's name the instant she heard it. "*Price,*" Eric said, and the panic ballooned in her, molten hot and instantaneous. She'd spent hours holed up in her room over the summer, tea lights burning, coffee cold, highlighting every last bit of her freshman curriculum. She'd worked color-coded deadlines into her phone, jotted earmarked project proposals into her planner. She'd memorized the names of all of Godbole's undergrad assistants, determined to find ways to weasel into their good graces.

Thus far, she was fairly certain she hadn't managed to succeed.

"Yikes," whispered a student as she passed by the front row of seats. "How'd you manage to get a nickname from Whitehall's TA so early in the semester?"

"No idea," she lied, mortification heating her skin. She hadn't thought anyone else had heard. At the desk, Colton Price busied himself sorting through a stack of papers. Framed by the towering whiteboard, the undergraduate senior seemed even more imposing than he had on the elevator. She didn't know how she'd missed it. He appeared to be only a year or two older, but the stark professionalism of his attire set him instantly apart from the rest of the students. His sweater looked dry-clean-only, his trousers freshly pressed. His shoes were finely tooled brogues, the same shade of brown as the neat curl of his hair. Only his tie sat askew.

She chose a seat several rows back, climbing the stairs and wedging herself into the rounded shell of a particleboard desk. Immediately in front of her was an explosion of ginger curls. The coils bobbed, ringlets springing every which way, and Delaney was met with bright hazel eyes, a face smattered with an abundance of freckles.

"Hi." The girl was solidly built and filled her frame well, dressed in a ruffled smock. A silver moon pendant hung around her throat. "For the record, I think you look much more like a Harley Quinn than a Wednesday Addams."

Delaney's spirits sank impossibly lower. "You heard that, too?"

"The door was wide open, Wednesday," she said. "Everyone heard."

"Great." Delaney focused on prying a pen loose from her bag. "My name's actually Lane."

"Oh, well, you look infinitely like a Lane." The girl's smile was feline sharp, her stare astute. "I'm Mackenzie. I really love your hair. You definitely shouldn't cut it."

Delaney frowned. "I wasn't planning on it."

"If you're done socializing, we can go ahead and get started." Colton Price's chilly tenor drifted over them, and Delaney swore the temperature in the room dropped several degrees. Peering toward the front of the room, she found Colton propped against the edge of Whitehall's desk, ankles crossed and palms pressed flat against the surface.

Silence fell at once, papers rustling to a standstill. Through an open transom window slipped the timorous trill of birdsong. Delaney felt it run through her, haunting and clear. All around the room, shadows shifted in the places where the light didn't reach, settling flat and heavy against the paneled carpet.

"*It's entirely normal,*" her psychiatrist told her parents once, "*for children to personify inanimate objects.*"

She was eighteen. *Eighteen.* The shadows were only shadows. She shut her eyes. Opened them again. Colton Price sat in her immediate

21

line of sight. He cut an impressive figure, the easy sag of his shoulders carrying the suggestion of old money and genetic arrogance.

She'd called him an asshole.

Right to his face.

He was responsible for overseeing her coursework, and she'd insulted him.

"Just like last year," he said, "my office hours are Tuesday and Thursday nights from six to ten. If it's not an emergency, I don't want to see you. If it *is* an emergency, I still don't want to see you, so seriously consider whether it merits a visit or an email before you interrupt my evening."

This was met with scattered laughter. At the front of the room, Colton didn't look like he was joking. He reached into his pocket and fished out a single nickel, holding it up to the light until it winked silver.

"Have you ever seen a magic trick?" The coin flipped between the knuckles of his left hand—there and gone in a flash of surprising dexterity. "The magician starts the trick by showing his audience something ordinary. Something easy to understand. Maybe it's a coin. Maybe it's a box. Maybe it's a clear stretch of sky." He held up his hand, now empty. "Next," he said, "the magician does something extraordinary with that ordinary thing. If it's a coin, he makes it disappear. If it's a box, he places his assistant inside it. If it's the sky, he steps clean through."

His eyes met Delaney's and stayed there.

"In the end, the coin reappears from where it was tucked inside his sleeve." Turning his wrist, he brandished the nickel between two fingers. "The assistant emerges from behind a trick wall in the box. But the sky? The magician doesn't reappear. There's no illusion. There's no sleight of hand. He's just gone—out of one reality and into the next."

A shiver thrummed through Delaney, and she swore Price marked it. His gaze darted instantly away. She was grateful when a commotion moved through the room, like wind bowing a field of feathered reeds. At first, it washed over her in a sea of indistinguishable sound. A dissonant rustle. A white-noise whisper. It took her several lagging seconds to realize that the cause of the upheaval was Richard Whitehall, sequestered in the open doorway.

The dean of Godbole was small and bowed, his eyes bottled by thick-rimmed glasses and his hair a neat crown of white. The red bulb of his nose sat nestled into a wiry mustache, which in turn curled around a pensive frown. He looked, Delaney thought, like someone's drawing of what a professor should be, down to the rectangular pads at his elbows.

"Off my desk, Mr. Price," he said.

"You got it." Pushing off the edge, Colton moved aside to make room for Whitehall. It took the old professor several lengthy moments to settle into place. In the interim, the room flooded with the ambient sounds of shifting bodies. Papers shuffled. A shoe scuffed carpet. Someone coughed. Adjusting his spectacles, Richard Whitehall peered up at the roomful of people.

"A full house this year," he noted. "Mr. Price has been injecting his usual brand of theatrics into the first day, I trust."

Delaney was warmed at once by the professor's pleasant disposition. Slowly, the chill in the room began to thaw. A bit of tension bled out of her, and for the first time since stepping inside Godbole's tower of glass, she relaxed into her seat.

At the front of the room, Whitehall pried his glasses off his face. "Mr. Price likes to talk about magic," he said, "but I'm afraid the truth is slightly less exciting. What we do in this room isn't magic. It's instinct. And it's in here." He tapped two fingers against the wall of his chest. "It's the feel of the worlds between heartbeats. Either you sense it or you don't. Pass through a door between realities without understanding its precise shape, its bladed edges, and, at best, you may never find your way home again. At worst, you'll come back in ribbons."

Silence fell heavily over the room. Outside the window, clouds clotted low across the sun. It brought the roomful of shadows into stark relief, as though the watchful dark might rise up and take on a corporeal shape. As if it might sprout teeth.

Delaney's heart beat faster.

Huffing a breath on his lenses, Whitehall set to polishing. "Time," he said, rubbing his glasses with a pocket kerchief, "runs much like a river. Every so often, shifts in the timeline cause that river to undergo a bifurcation. A single stream of events splits into a series of smaller distributaries—fragments into innumerable realities. Something small as a pebble can fracture a river in two. So, too, can the most seemingly insignificant of variables change the entire trajectory of human history—"

His voice was swallowed up beneath the rustle of garments, the fleeting tatters of a whisper. For several seconds, Whitehall's words became incomprehensible. All along the edges of the room, the shadows yawned, stretching out their limbs as though emboldened by Delaney's sudden severance from the fold. Reaching for her with dark, chilly fingers. Laughter broke out, and several students in the audience nodded along to an unintelligible joke.

Smiling just a beat too late, Delaney chanced a look at Colton to find him staring. He had, she noted, without quite meaning to, the kind of eyes that should have been warm—the sort of brown that turned to liquid gold in the light. Instead, his stare was hard and cold. The chill of his scrutiny trailed down her spine. She wished he would look anywhere else.

"This," Whitehall said, his voice sharpening into clarity as the room resettled, "is where each of you comes in. You'll make careers out of studying those metaphysical pebbles—examining the ripples they make across time and space. At Godbole, you'll spend the next four years learning to walk between worlds. It's no small undertaking. I advise you to seek out Mr. Price's assistance wherever possible, no matter what idle threats he may have doled out about eating up his office hours."

This was met with polite laughter, quiet and a little more than unsure.

Whitehall replaced his glasses and checked his watch. "I'm told by the board that this is meant to be an hour-long orientation, but I've no interest in that. My expectations were emailed out at the date of your acceptance." He glanced up at them, his smile aloof. "If you haven't already, be sure to read through the syllabus. We begin tomorrow."

A tepid stillness followed. No one moved. No one save for the shadows, quivering in their corners.

"He means get out," Colton said, and the room broke into upheaval.

4

When Delaney was still small and prone to daydreams, she'd peered out into the midnight pitch of her backyard and found a boy peering back. His nose and mouth were edged in moonlight, the inverse of his cheeks pooled with shadow.

"*Hello,*" she'd said, and the fast-fading memory of her voice sounded wrong in the uninhabitable space between her ears. She knew she ought to be afraid—she'd always avoided the dark—but something in the chilly abyss of the boy's stare kept her rooted to the spot. He'd looked, she thought, as frightened to see her as she'd been to see him. A little regal, a little hungry, with his chin upturned and his features gaunt, his arms too long and thin for the rest of him.

But when the wind moved through the trees, he was gone. Where his mouth had been, there was only the thin rictus of a branch. His unblinking stare was little more than the empty hollows of an elm.

For a while afterward, the dark felt less an enemy and more an ally. A friend to play with, alone in the quiet. She'd been tugged along after the shadows, like a fly lured to the glittering orb of a silk-spun web. Drawn to the topmost step of the cellar, where darkness seeped up the stairs like ink. Drawn to the woods at twilight, where moonlight played between the trees. Drawn to the mirror glass of her window, where night pressed its hungry face against the panes.

"*I see you watching me,*" she'd whisper, and feel a sickly sort of thrill. "*Are you lonely, too?*"

These days, she knew better than to follow the dark where it led. She knew it had teeth, and she had the scars to prove it. She was far too careful with herself to believe in things she couldn't see and touch.

That, more than anything, made Godbole feel dangerous.

Whitehall's seminar that morning had left her cold. Weak in the knees, the way she felt when she was staring down the shadows. Nothing about the curriculum was tangible. There was the sky, too tenuous to touch. There were other worlds, too distant to see. It felt like the luring dark, starving and staring. Waiting for her to stagger close enough to bite.

She'd known the reputation that Godbole carried. She knew that scholars of Howe University went on to publish their research in privatized annals, knew they specialized in the study of alternate historical outcomes—the sinking of the *Santa Maria*, a third world war, public health care without the discovery of penicillin.

She knew, and yet she hadn't truly believed. It felt like something out of a fairy tale—that there were places in the sky where the air grew thin enough to step through. Moreover, it felt more and more like a mistake, that something in her test results suggested she'd be capable of doing it.

Little glass Delaney, who'd never left her shelf.

She didn't like to take the T, for fear of mishearing the station announcements. She did her best to avoid ordering food at the deli counter, for fear of angering the shop clerks. The girl who couldn't ride a subway alone or order cold cuts by herself wasn't the sort of person who stepped through a tear in the sky.

And yet here she was.

She didn't feel so capable anymore.

Lying in the little bed of her dorm, she stared at the blazing wall of night-lights and wondered if Colton Price still slept with a light on.

Somehow, she doubted it.

Rolling onto her side, she peered across the room to where her roommate sat on the floor, legs crossed and arms slack, palms upturned atop her knees. The ocean blue of Adya Dawoud's hijab draped around her shoulders in a cerulean cowl, the ends tucked into the cream-colored stitch of her sweater. The warm beige of her oval face was gilded in the array of lights, gold carving out the prominent arch of her brows, the straight line of her nose. Her eyes were open and unblinking, her chestnut stare fixated on a point in the middle distance.

On a yoga mat in front of her sat a sterling silver handheld mirror, the handle adorned in pewter rosettes. A crystal pendulum lay against the looking glass, its planes bending the light, caught up in the silver trill of a necklace chain.

"Are you sure you don't mind all the lights?" Delaney asked, not for the first time. Her voice startled Adya into blinking, and her roommate's gaze refocused in a way that made Delaney's hair stand on end.

"Oh, hello," she said brightly. "I thought you were asleep."

"I can't sleep," Delaney replied, though the truth of it was that she rarely slept. She couldn't, with the shadows clustered at her feet, the night nibbling on her toes. "Did I interrupt something?"

"What, this?" Adya gathered up her materials and climbed to her feet. Her socks were mismatched, one pink, one yellow. "Not at all. It was a waste of time anyway."

Delaney tucked her hands beneath her cheek and watched Adya roll the mat back into a cylindrical bag. "What exactly were you working on?"

"This." Adya held her necklace up between them and glowered at the spinning pendant. "I've spent all afternoon trying to work out how to scry on command. I've downloaded apps, I've done meditation, I watched yoga tutorials. Did you know there are some classes that do yoga with goats? I can't imagine it's easy to access the astral body when there's something chewing on your sock."

"Sorry," Delaney said, ignoring the bit about the goats. "What do you mean by 'scrying'?"

"You know." Adya set the necklace down hard enough to plink the pendant against her desk. "Looking beyond the veil? Divination?"

Delaney shook her head.

Frowning, Adya picked up the mirror and angled it until the glow of a nearby night-light swam into its surface. "This is going to sound insane, but there's been something stuck in my periphery ever since I arrived on campus. It's like the beginnings of an aural migraine— there's just this pale, formless mass at the edge of my vision. I can't see it, not clearly, but I know whatever it is, it wants me to look."

Delaney sat up in bed. She felt suddenly cold, in spite of the considerable warmth of the cluttered dorm. All around her bed, the shadows chittered like katydids warning off a predator. She ignored them.

"And you think the mirror will help you see it?"

"I don't know." Adya dropped down onto her bed. Their bedroom door sat ajar, light from the hall spilling across the floor in a thin bar of yellow, and from the nearby common room there drifted the indecipherable chatter of students. "I need to figure out a way to get out of my head," she said, "but so far I've only been able to do it by accident. Usually, it happens when I'm mid-seizure, but my doctor has strongly advised against discontinuing my lamotrigine."

Delaney thought of staring into the dark and seeing a boy's face staring back. Of the scars that still constellated her kneecaps, white starbursts of skin that never properly healed. Softly, she said, "Maybe you shouldn't look. Maybe it's better not to know."

"Maybe." Adya turned the silver stem of the mirror over and over in her hand. "I spoke to Dr. Whitehall about it after class today. I have a supervision with him tomorrow. I'm hoping he'll give me some advice."

"I wouldn't count on it," came a voice from the open door.

Delaney glanced up to find the redhead from class wedged into the opening, the fiery halo of her curls coppery beneath the hallway lights. Adya scowled and tucked her legs up under her.

"How long have you been standing out there?"

"Long enough." Mackenzie elbowed her way into the night-lit haze of the room without waiting for an invitation, edging past a leaning tower of storage containers and dropping into the chair at Delaney's desk. "You know the adage 'Those who can't do, teach'? Rumor has it that's true for Whitehall. He's never walked through the sky a day in his life. His boy wonder does all the heavy lifting for him."

Delaney pulled a face. "Boy wonder?"

"Colton Price," Mackenzie said, as though it should have been obvious. "I've heard Whitehall treats him like a god, which explains why he has an ego the size of a planet. Some sophomore down the row told me Price can pry the sky open with his bare hands, whether he's close to a ley line or not."

Delaney waited for Adya to chime in with the most obvious next question. When her roommate stayed quiet, she asked, "Does everyone in this room know what a ley line is except for me?"

"Yes," Adya said, still squinting into the looking glass.

"You don't?" Mackenzie's eyes boggled.

"No," Delaney said, affronted by her astonishment. "My mom was a pretty unconventional teacher, but even her weirdest lesson plans never covered the occult."

"Ah." Mackenzie kicked her slippered feet onto Delaney's desk. "Scholarship kid?"

"Yeah." The admission made Delaney feel curiously small. Sinking deeper into her bed, she drew the sleeves of her sweater over her fingertips. "I'm starting to regret agreeing to go wherever they sent me. Today has made me realize just how out of the loop I am."

"You'll catch up." Adya set the mirror onto her bed. "Think of the ley lines this way—have you ever seen a longitudinal map of the earth?"

"Sure," Delaney said.

"It's like that. Only, where the latitude and longitudinal lines are used as travel markers, the ley lines are supernatural rivers of energy. The air only grows thin enough to cross through in places where the concentration of energy is the strongest."

"Unless you're Colton Price," Mackenzie said, inspecting the beds of her nails.

"Allegedly," Adya amended. "It's just a campus rumor. I doubt anyone's actually seen him do it. I'm Adya, by the way."

"Mackenzie. I'm just across the hall."

"I think I met your roommate earlier," Adya said. "She was doing pointe in the lobby."

"The one in the animal onesie? Yeah, that's Haley. She and I got paired together in the roommate lottery. She's a sophomore but couldn't find a single other person to live with. I can't imagine why." Mackenzie bent down and poked at the nearest night-light—a pale cluster of LED mushrooms. "What are the two of you doing in here with all the lights off, anyway? It's barely ten o'clock."

"I have a headache," Adya said, which was almost true.

Delaney, for her part, said nothing. She didn't want to tell them that she'd been desperate for company. She didn't want to admit that she'd crept out to the student social earlier in the night only to find the common room inundated with sounds. The room's muffled acoustics turned the conversations to echoes that ballooned, effervescent, against the ribbed ceilings. It left her head buzzing, her responses trundling along just a beat too late. Flustered, she'd fled as soon as she was able.

Not that it mattered. The longer she spent in the company of her new classmates, the more she felt as though she was the only one who'd gone her whole life without any true awareness of the preternatural. She didn't understand things like scrying and ley lines. She couldn't see beyond the veil. She couldn't tear apart the sky. She couldn't even sleep with the lights off.

Chances were, when it came time to step through the sky, she wouldn't be able to do that, either. Across the room, Adya had fallen back to staring into the mirror, her mouth puckered in a frown. Mackenzie scrutinized Delaney, her elbow propped on a pile of books, the painted stiletto of her nails trilling along her cheek.

"You'll make it through," she said when the silence began to grow uncomfortable.

Delaney stilled. "Excuse me?"

"That's what you were thinking about, right? Whether or not you'll be able to cross between worlds?"

"Yes," Delaney admitted. "But—"

"You'll make it," Mackenzie said again. "I grew up in Salem. My mom and aunt are members of a local coven there. They do readings out of the back room in the family shop, which they bought purely because of its proximity to a ley line. I did my first reading for a customer when I was six. The second Godbole opened its doors, I knew I was going to enroll."

Delaney frowned. "Is this supposed to be a pep talk?"

"No." Mackenzie rolled her eyes. "My point is, I applied for early admission. I interviewed. I wrote a killer essay. But there's no guarantee I have what it takes to step between worlds. Plenty of hopefuls drop out after the first semester. But you? You could have ended up literally anywhere, and the scholarship committee placed you at Howe. That means something inside of you says you belong here. Maybe more so than the rest of us."

The sound of shattered glass drew both of their eyes. Adya stood in the center of the room, the carpet around her feet fragmented in reflective shards. The mirror lay facedown, silver rosettes alloyed in the light.

"Sorry," Adya said, blinking too fast. "It's just that there was something in the mirror."

"Something," Delaney echoed.

"A face."

"Yeah," Mackenzie said, unimpressed. "Yours. You've been staring in that thing since I got in here."

"Not mine." Adya toed the mirror farther from her. "It was a boy."

The way she said it, her voice tight, made Delaney's blood run cold. She thought again of the twilit wood, the boy's face in the dark. The way he'd broken apart beneath the wind, there and then gone in the blink of an eye. She dragged her palms against her arm in an effort to rub heat back into her skin.

"The thing is," Adya said, still eyeballing the hand mirror as though she expected it to sprout fangs and lunge, "I think he was dying."

❧ 5 ❧

Colton Price had a carefully curated routine. It looked like this: It was 6:33. It was morning. It was Wednesday. He stood in the basement of his empty family town house, weight bar in hand, and finished his last set. In the flat silver of the wall mirror, his features were stark and pale. He blinked away swimmers and set the weights neatly on the dumbbell rack, rolling out a kink in his shoulder.

He woke each dawn at 5:30, without need for an alarm, though he set one anyway just to be sure. On Mondays, Wednesdays, and Fridays, he lifted. On Tuesdays and Thursdays, he jogged. Down along the Charles. Beneath the sagging boughs of honey locusts fat with fruit. Following his workout, he prepared a shake. After, he showered beneath the rainwater showerhead in the third-story bathroom, water beating down his back, the radio blaring classical music from its place on the marble vanity.

Classical, not rock or country or top forty, because he'd been raised on Handel and Tchaikovsky and because sometimes, when he was very tightly wound, the instrumentals were the only things that eased the tension in his chest. When that was done, he dressed, made his bed—tucking his corners in with the militaristic precision his nanny had demanded of him when he was still small and belligerent—and went downstairs to make eggs. Over easy, paired with whole-grain toast and a glass of orange juice.

He had his routine down to a science, and he did the same thing every morning.

Which was why he knew this particular morning was different.

He didn't know *how* he knew, only that he understood, with an uneasy sort of clarity, that something was about to happen. He could sense time slipping out from under him, wobbling slightly, as if it, too, wasn't sure what to make of the change. The thermostat shut off and the basement went cold, chilling the sweat against his skin. He didn't glance at his watch. He knew it was 6:37.

He'd always had an uncanny sense of time. When Colton moved between worlds, it felt like he was taking on water. His lungs went full and hard, his body cold. Pins and needles shot through his legs, rendering him useless until he'd pushed to the other side. Counting the seconds. Dreading each infinitesimal tick. Hyperaware of how long he'd gone without breathing.

It was an unfortunate by-product of drowning.

He sank into his hoodie and slapped his hands together once, twice, three times for warmth. His blood was ice in his veins. A lactic acid sting needled his calves. It was 6:38.

Upstairs, the doorbell rang.

Too early for visitors. Something in him threaded tight. Turning out the light, he took the stairs two at a time, rounding into the foyer and prying open the door to admit an unwelcome sight.

Mark Meeker stood on the threshold, sweaty beneath his canvas jacket. Meeker was small and wiry, prone to nervous tics and excessive hand-wringing. The Godbole dropout reminded Colton of a rat, all twitches and whiskers. Generally harmless, but the kind of creature that would happily gorge itself on your remains the instant an opportunity presented itself. Scraping his feet on the welcome mat, Meeker stepped inside without waiting for an invitation.

"Sure," Colton said flatly, hands in his pockets, "come on in."

Meeker sniffled in response. "Sky smells funny today." He tugged at the brim of his newsboy cap. "Like change. D'you smell it?"

"No," said Colton, though he felt it.

Running a finger under his nose, Meeker said, "Apostle's got a bone to pick with you."

Colton braced a shoulder against the wall. "I don't care."

Meeker blustered, hands spread wide in an are-you-kidding-me-with-this-shit pose. This was a routine they did. Meeker stammering. Colton dutifully playing the part of a rock, recalcitrant and cold.

"You should care," Meeker said. "Since he's got your balls in a vise."

Again, Colton felt that pull at his core, the feel of the earth slipping out from under him. If Lane were here, he'd ask what she heard, whispering in the corners. As it was, the shadows in the room fell in particularly menacing patterns, made stark by the rising sun, and Lane was somewhere on campus, possibly shoving pins into a poppet with his name on it.

The thought made him frown, and his frown made Meeker wring his hands harder.

The watch at Colton's wrist beeped—a needless reminder; he knew it was 6:45—and he said, "It's time for my shake."

Meeker goggled at him. "What? Right now?"

"Come on." Colton headed down the hall, socks scuffling marble. "Or don't. I don't care either way."

The kitchen was wide and vaulted, tiled all in black and white. He pulled a sweating carton of milk from the fridge and measured out three cups into the blender. Next came the rest, deposited in careful order: a half scoop of protein powder; frozen strawberries with the tops scooped off; a banana cut into thin, round coins; a spoonful of kale. Meeker procured a rolled manila file from the inside of his coat and flattened it on the counter. Colton eyeballed it sideways.

"What's this?"

"It's—" Meeker was drowned out by the sound of the blender whirring to life. The two of them sized each other up across the kitchen as the liquidizer pummeled frozen fruit into fluid. Colton pulled his finger off the button. The sound winnowed out.

"Sorry," Colton said, not sounding sorry at all.

"It's Peretti's autopsy report," Meeker finished, indignant. "Little homework for you."

Colton's phone beeped, signaling the arrival of a text. "Not interested," he said, ignoring the file in favor of glancing down at his cell.

"Not optional," Meeker fired back.

"Everything is optional." The text was from Hayes. Colton slid his phone back into the pocket of his gym shorts. "As it turns out, I don't feel like doing the Apostle's busy work today."

"No one asked about your *feelings*, Price." Meeker's smile was as twitchy as the rest of him. "You'll do what's expected of you."

Colton leaned against the counter and took a sip of his shake. He hadn't left the blender on long enough, and the consistency was too thick. "I'm not an errand boy."

"No," Meeker agreed. "You're not a boy at all, you little shit. Take the day. Look everything over. See if you can't piece together why these idiots kept turning up dead. The Apostle expects a call from you tonight."

When he was gone, Colton finished his shake. He went upstairs to take his shower. Paganini's 24 Caprices blared over the speakers, violin solo shivering through the soles of his feet. He didn't let himself think about the folder. He thought, instead, of the sounds the shadows made, far outside his capacity to hear them.

When he was done, he toweled himself dry and clicked on the news. A grim-faced reporter stood center-frame, discussing the latest in a string of tourist deaths out in Illinois. The newest victim was a student named Julian Guzman. All-American swimmer. Honors student. Beloved by friends and family. He'd been found on the side of the Chicago Skyway, his body crumpled up like roadkill.

Colton didn't know how the news made him feel. Empty? Annoyed? Afraid? A rising Godbole senior, Julian Guzman had possessed the uncanny ability to *sniff* out doors between worlds. One whiff, and he picked up on any nearby rips in the ether like a bloodhound. Once, in their sophomore year, Colton had asked Guzman what a thinning sky smelled like.

"*Sulfur,*" Guzman replied. "*Brimstone. It's not roses, man. This shit reeks.*"

On the television, a grim-faced woman with too many teeth looked directly into the camera and explained how Guzman bled to death on the pavement where he'd been discovered.

Colton wondered if bleeding out was slow.

Drowning took time.

He remembered the feel of slipping beneath the ice, cold ripping at his skin. The anesthetized dread of waking up several days too late, beneath a morning gone several degrees too warm. The commanding aura of a little girl all in rainbows.

His parents scarcely looked at him once he'd been medically cleared to come home. He knew they blamed him. Little Colton Price, always late. Always getting into scrapes. And Liam, the dutiful older brother, always there to pull him out.

He hadn't managed to pull Colton out of the pond.

Sulfur and brimstone. Shadows and ice. Drowning boys and a pound of flesh. One grisly accident after another. Godbole's legacy was being built on bones.

Colton clicked off the television. It was 7:30.

He checked his phone, opening the text from Hayes. The message was brief: *Did you see the news this morning?*

Yeah, he texted back, *just saw.*

The incoming reply beeped instantly: *Looks like Guzman struck out. Which of us is on deck?*

It was meant as a joke, but it left him cold.

Kostopoulos, he replied.

Setting aside his phone, he dressed in the clothes he'd ironed and laid out for himself the night before. He sat on the edge of his bed and pulled on his socks. He tried not to think about death. The silence of his room was all-encompassing. The quiet of the house threatened to swallow him whole.

Midway through the morning, he arrived at Whitehall's freshman seminar to find Lane already there. Another change. Another hiccup in his routine. He drew up short in the open door, caught off guard by her presence. She was dressed all in black, her hair a waterfall of color, and for several seconds he wasn't entirely sure which instructions he was meant to follow. He was expected to be in class fifteen minutes before students arrived. He was expected to stay away from Lane. He couldn't obey one directive without forgoing the other.

It was the coffee that convinced him. A latte sat on the edge of the desk, steam still rising from its white paper cup. He recognized the drink for what it was: a peace offering. He wouldn't accept it. He *couldn't* accept it. But turning tail and hiding somewhere else until class began felt too much like cowardice. It was, he surmised, in both of their best interests for him to have no reaction at all.

The moment he stepped over the threshold, he felt it—a pervasive ache that stitched beneath his ribs. A physical reminder. A Pavlovian response. He hadn't expected direct defiance to feel so palpable. Biting down a groan, he made his way toward the desk.

Pen between her teeth, Lane didn't glance up from her planner. She looked fully engrossed in her reading, and he wasn't sure if she hadn't heard him come in or if it was a part of her grand plan to pretend like he didn't exist.

He got his answer the moment he took his seat.

"I'm on time today." Her delivery came out too quiet for the theater's carpeted sprawl. Like she wasn't sure how powerfully she needed to project in order to be heard. Like she was worried about her voice taking up too much space. She sat with her legs crossed, one black boot swinging through the air like a pendulum.

"You're early," he corrected, prying loose his laptop. "It's a waste of your morning. And it won't win you any points. Whitehall doesn't give out prizes for being first in the door."

Her eyes darted in his direction. Scrolling through emails, he worked very hard to keep from meeting her gaze. Maybe, he reasoned, if he managed to look convincingly engrossed in his task, she'd lose interest. Instead, her stare lingered. He closed one browser and pulled open another, clicking aimlessly through his inbox. The force of her scrutiny clawed through him.

Finally, she said, "Can I ask you something?"

He deleted a counterfeit invoice from his spam folder. "Is it related to the coursework?"

"No." Her swinging boot fell still. "Not exactly."

"Then no," he said, though he was fiercely intrigued. "I have several things to get through before class starts, and your incessant talking is deeply distracting."

Softly, he heard her mutter, "I wouldn't call it incessant."

He glanced over the top of his laptop. "What?"

"What?"

"Did you say something?"

"No," she lied, frowning down at him.

"Good." He let a cold smile creep across his face. "Let's keep it that way."

The end of the week found him holed up in the student center, his books sprawled across the laminate surface of an empty conference table. Across the sun-drenched hall, Lane was laughing with her friends. Head thrown back. Eyes glittering. Reacting just a beat too late to something the redhead said.

He was, he knew, exactly where he shouldn't be. Testing himself. Parsing out his limits. He couldn't help it. The feel of her was an itch. He was torn between wanting to dissect the preternatural ache in his bones and wanting to claw it out of himself. Every time she glanced his way, he considered tearing out of this reality and into another. Shedding her presence like a skin.

Back home, the autopsy report went unread on the kitchen counter. Calls from the Apostle went unanswered. He knew better. He couldn't afford the distraction. Not with Peretti and Guzman dead. Not with Kostopoulos calling him in a panic in the night.

"I don't want to go. Do you hear me? I don't want to do it anymore."

He knew the risk, and yet the draw of Lane was a visceral, beating thing beneath his bones. He was a paper moth in the dark and she was a light. He knew himself well enough to know that he would continue to crash into her until everything burned.

A book slammed onto the table, and he glanced up to see Eric Hayes taking a seat.

"Does it hurt?" Hayes asked. "Being this stupid?"

"I'm just working on a paper," Colton objected.

"You've been at Howe for four years, and you've never once condescended to do your homework in the presence of underclassmen. Not even when you *were* an underclassman." Hayes slung off his backpack and let it crush against the seat next to him. "I don't want to have to babysit you, man. Don't make me babysit you."

Colton pried off his glasses and dropped the round wire frames into the open pages of his textbook. He didn't have a headache yet, but there was a budding pressure behind his eyes that told him he'd have a hell of a migraine later. "I'm not doing anything wrong."

"Maybe not yet," Hayes said, "but you've got a look."

"A look," Colton echoed flatly.

"A real reckless look." Hayes cracked the tab on his seltzer and took a sip. "I need your head in the game. Two of our guys have struck out in Chicago. The third is missing in action. If Kostopoulos fails, who's next? Me? You?"

"It's not going to be me," Colton said, because it was true. Colton knew it. Hayes knew it.

"Yeah." Hayes huffed out a humorless laugh. "Well, I sure as hell don't want to go. I found a leaked photo of Guzman online this morning. There was literal shit leaking out of his ears."

"Brain matter," Colton corrected.

Propping an elbow on the table, Hayes jammed a finger in his face. "The fact that you can say those two words together without flinching is sick. You're aware of that, right?"

Colton pinched the bridge of his nose. "We knew what we were getting into when we pledged."

"Did we?" Hayes peered over his shoulder, to where Lane and her friends had begun to pack up their things. Books shoved into bags. Arms slid into coats. Someone laughed, the sound high and clear. Glancing back at Colton, he said, "Because I don't think you did."

"What's that supposed to mean?"

"It means we're one week into the semester and you're already tailing her like a sad dog. This thing is bigger than you, Price. So do me a favor and start following orders before you screw this up for the rest of us."

The warning rang hollow. And, anyway, it didn't matter.

His mother used to call him strong-willed, when he was still small and whole and she wasn't afraid to look him in the eye. Contrary, how he'd pick the blue truck if someone offered him red. Relentless, how he'd insist on climbing all the way to the topmost branches of the old maple at the park if Liam told him he was too small.

How close he was determined to get to Lane, the more he was told to stay away.

❧ 6 ❧

Delaney's philosophy professor was an unsmiling woman with a shock of red hair and a presence like a bird. Her face seemed infinitely crafted into a tightly puckered moue that made it impossible for Delaney to discern whether her teacher was explicitly disappointed in her, or if that was merely her baseline expression.

"The study of fundamental truths lends itself to a Socratic approach," Professor Beaufort declared, peering at Delaney across the wide beak of her nose. "As such, I expect all of my students to contribute to the classroom discourse."

"I understand," Delaney rushed to say. The office in which they sat was brightly lit and absurdly floral, the shelves stacked with pale Grecian busts. Two weeks into the semester, and Delaney was already scheduling meetings to beg for additional amenities. It didn't feel good. "It's not that I don't want to participate. I'm just having difficulty keeping up with the flow of conversation in class."

A single one of Beaufort's thinly penciled brows stretched into a dramatic arch. "I have trouble believing that. You're a bright, articulate young woman. You and I are conversing now, and you're doing remarkably well."

It was meant as a compliment, though it hardly felt like one. Delaney struggled to maintain a smile as she muttered an unsteady, "Thank you."

Beaufort scrutinized her for a long moment, thin lips pinched. "All the same, if you feel the pace of my class is proving too much for you, you're still well within the drop period. You're a placement student, correct?"

Delaney's stomach bottomed out. "Yes."

"I thought as much." Beaufort steepled her thin fingers over the paper calendar on her desk. "Scholarship recipients are expected to maintain a 3.5 GPA in order to remain eligible for continued financial aid. Participation comprises a significant portion of your final grade. If you don't think you can find it in you to join the conversation, then I'd advise you to carefully reconsider your options."

"I'll keep that in mind," Delaney said, doing her best to keep a quaver from creeping into her voice. "Thank you for your time."

Out in the hall, Delaney stood with her forehead pressed to the plexiglass of the vending machine. Stuck in the coils, the sleeve of cookies she'd selected hung without dropping. She jabbed her finger repeatedly into the button. *B-6. B-6. B-6.* The cookies didn't budge.

Adya had promised Delaney it wouldn't take her long to catch up, and yet with each passing day Delaney felt further and further behind. The days bled one into the other, stuffed full of crowded classrooms and muffled acoustics, sounds that refused to be slotted into place, conversations that refused to be contextualized. She wrote down everything she heard, which, in the end, didn't turn out to be anything at all—only partially formed concepts and unfinished sentences, broken here and there with angry inksplots.

She sat in the student center and pretended to be a part of the conversation. She sat in the dining hall and pretended to laugh at Mackenzie's jokes. She felt, as she often did in crowded spaces, trapped along the periphery. One foot in the waking world with everyone else, the other somewhere quiet. Somewhere strange. Somewhere limitless and lonely. Without context to act as an anchor, sound flitted between her ears like dandelion fluff.

When the days were through, she dragged herself back to the neat row of freshman dormitories—to the messy haven of her room—and threw herself down onto her bed to rub away a headache. Her mother called and called and she ignored her, knowing if she answered the phone she was bound to cry.

Little glass Delaney, just a few weeks into the semester and already cracking.

It wasn't only her classes where she was falling short. Every morning, she woke in the dark of predawn and got herself ready. She arrived at Whitehall's theater as the sun crawled into the sky. She sat at the very front of the room and set her pens one after the other in a neat ballpoint row, a please-don't-hate-me coffee perched on the heavy desk at the theater's carpeted crux.

Every morning, Colton Price showed up like clockwork—five minutes after Delaney, ten minutes before class—his face screwed up in what she could only assume was disgust. He'd take his seat without looking at her. He'd cuff his sleeves without speaking to her. He'd slide a perfectly sharpened pencil behind his ear and set to critiquing papers. The coffee cooled, going ignored. It was a wordless message, its meaning clarion clear: *Apology not accepted.*

While Whitehall clicked through bulleted slides on the critical theory of diverse observable universes, Colton Price would sort through papers and watch, his eyes like twin thunderheads and a permanent scowl carved across his face. Delaney took her useless notes with her useless pens and tried to wonder what she possibly could have done to make him dislike her so deeply.

Surely, he'd been called an asshole before.

Still propped against the vending machine, she felt the waning patience of another student just over her shoulder. She hadn't heard him approach. She hadn't even been aware of him at all until he muttered something under his breath, his register too low to comprehend. A shoe scuffed tile. A sigh bloomed across the back of her neck.

"Can you help me?" she heard him ask.

"I don't know." She gave the machine one final, lackluster kick. "It ate my dollar. I think maybe it's broken."

But when she turned around, there was no one there.

The sun climbed bold and yellow in Godbole's towering glass face as she crept into the foyer just fifteen minutes later, Colton's coffee scalding the fingers of her left hand. In her right, she gripped her notebook, the dot-grid pages splayed open to reveal a large hand-drawn butterfly. The previous day, Whitehall had given a lecture on the mass implications of the butterfly effect in parallel universes. Delaney had spent the majority of class transforming her notes into doodles, a lump in her throat. Now, baking in the heat of the sun-drenched lobby, she made a futile attempt to decipher what she could before class began.

She was halfway to the elevator when Colton Price's voice barreled into her.

"Wednesday!"

A spike of panic rammed through her. She spun, not anticipating his proximity, and slammed directly into gray wool and burgundy silk. Coffee splattered, scalding the white ruffled bib of her dress. Colton reared back, similarly covered, the face of his watch winking gold in the light. For several seconds, they stood, wet and startled, and stared down at the empty cup on the floor between them.

"Oh," she said as the murky brown deluge bled into the paper wings of her butterfly. Then, because she felt she ought to say something more, she added, "I brought you a coffee."

"Yes," Colton said, inspecting the damage. "I'm wearing it."

"It's Lane," she sputtered out.

Those dark eyes rose to hers. "What?"

"My name. You called me Wednesday, but it's Lane."

He stared at her for a beat. For two. The coffee chilled against her stomach, turning her cold. "I know your name," he said. Then, "Whitehall wants to see you in his office before class."

An undercurrent of dread swam through her. "Me? Why?"

But he was already turning from her, picking up the fallen cup and chucking it into a nearby receptacle. She hurried after him, her pulse racing just a bit faster, supremely conscious of the too-loud click of her heels.

In the elevator, they fell back into their usual holding pattern. Colton tap, tap, tapped at the face of his watch as though it might have broken. Delaney blotted half-heartedly at her butterfly-encrypted notes. The air between them stood perfectly still.

"Ah, Ms. Meyers-Petrov," Whitehall said, the moment she stepped inside his office. The space was cramped and cluttered—the only spot of dark she'd seen in all of stark, clinical Godbole. Delaney was struck at once by the sheer cerebralism of him, all glasses and tweed and elbow pads, insulated in his office of dark mahogany and rich emeralds. "Thanks for coming in. I've been eager to speak with each freshman one-on-one. How are you getting on in your classes?"

Delaney considered her less-than-favorable meeting with her philosophy professor, the scribbled gaps in her notebooks. The way she

49

crawled into bed each night with her head ringing, both fearing the dark and dreading the dawn.

"Fine," she lied, conscious of Colton hanging on to her every word.

Whitehall pried up a crisp manila folder and thumbed through its contents. "Your file says you're here on scholarship."

"I am." She tried not to glance at Colton, with his glossy curls and his glossy shoes and his glossy watch. He'd probably paid his tuition bill in cash. He probably had a 4.0 GPA. He definitely didn't draw butterflies in his notebooks and personify the dark and miss out on half his lectures.

At the desk, Whitehall continued to peruse her records. "You must have excelled in your exams."

"Not exactly," Delaney admitted. "I wasn't allowed to finish the placement test."

Something in what she'd said caught Whitehall's attention. Intrigue flashed through his gaze, and he examined Delaney as though seeing her anew. "If you don't mind my saying so, you have a very intriguing accent. I can't quite place it. Where is it you're from?"

Delaney's blood iced over. She *did* mind his saying so, but she couldn't imagine embarrassing the dean of her department by pointing it out. Clutching the thin strap of her bag, she said, "Massachusetts."

"Ah." Whitehall's smile lingered. "And before that?"

Her stomach soured. Braced in the open door, Colton watched her like a shark, hands thrust into his pockets.

"Nowhere," she said, careful to articulate in the way she'd been taught. Tongue behind her teeth. Her consonants crisp.

"Really?" Whitehall sounded unconvinced. "Petrov—that's an interesting surname. What is it, Slavic?"

50

"Yes." She cursed the wobble in her voice. "But my mom grew up in New England."

"And you're sure you haven't lived anywhere else," Whitehall prompted, as though she might be misremembering her own childhood. "What about your parents?"

"She's deaf," Colton bit out, with an edge that brought both sets of eyes in his direction. Delaney's breath snared in her throat. She'd spent her whole life dancing around the word, too afraid to make anyone uneasy, too afraid to claim it for her own. In front of her, Colton didn't look afraid. He only looked annoyed. Propping his shoulder against the frame, he said, "I forwarded you the email over the summer."

"How completely embarrassing," Whitehall said, and spread his arms wide in an it-happens gesture. "My apologies. That'll teach me to ignore my backlogs. You'll have to excuse me for prying, but you're remarkably articulate. Am I correct in assuming your hearing loss was postlingual?"

Delaney wrenched her gaze away from Colton. "Yes."

"Ah. And do you sign?"

"A little. At home." She worried at a loose thread on her sleeve. Her skin felt hot, and she wanted desperately to sink into the floor. "I wear a cochlear implant."

"Spectacular," Whitehall marveled. "And do you hear things? In the quiet?"

Delaney blinked, surprised by the sudden specificity of his question. All around her, the early-morning sun fell in swaths of blistering yellow, driving the shadows to the in-betweens and underneaths, the corners and the crevasses. *We don't like it here*, they seemed to say. *We don't like it at all.*

"No," she said, a beat too late. All her life, that had been the correct response. This time—and for the first time—she had the distinct sense she'd said the wrong thing.

"Fascinating." The inflection in Whitehall's tone was strange, and Delaney thought she must have misheard it, muffled as it was in the airless chamber of his office. "Thank you, Ms. Meyers-Petrov. I think that'll be all for today. Again, please accept my sincerest apologies for my earlier blunder."

"It's okay." She felt out of sorts—uncertain what, aside from her abject humiliation, they'd managed to accomplish. "Was there anything else?"

"Not at all. Just a quick hello." Whitehall's smile was warm beneath the white curl of his mustache. He reminded her of a mall Santa—his demeanor a touch too merry, his sweater a shade too red. "We're doing something revolutionary here at Godbole, poking at holes in the sky. Because of that, we tend to draw a great deal of criticism from those who don't understand. It's incredibly important that our little department stick together. As such, I like to know who's sitting in my classroom. Put names to the faces."

His bespectacled gaze traveled to Colton, still framed in the door. Colton's stare was walled off, his mouth soldered in a tight line. He looked like a stone facsimile of a person, the lines of him too neat, too cold.

"I'm looking forward to getting to know you better," Whitehall said, distracted. Then, to Colton, "I'll see the both of you in class."

This time, Delaney was certain she'd misheard the inflection in his tone, because it sounded like a warning.

❧ 7 ❧

Delaney was seven years old the first time she woke in the woods. It was late June, the air magnolia sweet, and she'd opened her eyes to the oppressive quiet of the forest. Her feet were stippled in dirt, her fingertips gluey with sap, the long white of her braid adorned in winterberry brambles. Like she'd been born of the wood, clawing her way out from a belly of snarled rowan roots.

Her parents found her not long after. They'd carried her home like broken glass, swept up in pieces in their arms. They glued her back together, scrubbing the half-moons of dirt out from beneath her fingernails and phoning someone with enough letters in her credentials to give them an answer.

Her therapist was a stout woman with hair the color and texture of sheep's wool. That first session, Delaney sat cross-legged on the fainting couch and picked at her nails. She didn't want to tell the therapist about the boy in the branches, or the way she followed the dark wherever it led. She wanted to say all the right things only, so that the doctor would be pleased with her, but the right things were lies, and so it felt like a test she was predetermined to fail.

Somnambulism, the therapist called it in the end. Typical behavior for a child who'd undergone something as traumatic and as sudden as near death and a total hearing loss.

Giving it a name didn't stop it from happening. The next time, Delaney woke by a creek, knocked back into herself by the feel of her father shaking her awake. Her throat was raw, her fingers pruned by river water, and she'd been unbearably cold in spite of the mid-August heat. She'd been following the boy through the dark again, calling out for him to stop. Ignoring the bite of blackberry thorns. Awake now, the shadows fell around her like rain, spliced here and there with thin shafts of gold wherever light managed to breach the cedars. There was no boy. There was only the forest, dark and deep.

Her parents gave it a nickname—"episodes"—like she was a Saturday-morning cartoon. She'd wake in the woods, her hands braced against the coarse clefts of a redwood tree. She'd wake in the yard, feet black with mulch and rainwater needling her skin. Her parents put locks on her doors, a baby gate atop the stairs.

"Just give it time," the therapist assured Delaney's parents. *"She'll outgrow it."*

And then, one night, she did.

She woke in the street, her kneecaps bloody, pinned in the yellow headlights of their next-door neighbor's clunky Buick. Her heart looped in her chest and she felt more awake than she'd ever been in her life.

It never happened again.

It was as if the prospect of being mowed down by a car had startled the waking right out of her. As if whatever she'd been drawn to in the dark had finally given up and gone.

Delaney was lying in the night-light haze of her dorm. She was staring at a sliver of moonlight on the wall. She was thinking about dreaming. Even now, all these years later, she could still envision every detail of the boy in the wood: black eyes, dark curls, the legs of his pants wet where he'd tumbled into the creek.

"*Stop*," she'd cried. "*Don't run. I know you. I know you. I know you.*"

She'd spent years convincing herself it was only in her head.

Two weeks into the semester, and she wasn't sure anymore.

"Adya," she whispered into the dark. "Adya, are you awake?"

There was a telltale rustle, a sigh that was not quite as agitated as she felt it was meant to sound. "I am now," said Adya.

"What do you think it will feel like?" she asked. "Walking through the sky?"

Silence followed. For several moments, she thought maybe Adya wouldn't answer. But then her roommate rolled over. The light of the night-lights glazed her features, leaving her lips just bright enough to read.

"I had a seizure when I was thirteen," she said. "I was daydreaming in math, just staring out the window. My whole body jerked awake. You know that feeling when you're dreaming about falling and your arms and legs respond as if you actually are?"

Delaney thought of jolting awake in a wooded clearing, a chilly dawn gilding the leafless trees. "Yeah," she said. "I know the feeling."

"It was like that, only I'd never actually fallen asleep. Afterward, everything started to go numb. My vision tunneled. By that point, I was on the floor." She fell quiet, and Delaney let the silence fester. "The thing is," she said, "I knew I was on the floor, because I could see myself. The entire class was moving around me but I was perfectly still, standing on a desk in the center of the room. Not part of my body, but elsewhere. Like I'd been shaken clear out of myself." The mattress creaked as she rolled onto her back. "I imagine that's what it'll feel like."

"My roommate says it's a form of paresthesia," piped in Mackenzie from her makeshift cot on the floor.

Rolling onto her stomach, Delaney reached for the Tiffany lamp between their beds. The light clicked on, bathing the little dorm in a soft kaleidoscope of colors. Mackenzie lay curled on the top of a borrowed sleeping bag, a snowy plush owl propped beneath her head.

"I thought you were asleep," Delaney said at the same time as Adya moaned, "Bartleby is *not* a pillow, Mackenzie."

"I have too much stress to sleep, Laney-Jane," Mackenzie said, switching out Bartleby the owl for a pleated throw pillow. "I think I'm into my roommate."

Adya sat up in bed, her comforter pooling around her. "Haley? With the onesies?"

"I only have the one roommate," Mackenzie said dryly.

"I thought we don't like her."

"We don't, and I don't really want to unpack that right now, so can you please turn out the light?" Mackenzie sank down and drew the cover over her head. Her voice slipped out in a muffle. "I just want to lie here in the dark and brood."

Delaney stayed Adya's wrist halfway to the lamp. "First tell us what you meant before. About parathesia."

"It's *paresthesia*," Mackenzie corrected, reemerging.

"Mackenzie."

"Fine." Mackenzie rolled onto her back, curls sprawling in a fiery halo around her head. "Allegedly, crossing through the sky places intense pressure on our nerves. We'll each experience a distinct physical sensation. For Haley, it feels like spiders crawling up her skin, but it's different for everyone."

"So we have no idea what it'll be like," Delaney said. "It could be anything at all."

"It could hurt," Adya added glumly.

"It might." Mackenzie curled up onto her side, her knees drawn into her chest. "Alina Cho from the first floor heard a rumor that when Price goes through, it feels like he's drowning."

"That's awful," Adya said.

"Yeah." Mackenzie picked at her polish. "But it's not real. It's a tactile hallucination."

Delaney thought of the creeping dark, the way it murmured, waiting. She thought of the boy in the woods, his body wreathed in midnight, the way she'd pursued him through the press of trees. *"Wait, stop. I know you."*

She knew how real a hallucination could feel. How the imprint of it stayed with you, long after it was over. She couldn't imagine Colton Price carrying an ache like that. Not even the specter of one. He didn't seem the type of person to suffer anything, let alone pain.

"I have a calculus exam tomorrow," Adya said, breaking her train of thought, "and you're both disrespecting my rigid sleep schedule."

"What rigid sleep schedule?" Delaney kicked her foot out from under her covers, restless. Instantly, the shadows engulfed her toes. "You were up until three a.m. last night watching cat videos."

"And that's between me and the internet," Adya fired back. "Anyway, it's the only thing I can do to keep from thinking about that face in the mirror."

Delaney suppressed an empathetic shudder. "Have you seen it again?"

"No," Adya said, stretching across her bed. The lamp clicked off, plunging the room back into its night-lit haze. "And I don't want to. But I can't shake the feeling that it's still there, waiting just out of frame."

"That's deeply creepy."

"We're all a little creepy," Mackenzie chimed in. "That's why we're here."

Delaney curled into herself, cold in spite of the three layers of blanket she kept bunched beneath her chin. By the door, Mackenzie's phone screen lit the bow of her lips blue. The ceiling was awash with its glow. She stared into the treacle warmth of a half-shell night-light and counted back from one hundred, the way her parents used to do on nights when the ringing in her ears drove her to claw at her face. She made it all the way to the sixties before the first waves of sleep washed over her.

Just before she drifted under, she thought she saw a figure hunched over the end of Adya's bed, but when she woke in the dawn, she was sure it had only been a dream.

Delaney's midafternoon meeting with her human anatomy professor was turning out to be as discouraging as her philosophy meeting with Beaufort.

She waited before the wooden lectern, quiz in hand, and stared down at the angry red slashes across the top of her paper. Her stomach was a knot. Her hands were clammy. Outside the amphitheater, a crowd of incoming students had begun to gather in the lobby. Scattered bits of conversation droned through the room like the buzzing of bees. Flanked by the rigid chassis of a human skeleton, Professor Haas sat with arms folded over his stomach, the long stem of his tie adorned in twisting vertebrae.

"There's no hand-holding here," he said, his considerable baritone projecting through the empty theater at a volume that made her cringe. "You're not in high school anymore. It's the responsibility of the student to apply for any necessary academic adjustments ahead of their courses." He jabbed a finger at the papered flurry of his desk. "These weekly quizzes make up one-third of your final grade. I've seen your file. Your GPA can't afford to take the hit."

"I understand," Delaney said, determined to appear as amenable as possible. Her insides felt like shredded paper.

With a groan, Haas rose from his chair. "Now, if you'll excuse me, I have another class beginning in just a moment."

As if on cue, the dam broke and students began pouring into the room. Mortified, Delaney shoved her quiz into her bag, intending to flee. She didn't make it more than a half step before she drew up short, her stomach plummeting to the floor. There, planted like a rock amid the rush of seniors, stood Colton Price.

Their eyes met. For a moment, neither of them moved. Embarrassment ignited beneath her skin like a combustible as she replayed the last several minutes in her head. The open criticisms. The blatant condescension. Ears burning, she rocketed toward the door, hoping desperately that if she looked like she was in a rush, he'd let her pass by without remark.

Her hope flagged and died the instant she nearly trod right upon the toes of his shoes. She managed to careen to a stop seconds before slamming into his chest.

"You're in my way," she whispered into the gray knit of his sweater.

He didn't step aside. This close, his considerable height forced her to crane her neck up to see his face, and she felt infuriatingly small beneath the lean frame of his shoulders. She didn't recognize the thing that built inside her belly at the nebulous brown of his gaze. She only knew that she was seconds away from crying, and she didn't want to do it in front of him.

She shoved past him, her shoulder clipping his bicep as she went. To her surprise, he turned a half step with her, thrusting out a hand to catch the edge of the door before she could escape into the hall.

"Wednesday—"

"How much of that did you hear?" She hadn't meant to ask, but the question forced its way out of her anyway. Her eyes pinched and she pulled them shut, willing the sting of humiliation out of her skin. Acutely aware of the way his arm bent before her in a barricade.

"Enough," he admitted.

She didn't wait to see if he'd say anything else. She only pushed through his arm and out into the lobby, her boots clattering across the wide plank flooring. Through the windows, the mid-September sky deepened to a bruise. Not full dark, but too close for comfort. The long walk to the freshman dormitories would be sheathed in twilight, shadows crawling along the pavers.

The door caught on her way out, tugged from behind as though someone had reached out and stayed it with a hand. She felt the tangible weight of a body, the heat of another person standing much too close.

"Wait," said a boy's voice, soft enough to be a sigh.

She spun on her heels, fully prepared to come face-to-face with Colton. She wasn't sure what she'd do when she saw him. Chastise him? Burst into tears?

Only, it wasn't Colton who stood there.

It wasn't anyone at all.

The lobby was empty. The door to Haas's lecture hall was shut.

And yet, even now she felt it—a presence. The feel of eyes on her face. The temperature in the lobby was cold as permafrost, the air dense as wool. She didn't know how long she stood there, transfixed.

Staring back at nothing. She only knew that by the time the vibration of her phone in her coat shook her free of her trance, the lobby's motion lights had clicked off.

Outside the window, the sky was a deep and starless black.

Alone, and with an autumn chill wending around her ankles, she fled.

8

Colton was deep in the heart of the library, looking for a place to work, when he heard it. A single sniffle. He faltered a step, straining his ears against the archival hush. Beneath the crinkle of pages, he heard it again—a hiccup, the sound halfway to a sob.

He would have kept on—it wasn't the first time he'd come across someone crying in the stacks—if it weren't for the phantom pull at his chest. Taut as fishing wire, it reeled him in. He pushed deeper into the maze of books, peering down the nearest row. A napping couple lay sprawled atop a bed of navy-blue research binders. Nearby, a weary-looking underclassman sat dwarfed beneath an imposing stack of leather annals. The next several sections were empty. Spelled asleep, gilded motes suspended in animation where the sun fell through the deep-set windows.

Seven rows down, he found who he was looking for.

Lane, perched cross-legged on the floor, her face buried in her hands. She was dressed all in gray and girdled in shadow, the dark preening at her feet like a sad, sorry kitten. Instantly, that infernal ache carved into his bones. His molars ground together hard enough to crack. He knew he'd be expected to walk away. He knew it, but something in the slump of her shoulders kept him rooted to the spot. Raising his arm, he coughed once into his fist. Lane rocketed up, dashing at her tears with the back of her hand.

"Oh." Her face fell. "You."

"I came to tell you to keep it down." He pressed a finger to the spine of a book, feigning interest in the title. "There's a noise ordinance in the library."

She rubbed at the upturned tip of her nose and said nothing. Her total lack of a rebuke made his jibe fall flat. She looked as vulnerable as he'd ever seen her, swimming in a rumpled hoodie and joggers, sprigs of lavender springing from her bun.

He couldn't leave, but he couldn't stay, either. Not where anyone could happen upon them. Peering through the shelves, he reassured himself that no one was watching before dipping his chin in the direction of the hall.

"Follow me."

Lane's nose crinkled in suspicion. "Why?"

He didn't say. He only shouldered his bag and left, hoping she'd pursue.

By the time he reached the quiet cloister of study rooms, the tight wire of his chest had snared into a tangle. It left him short of breath, his teeth gritted. Lane stood just behind him, hugging her knapsack in front of her like a shield. Leering up at him through red, puffy eyes.

"I don't have a study room booked," she said.

He slipped a key out of his pocket and brandished it between them. "TA perk. Come on."

They filed inside one after the other, Lane giving him as wide a berth as she could manage. The door snicked shut behind him with a brittle click. He slipped the key back into his pocket. Several paces away, Lane stood braced before the whiteboard easel like an alley cat, hackles raised.

"What are we doing here?"

"I've got a paper on multiversal ethical theorems." Tossing his backpack down next to hers, he dropped into the nearest seat. A notebook stuck out of Lane's open knapsack, spiral bound and unfamiliar. He side-eyed the pinched scrawl and said, "You can feel free to keep crying, if you find that sort of thing productive. At least in here you won't draw an audience."

He didn't look up from his sideways perusal of the unfamiliar handwriting as Lane dragged out a chair and plummeted into it with far more force than the action necessitated. Jabbing an aching finger at the notebook, he asked, "What's this?"

Lane looked where he was pointing. "Adya's Latin notes."

"And why do you have those?"

"Because," she said, digging her thumbnail into a lewd drawing someone had chiseled into the table, "mine are useless."

Leaning forward, he dragged the notebook toward him. The instant he glanced down at it, he wished he hadn't. The top of the page was normal enough—the declensions of nouns, a list of vocabulary. Halfway down, the ink blotted. The beginnings of a phrase took shape.

Non omnis moriar.

Dawoud had written it forward. She'd scribbled it backward. She'd looped it upside down. *Non omnis moriar. Non omnis moriar.* Colton's stomach went cold. He set the notebook down, metal spiral clicking wood.

"These seem pretty useless, too," he said, striving for a detachment he didn't feel. When he glanced up at Lane, it was to find her a thousand miles away. Chin balanced on her fist. Staring out the wide oriel window on the eastern wall. Sunlight turning her eyes to liquid viridian.

"Wednesday," he said, softer than he'd meant to. Slowly, her gaze slid his way. "Why don't you just tell your professors the truth?"

"I'm not embarrassed about it," she said, "if that's what you think. It's just that in the moment, I'm always worried I'll make them feel like jerks."

"Maybe they deserve to feel like jerks."

"Never mind." She slumped forward, chin in her hands. "You wouldn't get it."

"Maybe not. But I know for a fact you emailed all their TAs over the summer. If they didn't read the email, that's on them."

She regarded him in silence for a long moment, pulling her legs into a pretzel.

"My parents wanted me to enroll in an online program," she said, once the quiet had stretched on for too long. "I pushed for more. I wanted the experience." She said it with derision, like experience was something laughable. Something worthy of scorn. "In the lecture halls, there's a thousand noises. Someone's turning a page. Someone has a cough. Someone keeps clicking their pen. I thought I'd be able to keep up if I just stayed on top of the note-taking. But there's no point if the notes are full of holes."

He thought of her penciled butterfly, the way the words trailed off and bloomed into wings spread wide. He saw now what else peeked out of her knapsack. An exam, an angry red SEE ME slashed across the top.

A scoff broke away from her. "Not that you care."

Colton wanted to tell her she was dead wrong. He'd never cared about anything more in his life. Instead, he stayed quiet, every last one of his bones aching. Outside in the hall, a cluster of students trickled past. A disembodied laugh pushed through the door in a muffle. His hands felt full of hairline fractures. Insubordination, ground deep. The legs of his chair stuttered over tile as he stood, indicating for Lane to do the same.

"Come here."

Her eyes tracked him as he moved toward the window. "Why?"

"I want to show you something."

Reluctantly, she joined him at the easternmost wall. Beyond the dormered roof of the student center there stood a sparse wood. Its belly of gnarled oaks clawed at the sky. Its edges were bordered in a tangle of evergreens.

"Look out there past the trees," he said. "What do you see?"

She rose up onto her toes, eyes narrowed. "More trees."

Resting his temple against the sun-warmed glass, he peered down at her. "For someone so opposed to stepping on toes, you seem to have no problem stepping on mine."

She traced a heart into the gray cloud of her breath and didn't acknowledge him. "Oh, wait." Her fingertip stilled against the glass. "I *do* see something. There's a little roof poking out of the trees."

He remained propped against the window, watching her. "How much do you know about Godbole's history?"

"I skimmed that portion of the welcome packet," she admitted.

"I'll give it to you in a nutshell, then," he said, "because it's important for what I'm about to tell you."

This got her attention. She angled her face up to his, her hands disappearing into the cuffs of her sleeves.

"Devan Godbole was a laughingstock well before he became an academic namesake," he said. "No one believed his theories on slipping between worlds. He spent years being laughed out of international science councils until Whitehall found him."

Lane stood rapt, dwarfed in his shadow. Knotting and unknotting the drawstrings of her sweatshirt. The first flurry of nerves ran through him. He wasn't telling her anything expressly forbidden, but he was skirting dangerously close.

"Godbole needed a financier," he continued. "Whitehall needed someone with vision. They spent the next several years following an EMF meter over the whole of the world, mapping out ley lines from one country to the next. They were in Wiltshire when they found it—Godbole's fingers hooked on a wrinkle. The way Whitehall tells it, it was a mild, sunny day in England when Godbole peeled back the sky and looked through to the other side to see that it was raining."

Lane frowned up at him, her tears dried and gone. "What does any of that have to do with the house in the woods?"

"Whitehall calls it the Sanctum. They were following an ancient coffin road through the countryside when they first found the rift. The tear was along the base of an old stone foundation. I don't know why they brought it back. Sentimentality, maybe. But they had the foundation dismantled and the stones shipped from England."

That was two years before Godbole's accreditation. Shortly thereafter, and six months before the ribbon was cut at Godbole's great glass monolith, Devan Godbole went missing. Without a trace. Without a warning. Vanished. Like a lark, as if he'd blinked out of one reality and into another. He'd never reappeared.

"Whitehall had the Sanctum erected in Godbole's honor," he said. "It was built with the same stones they brought with them from England."

She stared at him, her mouth screwing up to one side. He wished he knew what was going on in her head. What she made of him, in the quiet of her mind.

As if he'd spoken his wish right out loud, she said, "I'm trying to figure out how this circles back to me failing out of school."

"You're not failing out of school," he said. "Don't be so dramatic. And this isn't about you at all. It's about the notes Dawoud gave you. All those Latin ambigrams? She's experiencing a dissociative blockage."

Her fingers tightened over the drawstrings. "What is that?"

"I overheard some of her supervision meeting with Whitehall the other day. She's been trying to get out of her head, right?"

"Right."

He wasn't meant to get close. He wasn't allowed to know her. But no one had ever said anything about discussing her roommate. "The sort of astral projection Dawoud is attempting is similar to pushing at a revolving door," he explained. "The carriage won't turn if something else is pushing on the other side."

Discomfort crept into Lane's eyes. "What does that mean?"

"It means she can't get out, because something else is trying to get in. That's why her notebook is flooded with a dead language. The words aren't coming from her." He rapped a knuckle against the glass. "You should take her to the Sanctum."

She rose again to her toes, peering out the window and into the wood. "Why there?"

He shrugged. "Some people think the stones act as a locus of supernatural energy."

Her cypress stare locked on him. "And what do you think?"

"I think it's dirty and it reeks of weed. But if Dawoud is looking for answers, it's worth a try."

He knew by the crinkle in her nose that she was trying to puzzle out whether or not she should trust him. *No,* he wanted to tell her. *Definitely not.* He wanted to tell her that she should stay far away from him. She should stop bringing him coffees. She should stop showing up early to class. She should, at all costs, avoid being caught alone with him.

He'd never tell her any of that. This close, the nearness of her sank into him like teeth. That preternatural pain whittled at his bones. Understanding lit like a wick. He'd take it, he realized. He'd break the rules. He'd welcome this slow, impossible unraveling over the alternative.

Over never knowing her at all.

Flexing his fingers, he slid his hands into his pockets. He hoped she hadn't noticed how they shook. As nonchalantly as he knew how, he said, "I can help you with your classes, if you'd like."

9

Delaney hadn't always been able to hear a hum in the silence. When she first lost her hearing, and for a long time afterward, all she heard was that shrill ringing in her ears. Sometimes, later on, when she was tired or unfocused—when she hovered right on that liminal cusp between sleep and waking—the shrill vibrato of tinnitus would take shape. The sound would become the hum, the hum a word. A murmur. A sigh. By then she was too old for games. The cuts on her knees had faded to scars. She'd stopped whispering her secrets to the dark.

I'm dreaming, she'd tell herself, and shut her eyes. *Only dreaming.*

She wasn't dreaming now. She was wide awake. Standing in the wood, a late-afternoon sun falling sideways through the trees. In front of her was a house.

A sanctum.

It was, as a whole, a fairly unassuming structure. The mismatched gray stonework was set with fretted windows and capped in a steeply dormered roof. It looked like the love child of a modest chapel and Baba Yaga's hut—as though it couldn't decide whether it wanted to signal a call to worship or sprout a pair of chicken legs and take off through the wood.

Moreover, it was speaking to her.

The hum in her head sang through the whole of her body here, coursing through her in a river of noise. She hung back on the foot-trodden path and watched the darkness pour out through the yawning maw of the open front door. It bubbled forth like champagne, frothing at the lip, drunk and savage and beckoning. She didn't want to go inside.

She hadn't wanted to come at all, but Delaney had been custom-built into someone agreeable, and she hadn't managed to talk Adya and Mackenzie out of dragging her along, once she'd put the idea in their heads.

Inside, she found Adya seated on the buckled hardwood of the anterior narthex, sinking into the pleated knit of her sweater. The light of a nearby banker's lamp caught in the cerulean waves of her hijab, winked in the revolving faces of her pendant. A few feet away, Mackenzie sat at a white bifold table, lazily flicking through a deck of tarot cards.

"You should tell him you'll do it," Mackenzie said, without looking up.

Delaney paused in her examination of a rusted cart, stacked high with well-worn copies of waterlogged paperbacks and naked hardcovers. A laminated sign clung precariously to the side: DON'T BE AN ASSHOLE. IF YOU TAKE A BOOK, LEAVE A BOOK.

"Tell who I'll do what?"

"Price." Mackenzie gathered up the loose cards into her deck and began shuffling. "Tell him you'll study with him."

Delaney set a coverless copy of *The Catcher in the Rye* back among its peers. She hadn't told either of them about Colton's offer. She'd done her best not to think about it at all—about how close they'd stood, their toes nearly touching. The deep well of his stare. The tremor in his hands.

"Don't look at me like that, honey." Mackenzie flipped the foiled cards one after the other, setting them in front of her in a cursory *click, click, click.* The drowning man. The high priestess. The lovers. "It's not like I read your diary. I can't help seeing these things. It's like a sneeze. It comes out of nowhere."

"It's invasive," Adya said, without taking her eyes off the pendant. "You're like an invasive plant. Also, you're talking too much."

"It doesn't matter if I'm talking or not. You can't just *will* a psychic block away. It has to work its way out."

"Like a splinter," Adya mused.

"Sure." Mackenzie scooped up her cards. "Like a splinter." Shuffling the deck, she ran her thumbnail along the top in a sullen inspection. "I looked up that phrase you wrote in your notebook, by the way. *Non omnis moriar?* It's from the poet Horace. It means 'I shall not wholly die.'"

There followed a beat. Sound winnowed out, slipping sideways. Turning strange. Deep within Delaney's head, the ringing began. Timorous as birdsong, sharp as a whistle, enduring as a hum.

"Whatever's trying to get inside Adya's head," Mackenzie said, sounding as though she were speaking underwater, "it has a pretty intense motto."

The ringing between Delaney's ears reached a pinnacle that shuddered her eyes in their sockets. She pinched the bridge of her nose and exhaled slowly, regretting this excursion more and more by the minute.

"I'm going to look around," she said, already heading deeper into the empty building. Mackenzie called after her, but she'd moved quickly out of earshot, passing beneath an alcove framed in spindlework and into the vaulted nave of the innermost space.

Here, the waning light fell through the frets in thin spills of merlot, washing the whole of the room in red. A row of tin cans lined the floor, each stuffed full of writing utensils. Nearby, an overturned milk crate housed a swear jar on which someone had written the word *fubar*. The glass was packed full of loose change. The walls were covered in writing, and as she drew closer, she saw that they were names. She opened the flashlight on her phone and scanned the list, running her fingers over the graffitied roster until she reached a few names she recognized.

Eric Hayes was scrawled in permanent marker, the *E* substantially larger than the rest. Next to his name was a number. Nearby, someone named Julian Guzman had scribbled his name and a corresponding number in chicken scratch. Underneath sat a name she knew, the handwriting infuriatingly uniform.

Colton Price.

She traced the letters, dragging her fingertip over the neat slash of the *l*, the meticulous dot of the *i*, the careful loop of the zero beside it. Strange, that she'd spent weeks spinning out in his orbit only to keep colliding with him now in the oddest of ways. After how unsociable he'd been each morning, his sudden proposition to help her with coursework felt a little bit like whiplash, dizzying and uncertain. And yet, her grades were tanking. Her scholarship was at risk. On a campus full of extraordinary students, she was quickly cementing herself as someone entirely ordinary. Someone just a handful of C-minuses away from dropping out of school.

She wasn't in a position to refuse his offer.

She reached down by her feet and drew a permanent marker out of a dented tin can. The light from her phone cast the list in a silvery pall. On a whim, she added her name alongside Colton's. When she leaned in to blow on the still-wet ink, her eyes caught on a name directly beneath.

Nate Schiller, penned in a flourishing script that was more art than autograph.

"That's me," said a voice from directly behind her.

She yelped, dropping both her phone and the marker. She found the speaker splayed against a tired salmon love seat, his arms slung over bent knees. Pale, messy curls pushed out from beneath a hood, and from here she could see the white tangle of earbuds disappearing into his sweatshirt.

Plucking at a snag in the cushion, he said, "Sorry. I didn't mean to scare you. It's just—that's my name you're looking at. I thought it'd be funny to write it that way. My mom made me take a calligraphy course one year. She thought it might help with my shit handwriting." Stuffing pooled on the floor where he flicked it, and he added, "It didn't, though. Help."

Delaney pried her hand off her heart. "You're Nate?"

"Unfortunately," he said, his grin self-deprecating.

"I'm Lane."

"I know." Then, rushing, "I'm not a creep. I heard you and your friends talking."

"You're not a creep," she echoed, "and yet you're sitting here in the dark alone. Sorry, but that's the definition of creepy."

He sat up and stretched, scratching at the crown of his head through his hood. "In fairness," he said, speaking through a yawn, "it wasn't dark when I got here. And I said 'Hey' when you first walked in, but I don't think you heard me."

74

"Oh." She scuffed the toe of her boot against the floor. "Yeah, probably not. I don't have the best hearing."

He waved her off, prying his earbuds loose. "What are you doing adding your name to the dead pool?"

Faltering, she glanced back at the wall of names. "The *what*?"

"The dead pool," he said again, enunciating. "That's what the numbers are for. They're bets. Everyone up on that wall has either died or is going to die."

Unease flared in her chest. She gaped at him, unsure how to read his tone. Spotlit particles danced in the broad, silvery beacon of her flashlight.

"Kidding," Nate said when she didn't speak. "Kind of. We did place bets. Plus, Julian Guzman's up there, and he's dead. It's all over the local news in Illinois. Allegedly, he was killed in a collision. *Allegedly.* And there's others missing."

"Sorry," Delaney said, not following, "who else is missing?"

"Ryan Peretti," he said, and jabbed a finger toward the wall of names. "He was a rising senior, but he didn't reenroll this semester. And then there's Greg Kostopoulos. He and I have physics together, but he hasn't been in class all week. Someone said he has the flu."

"But you don't think so." Delaney scooped up her phone and shut off the light, leaving them in the purpling haze of sunset.

"I don't."

"Because you think they've both died."

Nate shrugged. "They *are* in the dead pool."

"So are you," she pointed out.

"So am I." He sounded wistful as he sat back against the couch and pushed an earbud into his left ear. "And now so are you. Didn't

75

your parents tell you you should never sign anything without knowing what it is you're signing?"

A shout flooded the hollow nave, reverberating between them. Delaney nearly dropped her phone a second time.

Nate frowned in the direction of the narthex. "What was that?"

"My roommate," Delaney said. "I think. I'm going to go make sure she's okay. Are you heading out? It's getting pretty dark."

He popped in his other earbud. His features were murky beneath the twilit haze, shadows swimming in place of his smile. From this distance, she couldn't quite make out the color of his eyes. "I'll probably hang out here a while longer. I'm not much of a people person."

"I get that," she said, because neither was she. She felt a funny sort of kinship with him—this boy who didn't mind a little bit of solitude. For the first time since the semester began, she felt as if she'd finally bumped into someone on equal footing. "See you around campus, then?"

His eyes flashed in the waning light. "Sure," he said. "I'll see you around."

She hurried off without him, the smell of marker vapors following her out.

She found Adya and Mackenzie where she'd left them, the latter passing the former a bottle of water, one hand rubbing circles into her back. The tarot cards were scattered about the floor as though they'd been pitched in a strong wind.

"What happened?" Delaney asked, drawing up short.

Adya didn't reply right away. Shutting her eyes, she rubbed at them with the heels of her hands. The pendant sat shattered on the ground in front of her, broken bits of crystal catching the light. Drawing a single, shaky breath, she said, "I saw him."

"The same boy as before?" Delaney bent down and began gathering up Mackenzie's cards, stomach curdling.

"I think so," Adya said after she'd capped her water. Her stare was black in the paltry light, the dark fringe of her lashes dewed with tears. "I couldn't see his face."

Delaney thought of the wall of names, Nate Schiller lit red by the drowning sun. *"Everyone up on that wall has either died or is going to die."* Suddenly, it didn't seem so far-fetched.

"You're okay," Mackenzie said as Adya let out a shuddering exhale. "You're fine, just keep sipping your water."

Delaney reached for another card and drew her hand back, quick. A tear of blood welled on the tip of her finger. Sucking the paper cut clean, she glanced down at the card. The devil smiled up at her, tongue forked and tail lashing.

"Did he say anything to you?" she asked, still sucking at the sting in her finger.

Adya's eyes were big and round as they met hers. "No," she said. "He'd been ripped apart."

≪ 10 ≫

The Apostle made the call at night, as he always did. He stood in his office on the second floor of his sprawling Newton town house, backlit by the silver-plate moon in the great bay window. As he always did. In the corner, the darkness convalesced. It grew arms, thin and reaching. It watched, waiting, its smile cut with moonlight.

As it always did.

He did his level best to ignore it.

He wore his bathrobe, the fine pima cotton emblazoned with his initials. His slippers, one size too small, had been a Christmas gift from his wife. The memory foam sweated against the soles of his feet. His phone was a burner. Tonight, it felt heavier than usual.

The phone rang once. Two times. Three. He didn't like to be ignored. He pressed his thumb to the polished glass casing to his left. It sat atop a heavy plinth, the bleached white of a bone shard nestled in a beveled snuffbox within. The curve of it caught ivory in the moonlight, its edges dagger sharp where it had been filed away. Material proof of the vast extent of the Priory's reach. Proof that initiating a boy who could rip open the sky between worlds had been a worthwhile investment indeed.

A fourth ring shivered in his ear.

He was getting annoyed.

He paced, circling the display, his eyes never leaving the necrotic shard. It was his genie's lamp, his Charon's coin. His bit of Koschei's soul, squirreled away inside a needle, inside an egg, inside a little wooden chest in a little glass case on the second story of a Newton town house.

A voice picked up on the other end. "I just absolutely beasted this level."

The Apostle shut his eyes. Opened them again. The bone gleamed with an unholy sheen. "This is the second time I've called you."

"Is it?" The Apostle heard the continuous beeping of a game. "The gods of Valhalla needed my assistance."

"I assure you I don't know what that means."

The Apostle heard the digital clang of swords, the computerized sound of someone dying a horrific death. *"Nailed him,"* Colton Price said, not to him. Then, "You should get into gaming. It might be good for your ulcer."

He could not see how hacking ogres to bits with a sword could be remotely good for his ulcer, but he refrained from saying so aloud. Instead, he shut his eyes and drew a breath. He counted backward from ten, which his therapist had politely suggested he try as a means of quelling his rage.

It wasn't that he was an angry man by nature; it was just that Colton Price was masterful at pressing buttons. The Priory had set eyes on Price the very moment he'd arrived at Godbole. They'd invited him to pledge, not because he'd rushed, but because he was the unequivocal best at what he did. A marvel, this boy who'd cheated death—who'd grown into a man capable of tearing open the sky.

But there was no denying Colton Price was difficult to work with.

"There's been a hiccup in the plan," the Apostle said.

Price sucked air through his teeth. "I'd argue Julian Guzman biting the dust is a little bit bigger than a hiccup."

"All is not lost. We've still got Kostopoulos."

More pinging; steel met steel. A voice screamed, high and tinny. "He won't do any better," Price said. "They're canaries in a coal mine. Maybe you should take the sign for what it is."

A twitch began in his eye. He rubbed at it with a finger, determined not to shout. "Remind me what it was Thomas Edison said about failure."

He knew Price would know. The boy was a walking encyclopedia, unforgivably smug in the understanding that he was, more often than not, the smartest person in the room. "'I have not failed ten thousand times,'" he said, speaking over the muffled clash of swords, "'I've successfully found ten thousand ways that won't work.'"

"One of them will take," the Apostle insisted, and said nothing else.

In the ensuing silence, Price let out a laugh. "All right," he said. "I can hear you stewing through the phone. Break a few more light bulbs. Kill a few more canaries. I don't care."

"You should. Need I remind you that the results of this project affect you as well as me?"

The game beeped. A winning bell sounded. "Maybe."

The Apostle scowled down at his phone. He didn't like that response. *Maybe.* It reeked of belligerence. Colton Price, with all that beat in his blood, needed to be very carefully controlled. He wasn't a boy; he was a weapon. And he knew it.

"I do hope you've been staying sharp, Mr. Price."

"As a tack," he replied, without missing a beat.

"Really?" The Apostle pressed his hand to the case. The bone shard winked up at him, milky with moonglow. "Because I've had reports that you've been spending your mornings with Ms. Meyers-Petrov."

For once, the wearisome Price didn't instantly supply a witty response. To anyone else, the silence would have seemed like contrition, but the Apostle knew better. Colton Price had never been contrite a day in his life. He was, as a rule, utterly disdainful. He wasn't the sort to bother with excuses. He most likely didn't even care that he'd been caught. In the background, the game began anew. Something snarled, the sound bestial in the quiet.

"You know the risks," the Apostle reminded him. "You know the price you'll pay should you become worthless to the Priory."

"I don't plan to become worthless."

"Then keep your distance. I trust Meeker gave you the reports?"

"Yeah," Price said. "I've got the folders."

"Study them. Look for patterns. Find out what the others did wrong. That's your job. It's the only job. Nothing else."

The line went dead.

The Apostle pried the phone from his ear. It was hot in his hand. Clouds had slipped across the moon during the call, muting the light so it fell in through the windows in obscure strips—too dark to see by. The bone shard blackened, turning obsidian in the gloom. It sent— though it should not have—a thrum of disquiet down his spine. He felt his way to the desk and slumped in his chair, startling slightly at the creak of leather beneath him.

At the far end of the room, the thin arms of dark dragged nearer. Talons dug into the floor. A head coalesced, the wrongness of it never failing to strike cold into his heart. He tried not to look at the figure directly as the darkness staggered to its feet, skull concave, mouth gaped like a wound. The smell of putrefaction permeated the room, mildewed and horrible and unyielding. He'd spent the past ten years trying to air it out. Windows open, candles lit, air fresheners hung. It was no use.

The stench of death was in everything he owned.

"Go away," he said crossly. "I'm taking care of it."

That terrible dark smiled a terrible smile. When it spoke, its voice was full of cold, slithering things. "It's you and it's me," it said. "It's me and it's you."

"You keep saying that," the Apostle said, "but I'm the only one doing all the work."

"All is as you wanted," sang the dark, which couldn't be, he thought, further from the truth. Nothing was as he wanted. That was precisely the problem. Something thumped across the far side of the room. It sounded heavy. He briefly considered turning on the lights and then thought better of it. It was far worse, he'd learned, to look upon that terrible face. To see it bashed in and broken. To see it laughing at him.

"The boy will follow where she goes," crooned the dark, dragging itself close. "He will follow her and follow her. And then," it said, all packed with glee, "and then, my dear, my darling, my Dickie, she will be your undoing."

11

The first time Liam let Colton tag along to a scrimmage, he'd been six years old. Too small to participate, he'd been happy enough to warm the bench and watch his brother play. Beside him sat the silver stereo Liam had carried with them from home. An old mixtape of their father's played through the oval speakers. Cupping a hot cocoa between mittened hands, he'd done his best to play DJ for Liam and his band of friends.

"We need something epic," Liam had shouted over at him, his breath turning to crystals. The day was gray and wet. The snow blew in sideways in flurries that landed like rain. On the ice, the blue of Liam's ski jacket turned black with slush. "Something we can win to. An anthem."

At six years old, Colton hadn't known what an anthem was, but he knew epic when he heard it. Their father's tape was full of songs from the '80s—heavy metal hits and hard rock ballads that made the whole bench shake. He stopped when he reached the opening notes of a clean guitar riff. There was something sinister in the sound. Something thrilling. The percussion of tom-tom drums beat in his chest. Sank into him like claws. On the ice, Liam's head picked up, and he flashed Colton a thumbs-up, stick in the air.

"That's it, C.J.! Leave it there!"

Whitehall's office was dark, lit only by the green glass shell of the banker's lamp. It threw the shadows into stark relief along the broad oak paneling, casting Colton and his open laptop in a sphere of yellow. His phone sat faceup on the desk, his earbuds in a tangle where he'd discarded them. The opening riff of a guitar solo echoed tinnily through the speakers. An E-minor chord, branded into his subconscious.

Say your prayers, little one, don't forget, my son.

He switched off his phone. Silence strung through the space. It felt spindled and cold. It left him uneasy. He glanced down at his watch to see only two minutes had passed since he'd checked it last. Two minutes, where it felt like ten. He didn't like when time dragged this way. When it slowed to a near still. It felt like being stuck inside a dream where his legs were made of lead. Unable to run. Unable to swim. Dark closing in. His mouth full of water.

When he looked up, a figure filled the doorway.

"It's creepy that you prefer sitting in the dark like this, you know." Eric Hayes didn't bother with a hello as he pushed into the office, flicking the overhead light on as the door clicked shut behind him. Instantly, the little space was flooded with a too-bright light. Colton fought the urge to shield his eyes. Their muddled reflections swam into the mirror dark of the great bay window, their outlines malformed. "Have you heard from the Apostle?"

"Unfortunately." Colton shut his laptop. "Have you?"

"Not since Guzman turned up dead. I don't like it. What are we listening to?" He scooped up Colton's earbuds and stuffed one in his ear. "Sick, Metallica? I didn't peg you as a metal fan."

"I'm not," Colton said. It wasn't a lie.

Hayes fixed him in a look. Colton ignored it and returned his attention to the laptop, scrolling through the discussion board for the previous night's assignment. Out of the corner of his eye, he saw Hayes pluck the earbud from his ear and spin it round between his thumb and forefinger. He could sense him chewing on his next words, preparing to spit them out.

"Look," he said, tapping the earbud against the desk, "my kid sister's big into musicals. Not my scene, but she eats it up. She's been a theater and dance kid her whole life."

"And this applies to me, because," Colton said, without looking up from his computer.

"I'm just saying. If she ever died, I don't think I could stomach it—listening to her show tunes day in and day out."

Colton fell quiet. His finger hovered over the touchpad of his laptop. Taking his silence as invitation, Hayes dragged out a chair and dropped into it, legs sprawled. "You're more tormented than usual today. It's bumming me out."

Colton shut his computer and leaned back far enough to creak the springs of Whitehall's chair. "Is there a reason you're here?"

Hayes's jaw tightened. "Can't a guy want to hang out?"

Colton's only response was an unwavering stare. Hayes relented with a groan. "Fine. I went for a run after classes yesterday. When I hit the wooded trails out back, I saw the lights on at the Sanctum and I thought I'd swing by and check it out."

"And?" Colton sat perfectly still. "What did you find?"

Hayes kneaded his knuckles until they cracked. "Pretty sure I saw your girl kicking it with Nate Schiller."

On the shelf behind Colton, the heavy bracket clock counted down the seconds. The epochal *tick, tick, tick* of it made him want to crawl out of his skin. "That's not possible."

Hayes sat back with a grimace. "She talked to you, didn't she?"

"It's not the same thing."

"Get over yourself, it's pretty damn close." Hayes kicked out the heel of his boot. "If she and Schiller are buddying up, you know what that means, right?"

He did.

He knew all too well.

A soft knock at the door kept him from having to answer. Hayes glanced over at him, frowning. "Did you change your office hours?"

"No," he said. Then, louder, "It's open."

The door pushed inward, and there was Lane, light from the hall spilling around her in an aura. That formidable ache pushed into his skin. It beat through him the way the opening riff of the ballad had pounded in his chest that snowy winter's day at the pond. He folded his fingers into a hasty fist.

"Wednesday," he said, as carefully as he knew how. "Can I help you?"

"Yes, actually. Can we talk?" Her green eyes flitted to Hayes. "Privately?"

With a grin that made Colton want to punch him in the mouth, Hayes leaned back and kicked his boots up onto the desk. "Anything you need to say to Price, you can say to me."

"Oh." Lane looked to Colton. He ground his jaw and stared back. "Okay." She dug the toe of her boot into the floor. "I've given some thought to your offer, and I've decided to take you up on it."

Colton could feel Hayes watching him. Waiting to see how thoroughly he could screw this up. He wanted to say a thousand different things. Instead, he said, "I'm not sure what you mean."

Lane blinked, recalibrating. "The other day," she said, as though he might have simply forgotten. "You said you'd help me study."

He'd spent enough time staring down his demons in the mirror to know the smile he gave her was bone-chillingly cold. "If you're having difficulty in Whitehall's class, you can make an appointment during my office hours like everyone else."

She gaped at him, her eyes perfect circles of surprise. Color rose into her cheeks. He'd never felt more like an asshole.

"Okay. Sure." She bit out her words one curt syllable at a time. "I'm sorry to have bothered you."

She didn't wait for a dismissal. Instead, she spun on her heel, the black hem of her skirt flaring out. The door slammed, the force of her departure juddering the knickknacks on their shelves. The sound of it felt absolute. Like a stone rolled over a tomb.

Colton shut his eyes. Listened to the muffled fall of her boots fading into silence.

"Wow" was all Hayes said.

"Don't start."

"That was brutal."

Colton sank deeper into his seat and opted not to respond.

"Be real with me for a second here," Hayes said. "Do you get off on being pushed around?"

"No one is being pushed around."

"Not yet, maybe. But what happens when she figures it out?" When Colton didn't offer up an answer, Hayes stood to go. "Just don't be an idiot. You're not the only one with something to lose. We're close to the end, all right? You know the stakes. We can't close without you."

Again, Colton was quiet. Hayes heaved out a sigh.

"Look, is she really that important?"

"Yes," he said, in answer to Hayes's question. One word. Too small to bear the impossible weight of the truth. Was she important? *Was Delaney Meyers-Petrov important?* The question was laughable, and so he laughed at it. The sound sawed out of him in an entirely unfunny rasp. "Yes," he said again.

Hayes frowned down at him. "Then leave her alone, Price. Before you get her killed."

❧ 12 ❧

Delaney was not going to pass her calculus exam on Monday. It wasn't that she didn't understand the correct order of operations, though her notes were mostly riddled in butterflies. It wasn't that she hadn't taken the time to study, though the table in front of her was currently littered with newspaper clippings.

It was, instead, that Adya was becoming increasingly certain she'd witnessed a murder.

"What exactly did you mean," Mackenzie asked, tipping back in her chair on the far side of the table, "by 'ripped apart'?"

Next to her, Adya took an audible sip of her chai and didn't respond. All around them, the campus coffee shop was packed full of students. A silver September rain drilled sideways against the windows. Delaney chewed on the cap of her pen and did her best to follow the broken flow of conversation.

Undeterred by Adya's silence, Mackenzie pressed on. "Would you say he'd been boned like a fish? Or was it more of a light flaying?"

Adya slammed her mug down on the table. "Mackenzie, if you keep talking about this, I'm going to throw up. Speaking of nauseating, what is on your head?"

Mackenzie readjusted the bill of her deerstalker cap. "It's a detective's hat."

"You look ridiculous. Where did you even find it?"

"The theater department. Focus, you're getting us off track."

"Nate said there's some students who haven't shown up this semester," Delaney volunteered, when there was enough of a lull for her to feel comfortable interjecting. The café was flooded with alternative rock, the rumble of the espresso machine, the clatter of silverware. All of it melded into an indistinguishable fuzz that swallowed up the voices of her companions.

"Let's circle back to that." Mackenzie flipped her chair around so that she was perched backward, arms slung over the spine. "Your antisocial friend—"

"Nate," Delaney interjected.

"—said the wall of names was a mark of impending death. That could be relevant. Did you recognize anyone on it?"

"Price," Delaney admitted. His name wedged like a lump in her throat. She didn't want to think about Colton. Not after last night. She didn't want to see him again, either—not unless it was to watch him trip over his stupid, expensive shoes and faceplant into a ditch.

"Maybe he knows something." Mackenzie jotted a note onto her yellow legal pad. "Lane, can you ask him?"

"Me?" Her voice squeaked out around the lump. "Why me?"

Mackenzie didn't look up from her pad. "The two of you have a thing."

Horror strung through her. "We do *not* have a thing."

"You do kind of have a thing," Adya said, poking at the ring of milk foam in her mug. "You spend all that time sitting in that empty classroom together. You might as well talk about something."

Delaney swung her boot beneath the table, making contact with Adya's shin. "I wouldn't even know how to bring it up."

"Easy," Mackenzie said. "You just say, 'Hey, I saw your name on a wall with a bunch of other names. Any chance one of them might have been deboned and, slash or, torn into pieces?'" Eyes brightening, the redhead flashed her a wide, feline grin. "In fact, you can practice right now. Price is on his way in."

"What?" Delaney froze, unsettled. "You can *sense* him?"

"Yeah," Mackenzie said. "With my eyes. He just walked by the window."

The door swung wide, bells jingling, and a chilly wind blasted over the threshold. There, on the welcome mat, stood Colton Price, a plaid scarf the color of tobacco leaf wrapped twice around his throat. His cheeks were pinked with cold and his hair was dark with rainwater, and—most disturbingly of all—he was looking over at her.

Mackenzie began gathering up their research, shoving stray papers into her bag. "Invite him over here," she ordered.

"I will not."

"You will, too." Mackenzie looped her arm through Adya's and hauled her to her feet. "Take one for the team, Laney-Jane."

"Wait," Adya protested. "I didn't finish my drink."

Delaney watched them go, panic building, and thought about packing up her things and chasing after them. Before she could reach for her bag, the chair opposite her was drawn out and Colton dropped into it, the cold spilling off him in waves.

Rubbing warmth back into his hands, he said, "You look nice today."

The unexpected compliment thrummed through her. Swallowing thickly, she made a careful show of examining her notes. "I'm busy."

"Hostile," he noted. He looked offensively like himself today—all hard lines and sharp angles, his mouth bladed and his eyes just a shade too dark. "You're mad at me."

"You miss nothing."

"Would it help if I apologize?"

"No," she assured him, "so don't waste your breath."

He ignored her, dragging her open notebook closer for inspection. The leaden wings of a butterfly were mortifyingly visible on the page. "Look, Wednesday," he said, examining her work. "You caught me off guard yesterday. I really do want to help you."

"I don't need your help, Price, but thank you." She leaned across the table and tugged at her notebook. It didn't give.

Colton flashed her a wounded look. "You don't mean that."

"I do, actually. Let *go*." She gave the notebook another tug, harder this time than before, and he relinquished his grip. The unexpected compliance sent her toppling back into her seat with an *ow*.

"Think about this rationally for a minute," he said, unwinding his scarf. She could see the smallest peek of his clavicle at this angle—the fine cordage of his throat. Her mouth felt dry. "I'm not exactly supposed to have one-on-one study sessions with freshmen in the class I'm assisting. It might look like I'm helping you cheat."

The way he was looking at her, his eyes swallowing up the light, made her nerves pop into sparks. "What are you saying? You want us to have secret study dates?"

"If you put it that way, sure." He glanced down at his watch. "The fewer people who know, the better."

"I don't know." From across the café, she felt the force of Mackenzie's stare drilling into her. She knew what her floormate would say, if she were here. She'd tell Lane a study date would be the perfect chance to find out more about the wall of names. She'd tell her to do a better job playing detective. She'd tell her to say yes. Instead, Delaney chewed at the cap of her pen and said, "Sounds risky."

"For me," Colton assured her. "Not for you."

"Then why'd you offer?" The question wobbled in the air between them, strung thin beneath the acrid smack of burnt espresso, the wet slap of September rain. When he didn't reply, she took the liberty of answering for him.

"Because you feel bad for me. You look at me, and you don't see a contender. You just see a kicked puppy. Poor deaf Delaney, who draws butterflies in her notebooks and can't even pass an open-notes quiz."

"That's not why," he said, with a severity that brooked no argument.

Delaney swallowed, her reply sticking in her throat. She wished he would leave. He was unnerving her—this too-communicative Colton, his smiles sharp enough to nick an artery. He was a far cry from the Colton she'd grown accustomed to—distant and mono-syllabic and determined to avoid her at all costs.

"You caught me in a moment of weakness the other day," she said, in a voice that was much too small for her liking. "I dumped a lot of personal information on you when I shouldn't have. I think it's probably best for both of us if we just pretend it never happened."

Flatly, he said, "No."

"Sorry?"

"You heard me, Wednesday. I don't want to pretend it never happened. I told you I wanted to work together. I meant it."

There was something alarmingly earnest in his gaze. She looked away from it, ignoring the stutter of her pulse. "Working together implies you get something out of this, too."

He hooked an elbow over the spine of his chair and regarded her through a too-level gaze. "Maybe I'm an altruist."

"*Hah.*" She stifled a laugh. "Try again."

A groan built in his throat. She saw it rather than heard it—evident in the way his chest expanded, the way his shoulders tensed. The way he said "Wednesday" one syllable at a time. *Wed. Nes. Day.*

"Lane," she corrected.

"Ms. Meyers-Petrov." His voice was imbibed with sweetness, an All-American-Boy sound that set her immediately on edge. "You want quid pro quo? I can do quid pro quo." Leaning across the table, he tore the butterfly from its binding and brandished it between them in a flourish. "I want you to paint this."

"A butterfly," she deadpanned.

"Oh, is that what it is?" He held it up for inspection. "I thought it might be a locust."

"I'm not an artist." She reached for the drawing, and he leaned back, holding it just out of her grasp.

"That's fine." His hair had dried into waves, several errant curls creeping forward at his temple. "You asked what I want. This is it. I'll let you use my notes if you paint this for me."

She surrendered the drawing. "Where?"

"An excellent question." He set the butterfly down and plucked her pen from her grasp, then jotted an address across the top of her open notebook. "My house," he said. "Tonight, after your classes are done for the day."

"Your *house*?"

He spread his hands wide, affronted. "What's wrong with my house?"

"Probably nothing," she admitted, wishing she hadn't reacted quite so fervently. On the far side of the café, Mackenzie and Adya were staring openly. "It's just that you give me a real Jack the Ripper vibe sometimes, and I don't think I should go home with you."

One corner of Colton's mouth twitched. "That's incredibly rude."

"But is it untrue?"

The subsequent arch of his brows gave him an unforgivably imperious air. "I'm not planning to kill you, Wednesday. I'm extending an invitation."

"I don't know." She poked at the handle of Adya's abandoned mug. "Sounds like something a murderer might say."

Colton stared at her for a single, silent beat, a muscle working in his jaw. Then, rising from his chair, he folded the butterfly drawing in half and slid it neatly into the interior of his coat.

"I'll see you tonight," he said.

"Maybe," she called after him, but he was already walking away, his scarf trailing, the college-ruled perforations of her paper peeking around his lapels.

"Be there," he mouthed, and then he was gone, ducking beneath the jingle of the bell and the bite of the wind and plunging into the campus rush.

It wasn't until he was well out of sight that she realized he'd absconded with her pen.

13

It was well into evening when Delaney finally arrived at the address Colton had jotted in her notebook. Huddled beneath her umbrella, she made her way down the little brick lane, staring up in wonder at the little brick houses. The neat baronial homes looked like something out of a postcard, all widow's watches and finely wrought iron.

She hadn't planned to come, but then her composition professor sent her a scathing email regarding her lack of classroom participation and her Latin exam came back covered in red slashes and Mackenzie wouldn't let up about the importance of putting a name to the face in Adya's head.

Now, and in spite of her better efforts, Delaney was standing on Colton Price's road, in front of Colton Price's house.

A car rushed past. The sun dropped out of sight, leaving the cast iron streetlamps to wink on one by one by one. The sleepy brownstones lit up like votives, bathing the whole of the maple-lined lane in a merry glow.

Only one house stayed dark.

The thought that Colton Price might not be home at all was what finally spurred her into moving. She'd knock, he wouldn't answer, and then she'd leave the way she came—worrying on foot, panicking by train, stewing in the stinking heat of Government Center. She'd have more than enough ammunition to remain furious with him for days.

She climbed the stoop and knocked three times on the door.

Silence rose to meet her.

She leaned in to listen—a learned behavior, she couldn't hear beyond the wood if she'd tried—and knocked again. Again, the door stayed shut. The house remained dark and silent as a tomb.

She'd just positioned her fist to knock a third time when the door wrenched open. It widened only a crack—just enough for Colton to wedge himself into the gap. He was dressed down in a white crewneck and jeans, his feet clad in socks. His eyes were guarded, the set of his jaw unreasonably stiff, as though she'd arrived unannounced on his doorstep, and not at all as if he'd singlehandedly provoked her into coming.

"I'm here," she said, a little indignantly.

"I can see that." He didn't invite her in. In the street behind her, a car slipped past like a silvery fish, windows catching in the lamplight.

"Are you going to make me stand out here all night?"

"Of course not," he said. Then, "Yes. Actually, yes—tonight's no good for me."

"Oh." Surprise gave way to annoyance. "You're serious."

Leaning his temple against the door's edge, he said, "I wish I wasn't."

Another car slinked past on whisper treads. Her annoyance grew into the first stirrings of anger. Fighting to keep her voice level, she said, "I came all the way out here at your insistence."

"Believe me," he began, "I am very aware of that. I—"

She held up a hand to silence him. "I'm not trying to be rude, but there's no way I'm walking all the way back to the T without at least using the bathroom, so I'm going to need you to open the door and let me in."

To her surprise, he pulled the door open at once, the movement like a reflex. Like she'd tapped his tendon with a percussion hammer and he'd wrenched awake in reply. Darkness spilled out from the foyer. Colton clung to the frame, his knuckles white and his glower accusatory—as though she'd shoved the door open herself.

"Okay." Her impertinence deflated like a balloon. "I didn't think you'd actually do it."

He stayed alarmingly silent in response. Uncertain, she tiptoed across the threshold, giving him as wide a berth as she could manage. She didn't make it more than a half step before drawing up short. The spacious hall was dimly lit, white walls dancing in the glow of a dozen flickering candles that slowly melted atop the hall tree bench.

It was lovely. It was exquisite. It was, she noted in fast-blossoming horror, distressingly romantic. The door clicked shut, and she rounded on Colton to find him a few feet in front of her, long fingers laced over the crown of his head. Lit from beneath, his features were stark and suffering as a saint's.

She flung an open hand at the provisional altar. "What is this?"

"A long story," he said darkly.

"Are you—" She faltered, frowning at the snapping flames. "Is this some sort of gesture?"

The look Colton gave her was deeply afflicted. "What kind of gesture?"

"You know," she said. "A *gesture*."

The whites of his eyes expanded, and he steepled his fingers in front of his lips, clinging to patience. "I'm not coming on to you, Wednesday."

His response delivered a devastating blow. Mortified, she kicked herself for bringing it up at all. She shouldn't have said anything. She should have ignored the candles. Better yet, she should have stayed on campus, where it was warm and well lit and there was a notable lack of Colton Price.

Feigning nonchalance, she asked, "Are you summoning a demon?"

An edge crept into his voice. "No."

"Holding a séance?"

"No," he said again.

"Do you do all your studying in the dark?"

"Jesus." His eyes were a shade too black, his features chiseled a touch too sharp. Gilded in the ecclesiastic flicker of the foyer, he looked almost inhuman. "If I say yes, will you let this go?"

"Sure," she said, aware that she was staring. "I'll let it go."

"Fantastic." He set off, beckoning for her to follow. "Let's get to work. I saw your calc notes out this morning in the café. I figured we'd start there."

Colton turned out to be as formidable a tutor as he was a teaching assistant. His notes were a study in diligence. Every subject was meticulously labeled, the pages pristinely bulleted, each notebook alphabetized and color-coded to the point of obsession. Each night they staked out a workplace and studied deep into the night, combing through his stenographer-worthy binders until she'd managed to flood the sizable gaps in her notebooks with everything in his.

Night by night, the lessons began to click into place. Half-finished thoughts became concrete concepts. Broken formulas became solvable equations. Misspelled words became legible Latin. Outside the broad bay window of the Price sitting room, the world changed. The leaves on the old maples turned brittle, darkening to the color of blood. The air caught a chill it couldn't shake, whittling the wind into an arrow, sharp enough to set the glass to rattling in its panes.

The lights stayed on after that first night. Colton kept Delaney corralled in the kitchen and the living room, never venturing any deeper into the house. In the busy warren of colonial-era corridors, every last door stayed firmly shut. No one came. No one went. There was no sign that anyone else lived there at all, save for a little boy's navy-blue jacket that hung from a hook on the hall tree.

"*Do you have a younger brother?*" she'd asked one night as they sat shoulder to shoulder at the kitchen island and pored through his Latin notes.

"*No,*" he'd said, and passed her a sheet of conjugations. He hadn't elaborated, and she'd been too caught off guard by the ice in his voice to press him for more.

It was early October, the afternoons twilit, when she finally cracked under Mackenzie's incessant pressure.

"You have to ask Price about the wall." Her floormate lay sprawled like a starfish across her quilt, picking the polish from her nails. "Every day you don't, Adya suffers."

"Adya is fine," Adya said, her features lit blue by her laptop. "I haven't had another block in weeks. Whatever was there, it's gone now."

"Because he's dead," Mackenzie countered. "Probably rotting in a ditch somewhere. And we could be the only ones who saw. We need to be putting one hundred percent of our focus into this."

Adya shut her laptop. "We don't even know if what I saw was real."

"Exactly." Delaney nudged Mackenzie's feet off the edge of her bed. "Plus, I sort of feel like we should be putting our focus into crossing between worlds. We only have a week left until trial runs."

She didn't tell them she'd been back to the Sanctum, and often. Sometimes, it was empty, and she'd while away the breaks between classes basking in the bliss of total silence. More often than not, Nate Schiller was there, hood up and earbuds in, air-drumming along to a song she couldn't hear.

"*This is a meditative space*," he'd announced the first time she returned, toting a brown paper bag of half-stale pastries. "*If you're going to make it your hangout spot, you need to respect the house rules. First, share your snacks. Second, maintain complete and total silence.*"

"*Way ahead of you*," she'd said, and set a pumpkin muffin on the pallet table between them.

Away from the dorms and the cafés and the classrooms, she finally felt free to click off her implant. There was an unspoken fellowship in their mutual solitude, an easy quiet she'd rarely found with anyone else. She read. Nate listened to music. They didn't speak. Several times, she'd considered mining Nate for more information about the wall, but to do so felt like a breach of trust—a breaking of the unspoken covenant they shared.

And so, she left it alone.

"Hello?" Mackenzie snapped her fingers in front of her face and Delaney became belatedly aware of the fact that she hadn't absorbed a word either of her friends had said. "We have a moral responsibility here, Laney," she insisted. "Ask Price about the wall."

Dusk found Delaney curled into the deep cushions of Colton's family room couch, the moon pressed up against the glass. Colton sat just opposite her, his long legs sprawled across the couch, their limbs all but tangled. She'd spent a better part of the night pretending not to notice.

"Adya and I went to the Sanctum a few weeks ago." She peered over the top of her borrowed notes, too acutely aware of the phantom brush of his foot against her thigh. "Your name was on the wall."

Colton didn't look up from his book. "That checks," he said, "since I put it there."

The crinkle of his turning page rustled all through the chilly grandeur of the house. Before she could think better of it, she said, "I wrote my name next to yours."

The fathomless dark of Colton's stare flicked to hers. "Yeah?"

"Does that mean anything to you?"

A muscle worked in his jaw. "I don't know," he said slowly. "Should it?"

Too late, she realized how she'd sounded. Like an underclassman with a crush. Pining and lovesick, carving their initials into the trunk of a tree. Penciling his name into her notebook. Fire ignited in her cheeks.

"It's just that Nate said the wall is some sort of dead pool," she rushed to say. "It's an infinitely creepy thought, and I wasn't sure if there was a real reason you all wrote your names up there. Maybe some sort of brotherhood thing?" She was veering dangerously close to babbling, and she wished desperately for the ability to scrub this conversation from both of their brains.

Across the couch, Colton had gone still. "Nate Schiller?"

"Yeah. Do you know him?"

"We used to be friends," he said. Then, "You shouldn't talk to him."

She withdrew her legs, swinging them onto the floor. "Why not?"

"For one," he said, mirroring her movements, "the guy is two bad theories away from becoming a Flat Earther. He thinks everything is a conspiracy."

"So you're saying he's wrong," Delaney pressed. "You're not all placing bets on who might turn up dead?"

Colton dug the heel of his hand into his eye. "I'm saying I don't think you should spend time with him."

Propelled by a burst of indignation, Delaney pushed herself off the couch. Colton followed, towering over her beneath the incandescent lights of the parlor.

"You're supposed to be helping me with my classes," she bit out, "not managing my social life."

"I'm not trying to manage anything," he countered. "I'm just giving you some friendly advice."

"Advice?" Her voice climbed an octave. "Fine. Let's hear it, then."

Colton hesitated, his throat working in a swallow. "Nate Schiller isn't someone you should trust," he said finally, with the slowness of someone cherry-picking his words. "He's dangerous."

14

When Colton first came home after the ice, his mother called him unnatural.

Unnatural, for a little boy to spend several nights alone in the winter wood and come back whole. Unnatural, the way he stared all day without speaking. The way he sat up all night without sleeping.

She kept away, leaving Colton to the maid, to the nanny, to the house packed with boxes. For weeks, he sat alone in his room and tried to rub away the cold in his skin. Tucked beneath a blanket. Shivering hard enough to chatter his teeth. In the mornings, he watched cartoons. In the evenings, he read. In between, he watched letters from the divorce lawyers pile on the kitchen counter.

One Saturday morning, when the silence grew too sharp, he made himself a peanut butter and potato chip sandwich on rye and took himself to the cemetery. A lonely little boy in the back of a lonely yellow cab, suffocating under the smell of cigarette smoke.

The April day was bold and bright and he wept on the dirt where his brother lay buried. The puck he'd carried with him sat wedged against Liam's headstone, an angry spot of black amid a bundle of yellow asters. His sandwich, twice bitten, lay forgotten in the grass. That scooped-out feeling persisted in the hollow of his chest. A vital piece, gone from the place between his ribs. He'd never felt so sorry in his life.

He'd learned, in his twenty-one years on earth, that he was the sort of person people left. And yet here was Lane. She was standing in his house. His mausoleum youth. His reliquary of ghosts. Hers was a world of coffee shop mornings and late library nights. Warm and structured and bright. It felt too cold for her here, in this empty house with its empty walls and its empty boy.

He hadn't expected her to come back. Not after last night. Not after the way they'd left things. But there she stood, her lavender hair wound in a bun and speared with a slender paintbrush. On the wall of his father's study, the broad, kaleidoscopic wings of a butterfly unfurled.

For the first time in a long time, the house didn't feel like a grave.

"I let myself in," she said when he continued to hover in the doorway. "I hope that's okay."

There was a smudge of gold under her left eye. A fleck of red on the bridge of her nose. He couldn't think of anything he was more okay with.

"It's fine." He pulled at his fingers until his knuckles popped. "It's not every day someone breaks into your house to paint butterflies on your wall."

"I didn't break in," she protested. "You told me I had a standing invitation."

He propped his shoulder against the butted frame. "Did I say that?"

She screwed up her face in response, scraping excess paint along the tray. "You did. I thought I'd surprise you. I figured this was the right room—I saw all the supplies piled outside the door last week."

In his pocket, his phone rang for the third time in an hour. He ignored it, too preoccupied in staring up at the wash of golds and reds and browns flooding the space where his father's framed accolades used to hang. Everyone else had gone and stayed gone. But Lane had come back.

Paintbrush in hand, Lane began to fidget beneath his silence. "Unless this isn't actually what you wanted at all," she said, back-pedaling. "In which case I can paint over it."

"It's perfect," he assured her. "I don't want you to change a thing."

She stood back and examined her work, hands on her hips. Spatters of vermillion dripped onto the drop cloth. Quietly, he joined her at the wall. For a long time, they stood side by side without speaking. Pinioned in the spotlight of a yellow painter's lamp. Colton studied the butterfly and thought about metamorphosis. About slow sinking beneath the water, cold and cocooning, and coming back as something new. Something strange.

Something a mother might be capable of leaving behind.

"I'm sorry for last night," Lane said, her voice a welcome intrusion on his thoughts. "I feel like I might have overreacted."

"Don't worry about it. I was out of line." He didn't mention Schiller, though he desperately wanted to ask whether or not she'd seen him again.

"You weren't." Lane knelt down and gathered up a second brush. "You said that you and Nate used to be close. Did you guys have a fight?"

The question set him immediately on guard. "Not exactly."

Wedging open a new can of paint, Lane peered up at him. "Whatever it was, I'm sure you just felt like you were looking out for me. That's what friends do, right?"

His chest gave a violent twist. "Are we friends?"

"I think so." Pinpricks of color rose into her cheeks. "Aren't we?"

He wondered what would happen if he broke down and told her the truth. If his bones would cleave in two from the strain. "Sure," he said. "We can be friends."

"Good." She thrust the second paintbrush into his unexpecting grasp. "You can take the left wing."

He didn't move. "I'm not an artist."

"Neither am I." She toed a tray in his direction. Paint sluiced over the sides in fat red globs. "It's easy. You just get some color on the brush and slap it on."

As if in demonstration, she shoved her brush deep into a nearby tray and fanned the bristles along the wall. Gold dripped down like rain. Colton fought a wince.

"Michelangelo just rolled over in his grave."

Lane bit down on a half smile. "Let's go, Price. If I'm painting, you're painting."

Her words tugged through him like marionette string. Inextricably tangled. Cutting off his circulation. He couldn't refuse her if he'd wanted to. Scowling, he wet his brush and dragged the barest tip of the bristles along the wall. A thin swath of red appeared like a wound. Glancing over at Lane, he found her beaming up at him. Eyes bright, her face constellated in gold.

"You're happy with this?"

"Ecstatic," she assured him.

They worked in silence after that. Focused on their tasks. Comfortable in the quiet. He couldn't remember the last time he'd been inside this room and not felt like he couldn't breathe.

He'd nearly run out of paint when Lane rounded on him. "Adya saw it, by the way," she said. "The thing in her head."

107

He set his brush in the tray. "Yeah?"

"It was a boy. Or, what was left of a boy. She said he'd been ripped apart."

His blood went cyanotic in his veins. "That's rough."

"It's *horrifying*." Eyeballing him sideways, she asked, "Does it remind you of anyone?"

It dawned on him that this was why she'd come back. Not to paint him butterflies. Not to be his friend. But because she was still digging into that infernal wall of names. He tried to summon the will to be angry. Instead, all he felt was relief.

"Wednesday," he said evenly, "are you asking me if I *personally* know anyone who's been ripped apart?"

She grimaced. "Yes?"

"No." It wasn't a lie. Guzman's autopsy report said his injuries were congruous with someone who had been dropped from a terrific height. Peretti looked as though he'd been dragged some great distance. There was no conceivable pattern, because patterns were for humans. And Guzman and Peretti hadn't been killed by something human.

He didn't want to think about what Dawoud's discovery might mean. Not with Schiller's name yawning between them like a chasm.

He didn't want to answer all these questions.

He didn't want to be her friend.

Glancing down at his watch, he rushed to speak before she could continue her interrogation. "It's getting late. There's no way you're making the last train. Let me give you a ride back to campus."

The drive home was quiet. No music. No conversation. Only the rumble of the engine, high beams carving a path through a new moon dark. Beneath his skin, hairline fractures charted a map along his vertebrae. He kept his hands on the wheel and tried not to think about Schiller, and what else he might have whispered in Lane's ear.

They were minutes from campus when Lane finally broke the silence.

"Will your parents be mad? About the butterfly?"

"I doubt it."

It wasn't much of an answer, but it was all he could bring himself to give her. In the cupholder, his phone lit the interior of the car with another incoming call. He rushed to kill it. The car cabin pitched back into starry dark. Next to him, Lane wasn't satisfied.

"They're never at the house," she noted as he pulled into the campus parking lot. "Where do they spend all their time?"

In the windows, the formless streak of evergreens turned to the string-lit twinkle of topiaries. "Don't dig into my life, Wednesday," he said. "You might not like me afterward."

"No risk of that," she assured him. "I already don't like you."

"Is that right?" Colton drew into a loading zone and put the car in park. "Is that why you spent your entire night painting me a butterfly?"

"Yes," she said, and the lie sank deep into his solar plexus.

Engine idling, he sat still and waited for her to climb out of the car. Every part of him felt like a bruise. In the cupholder, his phone blew up with one notification after another. He peered over at Lane and found her watching him, her face lit blue in the light of his screen.

For a few minutes, the only sound was the quiet tangle of their breathing. Along the base of the windshield, a streak of lamplit condensation began to bloom. She looked starlit in the dark, her eyes glazed gold, and he wondered how badly it would hurt if he leaned in and kissed her.

He was about to cave and find out when his phone rang anew. Cursing, he fumbled for it, silencing the ringer. Remnants of the chime clung to the air. When he peered back at Lane, a thoughtful frown had crept in at the corners of her mouth.

"What does it feel like," she asked, "when you go through a door?"

The wordless intimacy of the previous moment had severed. He couldn't call it back, and it was for the best. His infractions notched into his bones like a belt. He could taste his spine in his mouth.

"It feels different for everyone," he said, opting for a nonanswer in place of the truth. His voice came out garroted, and he hoped she hadn't noticed.

"I didn't ask about everyone," she countered. "I asked about you."

He hadn't misunderstood. He just didn't want to tell her. He didn't want her to know how he clutched at his throat each time, convinced there was water spilling into his lungs. How he cried like a child. How the cold bled into his bones.

Instead, he said, "You ask too many questions."

"You don't give me a lot to work with." She adjusted the right passenger vent, fingers splayed over the paltry heat. Visibly striving for nonchalance. "I'm worried I won't make it through the doors next week."

"You will," he said, and he meant it. "You're supposed to be here. You think you aren't, but you are."

She huffed out a disingenuous laugh. "Try telling that to my professors. I'm pretty sure they'll disagree with you."

"Who cares about them?" He traced the glossy logo of his steering wheel. "They see you for eighty minutes a day in a room full of faces. They don't know what you're capable of."

"Nothing," she snapped, and he heard the strain in her voice. "I'm capable of nothing. Adya can step right outside of her own body. Mackenzie can tell you what's going to happen days before it actually does. Every other student I've met is in touch with some special, arcane ability. And then there's me."

He held her gaze. "And then there's you."

The words hung in the air between them. He wished she knew the things he knew. He wished he wasn't bound to a lie.

On the windshield, the spot of condensation flowered outward in a widening oval of gray, shrouding them in a fog. It felt like they were doing something illicit. Parked around the corner from her dorm. The new moon climbing into the empty pinnacle of the sky. Her bright eyes shining up at him.

She must have felt it, too, because she unbuckled suddenly, reaching for her bag.

"I should go inside."

"Delaney—"

She paused with her hand on the half-open door, looking back at him. Cold buffeted in around her. Shadows seeped into every crack. Crawled into his skin and stayed. He wondered what she saw when she looked at him this way. If he even looked real.

He wanted to thank her for coming back. For painting him a butterfly.

He wanted to tell her he had no interest in being friends.

Instead, all he managed was "I'll see you in class."

15

Delaney and Adya were deep in the library, squirreled away in a cluster of wooden carrel desks, when Mackenzie found them. She dropped into an empty chair, her coffee spattering every which way and her curls in a snarl.

"Greg Kostopoulos," she said, without preamble.

Adya plucked an earbud from beneath the pink blush of her hijab. "Hello to you, too."

"Greg Kostopoulos," Mackenzie said again, as though they ought to recognize the name. "Yesterday, a hiker and his dog were hiking Starved Rock out in Illinois and they found a body in the woods. Guess who it was."

Delaney's stomach went cold.

"That's right," Mackenzie said. "*Greg Kostopoulos*. The official report says he tripped and fell while out for a run. But here's the kicker—he's not even from Illinois. He's from Ohio."

"Oh, wow," Adya marveled, peering around the divider at Delaney. "*Ohio*."

"That's definitely fishy," Delaney agreed.

"Will the two of you be serious for a second?" Mackenzie drew her phone out of her pocket and began scrolling through it. "Kostopoulos was an active student here at Howe. What's a college student from Massachusetts with roots in Ohio doing out in Illinois in the middle of the fall semester?"

"Slow down, Sherlock," Adya said. "He probably had family out there. Are the police even investigating it as a murder?"

"They're not," Mackenzie admitted, and shoved her phone into Adya's lap. "But I have a vibe, okay? Something isn't clicking. This is Greg. Do you recognize him?"

From this angle, Delaney could just see the grainy profile of a boy's face on the screen. Adya bent low over the phone, her nose crinkling.

"No," she said, and slid the phone back to Mackenzie. "That's not the boy from my head."

"I already asked Price about that," Delaney said. "He didn't seem to know anything."

"Unless he's lying to you," Mackenzie pointed out.

The thought made Delaney uneasy. Not because she was worried that he might be, but because she knew that he was.

He was lying and lying. And she was letting him.

The chair next to her gave a violent stutter and a body dropped into it. Startled, she glanced up to find the previously empty seat occupied by Eric Hayes, his face shadowed beneath a gray hood, the bite of an autumn wind clinging to his frame as though he'd been swept in off the quad.

"You need to leave him alone," he said, leaning over the arm of his chair.

Delaney knew who he meant, but she was feeling impertinent, and so she asked, "Who?"

"Spare me the clueless act," he said. "I know you and Price have been cozying up after-hours."

"He's been helping me with some things for class."

"It's literally his job," Mackenzie added.

"Not talking to you, Red." Hayes kept his focus trained on Delaney, and she did her best not to shrivel under his gaze. "I wasn't aware Price held office hours in a fogged-up BMW in the middle of the night."

The cluster of wooden desks went quiet enough to hear a pin drop. Delaney's throat squeezed tight. Her cheeks stung as if she'd been slapped.

"That's what I thought." Eric rose from his chair, swiping his hood from his head. "You want my advice? Find yourself another study buddy. Before someone gets hurt."

The three of them sat in silence as he stalked off across the reference lab.

"Unbelievable," Mackenzie said when he was out of earshot. "I'd bet every last one of my meal points that they've all gotten themselves involved in something they shouldn't have."

"His name was on the wall," Delaney said, watching Eric join a table of upperclassmen. "That can't be a coincidence. Maybe Greg Kostopoulos is up there, too. I can go by after class and check it out."

Adya suppressed a shudder. "I don't know, Lane. That place has a bad vibe."

"I don't mind it," Delaney said. "Plus, Nate's usually hanging around. Maybe he'll know something."

When the day was done, Delaney bundled up in a coat and hat and headed for the Sanctum. A hunk of black tourmaline weighed heavily in her pocket—to clear any malevolent energy, Mackenzie insisted. The days were getting darker, and already twilight had begun to deepen. She pressed on, hurrying down the wooded path at a clip, ignoring the gathering dark.

She entered the Sanctum to find the interior in shambles. The book cart was overturned, its contents strewn throughout the room. A beanbag had been rent from seam to seam as if by claws, leaving white polystyrene filling to flood the entirety of the space in snowy clings.

Alarmed, she pushed through the mess to the main chamber, where the wall of names rose up from a cataclysm of loose change and scattered pens. At the crux of it all knelt Nate, shirtless and hunched, his shoulders bowed. With a start, she realized he was crying. The sound came out of him in short, watery pulls.

"Nate," she said, as softly as she was able.

The crying stifled. The room went still.

"Get out," he said.

She stood her ground. "What happened?"

He bent forward, his fists pressed into the floor, rocking himself like a child. The sound that came out of him was low and strange. A moan, inhuman. She took a step, and a marker went skittering away from her, spinning out like a pinwheel. It rolled to a stop at the sole of his shoe.

He froze up like an animal, the hard ridge of his spine visible beneath his skin. Across his left shoulder blade, there was a single phrase done in bold, looping ink. *Non omnis moriar.* The sight of it bit into her like ice. When he spoke again, his voice came out strangled, like he'd meant to scream and found himself instead underwater.

"Get. Out!"

She staggered back, slamming into the wall and groping for the exit. Back through the polystyrene mess, little white balls clinging to her stockings. Out into the trees, where the waning light grew far too faint to pierce the branches. Alone and in the dark, she raced headlong down the leaf-slick trail. Branches tore at her skin. Her boots caught on the broad rivers of roots. She didn't stop. She kept on running, shadows tearing at her skin, until she broke at last through the thick juniper press and staggered onto pavement.

Up ahead, the moonlit quad was empty of students. She huddled beneath the feeble glow of a streetlamp and tried to catch her breath. Her beret was gone, lost to the wood. Her cheek stung where she'd run headlong into a patch of spruce. The hunk of tourmaline sat useless in her pocket.

Breathless, she was about to start off for her dorm when she heard it: a sound, severed and strange as a coyote's cry. It was the sort of far-off wail of something in deep distress, bone-chilling and distant. It carried in as though borne upon the icy crest of a winter wind. Only, there was no wind. The night around her was still and quiet as glass.

Somewhere in the dark, a foot fell on the walk. Her heart climbed into her throat, sour and thumping. A second step followed, dragging across the ground in a scrape. Step. Drag. Step. Drag. That pervasive wail continued. She froze, paralyzed—convinced that to step outside the fluorescent sphere was to enter the den of some ancient, unseen beast.

The pavement was mottled in shadow, the spaces between the lamp-lit concrete dark as a void. And there, beyond the reaches of light, something was approaching, its movements arachnid.

All the hair rose along her arms. Softly, she called out, "Hello?"

The disembodied wailing fell silent. At the far end of the sidewalk, a single lamp clicked off.

"Malus navis," whispered the wind.

She frowned, not trusting her hearing. "Nate?"

The sound that answered her was a snarl, primordial and strange. A second lamp clicked off. That terrible void widened, swallowing up the walk. Her heart clanged through her in a warning bell. With fumbling fingers, she drew her phone out of her pocket.

It rang only once before Colton answered.

"Wednesday. This better be good. I'm right in the middle of dissecting Dante, and he's just about to journey into the first circle of Hell."

"Where are you?"

He paused for the briefest of seconds. "The library. Are you okay?"

"I'm outside by the quad." Another lamp clicked off. The dark rushed toward her. She shut her eyes. On the other end of the phone, she heard Colton zipping up his bag. "I'm going to ask you for a favor," she said. "I need you to not make fun of me for it."

"Okay." His voice came out cavernous, like he'd stepped inside a stairwell.

"I'm serious, Price."

"Do I sound like I'm laughing?"

Something skittered past just out of sight. "Can you come out here with me?" She didn't know how to explain what she needed from him without sounding insane. Without looking breakable. Fingers shaking, she landed on, "I don't really like the dark."

"I'm halfway there," he said. "Don't move, I can see you."

The line went dead. She opened her eyes, phone still pressed to her ear. Another lamp had gone out. Winter moths flitted over her head in a frenzy, evading predators. Beyond the pale scope of fluorescence, she couldn't see anything at all.

A towering figure burst into frame, and she stifled a scream, scrabbling backward as a longboard went past, wheels snicking audibly over lips in the sidewalk. The rider, heavily bundled against the cold, threw her a cursory hello. One shoe to the pavement, he propelled himself back into the dark.

"Oh." The slow blush of mortification crept into her skin. She felt infinitely stupid, her implant useless. Of course that's what it had been. Nothing ancient. Nothing arachnid. Just a boy on a skateboard. She was about to call Colton back and tell him not to bother when the light over her head clicked off.

A blind dark fell. She clapped her hands over her eyes just as the shadows swarmed. They pried at her with frozen fingers. Pleaded in frozen voices. *Please, please, please.*

Two sets of fingers closed around her forearms. Just as cold but twice as firm.

"Wednesday," came Colton's voice. Gently, he pried her hands from her face. "Jesus. Open your eyes."

She did. The streetlamps were on, electricity fizzing. Colton stood before her, his brow furrowed, his hands bracketing her wrists. In a dizzying rush, all the nerve endings in her body gathered beneath the pads of his thumbs.

"You look like you've been in a fight with a holly tree." He said it like he was cracking a joke, but he wasn't smiling. Releasing her wrists, he worked something loose from the tangle of her hair. The scalloped green of a leaf came away in his hand, the stem clustered with tiny red berries.

Embarrassed, she said, "I put that there."

"And the cut on your cheek?"

"That too," she said meekly, touching a fingertip to the sting.

"You're a bad liar." He didn't prod her for the truth. He only took silent stock of her, his jaw gritted. She fidgeted beneath his scrutiny, making a subtle effort to work the knots out of her hair.

Finally, he said, "Let me walk you back to your dorm."

"That's really not necessary. I'm sure you have better things to do."

"Yeah, analyzing fourteenth-century poetry is a real gas. Seriously, let me walk back with you. I was heading home anyway."

"Really?"

"Really."

He handed her the sprig of holly and she took it. His fingers lingered. Her breath caught, the sound treacherous in the quiet, and his smile hooked. The brimstone of his eyes dropped to her mouth. She thought of Nate on his knees in the Sanctum, the bestial echo of his scream, the lies that built and built. Suddenly, and with the dark pressing in, Colton Price was the only thing that felt solid. An anchor, in the middle of a nightmare.

As though he knew it, he pushed his fingers through hers. The holly dropped to the sidewalk. With a tug, he drew her a half step— out of the light and into the broad swath of dark.

She braced herself for the onslaught of shadows, but nothing happened. She was positioned just beneath Colton, their breath crashing between them in clouds of gray, her face angled up to his. Her heart slammed into her ribs. The cold bled into her toes.

"Come on," he said. "Let's get you back."

Hands still threaded together, they made their way toward the twinkling lights of the freshman row, the night around them as still and quiet as glass.

❧ 16 ❧

Ronson's Do-It-Yourself Storage was located right off the Pike, two miles outside of Boston proper, and directly on a magnetic ley line. Once upon a time, the highly sensitive spot had been the location of a new age boutique, the owner a self-pronounced purveyor of charmed trinkets and tarot readings. Situated directly along a hum of energy, it was a great venue for the supernatural, less so for customers. The rumble of rush hour traffic persisted all throughout the day, ferrying in a steady soundtrack of truck brakes and car horns, the smell of exhaust, and the scream of police sirens.

It wasn't, in short, where one might choose to spend their Saturday.

When the shop closed, Ronson's storage rose up in its place. Godbole owned several rented units, each of them situated along the buzzing ley line, each of them housing an open door. Dust in the light. A hum in the head. A mirror ripple, the sky rent open to a mirror world.

Now, lit beneath a solitary streetlamp, the Apostle stared down the labyrinthine corridor of steel-plated units. The doors were much too bright, a festal motley of reds and oranges and blues. There was something sinister in its silence, foreboding in its emptiness. Somewhere in the dark, something clattered to the ground. The sound was followed by the soft *scritch-scritch* of dragging.

"Whatever you're touching," he called out, "don't."

The slow scraping silenced. A sigh lumbered out, filling the alley like something odiferous. Something rotten. He pulled his eyes shut and pinched the bridge of his nose. The hour was late—near dawn—and he'd left a pork roast warming in the Crock-Pot that was surely turning tough as rubber by the minute. His feet were losing feeling. His stomach was aching. He was quickly growing irritable with waiting. It was incredibly like Colton Price—a boy obsessed with timeliness—to be purposely late.

As though he'd summoned him, Price arrived, whistling an earsplittingly jaunty tune as he rounded the corner into sight. He was needlessly cheery for the godforsaken hour. This, coupled with the thought of a perfectly good pork roast gone to waste, soured the Apostle's fast-spoiling mood even further. He slid his hand into the pocket of his jacket and felt for the item within, the cold splinter of the bone shard sliding into his grasp. The talisman felt the way it always felt, like grabbing hold of a live wire. A jolt ran all the way to his elbow.

"No more of that," he said, and the whistling fell silent. Price's stare was inhuman in the dark, a stark opposition to the utter humanity of the rest of him, his smile cracked wide and his cheeks pinked with cold.

"Odd choice of a meeting place." Price rapped once on the wide serriform door closest to him. The sound pinged all through the wide alley of units. He knocked again, this time tapping out the first five notes of "Shave and a Haircut" with the backs of his knuckles. Again, the sound reverberated through the dark. There was a lull, and then the Apostle's infernal haunt tapped back: *Two bits*.

Price's grin widened. "I see you brought your friend."

The trivializing moniker rankled the Apostle beyond measure. The thing that loitered in the distance, rotten and reeking, was his unwelcome curse. His unholy affliction.

And Price knew it.

"Don't play with him," he snapped. "He's not a toy for your amusement."

"You're feeling defensive of the guy," Price said. "I get it. You spend a lot of time together." His grin was unwavering, his smile wolfish in the light. "Did you know prisoners of war used that call and response to identify fellow soldiers in captivity? We're not too different, your little buddy and I."

Somewhere nearby, that horrible thing was dragging itself, unseen, along the ground. The Apostle could hear the toes of its boots scuffing pavement. The boots it died in, water stained and peeling apart.

"He is not," the Apostle said, with far more rancor than he'd planned on, "my *buddy*."

"Yikes." Price slid his hands into his pockets with a level of indifference that only served to heighten the Apostle's annoyance. "I'm just making conversation."

"Well, don't," the Apostle ordered, his grip tight against the shard in his pocket. "In fact, don't say anything. I'll talk, you listen."

He was met with an obdurate silence and that glittering black stare. He took a moment to soak in the peace of it, knowing it was bound to be short-lived.

"A hiker found Kostopoulos at the bottom of a ravine. The official police report says he fell, but my source at the coroner's office says differently. I'm told he looked as though he'd been chewed up and then spat out—a fact that you might be aware of, had you not been too preoccupied to return a single one of my calls."

When Price said nothing, the Apostle reached into his back pocket and retrieved the rolled-up folder he'd brought from his car. Wetting his thumb, he made a show of padding through several sheets of bulleted notes, which Meeker had inexplicably compiled in Comic Sans.

"I've had Mark on a special assignment these past few weeks. You know how he gets restless without an activity to keep him occupied."

Price, as expected, continued to hold his tongue.

"Did you know," the Apostle began, feeling needlessly jubilant over this minor victory, "that Delaney Meyers-Petrov has an old family cat named Petrie?"

No answer rose to meet him save for the far-off peal of an ambulance siren, there and then gone. When he glanced up from his notes, it was to find all traces of that ever-present grin wiped clean from Price's mouth. Over his shoulder, the Apostle could just make out the knife's edge of a face, grotesque and hollowed, grinning a wide, winsome grin.

"Mark made a little note for himself in here," he went on, trying not to look directly at it. "He's written 'likes canned tuna.' It would seem he's earned the trust of the Meyers-Petrov family pet. Makes you nervous, doesn't it? Mark can be a bit volatile from time to time."

Again, Price was quiet.

"Let's see what else." The Apostle flipped to the next page. "She organizes her books alphabetically by author. She prefers morning showers to evening. She opts for sensible underwear, nothing with laces and frills." He peered up at Price again and found that the boy's face had gone bloodless in the dark. Fishing through the interior of his coat, he withdrew a rumpled woolen cap and lobbed it through the air like a Frisbee. "Say what you will about the fellow, but Mark Meeker is relentlessly thorough."

Meyers-Petrov's beret landed on the pavement between them. Price drew in an audible breath.

"That's neither here nor there," the Apostle said, satisfaction climbing through him. "I'm not interested in her sleeping habits or her family pets or her undergarments. No, what interests me is the fact that nearly every single evening, Meeker has followed her from Godbole's campus all the way to Park Street Station. Would you care to wager a guess as to where she goes from there?"

Still, Price was silent. The Apostle fingered the bone shard, clenching his teeth against the shock to his system. In front of him, Price's eyes had gone tightly shut. His hands balled into twin fists at his sides.

"Speak," the Apostle ordered. "I despise a one-sided conversation."

"Leave her alone." There was no smile in Price's voice—no glimmer of laughter, no streak of arrogance. Only the cold scrape of a plea dressed as a command. It should have thrilled the Apostle to see the vainglorious Price knocked down a peg. Instead, those black eyes opened and he felt chilled to the bone within the unflinching crosshairs of the boy's stare.

"You won't even deny it?"

"Deny what?" Price stood without moving, the air around him restless. "That you're stalking a student? It seems pretty clear to me."

The Apostle wasn't the sort of man to fly into a rage—wasn't the type to rend his garments or gnash his teeth when the going got tough. *Emotionless*, his wife called him once, during an argument. Her eyes had been jeweled in tears, her face misaligned in hurt. He'd been disgusted by the red blotch of her cheeks, the ugly way her mouth curled in on itself when she was sad. He'd always found crying to be such a waste of time.

"You were given a singular expectation," he said. "You haven't even tried to meet it. Need I remind you how very short your leash is, Mr. Price?"

"I guess maybe you do."

Off in the dark, his odious haunt hissed out a brittle laugh. For once, the sound served to revive instead of dismay him. Warmed him instead of leaving him cold. In that instant, he saw himself as something of modern-day Abraham, poised to drive a knife through little, weeping Isaac in order to gratify his god. The broken echo of the creature's laughter clung to the air. It reminded him that he was the sort of man who did whatever it took—who made the difficult decisions when the moment called for them.

This was, he presumed, just such a moment.

He permitted himself a single, sympathetic smile. "You carry yourself like a prince, but you're only a puppet. A wooden boy, desperate to convince everyone you're real. You and I know the truth, don't we? You can't do a damned thing without someone pulling your strings."

Price propped his shoulder against the serrated metal of a blood-red unit. "Is there a point to this speech, or do you plan to talk until the entire freshman class arrives?"

"Charming as ever." The Apostle rerolled the folder and shoved it back into his pocket. To the east, the first fingers of daylight clawed at the horizon. "I won't command you," he said. "You're a smart boy. And you're going to make this next decision all on your own. Cut ties with the Meyers-Petrov girl, or I'll see to it that when she dies, it's your hands around her throat."

❧ 17 ❧

Delaney was not going to make it through the tear in the sky.
She was going to drop out.

She was going to pack up her things.

She was going to go home and turn off her phone and sleep for a year.

Everyone else had gone and returned, one after the other, stepping through with trepidation and coming back bright-eyed and trembling, the blood gone out of their faces.

And then there was Delaney, lingering on the outskirts. Too afraid to walk home alone. Terrified of a skateboard. Paralyzed by the dark. She had nothing to show except for mediocre grades and a pair of ears that didn't work.

The last of the freshmen, she stood in the open unit of Ronson's and wished for the ability to turn herself invisible. She felt like a peasant in the story of the emperor's clothes—like everyone else saw something extravagant where all she saw was naked sky. In front of her, the garage was empty—devoid of all but air.

To her left, Whitehall watched her over the top of a clipboard. He looked as disheveled as usual in his oversized tweed and Coke-bottle glasses, the twirl of his mustache off-center.

Gently, he said, "There's no pressure here, Ms. Meyers-Petrov. There's no right or wrong answer. Just begin by telling me what you see."

But that was the problem. She didn't see *anything*.

When she remained firmly planted, Whitehall sighed. "You know," he said, "my wife used to be something of a folklorist. She was enthralled by the stories of people going missing at Clava Cairns, in Inverness—maidens snatched away in the night by the folk, newborn babes ripped from their cradles and swapped with changelings. Do you know what my dear friend Devan and I found when we visited Inverness?"

"What?"

"Sky clear enough to see clean through to the other side. A curtain, shifting in the light. Possibility, that maybe all the stories we'd been told as children were true. We found the same at the standing stones of England's Devil's Arrows, the Megaliths in Montana. All of them built on ley lines, all of them stretched thin as paper.

"If the average person stepped inside one of these units, they'd feel a chill. The faint whisper of an impossible breeze. The hairs would rise along the back of their neck, and they'd take their leave without ever understanding that they stood on the very precipice of another world. But you? You are no average person. And there are other ways to see. Perhaps you might try telling me what you hear, instead."

She glanced over at him, startled. "What I hear?"

"Yes." His eyes were bright behind his lenses. "In the silence."

Tentatively, she reached up and switched off her implant. The brassy tone of tinnitus chimed through her, the sound like a struck bell. And there, beneath it, was the faint shudder of something else. Something quiet.

She shut her eyes and the hum in her head swelled to a crescendo. It whittled through her in a foghorn scream. Slowly—impossibly—the sounds took shape, rising and falling in the wordless susurration of a thousand unknowable voices. As if the energy that snapped and sputtered along the ley lines was trying to speak to her, low and imploring.

She clicked her implant back on. "I hear it," she said, her eyes still closed.

"Good." Whitehall sounded pleased. "And what, precisely, is it you hear?"

"A hum."

"Very good. Now, open your eyes. Take another look."

She obeyed. Where there'd previously been nothing, there was now a faint sliver of gossamer. It reminded her of laundry hung to dry, diaphanous sheets swelling on a summer breeze. The hum in her head spilled out of her in a trill, dragging down her bones like she was a fiddle and the door was a bow, fiberglass edging pulled taut along her spine.

Whitehall smiled over at her, his eyes crinkling. "You are quite ready, Ms. Meyers-Petrov. No more dallying. Mr. Price will receive you on the other side. In you go."

And then that was it. He withdrew, leaving her alone in the empty unit.

In you go. As if she were stepping out of one room and into another, easy as pie.

In you go, as though it were as simple as crossing a threshold.

In you go, and she looked again at the place where the sky rent in two. Her heart beat out a painful staccato. This time when she stuck out her hand, she felt it. An edge, soft as spider's silk. Holding her breath, she stepped forward, following that incessant hum. Sound rose in a crescendo, running through her in a shiver that left her teeth chattering like castanets.

It could have been the blink of an eye.

It could have been an hour.

Her skin felt as if it were slowly peeling away. It didn't hurt; it only felt as though she were being gripped much too tightly, and by a thousand prying fingers. In her head, there were a thousand whispering voices. *Look*, they said. *Look, look, look*.

And then it was over, and she emerged onto the other side.

A half a step before, she'd been alone in a garage. Now she stood waist-deep in a meadow. The day was blue and bright, the sun a blinding corona of yellow. There was no storage unit, no chain-link fence, no nearby overpass. Only earth, wide and empty. The grass around her stood in colorless stalks, bowed low beneath prettily feathered heads. Somewhere in the distance, a bird warbled.

Nearby sat Colton, propped beneath the drooping boughs of a white oak, his forearms flung over his knees, a flash of something black in his hands. Over his head, the tree's alizarin leaves flickered like a living flame.

The sky tasted different here—clean and sweet. Beneath her feet, the ground was cracked asphalt, rivers of dark riven in fat clumps of mallow weed. Earth, reclaimed. She moved through it and wondered what sort of ripples made this world deviate so vastly from their own—what sort of event could turn the busy Bostonian rush she'd left behind to a sleepy muffle.

Colton rose to his feet as she approached, the inversion of his cheeks made stark by the sun. Slowly, it dawned on her that the thing in his hands was her beret, the felt clutched tight between his fingers.

"You're late," he said, and flashed her a private, steel-tipped smile.

"A little." Her legs wobbled. "But I made it."

"There was never any doubt."

His unwavering confidence in her made her feel a thousand things at once. It wasn't fair. Even when he wasn't trying, everything out of his mouth felt tailor-made to unravel her.

Striving for a detachment she didn't remotely feel, she said, "That's my hat."

"Is it?" He closed the remaining space between them, grasses bowing in his wake, and placed it on her head. His gaze was inscrutable as he leaned back to examine her. "Perfect."

A sudden wind tugged the leaves loose from their branches, and they were momentarily engulfed in a crimson flurry. She caught the beret against her head before it, too, was snatched up in the squall.

"Where did you find it?"

Colton's smile hitched up at the corners. "I wrestled it from a holly bush."

Frustration blossomed at the obvious lie, and she peered up at him, one eye pulled shut against the sun. "Is everything with you always a secret?"

"No." The word dropped between them like a pin.

"Prove it, then," she said.

His eyes went wide. "Prove it?"

"Yes."

"Right now?"

"*Yes*," she said again, more emphatically than before. "Before we go back. Tell me just three things that are absolutely true."

Sliding his hands into his pockets, he considered the stretch of sky beyond the trees. Finally, he asked, "Have you ever heard of Charon's obol?"

The question caught her off guard. "I haven't."

"It involves the ancient Greek practice of tucking coins into the cheeks of the dead to grant them safe passage through the underworld." He drew out a hand, and Delaney caught the alloyed wink of a nickel disappearing between his fingers. "The obols were meant as a bribe for the ferryman. Surviving family members wanted to make sure the deceased were able to pay their way across the rivers. Otherwise, they'd be stuck earthside for all eternity, left to wander back home to haunt the living."

"Oh," Delaney said, disappointed. "Okay."

Colton slipped the nickel back into his pocket. "There's one truth."

"But that was just a random fact," she countered. "It wasn't a personal truth."

His brows drew together. "Wasn't it?"

"Don't be cryptic," she said. "There has to be something you're comfortable sharing."

"Let's see." He pretended to mull it over. "Here's another—I'm allergic to shellfish."

"You're not taking this seriously."

The look he gave her was deeply affronted. "A shellfish allergy is incredibly serious. I could go into anaphylactic shock if I even make eye contact with a lobster."

"*Price.*"

"Fine." He pawed at the back of his neck. "You want the truth?"

"That's all I want," she assured him.

"Okay." He blew out a breath. "All right."

"This doesn't have to be a whole ordeal," Delaney said. "You're not being graded on the quality of your facts."

"Are you sure?" He pinned her in a look. "Because it kind of seems like I am."

"Just spit it out, Price."

"I don't want to be your friend, Delaney."

A bird swooped past in a rustle of wings. Delaney stared up at Colton. He glowered back down at her. He looked vaguely reproachful—as if she'd shoved her bare hand down his throat and ripped the admission out of him. All of the air rushed out of her on an exhale.

"Oh," she said.

"It's selfish of me," he went on, his voice like arsenic. "All I'll do is hurt you. I know it. Deep down, I think you know it, too. But you keep hanging around, and I can't figure out why."

Her heart tripped inside her chest. She knew it was her turn to say something, but her head seemed to have emptied out every last scrap of coherent thought it possessed. The wind picked up, bending the boughs of the old white oak. Ferried in on the red rush of leaves was a voice, low and broken.

Malus navis.

Delaney drew out from under Colton's shadow, peering around him to find the sky empty of all but cottonwood fluff. The way home was marked by little more than a sigh. There was no one there. Only her and Colton.

And whatever else waited nearby, murmuring in the meadow.

"Did you hear that?"

"Hear what?" Colton asked, an edge creeping into his voice.

Hurry. There it was again. This time, she wasn't sure if the sound originated in her head or out of it. *Help me.*

"Wednesday." This, from Colton, sharp and obtrusive. "Stop."

She hadn't realized she'd begun to walk away until he spoke. The earth cracked underfoot as she pushed deeper into the grasses, drawn to that incessant murmur. A twig snapped, startling a dragonfly into flight. A brace of blackbirds took screaming to the sky. They sounded faraway, as though she were hearing their cries through a wall of glass.

Faster, urged the voice, clear as cut crystal. *Don't leave me here alone.*

Something fractured beneath her and she wrenched her foot back, startled. It was a hand, fingers stiff with rigor mortis. A scream built in her throat. Stifling it, she pushed aside the feathered reeds. A boy lay flat in the earth, his face scraped away. A fat black fly crept along the bony hollow of his cheek. His torso looked as if he'd been cut all to ribbons, the ribbed white of several bones bared like teeth.

As though something had tried to claw its way out of him.

In front of him stood Adya. She looked as alarmed as Delaney felt, the sun falling all wrong across her face. Her pants were wet with mud, the palms of her hands slick with blood.

"I saw him again," Adya said. Her hands shook and shook. "Right in front of me this time, instead of out of view. He said he's been dead for weeks and no one came. No one helped. And so he found another way to stitch himself back together."

Her stomach was lead. "What does that mean?"

But Adya didn't appear to have heard her. She was staring at the body, her eyes wide with horror. Between them, some of the rigor mortis had begun to go out of the corpse. Sinew wove along bone in thin cords of red. Blooms of soft tissue formed, fibrous and white. A finger twitched.

"He was dragging himself on all fours." Adya's voice quavered. "I wanted to help, and so I went after him. I crawled right out of my head and followed him straight to you."

Unease crept through Delaney's veins. "That doesn't make any sense. Why me?"

"Something's coming," Adya answered, in a voice like a cave. Delaney glanced up, afraid, and found her roommate's pupils blown wide. "Something with teeth."

The lines of Adya blotted beneath a solar flare, and then she was gone, like a silk scarf snatched up by a sudden wind. In the place where the body had lain, there was only matted grass and the blue-green face of a lone penny.

Somewhere in the distance, Colton was calling her name.

Delaney didn't call back to him. She stood frozen in the meadow, staring down at the coin, the whispering dark flitting around her like fish breaking rank over the thin dorsal of a shark.

PART TWO

THE TRAGIC CASE
OF NATHANIEL SCHILLER

When chill death has severed soul and body,
everywhere my shade shall haunt you.
Virgil, *The Aeneid*

⚜ 18 ⚜

In a mirror world, in a looking-glass city, seated on a bench of lacquered walnut, Delaney Meyers-Petrov was falling asleep. The polished parquet was glossed to a sheen, the soaring walls papered in a bold red damask, and it wasn't so much that she was tired, but that the dull muffle of the gallery was lulling her into a daze.

She hadn't slept. Not in days. When she did, she dreamt only of skin sliced open in surgical precision, ribs pried loose like copper wire. Adya's voice in the dark: "*Something's coming. Something with teeth.*"

Outside, the mid-October streets of the other Boston were dark and colorless, the cobbled sidewalks alloyed in half-frozen puddles. Tucked away on the museum's third floor, the warmth was butter sweet. The walls were adorned in gilt frames that glittered beneath gridded downlights, the paintings of the old masters divided by soaring tapestry pilasters. It wouldn't have been the worst place to spend her days, if only she weren't plagued by the memory of the meadow.

Delaney set her pencil in the sketchpad on her lap and stretched out her cramped fingers, her skin silvered in lead. In front of her hung Nicolas Poussin's *Mars and Venus*, the god and goddess layered in rich reds and deep mahoganies, fat, dimpled cherubs gathered close.

She'd been working on her first lateral world assignment for just over a week, and so far all she'd managed to discover was that this Poussin looked precisely the same as the Poussin that hung back home in *her* Boston, in an identical gallery, under an identical spotlight. Not a brushstroke out of place, not a color substituted. A thousand doors away and four hundred years ago, this version of Nicolas Poussin had made the exact same artistic decisions as his mirror self.

She was meant to find the differences. It was paramount, Whitehall had explained, that his students master the ability to record subtle variances between worlds. He'd started them on something small—artwork—with the promise that by the end of their tenure at Godbole they'd be capable of observing differences on a far more significant scale.

She was expected to hand in a paper citing her observations by Friday at midnight, and yet all she could think about was that faceless body, the spectral black of Adya's stare.

Her notes thus far were mostly doodles—sketches she'd done in an effort to stay awake. A sinister-looking cherub, adulatory Venus, the upturned face of Mars, god of war.

His jaw was a hard line, his eyes a sharp, emblazoned brown. It was an inefficient rendering. She'd taken liberties with the sketch as her thoughts drifted to darker things, penciling in the neat curl at his brow, the knife of his mouth—too sharp to belong to dreamy Mars, lounging beneath Venus's affection.

Recognition dawned on her in a humiliating rush. Though she'd failed to capture the god, she'd somehow managed to delineate a near-perfect interpretation of Colton Price. She thought of him standing beneath the tree, wind-blown and sincere. *All I'll do is hurt you.*

"This sketch isn't half bad," came a voice from directly over her shoulder. "Although you've fudged some of the finer details on Mars."

Her pencil froze, lead tip poised over the wide column of a throat. She hadn't heard Colton approach. When he leaned in for a better look, she tore the page clean out. The rip sundered the rain-muffled quiet of the space. Balling the pulp paper into a hasty pellet, she shoved it deep down into the bowels of her bag.

"Unwarranted," he said, his mouth at her ear.

"What are you doing?"

"Facilitating." He leaned back and slid his hands into his pockets. Behind him, the museum's vast collection of Hanoverian silver sparked in the light, framing him in a tabernacle of polished flagons and sleek, alloyed trumpets. "It's my job to oversee the freshmen projects. Whitehall has you on the Poussin, right? Have you figured it out?"

"Not yet." She'd been at it for hours without success, her foot asleep, rain hissing against the roof. Staring without blinking at the layers upon layers of amoretto feathers. "They look exactly the same to me."

"Look again," he said. "He used a different shade of yellow for the sky. Lead antimonate, as opposed to silica and oxide."

Flustered, she threw down her pencil. "How am I supposed to notice that? That's the tiniest, most infinitesimal detail."

Colton's face cracked into a grin.

"Don't laugh at me," she said, her annoyance deepening. "I've been sitting here for hours. I can't feel my foot."

"I'm not laughing at you." He held out his hand. "Come on."

She drew back from him, suspicious. "Where?"

"Just come with me. I want to show you something."

Reluctantly, she slid her fingers into his hand and let him tug her onto her feet. He drew her after him into the vaulted corridor, passing through one room after another until they came to a stop in the carved rotunda. The empty pavilion was wide and bright, capped in an alabaster dome.

Disentangling his hand from hers, Colton headed to a wrought iron overlook and leaned into it, his weight on his forearms. She followed suit, the railing biting into her palms, her heartbeat unsteady. She hadn't let herself be alone with him—not since he'd found her shivering in the meadow, the shadows bounding around her like voles. Not since she'd backed him into a hasty confession beneath the knotted arms of an old oak.

"I don't want to be your friend, Delaney."

Beneath them, a crowd of tourists pushed in across the first-story foyer, scuffing shoes dry on the entryway rug and shaking rainwater from their umbrellas. For a while, she and Colton stood in silence and watched a mother shepherd her bundled children back out into the rain.

"Everyone down there looks exactly the same as at home," Colton said. "Most planes are like that. At a glance, they're hardly different. But they're all colored in different shades. Take that man there, for example." He pointed toward a stout visitor in a navy parka, who'd just emerged from the gift shop wielding an overwrought snow dome. "Why do you think he bought that?"

"Maybe he has an affinity for snow globes," Delaney said.

"Why? They're tacky."

"How predictably pretentious of you."

"People buy snow globes for the sentimental value, Wednesday, not because it's the height of interior design. Think about it. Maybe he had a wife. Maybe she loved it here. Maybe she died. Now he comes here once a year on the anniversary of her death and does the tour and then buys a globe. He takes it to her grave and leaves it by her headstone. He does it for himself, not for her—because it makes him hurt a little less. It makes him feel like he's keeping her alive."

She wasn't looking at the man anymore. Now she was staring at Colton. He stayed fixated on the crowd beneath them, his throat bobbing in a swallow. "Back home, he looks the same," he said. "Same eyes, same hair, same terrible blue parka. But his wife is still alive. He doesn't come here alone. His house isn't full of cheap commemorative glass. In another world, on another timeline, he's still a whole person, instead of half of one."

"Colton—"

"You can't always puzzle something out just by looking at it," he rushed to say. "Sometimes you have to dig a little bit to uncover the truth."

She frowned. "Are we still talking about the Poussin?"

"Obviously."

"Because it doesn't feel like it."

Silence fell again, and for a while they watched the crowd ebb and flow across the foyer—all shades of people, fractured in ways she couldn't see from her bird's-eye vantage. She felt a mounting pressure to say something, but before she could, Colton rapped a knuckle against the railing and asked, "Have you been avoiding me?"

"Maybe a little bit," she admitted.

He slid her a sideways glance. "You haven't come by the house."

"I've had a lot on my plate. Adya has been having a hard time since the incident at Ronson's."

It felt like an understatement. Delaney and Colton had stepped back through the sky to find ambulatory lights flashing, a nervous

Whitehall dispersing the gathered crowd of students. *"She's fainted,"* he'd said, signaling for a glass of water. *"Only fainted."*

But Adya hadn't fainted. She'd been flung outside of herself, tailing after a living corpse. The entire incident had spurred Mackenzie into investigating with renewed vigor, but for Delaney, it only kept her up at night. All she could see when she closed her eyes was that hollow stare, a face slowly grafting itself back together.

Next to her, Colton was still surveying the bustle of the foyer.

"Tell me something true," she said, because she needed a distraction.

A smile sharpened in the corner of his mouth. "I've named the butterfly Gregor."

"Gregor?"

"It deserved a name," he said. "It's my roommate."

"But *Gregor?*"

"Yes."

"That's a horrible name."

"That's your wrong opinion," he said, "and you're entitled to it. Gregor and I are very comfortable with the decision."

"So weird." They'd gravitated closer while speaking, elbows kissing atop the banister. "Tell me something else," she said. "Something embarrassing."

"That's an easy one. I've been keeping your chewed-up pens in the glove compartment of my car."

A startled laugh burst out of her. "I can't believe you just admitted to that. That is incredibly creepy."

His smile sharpened. "Bold words from a girl with a drawing of me shoved in her purse."

Heat burnished her cheeks. For a long time afterward, she

pretended to be deeply engrossed in the ebb and flow of the crowd. She was acutely aware of Colton's proximity—the way his arm brushed hers every time one of them moved even the slightest bit. There was something strangely intimate in it—standing side by side without speaking. Tucked away together in an empty alcove in a sleepy museum. A thousand worlds away from home.

When she finally snuck a glance in his direction, it was to find them nose to nose in the pale wash of daylight. Conflict swam in the frigid brown of his gaze.

"I have to tell you something," he said. "Something important."

"Okay."

His mouth twisted into a grimace. He looked as if he was bracing himself—readying himself for a blow. "It's about the day in the meadow. About the body you saw."

The loud clearing of a throat rebounded all through the marbled dome. She and Colton leapt apart at the sound. Mackenzie stood at the top of the main staircase, a sketchpad clutched to her chest. Adya loomed several paces behind her, the color gone from her cheeks.

"It was Nate Schiller," Mackenzie said. She was looking directly at Colton. "That's what you were about to say, right? That the body in the meadow was Lane's friend Nate?"

Confusion strung through Delaney like a web. "That's impossible."

Next to her, Colton didn't deny it. Instead, his response came out flat. "Yes."

Delaney's veins iced over. "What?"

"Someone found him this morning," Mackenzie said. "He was half-dead in a public park out in Chicago."

"Oh my *god*." Delaney's stomach curdled. "Is he—Will he be okay?"

"They don't know." Mackenzie hadn't taken her eyes off Colton. "He's been admitted to the hospital."

"They posted his picture on the news," Adya said, fidgeting with the champagne hem of her hijab. "Lane, it's the same boy from my visitations."

"But that doesn't make any sense," Delaney countered. "You told us you saw that boy get ripped apart—"

"The same day you met Nate," Mackenzie finished for her. "In the Sanctum."

Something cold crawled into Delaney's skin. She glanced over at Colton and found him watching her, his face bloodless. "Colton?"

"I'm sorry," he said.

"You knew?"

"I tried to tell you."

"Tell me what?" Her voice rose several octaves. She could feel herself becoming hysterical. "It couldn't have been Nate. Adya said the boy in her head was dead for weeks. Nate's been perfectly fine all semester."

"Lane," Adya said, in a voice that was disconcertingly tender. "Nate's mother filed a missing person's report back in June."

"He's been missing for almost five months," Mackenzie said. "Whatever you've been spending time with in the Sanctum, it isn't Nate Schiller."

19

Colton Price didn't answer the phone on the first try. Or the second. Or the third.

The Apostle stood stewing in his kitchen, overheating in his robe. He stood in the dark, listening to the kettle rattle on the stove. The only source of light came from the little blue nucleus beneath the burner. He stared into its depths and wished for a time when his kitchen didn't smell like rot.

"Do we think," sang the voice in the dark, "he is playing by the rules?"

"I don't want to talk to you," said the Apostle, holding tight to his mug. He'd already broken two this evening. One in a rage, when Price continued to ignore his calls. One in a fright, when his infernal haunt spoke directly at his ear. He didn't want to try for a third. Shards of porcelain lay scattered across the wide stone tile. The mugs had been a wedding present, a thousand lifetimes ago. Breaking them felt like breaking a promise to his wife.

"Who else will you talk to, darling Dickie?" crooned the voice. "There is you and there is me and there is we."

On the stove, the kettle began to whistle. In his pocket, his phone began to ring. He pried it loose, moving the whistling teapot to an unused burner to cool. Somewhere behind him, the nightmare thing dragged a finger along his wife's crystal stemware, hung from the broad buffet. Glass clink, clink, clinked together like a tuning fork struck against a surface.

"I wish you would stop that," the Apostle said, pressing the phone to his ear.

"I haven't even done anything," complained Colton Price.

"Not you." He moved the phone from one ear to the other, irate, and pressed two fingers to the pulse in his neck. "Where have you been? I've been trying to get in touch with you all night."

Price didn't apologize. "I've been busy."

The Apostle pinched the bridge of his nose until he saw spots. "I need you in Chicago tomorrow."

Price popped his lips. "I don't know."

"You don't know."

"I've got plans this weekend."

"Cancel them."

The pause on the other end was infuriatingly pronounced. In the interim, some of his wife's glassware shattered against the floor. Finally, Price said, "Does this have anything to do with Nate Schiller's unscheduled resurrection?"

"It has everything to do with him. Schiller's utter lack of discretion throughout this entire process has been abhorrent."

"I don't get the impression he electively respawned in the middle of a public park."

The Apostle chose to continue as though Price hadn't spoken at all. "His is quite possibly the first success we've had. I want you in Chicago when he wakes up."

"I'll have to think about it," Colton said, and the Apostle nearly smashed his third mug of the evening.

Through clenched teeth, he hissed, "He should be in our custody. We have no idea what state he'll be in when he wakes. He could be incognizant. He could be violent. I need someone there to make sure things don't get any further out of hand."

"All right." Price let out a whistle. "All right, calm down. I'll go to Chicago. The Cubs are playing the Sox this Sunday anyway. I'd love to see them get their asses handed to them on the home field."

"Excellent," the Apostle said, and he meant it, though it came out through gritted teeth. "I've already booked your flight on my charter. Be at Logan's at six a.m. tomorrow for check-in. And Price?"

"Yeah?"

"I'm certain I don't need to tell you that you do this alone."

A pause followed. Then, "Understood."

The line went dead. He was left to the silence of his kitchen, his mug empty and his kettle cooling and the smell of death at his back.

"He is lying," sang the ghoul in his ear. "He is lying and lying and lying."

"Boys like Price need to be handled," he said. "I am handling him."

The laugh that oozed out into the dark made him shiver. He shut his eyes, though shutting his eyes didn't do anything at all to rid himself of the slap of wet shoes against the floor, or the permanent reek of decay in everything he owned.

"We will see," it sang. "We will see, you and I and we."

❧ 20 ❧

O n Monday, Lane found Colton deep in the library, buried beneath a labyrinthine assortment of books. He didn't look up when she arrived, though she knew he'd heard her approach. For several silent minutes, she hung back and watched him work, the lines of him indistinct beneath pale fringes of midmorning light.

"I want to go see him," she said when she grew tired of waiting. Several shelves away, someone let out a scathing *shush*. It carried through the rows and rows in a disembodied sigh. At his desk, Colton continued to annotate the text in front of him, the round wire frame of his glasses slipping low on his nose.

"*Colton.*" She drew out the seat next to him and plummeted into it. "Did you hear me?"

"Yes," he said, highlighting a line of text. "I heard you."

"And?"

"And I can't have this discussion."

"Why not?"

"Wednesday, please." He fell back into his chair and peered over at her. He looked tired—his curls mussed, deep bruises like thumbprints beneath his eyes. "Don't push me. Not on this."

But she couldn't leave it alone. She thought of Nate on his knees, a scream ripping from his chest. The Latin inscription inked into his skin: *Non omnis moriar*, I shall not wholly die. She'd felt the oppressive weight of the dark, the watchful quaver of the shadows, and she'd run from it. She'd left him there alone to die. Or to come back from death.

She wasn't sure. She wasn't sure of anything, save for the fact that Nate had crawled to her, that day in the meadow. He'd wept. He'd begged. The plaintive specter of his cries haunted her in her waking hours. It chased her through her dreams.

"Don't leave me here alone."

"I have questions," she said, a little desperately.

Colton pried off his glasses and rubbed at his eyes with the heel of his hand. "Which makes this different from any of our other interactions how?"

She ignored the dig. "All those times I saw Nate at the Sanctum, was he actually—"

"Dead," Colton finished for her, when it was clear she felt too ridiculous to say it on her own. "Yes. It didn't stick. I told you the Sanctum was a locus of supernatural energy. I doubt he's the first ghost to hang around the place."

Ghost.

Ghost.

The word felt laughable, but then she was a girl who'd walked through worlds. A girl who'd spent her childhood whispering all her secrets to the shadows. Why shouldn't she also be the girl who befriended people who were dead, whether temporarily or otherwise?

A memory resurfaced, like the cresting of a leviathan through a flat, glassy sea. She thought of the boy in the dark behind her childhood home, of waking in the night to follow him over the dew-slick grass, through the winter-bitten wood, into the path of an oncoming car.

"I know you. I know you."

All this time she thought he'd been a figment of her imagination, but maybe the truth was something far more nefarious. Maybe he'd

149

been dead all along. Something tormented and afraid, waiting in the dark for her to stumble outside and catch sight of him.

Next to her, Colton kicked out his legs, draping the inside of his elbow over his eyes as though he meant to take a nap. His glasses dangled between his thumb and forefinger, lenses winking in the light of the drum lamps. It should have been her cue to leave, but Delaney couldn't bring herself to back down.

"Mackenzie said Nate is recovering at Amity General out in Illinois," she said. "I looked it up. It's only a three-hour flight. I'm going tomorrow, with or without you."

"Jesus." Colton dropped his arm and fixed her in a steely gaze. "What can I say to make you leave the Schiller thing alone?"

"Nothing," she snapped, and was met with a harsh "*Quiet*," the admonition flung from the far reaches of the third floor. Still thinking of the boy in the wood, she said, "I bailed on him once already. He was hurting, and I left him there by himself."

Some of the frustration softened around Colton's eyes. "There's no need to be this worried about him, you know. He's not even dead anymore."

He said it casually, as though death were a transplanted organ, and Nate had simply rejected it. Pushing it out, the way the body flushes out an infection.

"All the more reason not to turn my back on him."

"Do you hear yourself?" He tossed his glasses onto the desk. "He's not a kindred spirit; he was *haunting* you. You can't develop a kinship with something that isn't corporeal."

"Well, I did, okay. And this isn't the first time."

In his chair, Colton went unnaturally still. Instinctively, she traced her fingers over her knees, where the scars bloomed in pale, white starbursts beneath her stockings. Colton tracked her movements, the deep well of his stare impossible to read. Out in the corridor, a group of students shuffled in and out of view, arms laden with books.

"Did you know," Colton said, "that *The Divine Comedy* was first transcribed into English in the year 1802? In the years since, there have been more translations printed in English than in any other language."

"Don't change the subject."

"I'm not," he insisted. "Listen, as is the case with any iteration, not every translation is precisely the same. But these two books in front of me?" He shut the book he'd been annotating and placed it on top of another in a short, identical stack. "They were both done in 1949 by a mirror editor, for the same mirror imprint."

"I don't want to talk about your homework. I want to talk about Nate."

He continued on as though she hadn't interjected at all. "Theoretically, these two books should be virtually identical. But in this alternate version of Alighieri's work the final words in the tercets show an occasional variance. That means the source material was different. Whitehall wants me to write a paper convincing him that two different Dante Alighieris experienced two different visions of Hell, but it's a waste of time."

She slumped into the deep spine of her chair. "Because it has nothing to do with Nate?"

"Because," he said, "there may be an infinite number of worlds, but there's only one Hell."

He said it like it was a fact. Like he'd personally visited, just to confirm. Their gazes met and held. If he'd been trying to illustrate a point, he hadn't succeeded. The long tether of her patience snapping, Lane rose to go.

"Never mind."

"Wait." Colton mirrored her movements, tailing after her as she pushed into the maze of books. His shoulder clipped the stern bronze of a bust, nearly toppling it from its pillar. "Where are you going?"

"Back to my dorm." The broad double doors of the stacks spat her out in a spiral stairwell, her descent marked by thin iron balusters. Conscious of him tailing just a half step behind her, she said, "It's becoming increasingly clear to me that you don't plan to take me seriously."

"I *am* serious," he insisted, keeping pace. "Wednesday, look at me. I've never been more serious in my life."

He cut her off at the bottom step, jogging ahead of her and catching his hands on the railings. In the windowless light of the atrium, his stare almost looked earnest. Almost.

"Every time you open your mouth," she said, "another half-truth comes tumbling out."

"I know." He scrubbed a hand through his curls. "I know, and I'm sorry. I don't expect you to believe me, but I'd tell you everything if I could. It's just that some secrets aren't mine to give away."

"What's that supposed to mean?"

"It means I made a promise." The tendons in his throat moved in a swallow. "I took a pledge. And there are measures in place to make sure that pledge is honored."

A pair of upperclassmen entered the stairwell, and Colton was forced to step aside to let them pass. Delaney listened to the patter of their shoes on the stairs, the fading trickle of voices down the steps. Overhead, the doors to the stacks swung open and clicked shut.

When they were gone, she peered down at Colton. "Are you in some kind of trouble?"

An unfunny laugh cracked out of him. It ricocheted through the space like gunfire.

"Don't laugh," she bit out. "I'm serious. Should we be going to the police?"

"The *police*?" His voice was hard. "Jesus, Wednesday. What exactly do you think is happening here?"

"Three boys are dead." The words cracked out of her. "That's what happening. What if you're next?"

"Why would I be next?"

"Because your name is on the wall." When he didn't answer, she doubled down. "I'm booking a ticket to Chicago," she said. "And I'd rather not go alone."

The elusive invitation hung in the air between them. She expected him to refuse—to give her a dozen cryptic reasons why not. Instead, something wordless flashed through the bottomless well of his stare.

"Are you asking me to go with you," he asked, "or telling?"

"Telling," she said, though she hadn't been. She didn't know why, but it felt like the right answer. "I never met Nate while he was still alive. I don't know how this works. I don't even know if he'll recognize me. But he'll recognize you. So you're going to come with me."

"All right, then," he said, surprising her. "Let's go to Chicago."

❦ 21 ❧

Colton Price wasn't the type of person to admit to being afraid.

He wasn't the sort to wake sweating from a nightmare, his heart beating hard in his chest. He never left the lights on, wary of the unlit corners of his room. He didn't hide in the kitchen, trapped by his ghosts.

He was hiding now. Dressed in nothing but a pair of flannel pajama bottoms, his feet bare against the night-chilled tile. It was early in the morning. For once, he wasn't sure of the time. He'd woken in a start, without alarm, without rote, and stumbled blearily out of bed, a hangnail moon tailing him window to window as he headed down the hall and down the stairs.

He'd had a night terror, stark and clear, and now—awake and with his heart hammering—he felt as if time had been knocked clean out of him. Hands shaking, he helped himself to a cup of water from the fridge.

In his dream, he'd been trapped beneath the ice. On the other side was Lane. Her hands pressed up against the glassy shelf. Her eyes were wide and black. Not Lane's juniper stare, but something Other. He'd cried out, pond water whittling his lungs. It drew him away with icy fingers, down to the bottom, where he knew he'd find Liam. Eyes open. Goalie pads lashed with pondweed. Waiting for police sonar to ping his location.

He was awake now. The light in his kitchen clicked on, chasing away the dark. The clock read 2:13. His father used to set all the clocks in the house five minutes fast on purpose. It was, Christian Price loved to say, excellent practice to keep from being late.

In the Price family, tardiness was careless.

Carelessness was ugly.

Ugliness was unacceptable.

Colton had been late getting to Walden Pond the morning Liam died. So deep in March, the season had already begun to turn. The sun turned the ice slick with sweat. Pools of water formed in the shallow places, colored brown with sludge. Too late to skate. Too warm to try. He'd begged Liam to go out with him anyway. He'd been in second-hand gear, wielding a secondhand stick, following a secondhand dream, trying out for the junior hockey league the way Liam had when he'd been his age. At dinner the previous night, their father had ordered Colton to eat his broccoli, to sit up straight, to work harder at his assist if he had any hope of making the team. Like Liam, like Liam, like Liam.

The sign by the pond sat askew, speared in earth already thawing.

NO SKATING TODAY

It was 11:45 when they pulled Liam Price out of the ice.

It was 11:58 when they called it.

Now the clock said 2:15. He slid his phone out of his pocket. 2:10.

He didn't trust his eyes. All around him, time slipped and wavered. It slid past him in schools of thin, silvery fish, too quick to catch. His skin was cold. Pins and needles ran down his arms. He was drowning. Always drowning.

He slid open his phone and put in Lane's number.

The bones in his hands felt as though they'd been shattered beneath a mallet.

At his ear, the phone rang and rang. Outside the yellow reach of light, the shadows pressed close. When he'd been a little boy—still afraid of monsters under the bed—he would get a running start from the bathroom. He'd leap up onto his mattress without getting near enough to risk something grabbing his ankles. In the top bunk, Liam would fold himself over the edge and swat Colton with a pillow.

"Jesus H. Christ. Don't be such a baby, C.J. Monsters aren't real."

He knew better now. The truth pumped through his veins.

He shut his eyes. Braced himself for a voice mail.

Instead, he heard a soft "Hello?"

He let out a breath.

"Price? Hello?"

"I'm here," he said. "Were you sleeping?"

"No." She didn't say anything else. He could hear her computer keys click, click, clicking. He slumped down onto the floor, his knees pushed out. "I'm not going to miss the flight," she said, "if that's what you're worried about."

"What? Oh. No, that's not it."

"Okay." More clicking. Pages rustled.

"It's just—" He faltered, feeling supremely ridiculous. "Could you tell me what time it is?"

He was met with silence. Then, "It's two in the morning."

"I mean, specifically. To the minute."

Another pause. "It's quarter after."

"Exactly?"

"Exactly."

"Thanks." He leaned his head back against the cabinet, some of the tension bleeding out of him. On the other end, Lane had resumed typing. He listened to her work for a while without speaking. Outside the kitchen, the foyer was black as a void. "What are you working on?"

"That's none of your business."

"Defensive," he noted.

"You're not the only one with secrets." A pause followed, and she added, "This is going on my checklist, you know."

"You have a checklist?"

"I do. I call it 'reasons Colton Price probably keeps teeth in a kitchen drawer.'"

"Sounds unsanitary." A smile crept across his face, unbidden. "I'm not allowed to call you in the middle of the night to ask the time?"

"It's got a real Wes Craven feel," she said. "I'm waiting for you to tell me to look out my window."

"Your window?" He kicked out a leg. The bottom of his foot sat flush against the cabinet in front of him. "What's outside your window?"

"You, obviously. Probably with a hunting knife."

Knife aside, he wished that were true. He wished he were anywhere but here, in this empty mausoleum. A secondhand son in a throwaway home. He wished he were on campus, hand in hand outside her dormitory, the way they'd been the night he walked her home. He wished he could see what she was doing, how she was sitting—if she was at her desk or tucked up in her bed. If she worked by the overhead lights or beneath a tabletop lamp. If she was a pajama-set person or a recycled-T-shirt person.

"It was romantic when Romeo did it," he said.

Another pause. Then, "Romeo and Juliet died."

"Point taken." He wanted to ask her the time again, but he was awake enough now to realize how strange that would seem. How irrational. "I think it's nice, what you're doing," he said. "Going out to Chicago to see Schiller. It's a terrible idea, but it's nice. Not a lot of people would."

Quiet ensued. Then, softly, she said, "I know what it's like to wake up in a hospital bed and find out your entire life has been turned upside down while you were under. No one should have to go through that alone."

He shut his eyes and didn't respond. For the next several minutes, he sat with the phone tucked into his shoulder and listened to her work.

"Price," he heard her say, not for the first time. "*Colton*. Are you sleeping?"

"No," he said after a beat. "No, I'm still here."

"We have to be at the airport first thing in the morning. I should try and get at least a little sleep."

"Wait." His heart rioted against his ribs. He thought of slamming his hands on the wrong side of the ice. The cold knifing his bones. His brother with arms gone slack, slowly sinking out of sight. "Wednesday, wait a second. Stay and talk to me."

For a heartbeat, he thought it was too late. He thought she'd gone. But then he heard the sharp intake of her breath on the other line.

"Okay," she said. "I'll stay. But not for free."

"Fair enough." He settled back into the cabinets. "What's it going to cost me?"

He heard the scrape of a chair, the creak of springs as she climbed into bed. His throat felt like sandpaper. His stomach was a molten rock, hard and igneous. He kneaded his aching fist into the cool tile of the floor.

In a whisper, she said, "You have to tell me three more things that are true."

He pulled his eyes shut against the onslaught of his ghosts. "I can't think of any right now."

"Three things you don't like, then."

He considered. "I don't like coffee," he said after several seconds had passed.

"Are you serious?"

"As a heart attack. Which, coincidentally, you're sixty percent more likely to experience if you drink caffeine every day."

"Colton."

"What?"

"I spent weeks bringing you a coffee every single morning."

"And I didn't drink them."

"I thought it was just because you were being rude," she said. "I'm going to send you an invoice; those coffees weren't cheap. What's the second thing?"

He chewed on a half-settled smile, mulling it over. "I don't like that you don't come by the house anymore." She went quiet after that, and he wondered what she was thinking. He wanted to ask, but then he was afraid he wouldn't like the answer. Instead, he said, "Three—I hate keeping so many secrets."

It was a while before she answered—enough time for him to regret saying it at all. He didn't want her to be upset with him. He didn't want to fight again.

"I was reading about necromancy," Lane finally whispered, in a voice nearly too soft to hear. "When you first called."

"As one does."

"Do you think it's real? I mean, I know it's real as a concept, but do you think there are people out there who can manipulate the dead?"

He knew why she was asking. He knew the line of questioning that had led her there. It was the natural course of things, given what she'd witnessed in the meadow. Nate Schiller, knitting himself back together at her feet. He thought of little Delaney Meyers-Petrov leaning over him, her mittens full of stones. *"Get up; the water's too cold for swimming."*

"I don't know," he lied. "But I've clocked enough hours in other worlds to know that reality, as a rule, is limitless."

"So you're saying it's possible."

"I'm saying anything is," he said, and it was the closest he could bring himself to spilling the truth.

❦ 22 ❦

As it turned out, Colton Price had a very long list of things he didn't like. He didn't like crowded spaces, he informed Delaney, as the rented town car picked her up in the haze of an autumn dawn. He didn't like the smell of recycled air, he added as they zipped along the Callahan Tunnel, lights streaking past in bolts of yellow. He didn't like seats with little room for his legs. He didn't like proximity to strangers, public transportation, or bathrooms barely wide enough for his shoulders. An airplane, he argued, toeing out of his shoes in the security line, was all of these things.

"They pack you into a tiny metal box weighing ninety thousand pounds," he said, looping his leather belt into a plastic collection tray. "Then they vault you through the sky at thirty thousand feet. It's mathematically insane. Hi there. You look like a very reasonable person. Can I keep my watch on?"

On the other side of the belt, the TSA agent did not look remotely reasonable. She did, Delaney noted, look deeply tired of fielding passenger questions.

"No," she said, without batting an eye.

But Colton wasn't deterred. "It's just that I'm not entirely comfortable taking it off."

The agent stared. Colton scuffed his socks on the floor. On the belt, trays stacked high with belongings began to pile in a messy bottleneck.

"Just take the watch off, Price," Delaney said.

By the time they made it to their gate, both of them a little terse, there were only ten minutes remaining until takeoff. After scouting out the window seat, Delaney buckled herself in and watched Colton do the same. He was more casual than she'd ever seen him, dressed in jeans and a raglan shirt, his face obscured beneath the brim of a vintage Whalers cap. Even dressed down, he was in stark opposition to Delaney in her lavender space buns and oversized pullover, shredded black leggings disappearing into jodhpur boots.

He'd kept her on the phone for nearly an hour last night, until her head nodded forward and the phone slipped out of her hand. At some point, he must have hung up. When she woke to Adya standing over her, it was to find her phone battery close to dead and her implant still on, sound plugging the dull ache of overexposure in her head.

Now she tucked her legs up under her and asked, "Is it a family heirloom?"

Colton glanced up from wiping down his armrest with an antibacterial wipe—he didn't like germs, he'd told her in the boarding line, after a man in their immediate vicinity had sneezed six times in rapid succession. "Is what an heirloom?"

"The watch."

"Oh." He braceleted the timepiece in his free hand. "No."

He didn't say more. He didn't say anything at all until they were airborne, the seat belt light clicking off. "There's too many people on this plane." He tugged the brim of his ball cap over his eyes. "I can feel myself getting sick."

Lane glanced up from the book she'd snagged in the terminal kiosk. "Do you think that maybe, sometimes, you have a tendency to make a bigger deal out of things than necessary?"

He angled his chin just so, one dark eye peering out from beneath his cap. He didn't address her question. Instead, he said, with utmost solemnity, "If I catch a cold, it'll be your fault. I've been forced on this trip against my will."

"I highly doubt there's a single person in the world who can force you to do something against your will," she said, and returned to her book.

"You'd be surprised," he shot back. Then, a half a beat later, "I'm going to close my eyes."

Outside the window, the clouds streaked past in wind-whipped threads. For the better part of an hour, she lost herself in a chapter. When she glanced up, it was to find Colton awake and watching her. He didn't strike up a conversation. He didn't look away.

Desperate for something to do with her hands, she reached for the barf bag in the back of the seat, folding it into a clumsy origami swan. Testing out the aerodynamics, she tossed it into the air. It sailed dolefully across the armrest and landed square in Colton's lap. His eyes dropped to her misshapen creation.

"I've been thinking," she said.

"Yeah?" He picked up the swan, examining it from all angles. "About what?"

"I have this memory, from when I was small. I don't know if it's relevant."

"Tell me," he said, without missing a beat.

"When I was a little girl, my parents used to take me to Walden Pond to skip stones across the water. My dad was great at it. He always found the best pebbles for skipping. They would make it halfway across. Mine just sank. Straight to the bottom." She peered up at him to find him gone perfectly still. Something unidentifiable flinted his gaze. "One morning we got there early, before anyone else. I wanted to gather all the best pebbles before he had a chance, so I ran from the car. My parents were furious, because two boys had drowned there the week before."

Colton's throat corded in a swallow. The swan sat clutched between his fingers in a death grip.

"I managed to get a whole fistful of stones before I found the body," she went on. "It was a boy. He was lying half in the water and half in the mud, and I thought at first I was imagining him."

Sunlight glanced through the window in a golden lens flare and she could briefly see herself reflected back in it. She stared down at her fingertips. The nail of her index finger was nearly picked to the quick. Out in the aisle, the snack cart rattled past.

"Keep going," Colton said.

"You'll think I'm crazy."

"I won't."

She shut her eyes. It was too hard to look at him. Cold, disapproving Colton, with his smiles like a knife. She was certain he was judging her—little glass Delaney, her head packed full of daydreams. But all these years later, she could still recall every detail of that chilly March morning. She held on to them the way one clung to a dream. In fragments and in colors.

"He was dead," she whispered. "I was so sure of it. But when I called to him, he cried out. When I told him to move, he listened. When I reached out for his hand, he took mine. He was like ice. I've never felt anything so cold."

"What happened?"

"He disappeared." She opened her eyes to find him staring. "One minute he was there, the next he'd been swallowed up by the sky. By the time my parents came running, he was gone. They thought I'd been playing some sort of game. But it wasn't a game. I saw him. I felt him. And then—"

She tailed off, apprehensive. The way he was looking at her— sunlight turning his eyes a rare, honeyed brown—put a funny sort of thrill in her chest. He looked like a boy, for once, instead of something too sharp to touch.

"When Nate was coming back to life," she said, "Adya told me she followed him straight to me. I always thought maybe I imagined it, but what if that's who I am? What if I'm the kind of person who looks into the shadows and sees something dead looking back?"

With unconvincing nonchalance, Colton asked, "What if you are?"

She didn't want to think about what it might mean. Every little thing felt magnified, veering into too-sharp focus—the hum of the engine, the heat of the sun against her skin, Colton lifting up her paper swan and placing it gingerly atop the frayed nylon of her knee. He left it there, one fingertip balanced along the papery fan of the tail.

"This is a terrible swan," he said.

"It's a perfect swan, actually. I can also do a frog."

"Impressive."

"My mom's homeschool approach was very crafts based," she said as he nudged the swan just hard enough to flap its lopsided wings. "Instead of learning subtraction, I got macramé Mondays and water-color Wednesdays. It was a little bit ridiculous."

"It doesn't sound ridiculous," he said. "It sounds nice."

"At this point, it's a fire hazard." A ribbon of hair had come loose from one of her buns, and she worked to tuck it back into place. "She doesn't throw anything away. The whole house is stuffed full of all the do-it-yourself projects she made my dad and me take on with her over the years."

"My parents are divorced," Colton volunteered after another minute of fiddling with the swan. "Neither of them could stand to stay in Boston afterward, so I'm at the house on my own until graduation."

"Oh."

She thought of the sparse décor, the doors all shut up like tombs. She'd thought maybe they were in the middle of a renovation, not that no one lived there at all. No one but Colton. Next to her, the brown of his eyes was concealed beneath his cap.

"My dad's new wife has a tendency to burn through credit cards," he said. "When they open a new one, they don't always update their payment plans. That first night you came over, the electricity was shut off."

He said it so casually. Like it was a normal thing, to be forgotten.

Understanding pierced her like an arrow. The wall of candles. His attempts to turn her away at the door. "*God*," she breathed. "Why didn't you say something?"

A crooked smile overtook one half of his face. "To spare myself the humiliation."

"You let me make fun of you," she said. "Now I feel like a jerk."

Overhead, the fasten seat belt light clicked on. The pilot's voice filtered through the sound system in an unintelligible garble.

"What did he say?"

"He said we'll be starting our descent soon." Colton retracted his hand, letting the swan flutter down into her lap. "You can still change your mind, you know. You don't have to do this."

"But I do," she said. "There's a reason Nate found me. I don't know what it is, and I don't know if there's an answer waiting for me in Chicago, but I have to try. My whole life, people have defined me by one thing only. I came to Godbole because I wanted to see if there was another version of me out there. Maybe this is her."

Colton frowned. "A girl who can't fold a symmetrical swan?"

"I have to see this through to the end," she said, ignoring him.

"And what if you don't like what you find?"

"I don't know," she admitted. "I guess I'll deal with that when I get there."

❧ 23 ❧

The drive to the hospital was long and slow, hindered by the stop-and-go of traffic. An awful, crawling pace that made Colton sincerely consider opening the passenger door and throwing himself into the path of an oncoming vehicle. Sequestered in the back of a beetle-black town car, he and Lane sat with knees kissing, the city creeping past in cool concrete blocks and multifamily Greystones.

He shouldn't have come. Already, he could feel the consequences of his actions taking root. A migraine bloomed behind his eyes. Minor avulsions tore at his tendons. Every time he thought he'd become desensitized to the pain, it deepened. He wondered how much further he could push himself before his body gave out.

He couldn't help it. He went where she led, like a paper kite on a string. He was hopelessly caught, twisted in her branches. His line tangled. His spine splintered. His sail all in tatters. There was no clean way to work himself free.

Next to him, Lane stared out the window with wide, unblinking eyes. He liked the way she took the city in, lips pursed in a frown, spinning the braided ring on her finger round and round like a talisman. He'd been watching her do it for the past several blocks. Her hair was in twin buns, overlarge and preposterous. One of them was coming loose from the nap she'd taken during the final leg of their flight.

When they finally pulled up to their stop, the sun was big and round in the sky and Colton had missed seven consecutive phone calls in a row. His stomach was lead. His chest tight. The Apostle would be looking for him soon, and he was in exactly the wrong place, doing precisely what he'd been warned not to do. He didn't want to think about the repercussions.

They stopped at the coffee kiosk out in front of the hospital, and he ordered a hot latte.

Lane frowned up at him as he slid the steaming cup into a cardboard sleeve. "I thought you didn't drink coffee."

"It's not for me," he said, pocketing his change. He checked his watch as they headed into the visitors' entrance. Half past ten. His phone vibrated in his pocket. He ignored it.

The hospital's lobby was stark and clinical, lit by buzzing fluorescents. He'd always hated hospitals. He hated the way time came crashing to a halt. The way everyone looked just a little bit lost. The way, at any given moment, it was likely someone was dying.

But this hospital?

This hospital he hated because it housed something old and cold and nameless.

A beast, stuffed inside the body of a boy.

He checked his watch again. Next to him, Lane fussed with the cuff of her sleeve. She'd changed in the airport—out of her sweatshirt and into some sort of plaid apron and buttoned blouse.

Eyeballing him, she asked, "Do you have somewhere else to be?"

"No," he said. "Why?"

"This is the sixth time you've checked your watch."

"I want to make sure it hasn't stopped."

Her nose crinkled. "Your watch?"

"Time." He flicked the tip of her nose. "Obviously. Why'd you change?"

She tugged again at her sleeves. "I wanted to look nice."

"Got it." He fell into step alongside her, the cardboard sleeve doing little to protect his hand from the scalding latte. "You want to impress your undead boyfriend."

She skidded to a stop, heels clattering. "God, Colton. You don't have to be such a—"

"Back already?" The voice that rang out from the check-in desk was loud and maple sweet. Colton took the opportunity to evade Lane's ballooning wrath. Sidestepping her and her ire, he slid the latte across the counter. Behind a plexiglass divider sat a bottle-blond nurse in bold blue scrubs. Her smile stretched as she took the offered drink. "You remembered!"

"I wouldn't forget." He could feel Lane's glower on the side of his face. "I wanted to pop back in and check on our boy. How's he doing?"

Lane's stare knifed into him and twisted hard. A killing blow. He didn't look.

"He's in and out," the nurse admitted. "It's not technically visiting hours, but you can go on up. I won't tell. His mother's up there now. Hold on, I'll buzz you in."

He thanked her and led Lane away by the hand, drawing her down the hall and through the wide, open doors into the patient corridor. She made her displeasure known through short, stilted steps, so that he was forced to drag her along in his wake. The rocky pace was compounded by the rheumatic chafe of his bones. More than once, he considered scooping her up altogether and fireman carrying her the remainder of the way.

"Can you walk properly," he asked, tugging her around another corner, "or do I need to stuff you on a cot and wheel you? Because I will."

The air felt thinner here. The temperature several degrees too cool. Overhead, the lights ran past in thin strips of white. Motion activated, they flickered on one by one by one. Humming with electricity. Turning the accusation in Lane's stare to a cadmium green.

"You've already been to see him," she bit out.

"Yes." They were halfway across a yawning sky-bridge. Lane's reflection was briefly mirrored back at him in the wide plexiglass panels. He could tell by the look on her face that she was seriously considering the cost-benefit analysis of punching him square in the jaw. He wouldn't blame her.

They passed by a series of empty rooms, small and unlit and separated from the hall by thick-plated glass. Every once in a while, another person shuffled by. Sometimes dressed in a suit, sometimes in the sterile white of a lab coat. Always too immersed in their clipboard, their file, or their phone to take notice of two bickering college students.

"It's just that you made such a big deal over me wanting to come to Chicago," Lane said, wresting her hand free of his. He shook out his fingers, seeing stars. A deep, subchondral ache dug into his bones.

"I did do that," he agreed.

Lane made a face that could have curdled milk. "You didn't think that was pertinent information? Like maybe I'd—Hey!"

He'd stopped abruptly and Lane skidded into him with an indignance that bordered on violence. Shushing her, he gestured ahead. Outside a windowed room sat a lone woman, her head bowed, her eyes closed. She looked frail and thin, her hair shorn short.

Lane's irritation flagged. "Is that his mom?"

"I think so."

The air tasted wrong. There was something metallic in it—something sulfuric and strange. A sound clicked through the quiet. Not the turn of a hospital cart, the push of a wheel, but the slithering scrape of something old. A sudden panic gripped him.

He was making a mistake, letting her walk inside that room.

But he didn't have a choice.

"Listen to me," he said. "You need to be careful in there. You didn't know Schiller before. I did. The boy inside that room? He's wearing Schiller's face, but he's not the guy I pledged with."

A little bit of truth, wrenched free like a tooth. Tucked inside his jacket pocket, his pinkie popped out of joint with a single, bruising crack. He bit down a groan. Behind him, Lane craned her neck to the side, peering around him at the waiting room. She didn't look afraid. She only looked determined.

Softly, she asked, "How is that possible?"

"Because," he said, and his voice came out gritted, "people don't just come back from the dead by accident. Nathaniel Schiller died five weeks ago. When he went, he left an empty body behind. And now something else has crawled inside it."

❦ 24 ❧

Nate Schiller's mother was small and fair, her face a perfect oval and her hair styled in a neat sandy cut. She had the same nose as Nate—the same big, doleful eyes, only hers were a pale, powder blue where Nate's had been dark and turbulent. She glanced up as Delaney approached, her hands clutched as if in prayer.

"Hi," Delaney said. "Are you Mrs. Schiller?"

"Sarah," she corrected, and rose to her feet. "You must be a friend of Nathaniel's."

"I am," Delaney said, though she wasn't exactly sure that was true. "I'm Lane."

"Lane." Sarah's smile wobbled. Her eyes were fringed in tears. She reached for Lane's hand and held it, her fingers shaking. "It's so sweet of you to come all this way."

"It was nothing," Delaney assured her. "Really."

"I thought it would be good for him," Sarah said, dabbing at her nose with a tissue. "Howe. He was always a little odd, growing up." She let out a watery laugh. "He saw things that weren't there. He heard things no one else heard. It made it tough for him to make friends. When he started showing an interest in Godbole's program, I thought, 'This is it. This is the direction he needs.'" She sniffled, reaching into her bag for another tissue. "I'm sorry."

"You don't need to apologize." Delaney felt suddenly like she ought not to have come. She was an interloper. A stranger. She didn't know

Nate; she'd been haunted by him. She had no right to be here, comforting his mother.

But it was too late to turn tail and run.

"I'm going on and on," Sarah said. "It's just that it was always the two of us, at home. He was such a mama's boy. And then he went and found a group of friends, and I really thought a little bit of brotherhood might be good for him. He didn't say anything when he called home. He didn't say what they were making him do."

Delaney frowned. "What do you mean? What did they make him do?"

"I'm not sure." Sarah's eyes flooded with tears, and she caught them on petite fingers. "He pledged with a group he called the Priory. He said it wasn't a fraternity, but it was definitely some sort of boys' club. The police think he might have been involved in a hazing ritual."

"Oh." Delaney felt suddenly and deeply stupid. She glanced back at Colton. He stood at the far end of the hall, his phone pressed to his ear, his ball cap pulled low, his eyes fixed on her.

"I was about to run down to the cafeteria and get something to eat." Sarah's gaze flicked over and over again toward that wide, flat window along the wall. "Would you like to go in and sit with him while I'm gone?"

"I would," Delaney said, her regret deepening by the second. "If that's all right."

"Of course. I'm sure he'd like to see a friendly face."

Nate Schiller's hospital room was plain and cold. The walls were empty of adornment, the space lit by a single humming rod. The bed was thin and white, propped upright and edged in rails. Delaney stood in the open doorway and subdued a shiver.

The shadows here were obsolete, driven into hiding by the bald white of the overhead lights. *Stay away*, they seemed to say, cowering beneath the bed and the chair and the trays. *Stay away.*

Propped against a series of pillows, Nate dug into a tapioca pudding. Starchy white pearls lumped over the plastic edge of his plastic cup, spilling onto his hand. He didn't speak. Neither did Delaney. He looked the way he had in the Sanctum: aquiline nose and round jaw, his face dusted in freckles. His unwashed hair hung into his eyes in a row of pale Cs.

This close, Delaney could see the wrongness in him. There was something incongruous in the way his face didn't show the same signs of wear as the rest of him. There were no circles under his eyes, no waxen skin or sickly pallor to suggest exhaustion or stress.

He didn't look like someone who'd been dead. He looked content. He looked healthy. He looked stuffed full of pudding. His mouth was relaxed, his eyes bright. Beneath the thin paper of his hospital gown, a series of electrodes stuck to his chest in flat white circles. He picked up his head and regarded her coolly, and Delaney had the creeping sense that he was wholly unaffected by the passing time.

"Hi," she said, and immediately wanted to kick herself for it. "Do you know me?"

He didn't answer. He only set down his spoon, silverware clinking the laminate of his tray. Deep behind her eyes, the ringing began. It crackled through her skull like static electricity, white and galvanizing as a lightning strike.

On a whim, she reached behind her ear and clicked off her implant. Instantly, the room's ambient noises were extinguished. The steady hum of hospital equipment winnowed out and the thready huff of her breathing clipped to an immediate stop. In the hollow space left behind, her tinnitus flared.

"I'm Lane," she said. "Do you remember me?"

A lurid smile—one that was not, Delaney felt, entirely human—stretched across Nate's face. A feathery whisper of unease brushed the nape of her neck. She tried not to look afraid as something coiled between her ears. It sounded like a penny, rolled over stone. A presence took root, cold and alkaline. In the quiet of her thoughts, a voice crackled like static.

Yes, it said. *We remember. We hoped you would come.*

"We?" Panic gripped her by the throat. "What are you?"

There is no scope for me in your understanding. There is no word for me in your language.

Her nails bit into her palms. "And yet you're speaking my language."

Silence is universal, Delaney Meyers-Petrov.

She hesitated, her skin prickling. "You know my name."

I know a great many things about you. I can read the chapters of your life like a book.

The words dripped over her thoughts like ink, bleeding through her until she felt dizzy and a little bit sick. She'd grown used to hearing things in the silence, but this was nothing at all like the restless dark—nothing like the fuzzing hum of a door between worlds.

This was something new.

She fought the urge to turn tail and run, to leave behind that vacant stare and that insipid voice inside her head. Her skin itched all over with the feel of cold, crawling things, as if some small insect had crept inside and laid eggs. As if she were a host, and the voice a parasite.

Similar, said the voice, though she hadn't spoken aloud. *I suppose, in some ways, I am quite like a mouse.*

She held that blown-pupil stare, though she didn't want to. "Explain."

It didn't escape her notice that Nate had gone too long without blinking. As soon as the thought occurred to her, his lids blinked two times in deliberate succession. *Blink. Blink.* As if being human was voluntary. As if he was a doll, and it the ventriloquist.

Whatever *it* was.

I told you, it said. *I am like a mouse.*

"And I asked you to explain."

It is difficult to compose an explanation over your shouting.

"I'm not shouting."

Oh yes, you are.

She took a breath. She tried to still her thoughts. Her heartbeat raced through her like a rabbit in flight. In the quiet, the voice slithered through her skull. It writhed and it roiled. It hissed out an odious soliloquy.

I am that which slips into the secret spaces. When a door is left open too long, I am the thing that crawls inside. I am the beast who burrows in their hollows, the varmint who nibbles at their bones. This boy—

"Nate," Delaney couldn't help saying.

Nate's mouth stretched open in a beatific smile. Spittle gathered at the corners, but he didn't wipe it away. *This boy*, began the voice anew, *threw his door wide. He invited me in.*

"What does that mean? He wanted to die?"

No. He wanted to live forever.

His head quirked to the side in a movement that was not remotely human. Delaney recoiled from the wrongness of it, sliding back until she cracked into the IV pole and nearly sent it toppling. She set it to rights, heart hammering, disentangling herself from the drip chamber. Those empty eyes flicked over her face, moving faster, faster, white sclera bisected with the telltale red of burst vessels. A thin line of slaver tracked down his chin.

Delaney reached for the remote, about to page a nurse, and everything stopped. Nate fell stock-still, his palms slamming flat against the tray in a movement that made her jump. She felt the reverberation in the soles of her feet, in the walls of her heart. She stood gripping the metal pole—afraid to look away, afraid to get too close.

"Nate?"

He smiled up at her. This time, the voice in her head was a creaking floorboard in an old house. It was a stick snapping in the woods. It was leaves whispering on a cold October night. It whistled through the core of her.

Your door is wide open, Delaney Meyers-Petrov. I can see all your most secret spaces. I can see how you will die. I can see what stalks your sleep at night, the things that wake you weeping in the dawn. I can see the face of the boy in the window behind you, how you pine for him when you're alone. All twisted in your bedsheets.

She barely heard the voice over the rush of blood in her ears. Her eyes flitted toward the window. Colton stood on the other side, his features striped by partially closed blinds, his eyes glued to her, gaze assessing. Watching the one-sided conversation with the precision of a hawk. Discerning whatever he could.

Ah. The sound wound through her in chilly ecstasy. *Have I made you blush? The boy in this body blushed too. A pretty crimson, just for me. Blood heats the skin so nicely, and I like it warm.*

Her gaze jolted back to his. Nate—or the thing wearing his skin—had shifted on the bed, his bare feet sliding down onto the floor. He squared off across from her beneath the humming light, shoulders hunched. She fought the rising urge to flee.

"Why are you here?"

Because a door was left open.

"What door?"

You are asking the wrong questions, and I grow tired of answering them.

She didn't relent. "Are there more of you?"

His smile was watery—lopsided, as if the wearer was unaccustomed to its mask.

The boy in the glass knows these answers already, it said. *He has not told you the truth.*

A chill snaked through her. "What do you mean?"

The smile grew and grew. *I will not play a further part in this game. I am much too old and you are far too dull a quarry. I have my own matters to tend to.*

She flexed her fingers and found them shaking. "What matters are those?"

Those black eyes flashed. *There is a kindness in you, Delaney Meyers-Petrov. A quiet. I find it unduly sweet.* There followed a pause, pronounced and eerie. The smile on Nate's face caught at the corners. *Perhaps I will tend to my matters in another way.*

She tensed, sensing the change in the air an instant too late. "What does that—"

There was a clatter, the sound of metal striking tile. Nate was at her throat, cold fingers closing around her neck with a grip that cut the air from her lungs. Her back cracked against the wall and her head followed, smashing glass, pitching streaks of lightning across her vision in angry stabs of white.

Fingers scrabbling, she made contact with whatever she could. It didn't matter. Nate possessed a brute strength that was as inhuman as the rest of him. Somewhere nearby, she felt the reverberating slam of a door flying open. Felt it crack against the wall. Shoes pounded laminate and Nate was ripped away from her, laughing, laughing as he went.

The game, crooned the voice, too close, too close for comfort, *is in play.*

Delaney slid down the wall, cracking to her knees. She wheezed and she wheezed. Her chest didn't give. The air on her tongue tasted stale and useless. The room spun in disseminating flickers. Her head was a wraith.

A single face swam into focus.

Colton.

The world tilted, righting itself—or maybe it was she who was being righted, drawn into the fluorescent checker of the hall and guided into a chair. In front of her, Colton's face was drained of color. His mouth was on upside down. He pressed his palms to his chest and pulled them away. He did it again. He mouthed a single word. It took her several seconds to understand that he was signing.

Breathe, he signed.

That was it. One word.

Breathe. And she did. The first several tries yielded limited results, but on the third she felt her lungs flood with air. Her breath was tacky, her chest sore as her ribs cracked awake. Reaching up a shaking hand, she clicked on her implant. Sound came rushing back in hums and beeps and the steady, indistinguishable murmur of voices.

In the open door to Nate Schiller's room, a series of orderlies rushed in and out, radios crackling. And nearby, a spot of dark in the sterile white of the hall, stood a man she'd never seen, his newsboy cap pulled low. He studied Delaney with open bemusement, fishing through the pockets of his surplus jacket.

"You're a dead man, Price," he sang. "You know that?"

Colton ignored him, hauling Delaney onto her feet. Behind them, the stranger pressed a phone to his ear.

"You'd better clear out of here. They've called the cops."

"I don't care," Colton said, checking Delaney's pupils. She wrenched her chin out of his grasp, sick, dizzy, afraid. *The game is in play. The game is in play.* She could still feel the voice inside her head. It fluttered through her like a moth, ensnared. Smashing against her bones.

The man in the hat sniffed, disgusted. "You and your goddamned hubris. You really think you can get away with anything? I'm giving you an out. Take it. Let me clean up after Schiller. Get your girlfriend and get the hell out of here."

❦ 25 ❧

They'd circled the outskirts of Chicago twice, and Lane still hadn't said a word. The driver coaxed the car into the right lane, blinker clicking. Outside the window, a neat line of row homes slipped past, all stacked together in finely terraced plots of red brick and iron trappings.

"Another left up here," Colton said as they crept through Lincoln Park. He peered out the rearview window. A blond woman sat in the driver's seat of the black Honda CRV behind them, singing along to the radio. He didn't *think* they were being followed, but he couldn't be sure.

He glanced at his watch. The time was 12:23. The day had gone completely sideways. He needed space to think. He needed Lane to talk to him. To say something, even if all she did was shout.

He peered over at her, trying to be discreet. She sat with her head tipped into the headrest, her eyes closed. Her face was drained of color. Her hands were folded into her skirt, but Colton could see that she was shaking.

They passed through neighborhoods, through boroughs, in and out of districts. The cars behind them changed from trucks to coupes to SUVs, from four-door sedans to flashy exotics. None of them seemed to be tails. The next time he checked his watch, the hands read 12:35. Lane still hadn't spoken.

"Look," he said, beginning to feel a little bit desperate. He pointed out Lane's window. "Up there on the corner. That's the Englewood Post Office."

She opened her eyes slowly, as if the action pained her. He pointed again, indicating a completely unremarkable-looking building composed of completely unremarkable-looking brick.

"Oh," Lane mustered, unimpressed. "Wow."

"I think it deserves a little bit more fascination than that," Colton said as the car turned the corner. "This is the sight of several horrifically gruesome murders."

Lane shut her eyes again. "Over postage?"

"No." He wanted to keep her talking. He needed to keep her talking. "A man named H. H. Holmes built an elaborate hotel here in the late eighteen hundreds. Staircases leading nowhere, trapdoors, a laboratory in the basement. Supposedly he kept people in there. For experimentation."

"Nothing left of it now." The driver's sunglasses flashed black in the rearview mirror. The building slipped out of sight, replaced by a row of dogwood trees, leaves gone the color of pansies in the cooling autumn air.

"Too bad it burned down," Colton lamented. "I would have liked to see it."

Quiet followed. The engine hummed. Homes whipped by the windows in blocks of industrial gray. Without opening her eyes, Lane said, "I'm sure you would have thrived there," and he covered his smile with a fist.

The car slowed to a halt. They idled at a red light. It was, Colton felt, the longest red light in the continental United States. The pause made him infinitely restless. He checked the time. He bounced his knee. He checked the time again.

Behind them was an oversized Range Rover, every inch of it imposing. Colton's entire body went on edge. The SUV turned away—heading left as they went right—and he relaxed back into his seat. The town car rumbled over the edge of a curb and turned neatly into a parking lot. Outside the window, the shingled portico of a hotel came into view. The driver put the car in park and went around to collect their bags.

"And that," Colton said weakly, "concludes our tour of Chicago."

He hated that he'd said it the moment the words left his lips, but he'd been grasping for *something* to breach the quiet, and that was where he'd landed. In any case, it hadn't been the right thing to say. The look Lane fired off in his direction was cold enough to make even the hardiest of men constrict. She grumbled something unintelligible, sliding out the door and into the chilly autumn afternoon.

Buffeted into the hotel lobby by a Chicagoan wind, they found the service counter overseen by a much-too-cheerful woman in a tailored jacket and high ponytail. She checked them in with chirpy small talk, sliding two sleek keycards across the counter in a crisp white envelope.

At the far end of the lobby, they piled into the elevator, packed inside the lift with a crowd of tourists. An elderly couple in matching fanny packs. A woman in neon jogging gear. A tired-looking set of parents and their three children, armed with enough rolling carts for a small army. Colton and Lane waited on opposite sides as the elevator slowly emptied out. The elderly couple was the last to get off, shuffling out on the fifth floor. The door trundled shut, and then they were alone again. Colton watched Lane. Lane watched the numbers climb in little yellow lights over the door.

"You were right," she said, nearly too soft to hear. "There's something inside of Nate."

"I tried to tell you."

"What do we do?"

"Nothing," he said. "He's in hospital custody, surrounded by trained professionals. What could you and I possibly do that they can't?"

"We could be there for him," she bit out.

"For Schiller? You saw it yourself; Schiller's not in there anymore. He left a vacancy, and something else has taken up residence."

He saw the shudder run through her. Her eyes flitted to his. "What is it?"

It was a loaded question, but he couldn't lie to her anymore. He couldn't lie to her, but he couldn't tell her the truth, either. Not all of it. Instead, he carved himself up a little more and settled on "It doesn't have a name."

"Adya saw it." Tears fractured the cypress of her stare. "That day in the meadow, she said something big was coming. This is it, isn't it? This is what killed all the boys on that wall."

He swallowed. His throat felt tight. A mouthful of truths sat packed behind his teeth, big enough to choke on. He could give her a piece of it. Bone-whittled honesty, paid for in a deep, sutural ache.

"It was incredibly naive of Whitehall," he said, confessing what he could, "to think we could pass freely between worlds and not expect something uninvited to follow us home."

•   •   •

The room they'd rented was very sparse and very blue, the eastern wall framed in a window that overlooked a tight concrete garden. The furniture was mass-produced fiberboard, the walls adorned in framed geometric abstracts. He set their bags on the blue tufted couch. She dropped onto the blue paneled bed. Quietly, she began unstrapping her boots. She didn't say another word.

In the bathroom, he let the sink run until the water was piping hot. He rubbed the thin bar soap into a white lather. He scrubbed and scrubbed at his skin. Over and over, his brain replayed the sound Lane's head made as it slammed against the glass. The scream that cracked out of her.

When he looked up, she was standing in the open door. She'd changed into a sweater and a pair of shorts, so that she was all knit wool and bare legs. Her hair fell around her in a loose lavender spill. His chest laced unreasonably tight.

"You've been in here a while," she said, and he couldn't tell if she'd meant it as an accusation or an observation.

He took his time with the towel, refolding it when he'd finished. The smell of bleach clung to his skin. "Hospitals are full of sick people," he said, and reached for his watch. "I don't want to get smallpox."

"I'm pretty sure that was eradicated." She watched him fuss with the watch clasp. His hands shook, his fingers stiff with an arthritic ache from all the truths he'd chiseled free. On his left hand, his little finger was beginning to bruise.

"Here." She moved through the bathroom on black-stockinged feet. "Let me do it."

He relented with a muttered curse. The feel of her fingertips crept through him as she clicked the metal deployant into place and asked, "Is this part of your germ thing?"

His laugh came out in a disingenuous *hah-hah-hah*. "I don't have a germ thing."

"You do too have a germ thing."

He leaned back against the vanity. "Practicing good handwashing isn't indicative of a germaphobe, Wednesday."

"I don't know." In the mirrored lights, her pupils were reduced to pinpricks, black ringed in incandescent white. "You know who else was obsessed with cleanliness? Patrick Bateman."

"A fictional character."

"A serial killer."

"Fictional serial killer. Come here." Taking her chin in his hand, he angled her face toward the light. "You have a bruise."

"So do you," she said, indicating the purpling swell of his knuckle.

"This?" He flexed his fingers. "It's nothing."

"Same with mine," she lied. "I can't even feel it."

His jaw gritted hard enough to hurt. "*You know my name,*" he'd heard her say. He didn't like that. He didn't like the thought of what lived in Schiller's bones having a piece of her. Chewing on it.

His hand moved in direct defiance of his head, knuckles skating over the bloodless curve of her cheek, the underside of her jaw. Gently, he drew up her chin, baring her throat. Her neck was pocked in angry marks, the ghost of Schiller's chokehold already deepening to violet.

He thought very seriously about leaning in. About pressing his mouth to each bruise, one after the other. Licking clean her wounds. Instead, he settled on "Can you feel these?"

"Not even a little bit."

He let out a disbelieving *mmm* and nudged her hair over her shoulder so it spilled down her back. The lavender ends had begun to silver, fading. "Tell me what it said to you," he prompted, "when it got inside your head."

"It talked in riddles," she admitted. "Not all of it made sense. But it knew things about me. Things it shouldn't have been able to know."

His fingers hovered over the pulse beneath her ear. "What kind of things?"

Her cheeks caught fire. "I'd rather not say."

"Okay."

His head was a laundry list of shouldn'ts. Shouldn't have let her talk him into this trip. Shouldn't have assumed he could get away with it. Shouldn't have touched her, that frozen night on the quad. Now that he'd started, he was having trouble remembering how to stop.

Softly, she whispered, "Colton?"

He continued his inspection of her, his thumb trailing along the protrusion of her collarbone. "Yeah?"

"Are you in some sort of satanic cult?"

A laugh clawed out of him, and he tamped it down at the look on her face.

"It's not funny," she chided.

"Sorry." Christ, he wanted to kiss her. All his life she'd been his ghost, and now she was as corporeal as anything beneath his fingertips. "I am not currently, nor have I ever been, involved in a cult of any kind."

Out in the room, her handbag started ringing. They both froze.

188

The sound was jarring—a clarion fanfare of trumpets. He was met with Lane's stare, wide and a little bit panicked.

"That's Mackenzie."

"Ignore it."

"I can't." She slid out of his grasp. "It could be important."

Something cinched deep inside his chest as she slipped out of the bathroom. She toed across the floor and pried the still-trumpeting phone loose from her bag. A bolt of frustration ran through him. He wanted to take the phone and dropkick it out the window. He wanted to kiss her until she forgot about Schiller and the Sanctum and all the weeks and weeks of lies.

"Hi," he heard her say, a culpable edge creeping into her voice. "Yeah, sorry. I went home for a couple of days." She let out a feeble *hem-hem*. "I'm sick."

Colton peeked out from the bathroom. Lane was an atrocious liar. If he knew it, then Mackenzie Beckett definitely knew it. He watched her fidget, a stray beam of afternoon sun lancing through the jade of her eyes. Shifting her weight from her left foot to her right and back again, she did a guilty soft-shoe across the carpet.

"What? I—What?" She plucked nervously at a loose thread on her sweater. Colton had the sense she was trying very, very hard not to look at him. "*No*," she said, too defensive to be believed. "No, I'm at my— Mackenzie, why would you even ask that?"

A period of nervous listening followed. Lane went perfectly, absolutely still.

"Oh." A pause. "*Oh*."

Emerging into the room, Colton propped a shoulder against the wall. Lane's eyes flitted in his direction and away. The color was slowly draining from her face, leaving her ashen.

"Okay," she said. "I will." She shut her eyes. Took a slow, steadying breath. She looked as if a light breeze might be enough to bowl her clean over. "Okay. You too. Bye."

She ended the call. Her gaze met Colton's. He felt a million miles away from her.

"Mackenzie and Adya have been keeping tabs on Nate," she said. "According to them, he checked himself out of the hospital about a half hour ago."

❧ 26 ❧

The thing about men was that they always wanted to live forever, until they didn't. They wanted to open Pandora's box, peek in at what lay inside, and then close it back up, quick, once they beheld the ugly truth of what they sought. They wanted knowledge without travail, experience without suffering.

Discovery was not, the Apostle had learned, so easily earned.

There was always a cost. There was always a price to pay. Every step taken by man necessitated a sacrifice. An offering. An appeasement.

Devan Godbole had never quite grasped that concept back when he was still alive. He believed himself master of worlds, conqueror of time, god of space. He thought—as men of great intelligence often did—that he was clever enough to be rendered untouchable. Prideful, arrogant fool. He saw himself as a modern-day Victor Frankenstein, on the very cusp of creating life.

Much like Shelley's storied Victor, when he pulled back the covers and saw the horrible truth of his creation lying beneath, he'd become far too afraid to go on.

A coward. That was all Devan Godbole was, by the bloody end. Not a pioneer, not a trailblazer, but a man with his tail between his legs. Pandora, shoving buzzing moths of ugly truths back into the box. Failing to set loose the hope that sat, shivering, along the bottom.

For every discovery, there was a price. Nature demanded a balance, and the Apostle understood that. From the very beginning, he'd understood. Not Devan.

"I want to pull the plug," Devan had said one night over drinks. He'd been wild-eyed and ashen. He looked like he hadn't slept in weeks. Outside, rain drove sideways against the window. Wind rattled the glass in its panes. "I've already drafted a letter to Howe's board of accreditation. It's over. It's done."

The Apostle had held tight to his glass, nearly drained of scotch. His heart was a hard shell of grief back then, the losses he suffered yet unbalanced. He hadn't learned how to set wrong a right, how to nullify the constant ache of sorrow. At Devan's news, the shell in his chest gave an ugly wrench.

"You can't back out now," he'd bitten, a little drunk, a little sad, a little angry. "We're almost to the end. You don't get to change your mind."

"It's too late." Devan rose to go. He was fumbling, drunk already, his eyes glassy. Outside, it rained and rained. It was, the Apostle remembered thinking, a terribly easy night to get into an accident. "I already have," Devan said. "I won't make another door. Not in this lifetime. Not knowing what's waiting for us out there. Not knowing the truth."

Now the Apostle stood in front of a grave. Hours ago, the sky had turned sideways with a sunset, orange dusting the western edges of the world. He stood in his slippers—the ones his wife had given him for Christmas. It was a strange thing, he knew, to wear slippers to a graveyard. He did it anyway.

He'd sniped at her, that snowy morning as he peeled back the red tartan wrapping with the gold foil. The moccasins were too small, and didn't she know his size by now, after fifteen years of marriage? Her eyes had been round, apologetic saucers. The snow fell white and fat outside the wide bay window of their living room.

Now the bare backs of his heels sat in dirt. In his hand were flowers. Twelve white gerbera daisies, all of them limp.

He said, a little bit apologetically, "The store didn't have roses today."

The headstone bearing his wife's name said nothing at all. It sat—gray and absolute—in the mud. *Non omnis moriar* etched deep into the stone. A poem. A promise. He was not, he'd noticed upon arrival, the only person to leave flowers that day. Strewn across the stunted grass were twelve dead roses, each of them with the buds neatly snipped off in a macabre beheading.

Behind him, a single shadow detached from the rest. It dragged itself across the dirt.

The Apostle didn't turn around to see it draw near.

"I would appreciate it," he said, "if you didn't come here."

"I go where you go," said his haunt. Overhead, a bat fluttered by on leathery wings. The Apostle hated bats. He hated the dark. He hated Octobers. He hated graveyards, and the feel of the deep, interminable cold seeping in through the open backs of his slippers.

"Did you leave these flowers here?" He kicked at a blossom. Rosebuds went scattering in a midnight wind. The shadow laughed a wet, wheezing laugh.

"We are not the only players in this game anymore," it sang. "You and I. I and you."

He suppressed a shiver. This was his price. This was the cost of greatness. This dark, shuffling specter. This horrid, grinning wraith. Something dead, for something living. He bent low, brushing dying rosehips from the mound of earth where his wife lay buried. Twenty long years without her. Twenty long years looking for a back door.

She'd died surrounded by wires, by strangers, by monitors, and he'd spent the next two decades looking for someone who possessed the power to walk through worlds and bring her back to him.

Devan Godbole was supposed to have been that person. The Apostle put his money on the wrong horse. That was all. It was an easy fix. He had another. He had Price. He placed the daisies against the base of the gravestone. They wilted, white and insipid, looking half-dead already.

When he straightened, the shadow slumped directly in front of him. The gray marker sat between them like a bulwark. By the light of the moon, the figure looked nearly corporeal. Head concave. Its broad, smiling face a horrible thing.

It said, "The boy is not playing by your rules. Does it make you mad, so very mad, oh?"

The Apostle sniffed. He tipped his hat up on his head. "Price will be dealt with."

"The girl can hear us." The smile grew and grew. "She can hear us whispering, oh."

"Enough."

It must not have liked his tone—his shadow, his haunt, his curse. It got down on the ground. It lay in the dirt, shivering in a ball. Rolling side to side to side in a locus of pain. Its laugh came out high and thin, like a baby's wail. Like a man dying alone by the side of a highway. On a tree nearby, a barred owl took flight.

"Stop that," the Apostle said. "You're making a scene."

The figure flopped flat onto its back. Its maggot-bitten feet went scuffling, scuffling, and still. It smiled up at the Apostle. The Apostle stared back. They did this routine often—the creature reenacting its body's gruesome death, the Apostle waiting quietly for the spectacle to end. He'd grown used to it after so many years.

"They say she's a girl like a garden," it said. "All roses and lavender and spider mums. Too bright, too bright to be there. One foot among the dead, one foot among the living, like a little breathing bridge. Oh, how I'd love to see her. What a pretty, pretty sight she must be."

He snapped, "I hate it when you talk in riddles."

The shadow only laughed. It laughed and it laughed. "Every fiddler, he had a fiddle, and a very fine fiddle had he," it sang.

The Apostle pinched the bridge of his nose. "I am going home," he said. "Feel free to stay here in this miserable, wet necropolis. Lord knows you're perfectly suited for it."

But it didn't stay put. It never did.

It followed. All the way down the thin, winding trail. All the way back to the Apostle's Volvo, parked along the newly installed columbarium. Its feet dragged along at a scrape. It breathed long, rattling breaths. Sucking wind, like it was dying all over again.

He got into his car. He turned over the ignition. In his rearview mirror was that horrible smile, dark and wide.

"Home again, home again," it sang. "Jiggity jig."

He shut his eyes. When he opened them again, the face was still there, ghastly and unwavering. He put the car in drive. He said, not for the first time, "I wish you wouldn't look like that. Like him."

"This is where I live," it said, without blinking. It never remembered to blink. That was, the Apostle thought, the second worst part of the whole arrangement. The first was finding it standing astride him when he got up in the middle of the night to pee. It wobbled side to side as he took a left, clipping the curb in his haste. "Inside, inside," it sang. "Burrowed deep, deep, deep, deep, deep."

He let out a long-suffering sigh. "All right," he said. "All right, I get it. Don't sing."

Nature, he'd learned, demanded a balance in all things.

Non omnis moriar.

For every discovery, there was a price to pay.

The beast in Devan Godbole's bones was his.

❧ 27 ❧

Delaney was dreaming of holes.

The sky was black as sin. The earth underfoot was dead. The air smelled treacly and rich, like overturned dirt and lichen-kissed rot. She stood under the barbed shade of a leafless ash tree, the trunk hollowed out by clearwing borers. It was punctured with holes like a thousand winking eyes. Small holes. Large holes. Whole clusters of cavities, all black and empty. A pain persisted in her side. She rolled up her shirt, knowing already what she'd see.

A gash, claws dug deep.

A boring hole, raw and dark.

A clearwing moth fluttering, fluttering in her stomach.

The darkness *tsk*ed. It didn't approve. *Now look what you've done. We told you, we told you not to go near. We told you, we told you, not to play its games.* Overhead, the branches rustled in a fetid breeze. She scraped at her stomach, desperate to have that terrible fluttering outside of her. It didn't come away. It dug deep as a tick, fat and sated.

I am the thing that crawls inside. That strange, aeonian voice drowned out the leathery whisper of branches. *I am the beast who burrows. I am the varmint who nibbles at your bones.*

Wake up, Delaney Meyers-Petrov. Wake up and help me bring about an end.

Delaney woke to the lights clicking on. The room was too blue, the shadows too stark. Colton Price stood at the edge of the bed. She

197

sprang up, clutching at her chest, feeling a little bit attacked and a little bit startled. Attacked, because he was wearing nothing but his boxer briefs. Startled, because his torso was piebald with bruises. He wasn't looking at her. He wasn't moving at all. He was staring, instead, at the clock on her nightstand, the blanket from the couch pooling around his feet.

The time read 11:58.

She could feel, now that she was coming back into herself, the dull thud of bass moving through her box springs. She groped for her implant, lost between the pillows, and fitted it to her ear. It beeped. Once. Twice. Three times. The third beep was met with blaring rock from the radio, the volume cranked as high as it could go. She recognized the beat, but it took her several more seconds to slot the lyrics into place.

Colton still hadn't moved. The '80s anthem screamed through the paper-thin space. Delaney lurched across the bed, twisted all up in her sheets, and groped blearily at the clock. Mercifully, she found the correct button. Silence fell. Her heart thudded hard against her chest.

"The last occupant of this room must have had the alarm set," she said, though somewhere within her she felt deeply certain that wasn't the truth. She didn't want to think about that. Not now, with her stomach still turning, with midnight pressing its watchful face up against the window. At the end of her bed, Colton was silent, a slight twitch in his eye the only sign he was alive. She glanced up at him, concerned. "Colton?"

He started at the sound of his name, glancing down at her with eyes gone vacant. His pupils looked blown, and she nearly recoiled from the unblinking black of his stare.

"*Colton.*"

"What's the time." The delivery came out flat, a question without proper inflection.

"Eleven fifty-eight," she said, a little indignantly, because she felt she was owed an apology for the way she'd just been woken, and because, looming over her as he was, he could quite clearly see the clock for himself. She glanced toward the nightstand and amended, "Eleven fifty-nine."

Colton didn't blink. "On your phone."

"My phone?"

"Tell me the time on your phone."

She suppressed the very real and growing urge to throw something at him. But then his hands were fisted at his sides and his ribs were pocked with welts and she could tell that he was afraid.

"Okay," she said, and ran her hands beneath her pillows. "I'm looking. Don't have a conniption."

She found her phone down by her feet, tangled in a mess of blankets. Clicking it on, she was met with a wash of blue light. She squinted down at it, her eyes still struggling to adjust.

"It's midnight," she said, just as the clock on the table changed to match. "*Happy?*"

"Somewhat." He seemed to have picked up on her derision. Pressing the heel of his hand to an eye, he said, "Thank you, Wednesday."

She made a sound like *hmph* and flopped back, yanking the sheets up over her head. The lights were too bright. Her head was ringing, tinnitus pulling between her ears like a bow over string. The oddity of the wake-up call left her hyperaware, her heart beating like

199

a jackhammer. There was no conceivable way she was going to fall back asleep. Not with her head pounding. Not with Nate missing. Not with Colton hovering. Through the paltry thread count she could just make out the dark outline of him loitering at the edge of the bed.

Muffled by blankets, she asked, "Do you want to watch TV?"

There followed an interminable pause. For a moment, Delaney thought perhaps he hadn't heard her. Or, worse, that he had and was horrified by the suggestion. She was about to repeat herself when she heard him say, "Yeah. Okay."

She squirmed out from her tangle of sheets, making room for him as he grabbed the remote from the hutch and clicked off the light. There was something supremely ordinary about it—Colton Price in his underwear, Colton Price climbing into her bed, Colton Price clicking on the television.

That peculiar flutter came alive in her stomach, an errant moth beating against the walls of her. The flat-screen hummed to life, the blue light of a stock hotel menu turning the shadows from black to navy. Thinning them back, so they felt just a little less immediate.

The mattress was barely wider than a full, and they were brought close in the dark, elbows knocking together. The planes of his chest lit liquid crystal blue, the defined cordage of his arms limned in silver, then red, then yellow as he surfed through channels.

She occupied herself in fashioning a protective cocoon out of blankets, knees hugged to her chest, sheets double fisted beneath her chin. She tried—without success—not to think of the way he'd leaned into her in the too-blue bathroom, his hand on her throat, his breath at her lips. The way she'd convinced herself he'd been about to kiss her.

The way she'd hoped for it.

"That one," she said, pointing. "Go back, go back. *Go back.*"

"Christ." He fumbled with the buttons. "I'm going."

"There." She nudged the remote aside, hand pressed to his wrist. She could feel the hard beat of his pulse beneath his skin. "Stop scrolling, you're going to go past it again."

The epileptic flash of channels ceased. A sepia-toned reenactment began playing out across the screen. Colton went gimlet-eyed. "*This?* This is a true crime documentary."

"I know."

"This is what you want?"

"It is." Delaney settled back into her pillows. "Don't look at me like that. Just put the captions on."

"Yes, ma'am."

They spent the next forty-five minutes in relative silence, engrossed in a series of poorly scripted reenactments. She'd seen this one before, more than once—in the middle of the night, in the pale gray of a dawn, during the long, sleepless nights. She stayed cocooned in her protective nest and tried to give off the outward appearance of someone who was not grossly overthinking every little thing.

Which, of course, she was.

She was thinking about Nate, poured out of his body like water from a cup and then filled with something new. She was thinking about Colton, propped against the headboard, one arm crooked over his abdomen. The light of the television silvered the lines of him, illuminating the white starburst of a scar on the underside of his chin, the neat ink of a tattoo etched along his third rib.

All around the edges of the bed, the long-fingered dark sputtered blue and black and tried, as always, to catch her eye. She felt cold all over, the mothy dregs of her nightmare still churning in her stomach. The curtains were drawn, but she couldn't shake the feeling that Nate was out there. Waiting for her in the dark.

"Can I help you with something?" Colton asked when a commercial came on.

Her heart slammed hard into her ribs. She hadn't realized how intently she'd been staring. "I was just thinking," she said, too quickly.

He glanced down at her, the knife of his jaw thrown into stark, flickering relief. "About?"

"Well, this is excellent preparation for me."

"Oh yeah?" His eyes sparked black in the gloom. "How's that?"

"One day, when a producer comes knocking on my door asking me to do an interview for your true crime biopic, I'll know what to expect."

Colton didn't laugh. Instead, he said, "You're very mean to me, Wednesday."

She couldn't help it. The way he was looking at her left her wrung out and aching. She said, because she had to say *something*, "I was actually thinking about Nate. There wasn't even a trace of humanity behind his eyes. I don't understand how a person can be emptied out of themselves like that."

Colton didn't say anything in response. He was looking at the television again, the clean blue hues of a soap commercial reflected in his eyes.

"Whitehall doesn't teach on this," he said, "but there's a reason we can feel the doors and no one else can."

"Because we're weirdos."

His mouth turned up at the corner. "Not quite. Every single student at Godbole has had a brush with death. And when a body dies, even for an instant, the soul crosses between planes. Most people who die stay dead. But there are those of us who survive, shocked back into living in a hospital bed, or the back of an ambulance." His hands sat palm up in his lap, and he stared down into them, his fingers curled. His pinkie stuck out at an odd angle from the rest. "Death is the most natural thing in the world," he said. "Surviving it isn't. And so, we bring a little of it back with us once we've cheated Hell."

Delaney frowned. "A little bit of what?"

He shrugged. "Whatever's out there. Whatever it is that thrums along the ley lines. We carry it back in place of the piece we lost."

The hum in her head. The way it shivered in place of sound, timorous and strange. She'd flatlined in the hospital, her little glass body succumbing to fever. Her heart stopped and the world went dark and she was pulled back into herself by a well-timed jab of epinephrine. A shock to the system, stark enough to raise the dead.

Peering over at him, she asked, "What was your brush with death, then?"

Colton didn't answer. His fingers curled, tension cording the sinews in his arm. Delaney had the sense she was homing in on something deeply private, and she instantly regretted asking. Her pulse at a clip, she disentangled an arm from her bubble and ran a featherlight finger down the inside of his forearm. He watched her do it, his breathing accelerating as she worked open his fist and laced her fingers through his.

"You don't have to tell me," she said, "if it's too hard to talk about."

By the time the credits ran, Delaney had mostly managed to will away the lingering chill of her nightmare. Her head was a whirl, her thoughts spinning out like a top. She'd come to Chicago to see a friend and found a monster instead. And now it was out there, and it knew her name. She didn't know what to do next. She didn't know where else she could go but home. Back to her classes. Back to her night-lights. Back to pretending.

Burrowing deeper into the bed, she curled alongside Colton and watched the steady rise and fall of their interlocked fingers against his chest. The ink along his rib was a looping cursive, clearly visible to her at this angle.

Non omnis moriar.

The sight of it sank into her like teeth, and suddenly she was back in the Sanctum again, cowering in the open door, watching Nate try and try again to stagger to his feet. She disentangled her hand and walked her fingertips over the yellowing contusions on his torso. Along the curve of his third rib, there was a noticeable dip. A shallow divot, where there should have been bone.

"Colton," she whispered into the quiet. "What did you do?"

But when she glanced up, it was to find him asleep.

❧ 28 ❧

Everything was different, now that they'd come home. Colton knew it. Lane knew it. The understanding hovered unspoken between them as they stood outside arrivals, time rushing away and away, the chilly October air whipping past in the wake of terminal traffic. Colton tried not to feel guilty about the building wall of secrets as he stepped down off the curb and hailed her a cab.

She'd asked to rideshare, but he'd refused. For one, they were going in opposite directions. For another, he had a deep aversion to city taxis. He tried to imagine what the cab ride would look like. Stuffed into the back of a car that likely hadn't been cleaned in weeks, pressed knee to knee with Lane in halting Pike traffic. It seemed like a Herculean challenge to undertake before breakfast, and he didn't have the constitution for Grecian tragedy.

In any case, he'd already seen the SUV waiting for him at the far end of the loading zone.

"Do you think he'll turn up?" Lane asked. "Nate?"

She was trying to pretend like she wasn't afraid. Like the thought of Nate lurking just around the corner didn't terrify her. She wasn't fooling anyone. She stood huddled in her coat, her eyes darting from face to face. A businessman passed by, luggage rattling, and she nearly jumped out of her skin.

"Don't worry about Schiller," Colton answered, one hand on the rear passenger door. "It'll be taken care of."

He pried the door wide, but she didn't get in. "By who?"

"By qualified professionals," he said, feeling deeply tired. "Not a college freshman."

She still didn't budge. She looked very small, perched precariously atop the curb, her hair windswept in the breeze. "I'm worried about his mom."

"That's because you're a good person." He pried his wallet from his back pocket. From the saddle-stitched folder he slid two crisp twenty-dollar bills. "For the fare."

She eyeballed the cash like he was offering her a vial of poison. "I can't accept that."

"Don't be impolite, Wednesday." He held it under her nose. "Take it."

"No, thank you."

In the driver's seat, the cabbie hadn't grown impatient enough to yell, but he *had* grown impatient enough to hook his arm over the adjacent seat and glower back at them. "If you don't use it for the ride," Colton said, "then I'll spend it on flowers. Do you like roses?"

"They're not my favorite."

"Fantastic. Forty should cover just about a dozen."

She snatched the bills out of his hand. "You're insufferable."

"You're welcome." He held the door until she climbed inside. Once she'd buckled herself in, he shut it with all five of his fingers, soft and perfunctory. He watched the cab pull out of the idling zone. Watched it edge into the silvery line of MBTA buses, crossover SUVs, and transit cops. He thought about buying flowers anyway.

He didn't move once she was out of sight. He remained right where he was. Alone on the curb. A rock in a fluid stream of travelers. He glanced down at his watch. He studied the ebb and flow of people.

Postponing, until he caught sight of a familiar figure taking a seat on a nearby bench.

"Hayes." Colton slipped a hand into his pocket. "Good to see you."

Eric didn't return the sentiment. "I have to say—you've done a lot of stupid things in the time we've been friends, but this has to be by far the stupidest."

"Do you think so?"

"It wasn't a compliment." Eric sized him up across the chilly terminal. "Is your ego really so big that you thought you could bring Meyers-Petrov all the way to Chicago without getting caught?"

Colton thought of waking in the colorless shades of a silent dawn to find Lane sprawled across his chest. Her heart beat and beat into his skin. Every part of her felt perfectly, solidly alive, and for a moment he'd had trouble remembering what all of this was for.

"I didn't bring her to Chicago," he said. "She brought me."

Hayes crooked his head, studying Colton sideways. "Either way, the two of you royally screwed things up. Police have started asking questions. It won't be long before they're poking around in the other cases, too."

"Maybe they should."

To his surprise, Hayes barked out a bitter laugh. "Yeah," he said. "Maybe they should."

Colton frowned down at him. "What's with you?"

Eric shrugged. "Got a call from my sister last week. My grandmother's been moved into hospice."

"We're almost there," Colton said. "She just needs to last a while longer."

"Yeah, man, I don't think so." Hayes leaned forward, elbows slung across his knees. "I went to see her over the weekend. Nurses say she's been talking to my grandfather. They said older people do that some-times, when they're ready to go."

"No one is ever ready to go." The words cracked out of Colton before he could stop them. He thought of his chin cracking ice. The feel of water swallowing up his scream. The shadow of Liam break-ing through the surface.

"Maybe." Hayes palmed his jaw, looking conflicted. "Meeker's in the truck," he said. "Schiller, too."

Colton picked his head up and frowned over at the Range Rover. It sidled along the curb, hazards blinking. "How is he?"

"He's himself," Hayes admitted. "I don't know what you dealt with out in Chicago, but there's nothing inside of that body but a twenty-year-old boy."

Colton's stomach soured. "That's impossible. I saw him. He was gone."

Hayes huffed a breath into the double cuff of his palms. "I don't know what to tell you, Price. It's all Schiller in there. And he's a mess. He's been vomiting up everything we've tried to put in him since they got back to town. It's not looking good."

On cue, the door of the Range Rover was thrown wide. The keen-ing babble of a boy's voice pitched out, high and afraid.

"Malus navis," Schiller cried. "Don't leave me here. Don't leave."

This wasn't, Colton thought, how victory was meant to feel.

Meeker emerged from the back seat, shoving the cuffs of his sleeves up around his elbows. A sour smell followed him out.

"Schiller blew chunks all over my jacket," he griped.

"You can buy a new jacket," Colton said.

"Yeah, and maybe you can buy a new personality," Meeker fired back, stalking across the sidewalk. "I'm getting real sick of your shit, you know that? What the hell were you thinking?" Meeker shoved Colton back a half step, his hands reeking of sick. "Bringing her to the hospital? Huh?"

"Back off, Meeker." Hayes rose from the bench with a stretch. "You're making a scene."

Meeker tried and failed to shove Colton a second time, corralled by Hayes as the senior stepped neatly between them. Jabbing a finger in Colton's direction, Meeker snarled, "Boss has had it with you. He says it's time for you to pay the piper. You know what that means?"

Colton felt impossibly tired as he made his way to the curb and climbed into the back seat. Schiller sat beside him, eyes wide and features gaunt. Packed into the reeking Rover like corpses in a hearse. Both of them drawn to that same unfailing light.

"I know what it means," Colton said. "I'm just surprised you do."

"Price," Hayes warned, buckling himself into the driver's seat.

"What a typical response," Meeker spat, guiding the front passenger door shut. "You think you're smarter than me? You've been walking around acting like the rules don't apply to you, flashing that trust-fund grin. But that's all over now. When we get home, I'm going to carve the arrogance right out of your goddamned face."

"That's great," Colton said. "Can you shut up for a second?"

"Do you see this shit?" Meeker threw up his hands, looking over at Hayes for validation. "Do you see how he talks to me?"

Colton tuned him out, his focus trained on Schiller. The junior rocked back and forth on his seat, teeth chattering, a blue bucket clutched tightly in his hands.

"Nate," Colton said.

Schiller's eyes flicked to his. He went still as a rabbit. "That's me," he said. "Nate Schiller. Nathaniel David Schiller, Ten Cross Road."

Colton grimaced. "You feeling okay?"

"No," Schiller said. "I'm going to puke."

Hayes's eyes met Colton's in the rearview mirror. "See what I mean? There's nothing in there anymore. It's gone."

"Which raises the next most obvious question," Colton said. "Where did it go?"

❧ 29 ❧

Delaney was dreaming again. This time, she was standing in a field. The ground was riddled with divots, dug as if by a spade. She moved through them, bare feet pressed to patches of winter-dormant grass. Shallow graves stretched out in the dirt on either side of her. In the first, she found a femur, thin enough to have belonged to something small and mammalian. In the second, a skull, fanged teeth sharp as a cat's. In the third, she found a face. Eyes open. Mouth blue. Half-buried in sod.

Somewhere in the distance, water ran and ran. Something heavy was dragging itself through the mud. Closer. Closer. She stumbled backward and smacked into a figure, tall and solid. Turning, she found Colton Price rooted beneath a black hole sky. He was staring without seeing. He was speaking without making sound.

Non omnis moriar. He mouthed it over and over, in an endless litany. His eyes were a strange, spectral black. His mouth was full of teeth.

"Who are you?" she asked.

His eyes met hers. His stare was dark and cold. *Nobody*, he said.

She wanted to wake up. She wanted to wake up. She wanted to—

Open your eyes, Delaney Meyers-Petrov, said a voice. *We are going on a journey.*

She woke to sound, loud and immediate and very close. She was standing in her parents' living room. She was bundled in her coat and

211

hat. Her implant was on and the television was playing, bright and apoplectic, the volume cranked to a deafening decibel.

"Lane." Her father scrambled down the stairs, staggering into a pair of flannel pants as he went. "*Laney*. Hey. You all right?"

She slammed back into herself, the noises taking on an alarming shape—the snap of bone, the cry of something dying. On the screen, a pack of wolves ripped into a deer, muzzles blackened by steaming offal. Blood darkened the paw-crimped snow.

Her father clicked off the television and the living room was doused in instant dark. Delaney shuddered, stipples of white dragging across her retinas. Shadows nibbled at her skin, like little red garra fish. She couldn't remember coming home.

Across the room, her father edged through the dark, feeling for the light. The stairs creaked, and her mother's voice trickled down the steps.

"Jace?"

"We're all good, Mia," her father said, though he didn't sound terribly convinced. "It's just Laney." The lamp clicked on over the recliner. Jace, the chair, and Delaney were each washed in a circle of yellow. Her father peered over at her, his eyes crinkling in a frown. "You okay?"

"I—" She faltered, unsure how to answer. "Yeah. I'm okay."

Mia came into view, bathrobe drawn tight. She took a seat midway down the steps, her fingers fumbling through still-sleepy signs. "What are you doing home? Did something happen at school?"

"No." Delaney's stomach felt uneasy, skin prickling as if a spider had crawled across her belly. She didn't want to tell them she had no memory of coming home. No mental registry of putting on a coat and hat and heading out into the cold. No record of boarding the commuter rail, sitting on the train, walking the several blocks home alone in the frostbitten dark. Her blood knocked through her veins.

Settling on a lie, she said, "I just wanted to sleep in my own bed tonight. Sorry I put the TV on so loud."

"No sweat." Jace tucked an arm around her shoulder. "You can always come home, kiddo. Let's get you out of this coat. I'll make you a hot toddy."

In the kitchen, she sat in one of her mother's refurbished estate sale chairs and nursed her steaming mug of hot honeyed whiskey, careful to keep her scarf wound around the black-and-blue grip on her throat.

The counter was dusted with flour like snow, and a sticky residue was splattered across the backsplash. A stack of bills sat in a papered lean-to against the toaster, and the topmost envelope—bold typeface screaming FINAL NOTICE!—looked like it had been inadvertently buttered. The room smelled like frying oil and marjoram, and little by little some of the cold melted out of her bones.

"It's the middle of the night, Mama," Delaney said as Mia slid a plate of fried potato pancakes in front of her. "You really didn't need to make me food."

"Eat." Mia slid into a chair, signing as she went. "You look hungry."

"She looks tired," Jace countered.

"I'm fine," Delaney said, though neither of them had asked.

"Is it your classes?" Mia's fingers flew. "Are you falling behind? You signed up for too many courses this semester."

"I enrolled in the minimum required courses."

Mia snatched a pancake out of Jace's hand and set it back on the plate. "I don't like that you came all the way home at this hour—it's not safe. Anything could have happened to you. Remember Mrs. Davies's Buick?"

"I remember the Buick," Delaney said. "I told you, I just missed my bed."

"Are you sad? You look a little sad."

Reaching for another pancake, Jace asked, "Did you know the boy they found out in Chicago?"

Mia slammed her hand onto the table. "*Jace.*"

"What?" He threw his arms wide. "It was on the news."

"That doesn't mean this is the time to bring it up."

They'd stopped signing, the way they always did when the conversation became about her, instead of including her. Like she was still a toddler and not a college student. Like all they had to do was spell out their words and she wouldn't be able to u-n-d-e-r-s-t-a-n-d.

At her feet, Petrie wound in and out of her ankles. She set down her mug and scooped him up, sneaking him a sliver of fried potato. It took her a few seconds to realize her parents' focus had resettled on her. Jace's expression told her he'd just asked a question. She nuzzled her cheek to the fuzz top of Petrie's head.

"What did you say?"

Across the table, her father was halfway through his third pancake. "I said, 'Who's Colton Price?'"

Delaney schooled her features into careful detachment. "Where did you hear that name?"

Jace gestured to her phone, faceup on the table between them. "He's called about sixteen times since you've been home."

"Price," Mia echoed, frowning. "*Price.* How do I know that name?"

"You don't," Delaney rushed to say. "He's just a friend from school."

"Ah." Jace reached for another pancake. "And what's a friend from school doing calling you sixteen times in the middle of the night?"

"Dad."

"I'm just making conversation," he said. "Can't I make conversation?"

"That's it," Mia said suddenly, snapping her fingers. "That's where I know the name. You remember, don't you, Jace? *Price*—that's the name of the corporate attorney whose sons went through the ice out on Walden Pond. Oh, it has to have been years ago now, but at the time it was all over the news."

"Right. That's right." Jace palmed the salt-and-pepper scruff on his jaw. "Didn't the eldest son drown?"

On the table, Delaney's phone lit blue with another missed call. Colton, again. Something inside her went terribly cold. Setting Petrie on the floor, she rose from her chair.

"I have to take this," she said. "Excuse me."

Shut in her room, she sat on her bed and stared down at her phone. Every light she owned was on. The single incandescent bulb in her closet, the antique brass desktop lamp she'd bought for pennies at an estate sale, the square of winking Christmas lights that served as her headboard. Still, the shadows endured, sitting black and absolute against her floor.

The next time the phone rang, she picked up right away.

"I've been calling you." Colton didn't bother with a hello. His voice scraped through the receiver.

"You sound funny," she said. "Are you okay?"

"Sensational." He didn't sound sensational. He sounded like he was in pain. "I haven't heard from you since the airport. I wanted to make sure you made it back."

"Kind of." She glanced around at the clutter of her room, every available surface littered with mementos from her childhood. She'd only been gone two months, but already they looked like they belonged to someone else. "Colton?"

"Hmm?"

"I have something important to ask you. I need you to be honest."

Something clattered on his end. It sounded like pills rattling in a bottle, though she didn't entirely trust her hearing. "*Shit*," he muttered. Then, "Ask away."

She pulled her eyes shut against the conglomeration of light flooding her room. As if, shrouded in total dark, her late-night inquiry might feel a little bit less invasive.

"I asked you once if you had a brother. You said no. Was that a lie?"

He exhaled, long and slow, the air slipping out as if between gritted teeth. "You asked me if I had a little brother," he said. "Liam is older."

"Is?"

"Was," Colton corrected.

She shut her eyes. The rush of her pulse was dizzying. "What happened to him?"

He didn't answer. For several long minutes, she sat curled into her pillows and listened to the buzz of the open line. The shadows around her bed blinked up at her.

"Did you know," Colton finally said, "that goalie pads weigh fifteen pounds per leg?"

She wasn't entirely sure she'd heard him correctly. "What?"

"Goalie pads," he repeated. There was a rasp to his words, the edges scraped raw. She wished she could see his face. "Hockey gear. Padded shorts, shin guard, kick boots. Fifteen pounds on each side. That's thirty pounds of weight, easy. Not to mention the chest protector, neck guard, helmet, and hand mitts. In the end, you've got a goalie carrying about fifty extra pounds of equipment on the ice."

She drew up her covers. "I didn't know you liked hockey."

"I don't."

"Oh."

"It's just that you can't swim," he said, "with all that equipment."

Silence rose up again, dense and somnolent. She thought of the boy in the water, the way he'd clutched at her coat. *"Don't let go."*

"Colton." Her throat felt dry. "Did he drown? Your brother?"

A pause followed, long enough to be uncomfortable. "Yes."

Every student at Godbole was there, he'd told her, because they had a brush with death. He'd never told her how he'd almost died, but she knew the rumor—that when Colton Price stepped through worlds, it felt like he was drowning.

She could feel that she was encroaching on something deeply private—was aware that her line of questioning was entirely inappropriate. And yet she had to know.

"And what about you?"

"What about me?"

"Did you drown, too?"

This time, the answer came immediately, lashing out of him like a reflex. "Yes."

She bit her lip, hard enough to hurt. Impossible. It was impossible. "I told you the story about the boy in the water. About skipping pebbles at Walden Pond. You sat there and listened and you didn't say a thing."

A pause followed, barely perceptible. Then, "What's your favorite flower?"

The sudden change in topic left her spinning out like a top. *"What?"*

"Your favorite flower," he repeated. "You said you don't like roses, but there are over four hundred thousand types of flowering plants." He spoke in a slur, his words running all together. "It'd be easier if you told me which you liked to save me from having to buy them all."

"Colton."

"Mmm, yes?"

Petrie crept into bed, silent on padded paws, and pressed the top of his head into the underside of her chin. Misgiving stole through her. She wanted to tell him to focus. To stop evading the truth. Instead, she asked, "Did you take something?"

"Yes," he said.

"Why?"

"I have a headache."

Uneasiness bored into her. Drawing Petrie into her chest, she curled into a ball beneath her covers, staring up at the winking fairy lights until they stretched into streaky starbursts of gold. She thought about Colton alone in his bed on the other side of Boston, about how neatly she'd fit against him back in the hotel. The shadows fell, momentarily quelled, carpeting the floor out of sight. She closed her eyes.

She couldn't stop herself wishing for him.

"Wednesday?" Colton's voice was tacky with sleep. "I want to tell you everything."

"I wish you would."

"I can't," he said. "It hurts too much."

"Tell me what happened to you, at least."

A beat of quiet passed. Then another. She thought, maybe, he'd fallen asleep. Instead, he spoke, low and drugged. "I dragged myself out of Hell to you."

❧ 30 ❧

D elaney was the first to arrive at Godbole the next morning. She'd woken to an email from Whitehall, the message brief and perfunctory and, she felt—though she may have been projecting— deeply displeased. She hadn't submitted a written form detailing her intention to miss class, and she hadn't emailed with an excuse. She just hadn't shown up at all.

And now she was going to grovel. She stood in the elevator and stared at her reflection. A thousand disapproving copies of Delaney Meyers-Petrov stared back. She shut her eyes. Colton's voice, sleep-addled and strange, played on a loop in her head.

"I dragged myself out of Hell to you."

When she finally reached Whitehall's office—the only spot of dark in all of stark, polyhedral Godbole—she'd nearly sweated clean through her turtleneck. The day was warm for October, but the bruises dotting her throat had deepened to angry purple contusions, and so she had no choice but to keep them covered. She pried off her coat, baked to a crisp beneath the magnified sunlight at the windows, and took a moment to readjust the gray tattersall of her skirt. By the time she knocked on the door, she'd managed to bully herself into a semblance of composure.

"Come on in."

Whitehall stood sequestered at his desk, framed by his customary leaning towers of books. As always, Delaney was struck by the sheer cerebralism of him. He looked less like a professor and more like the caricature of one. Everything in his office was heavy and dark and old. The only pop of pastel came from a quaint but amateur painting hung over the back of his chair. It depicted a wooded glade, quivering aspens layered against an acrylic sunrise.

Moving through the room, she lowered herself into the wide leather wingback by the window. Light fell across her lap in caramelized swirls. At the desk, Whitehall removed his glasses and set to polishing them. "*It's not a habit,*" Mackenzie said a few weeks back, as they exchanged notes in the student center. "*It's performance art. He thinks it makes him look scholarly.*"

It worked. He looked every bit a scholar. He also looked, Delaney thought, angry. Some of her confidence began to wane. She wished she'd brought him beignets from the food truck by the quad. A white flag. A peace offering. Something that said *Please don't be disappointed in me.*

Inspecting his lenses, he said, "You are aware, Ms. Meyers-Petrov, of the ongoing police investigation out in Chicago, correct?"

Her stomach sank. "I am."

"Good. Good." He slipped his glasses back into place. "And are you also aware that Colton Price is considered a person of interest in the case of Nathaniel Schiller's alleged hazing?"

Her blood iced over. "Excuse me?"

"Make no mistake," he said, "I may look the doddering old fool, but I am certainly not one. I've known for a long time that there's something of an unsanctioned old boys' club here at Howe. It was bound to happen. You put a master key to the universe in the hands of men, eventually a few of them start to fancy themselves gods." Whitehall pressed a hand to a thin stack of files. "And Mr. Price, campus prince that he is, has been their ringleader from day one."

Delaney's palms were slick with sweat. She tried to piece together a counterargument—a reason why the allegations couldn't possibly be true—and came up empty. Colton Price had done nothing but keep secrets since day one. She'd let him ply her with bread crumbs, snatching up scraps of truth whenever he saw fit to share. Swallowing down lie after lie.

"All I'll do is hurt you," he'd said. Maybe she should have believed him.

"What happened to Nathaniel Schiller is deeply disconcerting," Whitehall said, and it sounded as though he were speaking through a tin-can telephone. "Police are following every lead, but I'm being told that Nathaniel disappeared shortly after you and Mr. Price took it upon yourselves to plan a field trip out to Chicago."

Delaney's stomach plummeted. "I'm sorry," she said, and meant it. "I truly am. If you'll just let me—"

"The reputation of Godbole hinges entirely on the conduct of its students," Whitehall continued, carrying on as though she hadn't spoken at all. "People don't like things they can't categorize. Can't put into a box. What we do here at Godbole doesn't fit into any of their neat little molds. Because of that, we have a great deal more enemies than allies. There are people out there who would love to see us lose our accreditation."

"I know," she said, too quiet to hear. "And I'm incredibly sorry. I didn't think it through."

He regarded her over the rim of his glasses. "Am I correct in assuming you received a copy of the student handbook at the start of the year?"

The question caught her off guard. "Yes."

"Then you're aware," he said, "that there are certain codes of academic conduct to which all students at Howe are expected to adhere."

"Yes," she said again.

He plucked a file off the top of the stack and thumbed through it. "While there are certainly no rules against engaging in a relationship with Mr. Price outside of class, it is in vehement opposition of the university's code of ethics for a teacher's aide to show favoritism to individual students within the confines of the classroom."

Her stomach wavered. Her head was static. "He didn't—That's not—We're not in a relationship." As soon as she'd said the words aloud, they zinged back through her, arrow sharp and mortifying. She was certain none of the other freshmen had shared a bed with Colton. Hands entwined, knees kissing, listening to each other breathe in the flickering dark. "We're friends," she admitted, a little too weakly for her liking.

"Is that so? And what about the allegations of favoritism?" He tapped at a set of papers in front of him. "I have a report here that claims Mr. Price has been providing you with the answers to exams in your core classes."

"What?" Panic shot through her in a dizzying rush. "That's not what happened. I'd been struggling to keep up in my classes. He let me borrow his old notes to study."

Whitehall dragged out his chair and settled into it. For a long moment, he sized her up without speaking, as though determined to discern the truth by osmosis. She'd never felt more breakable, pinned in the steady disapproval of his stare.

"If you're having difficulty in your classes," he said, lacing his fingers over his stomach, "the Student Aid Center can be found on the second floor of Gibbons Hall."

"I know." Her throat felt tight. "They offered the services of an interpreter."

"And that was not sufficient?"

"Well, I—" The room felt too small, the air too tight, and she was once again diminished to little glass Delaney, all full of cracks. "I'm not fluent," she said. "In sign. I know enough to use at home with my parents, but not enough to keep up in school."

Pushing out a sigh, Whitehall readjusted his glasses. "I regret to say, Ms. Meyers-Petrov, that while I can certainly empathize with your situation, students who've been caught cheating on exams face immediate expulsion from the program."

"But I *didn't* cheat."

"So you say." He rose from the desk and headed for the door, then pried it open. Sunlight fell inside in a blistering swath of gold. "Consider this meeting your one and only warning. I can't entirely fault you for being so misguided—Mr. Price was meant to act as a mentor, and he failed spectacularly. The way he's conducted himself is unacceptable. He's been relieved of his duties as teaching assistant and placed on probation for the remainder of the semester."

She understood by the way he hovered at the door that she was being dismissed. Her heart hammered in her throat. Her hands had gone clammy. She felt very sincerely as though she ought to be on the verge of tears. Eyes pinched, throat tight.

Instead, deep in the core of her, something sinister bled into her veins like a poison. Something old and cold and violent. A little unsteadily, she rose from her chair, weak-kneed and wobbling and wishing to be almost anywhere but here, caught under a microscope of disdain.

Whitehall stopped her at the door, his hand closing over her shoulder in a way that was not entirely welcome. "I'd like to offer you a piece of unsolicited advice," he said, "if I may."

That sinister something lashed out like a whip, and she was met with the sudden, startling urge to scream right in his face. To tear down his books one by one by one. To claw at the walls until the paneling came loose.

Instead, she said, "Of course."

"You're a good student," he said. "And I can tell you've got a good head on your shoulders. The behavior exhibited by Mr. Price is more than just a disappointment; it's dangerous. If I were you, I would think very carefully before having any further contact with Colton Price."

❧ 31 ❧

In a storage unit at a storage yard on a side street in a sleeping neighborhood of Boston, there was a door.

Not a corporeal door, nothing so simple as that. Nothing hewn from wood, fashioned out of the bones of trees. Nothing pieced together with rails and stiles and screws. Nothing built with mullion-split glass, sleek transoms, and crossable thresholds. Nothing pretty. Nothing ugly.

Just nothing at all.

It sat in the dark, a sliver in space. It was the air of a faraway breeze rippling through the ether. It was the hiccup of gas where nitrogen and oxygen collided.

It was a door, and on the other side was a storage unit, quite a lot like the first, on a mirror side street in a mirror borough in a mirror Boston, under a mirror night sky dusted with thousands of mirror stars. Farther away, past sleepy Chinatown dotted in white-tented food markets and under the gold-leafed magnolias of Post Office Square, there was a neat paved street lined with neat brick houses.

Out of the second-to-last house stepped Liam Price.

It was late. It was cold. All morning long, the October sky had been flat and gray, but now the sliver of sky overhead was sugared in starlight, the wind off the harbor winter bitten. He drew up his collar tight and descended the iron rail steps to the street, an athletic bag strapped over his shoulder.

He was in a mood, though just to look at him wouldn't have made it immediately clear. He'd never been the kind of person to wear his emotions in his face, or to carry them in his shoulders. Allison said—once, in an argument—that talking to Liam was like trying to process with a rock. He'd thought, then, that it was a very insensitive thing for a wife to say to a husband.

It wasn't that he didn't feel things; it was just that he was the sort to work his feelings out through physical activity. Life was, he liked to tell Janine in the adjacent cubicle, all about the little things. For him, it was a brisk run along the Charles, a cold beer and a round of darts, an hour or two on the rink. The last was where he thrived: skates kicking up sprays, his stick in his hand, the black spin of his puck hitting net. For an hour or two, he'd take out his frustration on the ice and pretend things were as simple as they'd been when he was small and C.J. was alive and he didn't know every last name of Janine's thirteen cats.

And, anyway, it wasn't that he'd had a *terrible* day, it was just that it was the same as every other. He'd spent the first half of it sitting through meetings that could have been emails, the second half reading emails that could have been texts. His last hour was occupied by the incredibly mind-numbing task of spinning in his overpriced ergonomic chair and listening to the harrowing details of Bing Clawsby's brush with ear mites.

So now, to counteract a day of absolute mediocrity, he was headed to the ice.

He drew short as he rounded the corner, a prickle building at the back of his neck. He was by a crosswalk, alone in an empty intersection. A car drove by, headlights carving through the dark and disappearing around the corner. He watched it go, red brake lights like lit cigarettes. He felt deeply uneasy.

Liam Price was, for all intents and purposes, a thoroughly unexciting person. He didn't deviate from his norms. He went to and from work. He went to and from the grocery store. He went to and from the pub down on State. Sometimes, when Allison's lingering Catholic guilt reared its ugly head, he went to and from church.

He'd never been in a bar fight, or arrested, or engaged in any sort of violence. He'd never taken self-defense or martial arts. And yet, he knew. He knew right away. He thought, fleetingly, that there must be something innately programmed into a man to recognize when he was being followed.

Another car zipped by, heedless of the speed limit. In the rush of wind left in its wake, Liam turned to stare at the dark.

The dark stared back.

It took a moment for him to slot into place what he was seeing. A boy, or perhaps a man—broad shoulders slumped beneath a gray wool coat with the collar pulled high. He stood in an alcove, out of reach of the streetlamps, his face halved in shadow. He wasn't smoking a cigarette, though he was standing the way one might when out for a smoke. He wasn't, Liam noticed—with growing diffidence— doing anything at all. Just watching.

The moment grew. The boy in the dark said nothing. A car flew down the street, illuminating the night in lightning white, and for a moment Liam could see his face in stark relief. Dark eyes beset with purpling contusions, a mouth split bloody. Something familiar lanced through him, and then the car was gone and, with it, the light. The boy's features sank back into obscurity.

He was left a little shaken.

It had been, he thought, like looking in a mirror.

No.

It had been like looking at a ghost.

Impossible, he thought, shaking himself free of the sudden and sticky feeling of cobwebs. His ghost was nine years old. His ghost was sleeping in a columbarium in Mount Auburn Cemetery.

"Hey," Liam called, thinking of Allison at home in their living room. She'd been reading when he left, her legs propped up on the plush arms of their couch, her belly extended. He could still see the yellow square of light from their kitchen window from here. "Hey, buddy, you all right?"

"You're having a kid," the boy said.

Cold struck Liam's heart. His fingers closed around his stick. He could reach for his phone—could call the cops—but something about the way the boy was standing, his shoulders slumped against the wall, made him hesitate.

"Who the fuck are you?"

Another car flew past, this time in the opposite direction. Light popped and flared, winnowing back into dark. He was met again with that face, dark eyes sharp and familiar beneath swollen lids. *Impossible.* This was a practical joke. This was a cosmic error. Several blocks away, police sirens warbled through the sky.

"I'm not kidding here," Liam said, the Boston brogue of his youth creeping back into the edge of his voice. "Why the hell would you say that to me? Do you know my wife?"

The stranger slipped his hands into his pockets.

"No," he said, too brusque to be believed. Then, "Sorry to have bothered you." He pushed himself up from the wall. He walked away without a word. Liam was left gripping his hockey stick like a sword, watching the boy step down into the street and head across to the other side.

"Hey!" His shout cut through the quiet. "Hey, I'm talking to you!"

But the stranger didn't stop. He'd rounded the corner by the time Liam's senses caught up to him. By the time he started running. His sneakers hammered pavement, carrying him down the road, athletic bag slamming into his side.

But by the time he came through the intersection and out into the busy street beyond, the boy was gone. The night was dark and crowded. Buildings hemmed him in on both sides. Traffic barreled down the street in all directions. The wind drove between the bricks, chilling him to the bone. Overhead, the thousand stars winked down at him, unseen, their light swallowed up in the dazzling glow of the city.

He was alone, alone, the city moving and breathing all around him, unable to shake the tightening vise of fear around his heart, unable to forget the slow resurfacing memory of C.J. Price's face sinking beneath ice.

❧ 32 ❧

Lying with her forehead pressed into the open spine of her book wasn't going to help Delaney pass her Latin exam on Friday, but she was committed to doing it anyway. She'd been wholly engrossed in the act for an hour and counting—long enough for the motion lights in her corner of the campus library to click off. Long enough for her eyes to close. Long enough to dream.

The stacks hemmed her in, turning oblong. The spaces between the books became bottomless runnels of black. Somewhere unseen, something skittered across the floor. Something small. Something with claws. A mouse. A shadow.

I'm inside you now, hissed a voice. *Mice in your walls. Mice in your floorboards. Mice in your head. If I wanted, I could chew your wires all to pieces.*

She jolted back, hard enough to topple her chair. Pinned against the chuffing metal grates of the space heater, she peered into the gaps between books. Nothing. Nothing. Nothing. And then. She drew up short at the sight of a face, wedged between two leather-bound tomes. He opened his eyes and she recoiled, slamming the shelving. Books toppled down without a sound, falling in slow motion. At her feet, water rushed in and in around her ankles.

A brother for a brother.

Something laughed, long and low.

Non omnis moriar, whispered the face in the shelf. *Non omnis moriar.*

Something tapped her on the shoulder. She let out a soundless shriek and whipped around. Nothing was there. Nothing but rows and rows and rows of books. Nothing but the slow-breathing dark.

We are searching for someone, sang a voice, now more familiar than it had any right to be. *Someone among the living. Someone among the dead.*

Wake up, Delaney Meyers-Petrov. Someone is watching us.

Delaney opened her eyes to find herself staring into a shelf. Only, instead of a dead boy's face, there was only dust. The air smelled like old paper and binding glue. Books sat in piles around her feet, as if she'd clawed them away one by one, casting them aside. Her heart skipped beats in a too-slow stutter.

"Lane?"

She spun on her heel, a cry eking out of her, and found Mackenzie and Adya standing at the far end of the stack, holding steaming coffees and studying her as though she'd just crawled out of a grave. She felt as if she might have. Her arms were aching, her fingernails scraped to the quick. The blood in her veins felt cold and stiff. Stagnant, like every piece of her had gone asleep when she did, even the parts meant to be involuntary. Mackenzie and Adya's matching expressions put her immediately on the defensive, though neither of them had said a word.

"What?"

"Oh, nothing," Mackenzie said as Adya sipped her coffee and remarked, "You've destroyed the library."

She pawed at her eyes. "I was looking for something."

"That's patently obvious." Adya pushed past her and set her coffee on the empty shelf, plucking one of the leather-bound books from the pile. Flipping through it, she asked, "What's 'sequestrum'?"

Delaney's stomach hooked. "What do you mean?"

Adya shoved the book under Delaney's nose. The words on the page were obscured beneath the black ink of permanent marker, her unmistakable handwriting cramped to the point of illegibility. *Sequestrum.* She'd written it into the margins. She'd written it into the end notes. She'd scrawled it across the chapter header.

Adya's dark eyes met hers over the top of the fanned pages. "What does it mean?"

"I don't know." Her head felt all full of weevils, her skull packed with a buzzing that wouldn't abate. "I fell asleep studying Latin."

"That settles it." Mackenzie thrust a coffee into Delaney's hand. "Pack up your stuff. Have some caffeine. We're getting off campus for the night."

Delaney glanced again at her feet, at the disorder she'd created. "But—"

"No buts." Mackenzie waggled a finger in her face, silencing her before she could protest. "Let's go. Let's go, let's go, let's go."

Thirty minutes and a crowded T ride later, they were expelled into the hellish heat of Kenmore Station. The crowd juxtaposed tired businessmen streaming in with the weekend crowd streaming out. They rode up the escalator in a crowd of commuters, all packed together like sardines, and then departed into the nipping wind of Beacon Street. She let herself be carried down the road toward Lansdowne, the middle chain in a human link—Adya chattering in Arabic on the phone with her mother and Mackenzie furiously engaged in a flip-off contest with a man who'd wolf-whistled at her a half block back.

The bar was no less crowded than the street, but at least it was warm. Bodies thronged together in a sweaty mess, and the amplified sting of a guitar shivered through the dizzying tumult. Already, Delaney felt the press of encroaching dark, the creep of shadow. With the remnants of her dream still clinging to her, the blackened corners took on a malevolent rigor.

It left her feeling unsteady and a little sick, her stomach cramping the way it used to when she was small and impulsive, chocolate-drunk on Halloween candy in her parents' kitchen pantry. She followed Mackenzie and Adya's lead, taking her seat at a bar top table and doing her best to follow the unraveling threads of conversation.

After ordering a plate of spinach and artichoke dip, they divvied up and split a pitcher of seltzer water between them. Delaney swirled her straw through her glass until the ice sloshed over the side, wondering if she was somehow doomed to perpetually feel half-asleep. One foot stuck in reality, the other in dreaming.

Maybe she was coming down with something.

"Heard you got Price fired," Mackenzie said, catching Delaney's eye.

Panic punched through the haze of her thoughts. "Where did you hear that?"

"The two of you are the campus scandal," Adya said, poking at the still-steaming dip in its skillet. "Some girl in the library asked me if you're being kicked out of the program."

Delaney groaned, burying her head in her hands. "Great. That's great."

"What happened in Chicago, anyway?"

Delaney picked up her head to answer and was hit with a rush of blood to the head.

In front of her stood a mirror Delaney. Hair wild, eyes wild, framed in lipstick-kissed glass and slow-blinking in surprise. She was alone. She was cold. She was in an unfamiliar bathroom, filled with unfamiliar sounds. Adya and Mackenzie were nowhere to be seen.

Her vision felt strange, like she'd put on a pair of 3D glasses and the room had suddenly gone fuzzy with light. Distant bass pumped through the cracked tile underfoot, moving through the graffiti-splashed lavatory in a feeble pulse. She had a vague memory of elbowing her way through a crush of bodies, the floor beneath her beer-slick and sticking.

In a rust-ringed sink, the water ran and ran in paltry spurts. Cold spat into her palms, tracking down her wrists in spears of ice. She brought a cupful to her throat, pressing chilly fingers to the fever in her skin.

When she glanced up, water running down her neck in thinning rivers, it was to the sight of Nate Schiller's face in the mirror. Her breath caught, every bit of her seizing up. He was gaunt and grinning, his skin gone gray in the bald bulb glare of recessed lighting. He looked half-mad. He looked like something dead.

"How did you do it?" he demanded. "How did you swallow it whole and live?"

"What?" Her voice came out of her in a rasp. "What do you mean?"

His head canted to the side in a wholly inhuman lean. The wrongness of it caught her cold. "It's in your skull, boring holes into your head. In your chest, fluttering like a moth. It's in your belly like a

234

spider, spinning its sticky, sticky web. Doesn't it tickle? Doesn't it itch? Doesn't it make you feel just so goddamn fucking mad?"

One moment he was still as a shadow, pitted in dark inside the narrow walls of a slung-open stall. The next he was running for her, head down, arms flung wide.

Delaney screamed and sat up straight. The motion lights clicked on overhead. Her leg was asleep. Her back was stiff. She was in the library, hemmed in by the stacks, her heart beating, beating, beating in her chest.

"Hello," said a girl's voice, with the distinct impatience of someone who'd already repeated herself several times. Delaney glanced up to find a disdainful blonde in a zebra onesie and a septum piercing. She stood framed in the mouth of the stacks, clinging to the straps of a yellow backpack. "You've been yelling in your sleep. Everyone else is getting super uncomfortable."

"Sorry," she said. "Thanks for waking me."

"I drew short straw."

"Oh." Delaney rubbed at her eyes. She felt scooped clean, all raw on the inside. "Well, thanks anyway. You're Haley, right? Mackenzie's roommate?"

"That's me." Haley's brow arched. "You're Mackenzie's weirdo friend who talks to dead people."

"I— Okay. Only once or twice." She wasn't sure that's who she wanted to be. Delaney Meyers-Petrov, the dead people girl. At the window, the sky was black as a void. "What time does the library close on Thursdays?"

Haley scowled down at her. "It's Friday."

"What? No." She scrabbled for her things, shoving them into her bag as she went. Her stomach gnawed at itself in protest. She couldn't remember the last time she'd eaten. "That's not possible," she said. Then, with a sinking feeling, "I think I'm losing time."

Haley looked unimpressed. "Same." Her voice winnowed in and out. "I feel like I haven't left the library in days."

"No, I mean I really think I'm losing time. I—"

Her words were snatched up in a whine. She stood shivering in the middle of the wind-bitten quad, spotlit in a single oval of lamplight. The distant trees rustled, bare branches clicking like teeth. She fumbled for her phone only to find the battery dead. Her fingers shook. Somewhere nearby, something whispered her name.

Her heart climbing into her throat, she broke into a run.

❧ 33 ❧

Colton's front door was open. The portico was dark, unlit by the merry twinkle of the wrought iron porch light. The stairs were unswept, concrete cluttered with thick clumps of wide, wet leaves. No one had set out pumpkins. No stacks of hay sat twined against the bone-chilled brick.

The door hadn't been thrown wide, but left ajar, as if some sneak thief had slipped in through the crack. The street was gilded in the hazy glow of streetlamps, the tree trunks girdled in yellow-gold fairy lights.

Inside Colton's house, it was dark.

Delaney dithered on the walk, leaves slick under her boots, and felt the creeping sense of being watched. It started as a shiver, moving down her spine in a slow tiptoe, like a spider had dropped off the leafless branches overhead and wiggled its eight long legs down the back of her shirt.

The other brownstones yawned away from her in a row of cheery brick, buttery light spilling out onto the sidewalk. The only thing that watched her was a scarecrow, set out by a lamppost and swinging just so, his rope unspooled. He reminded her, chillingly, of Nate. His button eyes were empty, his smile stitched into place.

Too afraid to linger, too afraid to continue on home alone, she took the steps to Colton's house two at a time, her dead phone clutched to her chest like a shield. Putting one boot through the open door, she wedged herself inside.

"Hello?"

Her voice catapulted across the foyer. Several leaves blew in through the opening, scraping over the floor in brittle cups of brown. She pushed the door shut behind her.

"Colton?"

The house was silent as a tomb. A fat October moon shone in through the window. It flooded the space in a funny sort of light, turning the shadows indistinguishable. She pushed forward, uneasy.

"Colton, are you—"

The crunch of bone beneath her boot stifled her inquiry. No. Not bone. Glass. Not glass, stone. The crack shivered through the space and she dropped her phone, letting out a curse as it skidded out of reach. Squatting down, she felt though the dark with blind, fumbling hands.

Her fingertips brushed something solid and she grabbed for it, thinking it her phone. Instead, her fist closed around something shattered. Something sharp. Pain bit into her palm, and she dropped the object with a yelp, launching back to her feet as the first well of blood rose along her skin.

Across the foyer, a foot scraped over tile. She was at once interminably conscious of how stupid she'd been, entering Colton's house without any sort of protection. Break-ins happened all the time in the city. What was she planning to do? Beat the intruder with her fists? She took a step backward, hoping she was moving toward the door. A few feet away, a figure stepped into a trickle of moonlight.

"Wednesday?"

Her relief at hearing Colton's voice was immediate and tenfold. She took a big swallow of air, clutching the cut-glass bleed of her hand to her chest, willing her heart to slow. In the open door, Colton stood with his hands thrust into the pockets of his overcoat, the collar pulled up around his throat. He angled his head, regarding her across the foyer.

"What are you doing?"

"What are *you* doing?" she shot back, though she knew it was not at all the correct thing to say to someone after entering their home uninvited. Colton's face looked strange, pitted in shadow as it was— his left eye diffused with a dark that didn't quite match the fall of moonlight on his face.

"I live here."

"In the dark?"

"Sometimes," he said wryly. "As you've seen."

"With the front door left wide open?"

He didn't reply right away. She saw him scuff the floor with the glossy toe of a shoe. Something small and shattered went skittering toward her, like a pebble skipped across a frozen pond.

"Maybe I was hoping you'd come through it," he lied.

She couldn't stop the scoff that came out of her. "Don't do that. Don't be insincere."

She was met with his laugh, though the sound came out strained, like he'd recently taken a kick to his windpipe. Pushing out of the door, he shoved it all the way shut. A light clicked on, flooding the space in too-bright yellow. Delaney felt suddenly and supremely ridiculous, pressed against the wall with her scarf coming undone, wet, skeletal leaves suctioned to her boots.

A few feet away, Colton looked like Hell itself.

His face, which she could now see clearly, was discolored with a myriad of contusions. His left eye was swollen shut, the skin puckering around an angry cut just below his temple. A bruise flowered at the corner of his mouth, an angry wound splitting the skin in an interrupted joker's grin.

"Colton." His name came out of her on a breath. "What happened?"

"It's not as bad as it looks."

"Yeah? Well, it looks like someone stuck a knife in your mouth."

"Huh." He brought two fingers up to his cheek and prodded, resulting in a wince. "I forgot about that."

Delaney took quick stock of the foyer. With the lights on, she could clearly see the damage that had been done. A heavy vase lay in fragments across the floor, hand-pinched clay severed into jagged puzzle pieces amid a heap of potting soil. Uprooted, the plant reached sad snake-grass fingers toward the ceiling.

When she looked back at Colton, it was to find him watching her in a curious sort of way. As if he were at a zoo, and she were a predator in an enclosure. As if he expected her to lunge. He hadn't come any closer.

"You've had a break-in," she said.

"Well, yes," he agreed after too long of a pause. "That's patently obvious." The look he gave her was wry, the hollows of his cheeks colored wrong, as if someone had tried to paint him from memory and failed. "I didn't see who it was, though. You chased them off before I could get close. Thank goodness you're so frightening."

She scowled. "What do you mean, you didn't get close? Looks as if they got a pretty good look at you."

"What, this?" He jabbed a finger at the mess of his face. "No, this is unrelated."

She let out a huff of air. "Of course it is."

For several moments afterward, they took silent stock of the mess. When Delaney chanced a look in Colton's direction, it was to find him scrutinizing her with that same enigmatic stare. He looked skeletal this way—as though he'd been hollowed out with a chisel, the curve of his mouth carved into a bloodied grimace.

"At the risk of sounding trite," he began, "you look like you've seen a ghost."

"Not a ghost." She tugged at the sleeves of her coat. Blood seeped through her fingers in thin rivers of red. Before she could think better of it, she said, "I think there's something very wrong with me."

⋄ 34 ⋄

Stepping back through the space between worlds always left Colton breathless. Dizzy, like he'd been suspended much too long in ageless, streaming dark. Throat raw, eyes streaming, his lungs packed with pond water. It took him a while to get his bearings.

This time, he'd come to in the tapering alley between his parents' home and the Morrisons', wedged neatly beside a woman's locked bicycle and two metal trash bins, the nearer of the two fender-dented beyond repair.

This time, he was instantly aware of a problem.

The issue wasn't so much that he hadn't immediately recognized where he was, stumbling like an amnesiac down the pavers. It wasn't even that he had reappeared—quite worryingly—in an entirely different place than he'd left. It was, instead, that from his vantage point beside the soot-blacked grout he could just make out the too-familiar figure of Delaney Meyers-Petrov standing in the street outside the alley.

She'd looked the way she always did—a little stunned, a little lost, the spiral of her hair coming unbound from its bun. Beautiful and bewildered and, he noted, woefully out of place. She'd been haloed in the yellow gold of the tree-strung lights, the night buzzing around her with all the effervescence of an electric live wire. She'd been standing on her toes.

She'd been staring up at his house.

He hadn't known what made him hold his tongue. Maybe it was the look in her eyes—the way they'd glazed over, shining like glass in the lamplight. Maybe it was the way his encounter with Liam still clung to him in cobwebs of grief. Maybe it was the phantom feel of water in his lungs.

He'd crept forward, one foot in front of the other, and watched as Lane made her way up the empty steps to his home. He'd thought for certain he'd locked the door, and yet when he'd rounded the corner on her tail, it was to hear the give of wood, the creak of hinges.

And then she was inside.

He'd been halfway up the steps himself, cautious and confused, when he heard the smash of something heavy. He knew, intuitively, that it was the planter, set as it was between the foyer and the hall. When he'd stepped inside, it was to find Delaney crouched over the mess. The toes of her boots made divots in the dirt. Her hands ran through rubble.

And, strangest of all, she'd been whispering.

Now he stood in the open door of the upstairs guest room and watched her rifle through his things. The tips of her ears and nose were winter bitten—as though she'd raced all the way here through the frozen streets of Boston. She looked otherworldly, like something he'd dreamt up, half-awake. Some strange, ephemeral haunt to be chased in the quiet gray of dawn.

She stood on her toes in front of the dresser and lifted the vine-beveled top of a sterling silver snuff box. Peering within, she poked at the black velvet interior. Her injured hand remained clutched to her chest. Blood seeped between her fingers, jeweling against her knuckles. He tucked the first aid kit under his arm and cleared his throat. Instantly, Delaney slammed the top back into place. The clink of silver eddied through the room like a shot.

She made no effort to lie about what she'd been doing. Instead, she looked visibly disappointed as she said, "There's nothing in there."

"What did you expect?"

"I don't know." She dragged a stocking-clad foot through the thick eggshell rug. "Teeth."

"That's not where I'd keep them."

"Oh." She didn't look at him. Poking at the brass patina of a drawer pull, she said, "Professor Whitehall told me you're being investigated as a person of interest in Nate's case."

"Allegations were made," he admitted. "They've been dropped."

Dark green eyes darted to his. "It must be nice to have a family lawyer on retainer," she bit out, too sharp. The moment the words were out of her, she shut her eyes. "Sorry. I don't know where that came from."

"You don't need to apologize. You're not wrong." When she was quiet, he added, "I didn't do anything to Schiller. You know that, right?"

"I know," she admitted. "I do. It's just that everything is upside down. I feel like I'm losing my grip on what's real and what isn't."

He held up the first aid kit. "Let's get you cleaned up. Then we'll deal with the rest." Gesturing for her to follow him, he headed toward the door at the far side of the room. It swung open at his coaxing, revealing the bathroom, tiled all in white. Beneath a quatrefoil window sat a clawfoot tub, deep enough to drown in.

Colton glanced back at Lane and found her frozen, her frame small and dark beneath the doorway. Something steel and cold and entirely un-Delaney-like glittered in her eyes. It caught him like a snare, this odd, interminable look.

"Lane," he said, louder than he'd meant to. She blinked just a tick too slowly, her gaze refocusing. Patting the porcelain lip of the tub, he said, "Take a seat."

She obeyed, the gray tattersall of her skirt pooling around her waist. Above the knit wool of her stockings, her bare legs were webbed in celestial fishnets. His jaw set and he lowered himself to the tile in front of her, setting the first aid kit down as he did. Lane's eyes remained glued to his face, her stare drilling into the scabbed-over gash at the corner of his mouth.

"I've been losing time," she said when he reached for her hand. He set it palm up, fingers splayed in the sling of her skirt. Up close, the cut didn't look quite so bad. It slashed her palm in a single, shallow stroke. As though she'd taken a dagger to herself in a ritualistic bloodletting. "Whole chunks of it," she added, and snapped the fingers of her good hand. "Gone."

He stayed quiet, tearing open a sterile wipe. He thought of the ride home in the reeking back seat of Meeker's Rover, careening through Boston traffic. Nate Schiller clutching a painter's bucket, his face several shades off-color.

"*It's gone,*" he'd babbled, tears streaming down his face. "*It's gone. It's gone. It's gone away.*"

Stabilizing her open hand in his, he pressed the wipe to her palm. He heard her suck in a breath. He kept his head down, focused on his task. A clean, dry cloth. A sterile strip of gauze. A dab of antiseptic.

If she showed up at his house, he was supposed to turn her away. Those were his instructions, etched bone deep. "*Don't open the door for her,*" the Apostle said. "*Don't let her inside. You've wasted more than enough of our time playing at being a boy. We can't afford another setback.*"

He hadn't opened the door; she'd forced it on her own.

He hadn't let her inside; she'd invited herself. And now she was here and he was crawling out of his skin. He felt her all along the splintering stria of his bones, like he was a mortar and she the pestle. She was grinding him all to powder.

Not at all lightly, she nudged him in the side with her foot.

"Colton." His name scattershot across the tile. She nudged again, harder than before. "Did you hear me?"

He caught her foot before she could prod him a third time, pinning her ankle to his ribs. "I heard you," he said.

"And are you ignoring me?"

He lifted his eyes to hers. "No."

Whatever she saw on his face softened the corners of her scowl. Inch by inch, he ran his hand up the underside of her calf, until his fingers cupped the back of her knee.

A little breathlessly, she said, "Don't look at me like that."

"How am I looking at you, Wednesday?" The question came out casual. Cavalier. His heart was all thunder.

"Like you think I'm crazy."

"I don't." His hand skated higher, over black nylon moons. Over thin, gauzy stars. "I don't think that."

When she was quiet, he traced a finger along the thigh-high sliver of a crescent moon. She let him do it, the color in her eyes deepening to an inky emerald. An implacable want for her crowded his gut.

"Colton." The tip of her index finger landed featherlight on the bloodied starburst at his temple. "Tell me who did this to you."

The answer skipped out of him like a heartbeat, involuntary and immediate. "Meeker."

He could tell by the surprise on her face that she hadn't expected him to offer up an answer so readily. Tentatively, she probed the purpled lid of his eye. "Who's Meeker?"

A question, this time. Not a command. A modicum of control crept back over him and he gritted his teeth hard enough to hurt. She frowned at his silence, continuing her careful ministrations. Her touch slid over the plane of his cheek, dropping to the angry pinch of his mouth.

Quick as a shot, he caught her wrist. "Don't."

The breath that tore out of her was a lit match, his veins kindling. All of him caught fire at once. He'd been cold for so long that the sudden spark left him fevered. Sweat cropped up along his skin. His vision swam.

"There's something inside of me," Lane said. "I can feel it fluttering in my chest. I dream, and it's all nightmares. I wake, and I'm not always in the same place as before. I keep saying things I don't mean to say and doing things I don't mean to do."

Too late, he began to understand. The pieces clicked into place.

Capax infiniti, he thought, his grip tight around her wrist. *I am holding the infinite.*

Something deathless, beating beneath his thumb. Something he'd waited for his entire life. Something that carried divinity in her chest like pictures in a locket. All twined in bone, like she'd been made for immortality.

Everyone else had died.

Everyone else had cracked beneath the strain, but not her.

Not Lane.

"It talks to me." She squeezed her eyes shut, suppressing a shudder. "It whispers to me at night, when I'm trying to sleep. And I recognize it. It's the same voice that spoke inside my head back in Chicago."

He angled his face toward hers, his chest strung tight. He was torn between a sick, sorry euphoria and slow-budding horror. He wanted to gather her up in his arms. He wanted to swing her around and exalt her with kisses. They'd done it. *She'd* done it.

Victor Mortis. Conqueror of death.

But then, there was nothing euphoric mirrored in her stare.

Instead, her gaze was unfocused, her pupils flat circles of black. Blown wide the way they'd been that night in the hotel, when the sting of a guitar screamed through the room. She'd told him the alarm must have been preset, but he'd been lying awake just before it happened. He'd seen her sit up and reach for the radio.

"Wednesday," he said. "Delaney, look at me."

She blinked, her eyes refocusing. Her hand went limp in his grasp. She didn't look elated. She only looked afraid.

"It's like it's fighting for space inside my head." Her whisper came out strained, as though she was afraid it might hear her. "You have to help me. You have to help me get it out."

✣ 35 ✣

Colton woke to hands around his throat. At first—caught in the delirium between sleep and wake—he thought it was Meeker, come back to finish the job.

But then the hands were too small, the fingers too slender, one palm roughened with gauze. He woke slowly and then all at once, awareness rushing over him in pinpricks. Lane's legs over his middle. Lane's hair tickling his cheek.

Lane's hands around his throat.

He reached for her, cuffing her wrists. Her bones bit into his palm. "Lane," he said. "*Lane.*"

The lines of her were starlit and feral. Her mouth hung slack. She looked markedly inhuman, though he could smell the faint lavender of her shampoo, the spearmint kiss of her breath.

Lane, he thought, unnerved by the alien pall of her stare. *This is Lane. Lane.*

"Lane," he said a third time. He barked it like a command. He barked it like, *wake up.* On his bedside table, the clock clicked from 11:57 to 11:58.

At his throat, Lane's grip turned raptorial.

"Halfling," she whispered, her voice arachnoid. He went still beneath her. Still as stone. Still as death. Still as a boy sinking much too low beneath sweating sheets of ice. Above him, Lane was haloed in moonglow. Her hair was spangled silver. "Oh yes. I know what you are. And I know what you'll become. I know you'll carry the shroud of death all your life."

His heartbeat was a violent thing. "Lane," he urged. "Look at me. Wake *up*."

"You wake up." The words came out of her in a hiss. Low and mocking. "C.J."

His breath stuttered to a stop and he thrust her off him, flipped her so their positions were reversed. Pinned to the mattress, she writhed like some starveling thing. The sound that came out of her was half laugh, half whine.

"Little C.J. killed his brother," she sang. "Yes, he did; yes, he did. Let him sink beneath the ice, yes he did."

"Stop it." The command came out garroted. "Enough."

Those black eyes bored into him. Her lips stretched into a wide, beatific smile. Against his chest, her heart beat with the slowness of someone dead asleep. Desperate, he reached for the only words he knew, buried deep in the back of his subconscious. The words he'd learned in the Priory, words that had been drilled into his brain. He'd never expected to need them with her.

"*Astra inclinant*," he whispered. His voice shook. "*Sed non obligant*."

The void of Lane's stare didn't abate. "This is what you wanted," she said, and a chill settled along his spine.

"You can't have this one," he said, firm and solid and more afraid than he'd been in his life. "She wasn't what was offered. *Astra inclinant*."

The thing inside Lane let out a high, clear laugh.

"*Sed non obligant*," he commanded.

Lane let out a gasp, keening up and into him until they were pressed together, her back arching off the mattress in a startling locus of energy. He felt it like a shifting wind—the exact moment she woke. Her pulse turned rabbit quick beneath his thumb. She fell flush against the mattress, her limbs gone limp. Moonlight flooded her irises, silvering the sea glass of her stare.

"Colton?" It was her voice, her surprise, her confusion. He wanted to bottle it up, small as it was. A laugh of relief hiccuped out of him. He sank lower, pressing his forehead to hers.

"We're okay," he said.

"Oh," she breathed, taking stock of their positioning. "Did I do something? Did I hurt you?"

"Only a little bit," he assured her.

She moved with intent, and he felt the sideways writhe of her trying to slip away. In a panic, he caught her to him. He wasn't sure what he meant to do, only that he couldn't let her leave. Couldn't let her dream. Not here, with the clock running, running, running and the specter of wrongness still tainting the air between them.

She lay perfectly still in his arms, awash in midnight and in athanasia. Leaning in, he ran the tip of his nose along the bridge of hers.

"Stay here with me," he said.

"Okay," she whispered.

Something wordless pulsed through him. Her heart against his chest. His heart beneath his bones. All the impossible, inexorable ways in which he wanted to crawl inside her, the time beating at an impetus.

"Asphodels," he said, without entirely meaning to. He propped himself onto his forearms, fists curled in the sprawl of her hair. Beneath him, her eyes shot through with confusion.

"What did you say?"

251

"Asphodels," he repeated, and hated his voice for cracking. "It's a perennial flower. Known, famously, for growing in the meadows of the underworld."

Lane's eyes narrowed. "Haunted flowers."

For a haunted girl, he thought but didn't say. The memory of her eyes flooded black still ebbed at him. "In some stories, Hades crowns Persephone in a garland of asphodels. He knows his Hell isn't where she wants to be, and so he does whatever he can to make it a little bit more bearable in winter. A little lovelier. So maybe she won't be so afraid of him in the end."

Silence rose up to meet them. The only sounds in the house were the distant tick of his mother's Langston grandfather clock, the muffled rumble of a car going past in the street. Their breath crashing between them.

Slowly, Lane brought a hand to his cheek. He sucked in a breath, willing himself still.

He'd never felt more like a tragedy.

"I guess what I'm saying," he whispered, "is that I've decided asphodels would be far better suited to you than roses."

PART THREE

THE EXORCISM OF DELANEY MEYERS-PETROV

And as he spoke he wept.
Three times he tried to reach arms around that neck
Three times the form, reached for in vain, escaped
Like a breeze between his hands, a dream on wings

Virgil, *The Aeneid*

❧ 36 ❧

Colton had spent the better part of his Monday morning trying to talk Lane out of going to school.

He sat on a stool at the kitchen island and watched her poke at the empty husk of a ripe autumn pomegranate. Her eyes were ringed in shadows, her sweater rumpled. A coffee stain darkened the thin plaid of her skirt. The countertop was jeweled in a spill of red seeds, piled with several haphazard stacks of textbooks. The entire kitchen smelled like espresso.

"You know," he said, trying another angle, "there are students who skip class when it rains."

Lane skewered him in a look. "If you have a point to make, then make it."

"My point," he said, "is that harboring an ancient entity is a valid reason to take a sick day."

She slid the pomegranate into the trash, crossing the kitchen to set her dish in the sink. "If my grades drop any lower, I'll lose my scholarship."

"It's just a piece of paper, Wednesday."

"It's not," she countered. "Not to me."

There was something ferocious in her gaze. Something he knew better than to cross. He knew it was eating at her—waiting around for a solution. Finding nothing. All that time looking for a way to invite something in, he'd never anticipated needing to cast it out. He and Lane spent the weekend holed up in his house, scouring the

255

internet. Poring over books. Reading ancient texts and religious texts and firsthand anecdotes until their vision blurred. Until they fell asleep tangled in his bed.

Until midnight crept in, and she woke.

It happened each night like clockwork. The witching hour arrived and the beast stirred beneath Delaney's bones. She sat up in bed, her eyes strange, her smile a wholly un-Delaney smile.

"Poor C.J.," she'd said on Saturday. Her voice was all wrong, bubbling as if the pond itself lived within her. She'd hummed a tune, tapping her fingers against the bedspread. "Can't save anyone, even yourself."

On Sunday, he'd fallen asleep facedown on his desk, glasses askew, an open page crumpled beneath his chin. He'd woken to Lane standing over him, a kitchen knife at his throat.

"What if I killed you?"

At the kitchen counter, Lane struggled with the zipper of her bag. Oblivious to the way she toyed with him in the dark. The way she taunted him, bold and leering.

"Okay," he said. "Focus on your classes if that's what you need. I'll stay here and keep picking away at the research. I'll call you if I find anything."

By the time Lane returned, night had fallen. Colton sat buried beneath a mountain of books in the family room. He'd spent the entire day searching for a solution, and he had nothing to show for it aside from a fraying temper and a tension headache.

He was about to head to the kitchen and heat up a plate of leftovers when, without warning, Lane exploded into the room. She dropkicked her bag onto the floor, then sank onto the couch. Her movements were exaggerated—not quite hers—and the thought left Colton unsettled.

"I stopped by the student health center," she said. Color had crept back into her cheeks in a flush. Her eyes were glass. "The nurse said I most likely have mono. *Mono*. Isn't that the most ridiculous thing you've ever heard?"

"I'm not sure what you expected." He shut his book and tossed it onto the growing pile of discards. "How do you feel?"

"Tired." She didn't look tired. She looked restless. Agitated. Her nails were picked to the quick. Covering up an overexaggerated yawn, she said, "I'm going to go to bed."

"Did you eat?"

She rose to go, toeing out of her boots as she went. "I'm not hungry."

"I didn't ask if you were hungry," he said, hooking his arm over the back of the couch. "I asked if you ate."

But she was already gone, the wooden creak of the stairs marking her departure. Quietly, he gathered up the piles and piles of books and set them on the coffee table in neat stacks. He gathered up her shoes and set them by the door. He sat at the kitchen island alone and ate a plate of lasagna. When he was done, he got two cups of water from the kitchen and headed upstairs.

The moon was perfectly framed in his window when the clock clicked over from 11:57 to 11:58. Seated at his desk, he felt the tug of it. Like he always did. Like a shoestring pulled loose from a grommet.

On the bed, Lane stirred. Drawing a breath, she sat up in a stretch. For a moment, it was so perfectly Delaney-like that he'd thought she really had woken. But then the wild spill of her hair fell back like a curtain and he was met with the otherworldly dark of her stare.

"Awake again," she said. "Don't you get tired?"

"I'm exhausted," he admitted.

It was the truth. He'd never been so tired in his life. But he'd done this to her. He'd refused to leave her alone. He'd kept too many secrets. He'd followed her to Chicago. He'd let her get too close to Nate.

He'd known better, and yet he still made the exact wrong decision at every possible juncture. And now it was up to him to fix it.

"Ego mittam te," he said. *I cast you out.*

The look the creature gave him was decidedly unimpressed. "You tried that last night."

"I'm trying it again."

He didn't know how to exorcise the beast. Not permanently. Not in any way that mattered. Schiller, like the others, had invited it in. There'd been no need for counteraction.

On his bed, Lane sat with the blankets pooled around her waist. His white undershirt was too big on her. It hung limply off her shoulder, as if she'd clawed at it in her sleep. She was inhumanly still. Statuesque, the moon painting her silkworm silver. She looked, he thought, more like a painted icon than a woman—made for worship and for offering. Blood rite and candlelight.

"You're staring," said the thing in her bones.

"*You're* staring," he shot back. The lack of sleep was making him petulant. Pushing up his glasses, he pawed at his eyes. None of the other hosts had spoken a word aloud, once it was inside them. Lane didn't stop talking.

"You find me unsettling."

He sighed, weary. No point in lying. "Yes."

Silence ensued. The minutes were like water in a drain. Swirling away from him without possibility of retrieval. The creature regarded him through cold, inhuman eyes. Borrowed eyes. Lane's eyes. There was no trace of jade anywhere in them.

"Why won't you tell the girl in this skin the truth about the pond?"

He stilled, halfway through reaching for the open book on his desk.

"Little drowning boy," whispered the beast. "Too afraid to pry himself open and show her what he's made of."

"What do you know about any of it?"

"I know a great deal, Colton James Price." It sounded gleeful. Happy to share. Happy to talk, to be rendered able to communicate. "I have ripped apart so many of your peers. Sucked the marrow from their bones. Split their ribs and eaten their dreams. Pitiable, gamey things. None of them sweet as she. None of them as strong."

He met those strange, dreamless eyes. His heart beat like it was afraid to make sound. "Et disperdam te."

A laugh followed, cold as the dead of winter. "I will not be banished by a mere halfling." The rictus of its smile put a shiver in his bones. "But if it's Latin you like, *auribus teneo lupum.*"

Colton frowned, mulling it over, and said, "You hold a wolf by the ears."

It made a low, pleased sort of sound. Like a purring cat. "For a boy only half-alive, you are twice as bright as most."

"What does it mean?"

"The others he sent," the creature said. "They were, all of them, fawns."

"You're saying Lane is a wolf?"

The smile stretched, turning to a grin that was nearly feral. "You know precisely what the girl is. It's why you sit here. It's why the dead gather. Night after night. Death after death." Her head canted to the side. Again, it asked, "Why won't you tell her? What she is? What you are?"

The October wind picked up outside, setting the trees to rattling. Whistling through the rafters. The shadows danced across the floor in streaks of wild, wavering dark.

Lane's eyes went wide. "Can you feel them? The shades? They're gathered all around." That eldritch voice dropped to a whisper. "They do not like me here."

"I don't like you here, either," Colton said.

Another laugh cracked out of her, high and strange. "They want me to leave."

"We have that in common." He swallowed, tired, wishing for sleep, and jabbed two fingers to his temple. Slowly, Lane rose from the bed. The shadows shivered, retracting. Skittering away from the places where she stepped. He remained perfectly still and watched her approach.

Gingerly, she slid into his lap. Her knees dug into the leather on either side of his hips. His flannel pants hung loose around her waist. He held his breath as she took his pencil from his desk and slid it behind his ear.

Slowly, slowly, she leaned in and brushed her lips along the broken corner of his mouth. "I don't much like you, either," it whispered into his skin. "But you invited me. You and your companions. And now I have something to take care of, here on this infernal plane."

"And what's that?" His voice was a crack, barely sound.

In lieu of an answer, the creature said, "I'm going to help you tell her the truth. You'll see. I can be benevolent. I can make it so you get everything you want from pretty little Wednesday."

Without warning, she sucked his lower lip between her teeth. He jolted beneath her, his hands flying to her hips. Revulsion curled through him as she rutted against him. A game. This was all a game to the thing in her skin.

He thrust her off him with a snarl, hard enough to send her sprawling to the floor. Her tailbone cracked audibly against the hardwood. She'd have a bruise there tomorrow, angry and dark, but for now the creature at his feet seemed wholly unfazed. Her beetle-dark stare flashed with amusement. Her smile was a cruel, jagged thing.

"It's so easy to pull your strings, puppet."

"Tell me why you're here," he demanded.

"Because," it said, "much like you, I am searching for my brother."

Laughing, she began to scrabble upright, her limbs at odd angles, her hair falling around her in pale cobwebs. His heart rammed so high in his throat he thought he'd choke on it.

"Enough," he said. "Affatim."

Her blinks were entirely for show. "Do you grow tired of sparring with me, C.J.?"

"Sed non obligant." A nightly goodbye, not a permanent one. He said it again, for good measure, clearer this time than before. "Sed non obligant."

A gasp followed. A shudder. Her eyes rolled back in her head. This time, when she fell, she fell with grace. Like a storybook maiden, spelled by poison. Finger pricked. So very small. Her eyes fluttered, heavy with sleep.

"Colton?"

He was at her side in a second, looped her arm around his shoulders. "You flopped right out of bed." A lie. *A lie.* He was so tired of telling them. "Poorly done, Wednesday."

"Hmm." She was lost in the haze of sleep, her face tucked into his chest. Her breath curled, low and slow, against his sternum. He climbed into bed alongside her, conscious of the ticking clock, the sinking moon, the pink flush of her cheeks. The shadows crowded, drawing near, and he felt like one of them—clinging to her, desperate and afraid.

He was aware of the irony. Aware of how selfish he was. Seeking comfort from her when it was his fault, his fault. But then he'd spent his entire life drawing as close as he could to her warmth. He couldn't stop now.

"I think I fell out of bed," she murmured, and he remembered, then, that she couldn't hear—that she'd left her implant on his bedside table. Yawning, she folded herself into the curves of him, feeling for her backside. "I'm going to have a horrible bruise tomorrow. I can already feel it."

❦ 37 ❧

Delaney woke to sunshine in the middle of the night.

The hour was late. She could feel it in the muddy silence of her head, the tired sludge of her bones. Late, and yet her skin was painted gold, gilded in an inconceivable sunrise blind that set her scrabbling back from its brilliance. Her heel struck the heavy tin of a can and she wobbled, teetering hard into a wall. Every part of her felt sticky and wet and cold. She shaded her eyes and peered into the sun, her heart rate climbing. There, in the unwavering miasma of light, stood the tapering shadow of a man.

The sun clicked off.

An overhead light clicked on. Delaney was left staring into the cooling bulb of a painter's lamp. In front of her was Colton, his irises ringed in white. His mouth was a hard, unsmiling line. Casting out her thoughts, she tried to piece together the detritus of her subconscious.

She couldn't remember dreaming. She couldn't remember waking.

Shifting, she found her ankles twisted in the paint-spattered linen of a drop cloth. Her skin was tacky, her bare arms cracked in plaster. She was in Colton's T-shirt, Colton's boxers, her skin smeared in paint like tar. She made a feeble effort to rub it away. The colors smudged deeper, ruining the white cotton of his shirt.

A pair of paint-free hands found her face, cradled her jaw. Her chin was guided up until her eyes met Colton's. Brows pinched, he conducted a careful search of her, his fingertips coming away in

263

shades of red and gold and black. Again and again, his gaze flicked to the wall over her shoulder.

"What?" she asked, and felt the scrape of her voice all through her. "What is it?"

Turning, she caught sight of the wall. Where the butterfly had once unfurled, golden and unfinished, there was now an angry ouroboros of black. Beneath it, she'd fingerpainted a single word in red. *Sequestrum.*

Her stomach bottomed out. Her knees wobbled.

"God, Colton. I'm so sorry—"

He brought his thumb to his chest in a five-fingered spread. *It's fine*, he signed. *It's okay.*

Her breath caught, and she frowned up at him. Her nerves were shredded paper. Her head was a heavy metal scream. "It's not fine," she said. "What about any of this is fine?"

His only answer was to fold her sticky hand into his and lead her out of the office. Into the hall, where they tracked painted footprints all through the pristine foyer. Into the upstairs bathroom, where he turned the valve on the shower until it spat water over the empty tile in a scalding rush. He stepped inside, drawing her in after him so that they were both standing, fully clothed, beneath the rainwater stream.

He didn't speak. Instead, lathering a washcloth, he took hold of her wrists and set to work. He scrubbed between her fingers, where the paint had already begun to flake. Along her forearms, where colors ran in muddy rivers. Beneath her chin, where her pulse hammered so hard it became difficult to draw breath. She watched the water swirl black atop the drain and did her best not to cry.

Eventually, he finished, setting the cloth aside. Water drilling into her shoulder blades, she became too-acutely aware of the way his borrowed T-shirt clung to her in an opaque second skin. She didn't bother trying to cover herself. There was a strange sort of comfort in knowing he could see her—in knowing she was there. Something corporeal. Something that took up space. The water fell and fell without sound, and she'd never felt less at home in her own bones.

"I don't want this," she said, unsure if he'd hear her over the rush of falling water. His dark eyes flicked to hers. His curls were dark Cs against his brow, his cheeks flushed in the heat. "Maybe Nate and the others went looking on purpose," she whispered, "but I didn't. I want it out."

His only answer was to take the hem of her shirt and tug her to him, dragging her over the slippery tile. They collided, forehead to forehead, nose to nose, mouth to mouth. Water spilled over her tongue, and for a moment she thought he meant to kiss her. To swallow down whatever it was that beat inside her chest. She wished he would. She wished he'd drink it from her tears. Wished he'd bite it from her lips. Instead, he only drew her into an embrace. Her ringing head pressed against his sternum; his ruined mouth grazed her temple.

They stayed that way, twined together without a word, until her fingers pruned and the sun came up and the water ran clear and cold.

She was in the kitchen, halfway through her second mug of coffee, when Colton found her. The patch of sky in the window was a bright sapphire blue, the morning winter crisp, and she'd taken it upon herself to pilfer a sweater out of his closet. Now she perched, birdlike, atop a stool and sank deeper into the warm burgundy wool, watching him prepare himself a shake. He did it the way he did everything—in thoughtful, measured strokes. Checking his watch between intervals.

When the whir of the blender finally silenced, he peered at her across the granite island. His cheeks were flushed beneath the bill of his cap, his T-shirt dark with sweat. He looked, she noticed, nervous.

Quietly, he asked, "Do you trust me?"

"Not always," she admitted.

The pinched corner of his mouth quirked in a half smile. "That's fair. Would you trust me today? I need your help with something."

"Okay," she said.

He didn't look convinced. "You're probably going to have a lot of questions."

"I always do."

"I'm not going to be able to answer most of them."

"You never do." She set down her mug and slid off the stool, still a little unsteady on her feet. "What are we doing?"

What they were doing, it turned out, was breaking and entering.

The house in question was a cozy colonial of whitewashed brick and stone pavers, neatly mulched gardens dotted with bushes someone had lovingly covered in burlap to ward off the frost. The driveway was empty. So, too, was the detached garage with its shuttered windows and pitched roof, empty flowerboxes prepped for spring.

"I don't know," Delaney said, peering up at it.

Colton slid his hand into the small of her back, sweeping her with him down the pavered walk. "Now is not the time for second thoughts."

"I'm just not sure I'm comfortable breaking into someone's house."

"Why not?" They'd reached the front door and he checked the knob to find it predictably locked. "You broke into mine."

"I already told you," she protested, kicking at a squat stone toad on the steps, "the door was open."

"No," he said, and pulled a set of keys out from his pocket. "It wasn't."

He fitted several keys into the lock before he found one that worked. With a creak, the door swung open. Colton did a small magician's flourish and waved her inside.

"Am I supposed to be impressed?" She dug in her heels. "You had a key all along. Whose house is this, anyway?"

"Just go inside," he said. "Before the neighbors decide we're being suspicious."

In a tight, carpeted foyer, she found herself face-to-face with a vast assortment of cut-glass animals. They sat in a stacked glass case, smiling anthropomorphic glass smiles, winking in the late-morning light. She moved through the space on her toes, feeling a creep in her skin that had nothing to do with the decor. It was the smell. An antiseptic sting. A waxy candle melt.

And then, beneath, the enduring smack of something rotten.

"Whose house did you say this was?" she asked, inspecting a painting on the wall. It was a neat, pastel piece that featured three scaled nyads sunning themselves in a shallow loch.

Colton's response came from halfway up the stairs. "I didn't," he said. "Quit dawdling, we're on borrowed time."

Upstairs, the hall was similarly carpeted, the walls done in a dark wood paneling that was several decades outdated. Colton ushered her past rooms with doors pulled shut, egging her along with a series of whispered chastisements. Behind the third door, there came a single knock. The clear scrape of fingernails dragged over wood.

Delaney drew up short. "What was that?"

Colton didn't seem to notice. "You're the worst thief of all time." He prodded her in the side with a finger. "Head toward the last door on the left."

She thought she must have misheard the giggle, low and giddy, that gurgled out into the hall behind them. The hairs rose along the back of her neck. Rounding on Colton, she whispered, "I'm never going anywhere with you again."

"You don't mean that. In here."

He hurried her into a wide, well-lit office. The space was sparse, save for two prominent features. A single executive desk sat anchored before a wide bay window, empty of all but a lone Newton's cradle. In the middle of the room, there rose a single white pedestal.

"There's an item on the podium." Colton hung back, hovering on the threshold. "I want you to get it."

She frowned over at him. "And what are you going to do? Stand there like Dracula?"

"I'm not allowed in." It was an admission, however vague. A confession, however small. Something wide-eyed and desperate clung to his features. "Delaney, please. Just get it."

"Okay," she said. "Okay, I'm going." She toed her way across the floor, cringing at the groan of old hardwood. The pillar was solid oak, the top capped in a clear glass vitrine. Inside was a pillow of crushed black velvet.

And there, nestled in the center, was a single shard of bone.

She peered down at it, confused. "What is this?"

She half expected to be met with silence. Instead, Colton offered up another grudging admission. "You wrote a word on the wall back home. *Sequestrum*."

A shiver moved through her at the memory. "What does it mean?"

"It's a type of necrosis," he said. "It's a contemporary Latin term for a piece of dead bone that's been separated from something living."

"Gross." She inched closer, her breath fanning over the case. "And I thought the glass collection downstairs was creepy. What did it come from?"

"Me."

Startled, she glanced up at him. She found him checking his watch, his finger tap, tap, tapping out the ticking seconds. "Let's hurry this up," he said. "We're running out of time."

Carefully, she lifted the glass off the top of the pillar. It was heavier than she expected, and she nearly dropped it. Setting it aside, she turned her attention to the shard of bone. It was as long as a pinkie and curved like a paring knife, the tip sharp enough to cut. Splintered like wood beneath an ax.

Colton's stare drilled into her as she pried it off the little pillow. Immediately, the feel of it sang through her skin in a funny, phantom pulse. She glanced back at Colton to find him breathing hard, his eyes gone black. Somewhere in the house, something began to stomp its feet. Faster, faster, the sound dull and exultant.

Get out, crawled a voice through her head, loud and close. *Get out now.*

"Colton?"

He blinked, his gaze clearing, his breathing steadying. His eyes found hers. "Let's go," he said.

. . .

They were halfway home, the trees slipping past the windows in veins of leafless dark, when Colton finally spoke. She sat in the passenger seat, her hands in her lap, the funny splinter of bone in her upturned palm. It hummed into her skin. It thrummed all through her.

"Keep it," Colton said, startling her.

"What? Why?"

"Because I can't," he explained, "and someone needs to take it. Someone I can trust. Someone I—" His throat corded in a swallow. "Keep it," he said again.

She stared at him across the cabin. She thought of the dip in his rib, the impossible cleft along the curve of his bone. "Whose house was that, Colton?"

His knuckles were white against the steering wheel. "Someone who doesn't control me anymore."

❧ 38 ❧

"You're going to have to ask me that again."

Mackenzie's voice was rendered tinny by the speaker of Delaney's phone. Delaney sat in Colton's bedroom; the walls were painted in hues of early-morning yellow. Down in the kitchen, the smell of coffee grounds wafted up to meet her.

It was Thursday, and on alternating days, she'd learned, Colton went out for a jog. He'd leave before the sun, returning hours later in a sweat, carrying the brisk October air in on his shoulders. He didn't deviate.

Outside the window, the sun had barely begun to peek over the horizon. He wouldn't be back for another hour, at least.

"Is it possible," Delaney repeated, "for someone to exert a supernatural control over someone else?"

On the other end of the phone, Mackenzie sounded as though she was stuffed under a pillow. "It's too early for this, Lane."

"It's important."

Mackenzie let out a long, drawn-out groan. "I don't know. Maybe through hypnosis?"

"No," Delaney said. "Not hypnosis. With an object."

"What sort of object?"

Delaney peered over at the silver snuff box perched at the edge of Colton's duvet. She'd tucked the sliver of bone within, out of sight in the soft velvet interior. "I can't say."

"You can't say," Mackenzie echoed. "Laney, I love you, but I don't like you very much right now."

271

"Sorry." She fell back onto the bed, one arm flung wide. "I didn't mean to wake you. It's not important; I'll figure it out on my own. See you in class?"

She was met with an incoherent grumble, the sound of the line going dead. Rolling onto her stomach, she reached for the box. She pried it open and poked at the shard of bone within. Instantly, the feel of it crept through her. It lingered in her skin. Lifting it out, she ran a fingertip along the fractured edge, the tip as sharp as a tooth. Her phone dinged and she dragged it toward her, still examining the splinter.

The text was from Colton. *What are you doing?*

Her stomach flipped. Shoving the bone back into the box, she slammed the cap in place.

Nothing, she texted back. Then, because her first answer hadn't been entirely true, she sent *Can you feel that?*

His reply was instantaneous. *Yes.*

That persistent flutter whispered through her chest. The voice lay dormant inside her head, her thoughts all snarled up in sound. She stared at the silver box, her thoughts racing and racing.

Finally, she texted, *Does it hurt?*

Her phone didn't ding again until she was midway through dressing for class, tucking the sheer cuffs of her blouse into the black knit of her cardigan. Her screen lit up, skipping along the vanity. Colton's response was short. Only two words.

Not anymore.

Delaney made it halfway into the kitchen before she realized she wasn't alone. She smelled the cigarette smoke seconds before she saw the intruder.

The exhaust hood was on over the stove, sucking wind, and the sound of it put a dull whir in her head. A window was thrown open, and it was here the stranger stood, expelling smoke through the open slat. The frosted October morning pushed chilly fingers of cold onto the floor.

"Hello there, beautiful," he said, and she realized she'd seen him before—outside Nate's room in Chicago. Smoke eked out from thin lips, a red bulb nose. He was stout and nervy looking, his eyes wide set. "I'm looking for Price."

"He's not here."

The man's smile was as twitchy as the rest of him. "I'm happy to wait."

She set her clutch on the counter and headed toward the coffee machine, eager to appear as unperturbed by his presence as possible. She took her time pouring out a cup. The stranger took his time with his cigarette. The fan chuffed and rattled in a wheeze.

Nursing her steaming mug with both hands, she turned to face the man by the window. "I'm Lane," she said.

That twitchy smile endured. "I know."

"And you are?"

"Mark." He flicked ash from his cigarette, letting it fall into the farmhouse sink in fat gray flakes. "Mark Meeker."

Meeker. Understanding stole through her. "And are you part of it?"

"Part of what?"

"The club," she said. "Price, Hayes, Schiller, the others."

"It's not a club," he spat, visibly annoyed. "It's a group of bored little boys who think they're important enough to earn immortality. They found someone to help them do it, and he found me. When they step out of line, I keep them in."

She gripped her mug tighter. "Is that what you did to Price? Keep him in line?"

A laugh coughed out of him in a rasping *ho-ho-ho*. "Does that upset you? I ruined your boyfriend's pretty face? Take my advice: Cut your losses and run. Little girls like you shouldn't be playing around with the likes of him."

A spate of unease stole through her. The cold air from the window pushed through her stockinged feet. "What's that supposed to mean? Little girls like me?"

"You know," he said. "With the dead crawling at your feet."

Her stomach turned. The blood leached out of her skin, leaving her cold.

"Ah." He waved her off, crushing the nub of his cigarette in the sink. "I've said too much. I always talk too much. Do me a favor, will you? Tell Price I dropped by." His eyes flashed with exuberance. "And you can go ahead and add that Meeker said he's a dead man."

When he made for the door, so did Delaney.

"Don't go," she said, blocking his path. "First tell me what you meant. About the dead crawling at my feet."

But something in his expression had changed at their proximity. He sniffed up at her, a crease forming between his brows. Without warning, he reached out and grabbed hold of her wrist. The mug was flung from her grasp, shattering over the floor. Coffee bled into the grout in muddy rivers.

"Hey!" She pulled back, heart hammering, but his grip was like a vise. They stood uncomfortably close in the sprawling kitchen, the cigarette reek of his breath stinging the air between them.

"I smell it on you," he said.

The hairs rose on the back of her neck. "What?"

"Holy shit." He let out a low whistle. "You're goddamn flush with it."

She swallowed, her throat thick. "Flush with what?"

"Immortality."

"Meeker." Colton's voice cracked through the kitchen like thunder.

Meeker dropped Delaney's wrist at once, drawing clear. Colton stood in the archway, sweating through his running clothes. His jaw was a tight line, his expression unreadable. He didn't look at Delaney. Only at Meeker, who had begun to wring his hands in earnest.

"Ah, buddy," Meeker said. "You're home. You look good. Healing nicely. Cold for a run today, though."

Colton stayed silent. His stare was a wall, dark and lethal. His chest rose and fell in measured breaths. Meeker blinked, recalibrating, and darted for the door, only to have Colton swallow up his exit.

"Where are you going?"

Meeker took a too-big swallow of air. "Home," he said. "Recorded last night's game. There's an ice-cold beer and a plate of wings in the fridge with my name on it."

Colton's eyes flitted to Delaney and away. "I can't let you take this to the Apostle."

Some of the color bled out of Meeker's face. "You're unbelievable, Price, you know that? You know what she is and you're letting her wander around like it's nothing."

"I'm handling it."

"*Handling it?*" Meeker barked out a laugh. "It reeks like the depths of Hell in here. She's practically got brimstone coming out of her ears. She's not yours to keep, you know. This win belongs to all of us. You think I'm not taking this little piece of news to the boss, you're insane."

A muscle ticked in Colton's jaw. "Stop talking."

"*Insane,*" Meeker said again. "I always knew it. You know what I said? I said, give him enough rope, Price'll hang himself. And look at you now, you selfish asshole." He jabbed a finger in Delaney's direction. "That girl's a noose around your goddamned neck."

Pushing forward, he strong-armed his way past Colton.

"Should have left her alone, Price." His shout rebounded all through the empty house. "Once the Apostle gets wind of this, he's going to come after his creature. It won't be long before your little girlfriend here is six feet under like the rest of them."

There was a beat—a sliver of hesitation. A fraction of a pause. Colton's gaze met Delaney's across the chilly kitchen. His breath had gone serrated, the whites of his eyes visible. She could see what he was about to do written on his face, sure as she knew her own heart, her own head.

"Colton—"

The sound of his name jarred him out of repose, and all at once he was moving. Out of the shadow-bitten arch of the doorway. Into the foyer, his sneakers silent against tile. Delaney tailed after him, her heart in her throat, her skin needled in a chill that had nothing to do with the wide-open window.

"Colton," she called. He didn't look back at her. "Colton, just—"

He caught up to Meeker beneath the chandelier, where daylight sparked through the endless crystal seeds. He didn't make any effort to reason with him, he only crooked his elbow around Meeker's throat. There was a grunt, a curse. Boots scuffled over tile. Both of them slammed hard against the ground.

"*Colton!*"

His name wrenched out of her. He didn't look. He didn't stop. His hands were fists, knuckles white, the muscles in his arms corded tight. Trapped in a chokehold, Meeker gasped for air. The thick tracery of his veins rose in his skin in angry, broken vessels. The heels of his boots kicked wildly, scraping tile, scuffing grout, scrabbling for purchase where there was none to find.

And then it was over.

In one minute, or perhaps ten. An instant, or an hour. The struggle quelled. The foyer lapsed back into silence. Delaney stood frozen on the kitchen threshold, her heart behind her teeth. On the floor, Colton shoved Meeker away from him. The body fell with a thud into a pool of refracted light, arms akimbo.

The body.

The *body*.

Not a man anymore, but a corpse.

Her knees wobbled. She slid down the striated pilaster, hitting the floor. The sound seemed to jar Colton back to awareness. He turned to her, still seated beneath the fractured prisms of sunlight. His hands sat upturned in his lap. His cheeks were flushed, his breathing ragged.

Her voice scraped the air between them. "What did you do?"

He drew to his knees, picking his way toward her, half crawling across the floor. Behind him was the body, unmoving. The shadows quavered out of sight, teeth chattering and so very afraid.

"Delaney." He'd drawn near enough now to press his brow to hers. "Lane? Look at me."

She only stared past him, where the body lay with eyes open, mouth agape. The question wrenched out of her a second time. "What did you *do*?"

"Don't—" His fingers trembled against her cheeks. His touch was ice. "Don't look at him. Look at me."

She did. Against every last one of her better instincts, she did. His breath sawed between them. He felt like a stranger, and yet his face was the same. So brutally familiar, it hurt her to look at him.

He can't help it, thrummed a soft, aeonian voice deep within her head. *It's what he is. His true nature. Wherever he goes, death follows close behind.*

"I had to do it," Colton said, and let out an unsteady breath. "I had to. I didn't have another choice."

☙ 39 ☙

Delaney was looking in the mirror. She was staring at a ghost.

The subway-tiled bathroom of her family home was tight and cluttered, the countertop packed with hair product and brush kits and makeup bags, a coffee mug stuffed with toothbrushes, the open tube of toothpaste her father never bothered to squeeze from the bottom. A pair of kitchen shears sat discarded in the sink.

The mirror in front of her was a wide oval, the frame unfinished wood. Her mother had painted a thin train of ivy along the border, leaves unfurling in emerald fans of green.

She shut her eyes. She opened them.

The ghost was still in the glass.

Bright jade eyes. Stark white hair. A pale, pinched face.

Immortal.

"Say something," she ordered.

Her reflection went silent when she did. It went still when she stilled, moved when she moved. It was, for all intents and purposes, her—dressed in a black tank and joggers, a mismatched pair of Colton's dress socks pooling around her ankles.

Her hair was short, the purple hacked away. The ends fell just beneath her chin in a choppy bob. She'd taken the scissors to it in a fit, sawing through violet coils until they spooled at the floor by her feet. As if in changing herself on the outside she could saw away the hidden bits that made her itch.

That was yesterday. Or maybe the day before.

She couldn't remember. She hadn't slept.

In the days since she'd fled Colton's house, she hadn't done anything other than stare and stare into the depths of her reflection and will the thing in her bones to show its face. Its flutter in her chest had become synonymous with her heartbeat. The hum in her head had whittled to a shrill, loud and clear as a whistle. The shadows stayed away, away.

She slammed her hand against the granite countertop, sending bobby pins scattering over the bath mat. "Say. *Something.*"

"That hasn't worked for you yet," Adya said, from her place in the empty bathtub. She flipped through a thick leather book, pages rustling. "I can't imagine why you'd expect it to work now."

"I don't know what else to do."

"I don't know, either, but the definition of insanity is doing the same thing over and over and expecting a different result." Adya sat up a little straighter, her face brightening. "We could call an exterminator."

Delaney slumped down onto the toilet lid. "I'm not infested with roaches."

"Fine. We'll table that idea for now." Adya flipped to another page. "How about a Catholic priest? In all the movies they always come and do the thing with the water."

Delaney let out a groan and dropped her head into her hands. Somewhere unseen, her phone rang. Again. She ignored it. Again. The voice inside her remain silent.

"You don't want to talk to me?" She jabbed herself in the temple. "I heard you. I know you can speak."

Silence, again, save for the sound of Adya tossing yet another book on the growing pile of discards. Delaney slid down onto the floor. Her bruised tailbone thunked tile, and she barked out a laugh that felt entirely wild. Her stomach gnawed at itself, like a starveling winter's wolf running its teeth along a bone.

On the floor in front of her sat the silver snuff box she'd taken from Colton's house. She opened it and stared at the sliver of bone within. Picking it up, she turned it over and over, inspecting it from all angles, careless of whether or not Colton could feel it. She hoped he would. She hoped it made him crawl out of his skin, the way she was close to crawling out of hers. At her feet, Petrie wound in and out of her legs in a lazy figure eight, mewling contentedly.

"It's kind of creepy," Adya said, folding her arms over the lip of the tub. "How do you think he got it out?"

"I don't know."

"Maybe he had some sort of surgery and asked to keep it after. I have a friend who kept her appendix in a jar after her appendectomy."

"Gross."

"You're literally holding a severed piece of our TA," Adya said, resting her chin on her forearm. "You're not allowed to judge."

Delaney didn't answer. She only ran a finger along the outer curve, where the bone was smooth and white as a shell. She pressed it into the tip of her thumb, hard enough to puncture skin.

If we carved a piece of you away, what do we think would come out?

The voice thrummed through her head like a clarion bell. She tucked the bone into her pocket and leapt to her feet, nearly earning a claw to the ankle from Petrie as she went.

"I've been talking to you for hours," she snapped.

"Me?" Adya looked momentarily affronted. Then, realization dawning, she sank back into the tub. "Not me. Got it."

Deep inside Delaney's head, the voice said, *I am not a plaything.*

"What are you, then?"

Today, I am Delaney Meyers-Petrov.

Downstairs, the doorbell rang.

Adya frowned, halfway through scooping Petrie into her arms. "Who do you think that is?"

"I don't know." Delaney's heart was a hammer, her ribs the anvil. The feel of the bell reverberated all through her. "I'll be right back."

Fumbling out into the narrow hall, she all but tripped down the steps. She was aware of how wild she looked—how feral and on edge. The doorbell rang a second time. A third. A fourth.

She wrenched the door ajar to find Colton standing on the stoop, a garment bag hooked over his shoulder, his finger poised to jab the button again. He stared up at her, his pupils dilated and the tips of his ears a bright, bold pink. In her pocket, the shard weighted against her thigh like an anchor. He opened his mouth to speak, and she promptly slammed the door in his face.

"Delaney." His fist hammered wood. "Delaney, open the door."

"I'm not home."

"You—" His hand slammed into the frame and stayed there, silenced. "Please just open the door."

She pulled it open—just enough to see his face. Cold drove in through the crack and his relief mushroomed between them in a cloud of gray.

"You cut your hair," he said.

"How did you know where I live?"

He huffed out another breath, gray fragmenting between them, and moved to slip his hand into his jacket pocket. His fingers brushed the edge of a little blue box bound in ribbon and he let his hand drop.

He didn't answer her question. Instead, he peered up at her and asked, "Are you afraid of me?"

"No," she said, though it wasn't entirely true.

"Angry, then."

"No," she said again, though that wasn't entirely true, either.

"Well, I'm not sorry," he said. "I'm not sorry for what happened. You have no idea what the Apostle would have done to you if he found out what you've managed to do."

Managed, he said. As if she'd set her mind to it. As if she'd opened her mouth and swallowed this fluttering, insidious thing down like cough syrup. The laugh that cracked out of her was half-mad. A cardinal took off from a low-hanging poplar branch, winging through the sky in a brush of violent red.

When she fell silent, it was to find him frowning down at the pocket of her pants. The shard curled out of the top like a fang. She wondered if he felt it—the slide of bone, like the phantom tickle of a severed limb. A hollow ache where a piece of him ought to be. She tried to ignore the marked shift in his breathing. The way he braced his hand against the railing.

"I don't care," she said. "I don't care about your mysterious Apostle or your secret club or your wall of names. There is something *inside* of me, Colton."

His jaw feathered in a grimace. "I know that," he said. "You think I don't know that?"

"It's talking to me. It's stealing things from me. It's chewing me up. And it's your fault."

He hesitated for the barest fraction of a second. Then, scuffing a shoe against the leaf-impaled welcome mat, he said, "I feel like this might be the wrong time to remind you that I was vehemently against going to Chicago."

This time, when she slammed the door, it closed on his foot. He swallowed a wince, sliding the garment bag from his shoulder and propelling it through the crack. "Wait," he said. "This is for you."

She hung back, suspicious. She felt stiff as cardboard—like she was very carefully going through the motions of talking, blinking, breathing. Like if she were to stop, her body would carry right on without her.

"What is it?"

"A dress," he said, "not a viper. So you can stop looking at it like it's getting ready to bite you."

"What's it for?"

"An outing. Of sorts." He let the garment bag slump in his grip. "You left so fast the other day. I didn't even have a chance to talk to you."

She frowned. "You *killed someone*, Colton."

His foot remained determinedly wedged in the door. He looked, she thought, very tired. "I know," he said. "I was there."

"God." She pushed the door harder into his foot. It didn't budge. "It's not a joke."

"I'm not making a joke," he said, something plaintive creeping into his voice. The garment bag hung limp and dark between them. She thought of the way he'd trembled, the way he'd crawled across the floor on his knees.

"*I dragged myself out of Hell to you,*" he'd said the other night. All this time, she'd assumed it was a metaphor. Now, with the shard of bone digging into her thigh, she wasn't so sure.

Something sick and nameless roiled in her gut. Something she didn't understand. Something she wasn't ready to pick apart. After she'd come home from Colton's that day—fighting back tears on the T, racing along the iced-over sidewalk—she'd shut herself into the second-story bathroom and thrown up until there was nothing left inside her but air.

Air, and that ageless fluttering.

The haunt like a clearwing moth.

The skitter of something strange along her bones.

"Delaney," he said, working now to pry his foot free. "Please just take the dress."

She recognized it for what it was. A peace offering, laughable in the face of all that had happened. Something expensive for something unforgivable.

She scrutinized the bag for another several seconds before snatching it through the crack. It came to her in a rustle, as if it were protesting the changing of hands. As if it knew it was being passed on to someone who couldn't possibly afford it.

"What's in the box?"

His gaze followed hers to the little blue square in his pocket. The ribbon trailed out in an iridescent coil. "Nothing," he said, too quickly to be believed. Then, "Nothing important."

"Okay."

Silence, again. Neither of them moved from where they stood. She stood shivering in the doorway, peering out at him. He stared back, his pulse hammering in the triangle of his throat. The sun speared through the clouds in pinpricks of new-November white, turning the leaf-cluttered stoop into an oven. Between them, three lopsided jack-o'-lanterns grinned up through gaping, pulpy maws, their eyes squirrel bitten and strange.

"We've been researching for days," he said. "We haven't found anything useful. It's time for plan B."

"Is this dress part of plan B?"

"It is. It's the start of it, anyway." He fastened a button on his coat, checking his watch as he did. She'd never seen him so restless. "Will you come by my house tonight? Around seven?"

"What for?"

He proffered his shoulder in a half shrug. "I'll tell you when you get there."

"I don't know," she said. "I think it's a bad idea."

"Why?" He didn't sound angry, only curious, and she couldn't deny him the truth.

"Because," she said, "every time I get too close to you, everything starts to fall apart."

His face fell. "Not everything."

"*God*, Colton. Look around. Because of you, I'm being threatened with expulsion from Godbole. Because of you, a person is dead. Because of you, there is something living inside of me. You told me once that all you'd do is hurt me. I should have listened."

"Okay." He didn't offer up a clever retort, didn't push and cajole, didn't ply her with platitudes. He only looked quietly crestfallen, his throat cording in a sticky swallow. "Okay," he said again. He backed down the steps, one hand trailing along the railing. Leaving without a fight. "I get it. I'll leave you alone."

He was halfway down the walk when she called out to him, her heart in her mouth.

"I said I should have listened," she said. "I didn't say I would. I'll be there at seven. Let's try for plan B."

❧ 40 ❧

Delaney stood outside Colton Price's house in a beige chesterfield and black beret, the lapels of her coat clutched tight against the chill. It was just before twilight, and the sky was aflame with a sunset, the Boston skyline lit red by the sun. One by one, the streetlights began to come on, twinkling awake in filaments of branch-strung gold.

She'd been out here for nearly ten minutes.

Already, her feet were losing feeling. Her fingertips were numb. Her dress was cocktail length—perfect for the sort of upscale outing that matched the much-too-expensive dress Colton had gifted her, less so for idling in the path of a sharp November wind. The chill bit through her nylons with interminable force. She didn't feel like something new. Something remade. She only felt cold.

The door fell open just as she raised her fist to knock. Colton stood on the threshold in a three-piece suit and overcoat, his jaw wired tight, every inch of him immaculately tailored.

"I've lost patience," he said, winding a scarf around his neck. "If you're not going to get up the courage to knock, we might as well move on with our night."

"Oh." She fussed with the shorn ends of her bob, unused to the length. "Sorry."

"At least you're chronically early." He headed down the steps and into the street. "I've calculated in plenty of time for you to experience multiple instances of cold feet."

She fell in line with him, her heels clattering. "I don't have cold feet."

"Not yet, maybe." He flashed her a grim half smile and beckoned her down the backstreet between his house and the next. The street here was thin and tapering, empty save for a row of tired trash barrels and a newly emptied dumpster. "After you."

She peered down the unlit walk, her heels precariously balanced atop the cobbled stones, the shard of bone biting into her leg where she'd tucked it. "*Here?*"

Next to her, Colton was uncharacteristically agitated. "Where else?"

"This is an empty alley."

"Which makes it the perfect place to step through the sky unnoticed." He ignored the shock on her face in favor of glancing down at his watch. "Let's get started. I don't have you scheduled for another moral crisis for at least three minutes."

Placing a hand on the small of her back, he guided her deeper into the windswept alley. A car went past, briefly igniting the soot-addled bricks. Slicing across the dark in a silver freeze-frame. She drew back from him, her vision webbed in floaters.

"I don't hear anything. We're not on a ley line."

"That's correct," he said. His fist opened and closed like he was working out a cramp.

"I thought that just was a rumor. About you being able to open doors with your bare hands."

His features were muddled beneath the elusive blue of newly fallen night. She caught the corners of a wry smile as he said, "We all have our talents."

"And you can take me with you?"

"I can." He stood farther from her than usual, his stare dark as Erebus. "But there's a caveat. Going through two previously opened doors and creating an entirely new set of doors are vastly different experiences."

"How so?"

"At Ronson's, the way is already opened for you. You pass right through two abutting thresholds. Easy in, easy out." He pressed his palms together. "Do you follow?"

She frowned. "I follow."

"Tonight's different. We'll need to cross through the space between the doors." He pried his hands apart, leaving a wide gap of dark between his palms. "It'll be different than what you're used to."

"Okay." She tried not to let her nerves show. "Have you done this before? Taken someone else through with you, I mean."

Colton's brows drew together. "Yes," he admitted.

"Oh." She drew her lower lip between her teeth. "Does it hurt?"

A humorless grin knifed across his face. "Like hell."

"Well, great." Restless, she fiddled with the straps of her purse. "Let's get it over with."

Colton regarded her for a moment more, his eyes inscrutable in the gathering dark. Finally, he held out both his hands. His fingers lay flat, and twin silvers winked up at her in his open palms. It took her a second to realize they were nickels.

"I'll need two things from you," he said. "First, no matter what happens, the coins cannot fall. Not until we're all the way through."

"Okay." Slowly, she placed her hands over his. The coins were cold against her palms. His hands were colder. There was something odd in his expression, something nameless in the flinted dark of his stare. "What's the second thing?"

"You might be tempted to look around. Don't do it. Look only at me."

"Okay," she said, again.

"Only at me, Delaney."

"I heard you. I won't look around."

"Good." His jaw set. Over his shoulder, there was brick and there was dark. She couldn't even feel the hum of an open sky. Nothing twanged through her. Nothing rattled, nothing whined. Inside her head, the voice was silent. Evenly—as though he were explaining how to parallel park—Colton said, "I'm going to step through. I'll draw you in after me."

His elbows crooked and he guided her gently into him. Palms pressed tight, they melded together like lovers on a dance floor. First, there was nothing. Only the distant honk of a horn, the muffled rush of city traffic, the faraway mewl of a siren.

And then she heard it. The hum along her bones.

A soft staccato. A tug, like she was strung all up like a marionette. Colton's face had gone white as a ghost, the lines of him cut steel. The air around them grew thin as vellum and he took a single step backward. Out of the corner of her eye, she saw a flash, a rush of movement, like something running toward her.

"Don't let go," Colton ordered. "Don't look away."

"Okay," she whispered. "I get it."

He stepped again and she was drawn after him, plunged into cold like ice. A thousand sensations speared into her at once. The air around them hummed, but this time the sound was clear. This time, her head was full of moans. Her name was uttered like a prayer. It came to her in snatches and in screams. In whines and in whispers.

Delaney. Delaney. You're here with us, Delaney.

Fingers tore at her coat, at her skin. Colton drew her hard into his chest—hard enough to leave her breathless.

"Look at me," he ground out.

"I'm looking." Her voice was snatched away by the moaning both in and out of her head, the sundering of sensation in her arms and legs. Something coalesced in the air beside her face, something ink dark and skeletal and built all of sighs.

Malum navis, it whispered in her ear. *Look at us, Delaney.*

It came at her again, this time from the other side. She felt, more than saw, the wide gape of a jaw, the hollow points of two empty eyes. It caught her by surprise and she turned, just a fraction—just enough—breaking her eye contact. Somewhere in the distance, far off beneath the ceaseless murmurs, she heard Colton bark out her name.

There, Delaney Meyers-Petrov. Look us in the eye.

We have been waiting, waiting, waiting.

Waiting for you to see.

Colton's fingers closed around her wrists and he hauled her into him. The nickels bit into the heels of her hands as he brought his mouth crashing down against hers. The kiss was a surprise, immediate and immolating. There was nothing sweet about it. Nothing soft. Only the clash of mouths, the scrape of teeth. They collided the way they always had—like they were going to war—and something in Delaney tightened at the awareness. Her eyes fluttered shut against the skeletal haunts as Colton kissed her like an ache, his breath skating across her tongue.

And then there was silence.

Silence and snow.

It was as if all the world had snuffed out but them. The ground beneath her solidified into stone, the air turned winter crisp. She felt the soft flurry of a light squall, the fast melt of flakes against the heat of her cheeks.

The coins plinked soundlessly to the ground as her hands found their way to Colton's lapels. She held tight to him like a tether, white-knuckled and trembling. The snow fell and fell, and the kiss remained unbroken. It deepened, turning slow and coaxing. His touch trailed up to her jaw and hovered there, butterfly light against the flame in her skin. When at last they broke apart, the space between them was left flooded with gray, their breath turned crystalline in the chill.

"I told you not to look away." His voice came out sandpapered.

"And I didn't."

He tucked a short lock of white behind her ear. He didn't linger. "You were about to."

The moment severed, she felt suddenly desperate to be out from beneath his shadow. Out of reach of his caress. Away from the beat of his heart, visibly racing in the hollow of his throat. Shutting her eyes, she swallowed several lungfuls of air.

"What were those things in there?"

"That's what you hear." His eyes were black as an abyss. "When the shadows speak to you. When you hear that hum in your head. It's all of that, just unmuffled."

"So those faces, they were—"

"Ghosts," Colton finished for her. "Shades. Spirits. You can say it, it won't summon them. They're already here."

She reared back and glanced around, eyeballing the dark. The dark that had been her friend. The dark she'd carried home in her hands, cupped tight like a fluttering gypsy moth. The dark she'd feared, late at night when it wouldn't stop watching.

"*Mackenzie's weirdo friend*," Haley called her. "*The one who talks to dead people.*"

Dread slunk through her veins. In front of her, Colton's mouth thinned. "Don't look at me like that. You knew what they were."

"I didn't."

"You did," he said. "Deep down. Or did you think Schiller was the only one?"

She felt breathless, as if she'd run a mile full speed. She wished Colton would look somewhere else than at her, his gaze still swimming with the dregs of their kiss. His collar was rumpled, his curls dusted with snow. He looked like something stark and unholy, backlit as he was by the string lights of the street beyond.

"Why me?"

His brows cinched together. "Do we have to do this right this minute? We're on a schedule tonight. I don't want to be late."

"*Colton.*" His name cracked out of her like a whip. "Why me?"

Slipping his hands into his pockets, he regarded her through the sidelong rush of flurries. "Dead things are drawn to liminal spaces," he said. "They like to congregate in the in-betweens. Between light and dark, between worlds, between midnights." He hesitated and then added, "Between silence and sound."

She was a girl of quiet—little glass Delaney, caught between the hush and the hum like a translucent moth fluttering in a silk-string web. Just a click away from silence. Just a button away from sound. Her entire world was a liminal space. Somewhere she'd always thought herself infinitely, maddeningly alone.

Her head was an impossible tangle. She peered into the snow-laced dark of the alley. For once, the shadows lay dormant. They didn't spool at her feet, didn't cling to her ankles, didn't pluck and preen and leer.

They're keeping away, crept that damnable voice through her bones. *They do not like me here. They want me to leave and to leave you alone.*

"I wish you would," Delaney said aloud.

Colton's eyes snapped to hers. He spoke, but the sound was lost to her—muffled by the falling snow, snatched away by the formidable presence twining roots along her ribs.

I am not yet ready to go, Delaney Meyers-Petrov. I must see this through to the end. And you are the only mortal creature that has borne the weight of me without cracking.

She wanted to cry out. She wanted to claw whatever old, interminable thing this was away from her—to scoop it out with a scalpel and leave it shivering in the frozen earth. She'd spent hours standing in front of her mirror ordering it to speak, and now that it had, she wished it would be silent. Hugging her arms to herself, she blinked back the wild pinch of tears.

"Tell me what it is," she said. "This thing inside me."

"It doesn't have a name," Colton said. "Not in any known language."

"Is it something dead?"

The voice plinked through her with discernible scorn. *Death cannot touch me.*

"I didn't ask you," she snapped, "I asked him."

In front of her, Colton looked as if she'd struck him, palpable guilt etching lines around his grimace.

"Where were we?" She shut her eyes. Opened them again. She wasn't entirely sure she wanted to know. "Just now, in the space between worlds. Where was that?"

"Another liminal space." Colton didn't move as he said it. Not a blink, not a twitch. "Every mirror plane in every mirror world intersects along exactly the same line."

The wind pushed through them and Delaney suppressed a shiver. "And that line is?"

"The road through purgatory," Colton said. "You and I just crossed through Hell."

❧ 41 ❧

The taxicab had taken them almost six full blocks before Lane spoke again.

"Why didn't you tell me?"

She was looking out the window. The city wedged past in streaks of light. A snow-melt mosaic of yellow and red and green. Colton could still taste her on his tongue. He would never be rid of the memory of her mouth.

"I'm telling you now," he said, as quietly as he could. Already, the cabbie had given their taciturn silence several sideways glances in the rearview mirror. Colton was certain he looked like the asshole here, with Lane's doe eyes spangled in tears.

Next to him, Lane's beret was still jeweled in half-melted snowflakes. With her hair shorn all to white, she looked like some wild winter's queen. He wanted to gather her up in his arms and kiss her again. He could feel the shard somewhere on her person, nylon-scraped and blinding. It was driving him out of his mind.

"Let me pose that question in a different way," she said, studying him. "Why now, and not before?"

He hooked his left elbow over the back of the seat. "I couldn't," he said, with as much nonchalance as he could muster. "Before."

"Because of your mysterious Apostle."

That infernal scrape of bone was like nails dragged over slate. Teeth gritted, he said, "Yes."

"Because of the bone shard."

The snowy night slipped past the window in spotlit flurries. He readjusted his seat and tried his best not to look like someone whose skeleton was currently attempting to climb clean out of his body. "Yes," he said again.

"And how does that work, exactly?"

He checked his watch. "I don't think I'm comfortable having this conversation in the back of a taxicab."

"Is there a time you *would* be comfortable talking about this?"

"I don't know," he said. "I'll have to consult my calendar."

Her eyes flashed with an unholy fire. "Price, I swear to God." Her hand fell to her lap with a twitch, as if she were considering slapping him. "Please don't be yourself right now."

He fiddled with a button on his coat. "Who else would you like me to be?"

She let out a groan that was, he felt, needlessly theatrical. With a huff, she turned back to the window. The cabbie shot them another discerning glance in the rearview as he rounded the corner, weaving in and out of slippery roundabouts.

"I don't know why I bother," Colton heard her mutter, and he wasn't entirely sure if she was speaking to herself or answering the voice inside her.

He'd tell her everything, in time. About the Apostle. About the Priory. About Liam. About the pledge they all made, the thin lip of Hell they'd found in the outskirts of Chicago. About nine-year-old Colton, who'd thrashed his way through the frozen Cocytus itself to lay himself at her feet. Drawn to her, drawn to her, the way every other dead, shivering thing drew in close.

A winter's queen.

A graveyard's queen.

The Apostle would have eaten her alive if he'd discovered what she'd managed to do. He'd have opened her up like a little tin toy. A doll with an incubus keeping warm beneath her skin. And so, Colton buried Meeker's body deep in the woods. He'd thrown up his breakfast, kneecaps snarled in the knotted roots of an ancient elm, his hands calloused from hours of shoveling earth gone hard with frost.

The cab took another turn, careening sharply into the November-dazzled lights of Newbury Street. With the squeal of brakes, the driver pulled off to a no-parking zone. Several horns honked as they wove around them, tires leaving black gashes in the slow-gathering snow. The cabbie turned around to peer at them. His voice was thick with a Saugus brogue.

"Here work?"

"Here is perfect," Colton said, leaning forward to hand over a tip. "Thanks a lot."

He slid out into the snow and jogged around to the other side to get the door. Lane burst out in a fury, clutching the strap of her purse as though it were a shield. She didn't look at him. Not as she trudged through the dirtied heap of snow along the curb. Not as she nearly lost her footing along the old brick pavers. Colton fell into step alongside her, offering his arm. She declined, and the snub stung as if she'd slapped him.

The gallery was located on the third floor of an old brick building packed with whitewashed mortar. Tucked between a coffee bistro and a consignment shop. The double doors were solid, heavy oak, and the hinge creaked as Colton pulled the right door open. Stepping aside, he held it wide for Lane to pass through. She regarded him coldly, as if he were offering up a rat.

"After you," he said.

She pushed past him, pulling open the door on the left. The noisy click of her heels followed her into the lamplit foyer. The severed shard jostled repeatedly against her as she walked, thud, thud, thudding in a way that made his blood roar in his ears.

He caught up with her at the elevator, where she was working silently and indignantly to peel off her coat. Wordlessly, he helped her shrug out of it. She spun away from him in an angry pirouette. Like he was Midas, his touch gilded poison. One ankle wobbled precariously over tile as she struggled to reposition the thin strap of her bag.

He was grateful for her momentary distraction, aware that he was staring.

She stood before him in a long-sleeved dress of fitted black velvet, the hem interrupted by a subtle slit up her left thigh. He slung her coat into the crook of his elbow and cleared his throat as quietly as he knew how. The sound ricocheted through the foyer like a gunshot.

"That's not the dress I gave you."

"Oh?" She glanced down at herself as if she'd only just noticed, smoothing her hands over the flat of her stomach, the velvety protrusion of her hipbones. "I guess it isn't," she said, her tone dismissive.

The elevator doors opened and she turned on her heel, crossing into the lift without a backward glance. He didn't know what made him snap—that incessant scrape of the shard against her skin or her unearned fury—but by the time the doors shut behind him, the hammering of his heart against his chest rendered him incapable of rational thought.

In front of him, Lane stood in the wide, rusted mirror. Her clutch sat balanced on the flat-plated handrail. Her attention was trained on reapplying the deep mauve of her lipstick.

Without thinking it through, he jammed the emergency stop. The elevator gave a sickening lurch and then juddered to a standstill. The emergency light clicked on overhead. Instantly, the little space was flooded red as blood. Lane glanced up only briefly before continuing her application.

"Don't be so dramatic, Price." There was a wobble in her voice, hardly perceptible to anyone who hadn't spent a lifetime pretending not to know her. She capped the lipstick with meticulous care. "I looked at the dress you brought over. This one is perfectly comparable."

Surely, there were words—real, cognizant, intelligent words—he could say here. All he could think of was that maddening slide of velvet over bone. He was seconds away from breaking out in hives. Stalking up behind her, he dumped her coat on the floor and braced his hands against the rail on either side of her hips. Boxing her in against the glass.

Her eyes flew to his reflection. "*Excuse* you."

The emergency tone sounded. He didn't move. "Tell me why you're so angry with me."

"I'm not angry."

"But you are. You can't even look at me." He swallowed hard. "Is it because I've told you too much or because I haven't told you enough?"

"It's because you're unknowable." Her breath fanned red over the glass. "And I can't understand why you won't let me see you without a mask."

His chest ached. Slowly, he ran the backs of his knuckles up her sleeve. Her breath caught. The sound slammed through him as his fingertips skated over the pale protrusion of her collarbone. Closed around her throat. Her chin arched upward at his coaxing.

300

"Look at me," he said. "There's no mask."

Cypress eyes met his in the mirror. Her stare was dark with invitation. God, he wanted to take her up on it. Against the looking glass. Velvet crushed around her waist. A crowd of people waiting just outside. The dead closing in.

Instead, he said, "I know you brought it with you."

Her focus didn't waver. "Brought what?"

"Don't play with me. I asked you to keep it somewhere safe."

Her eyes were big and round as she asked, "Where's safer than with me?"

Understanding turned his insides to smoke. "Where is it? In your dress?"

"My tights," she admitted. "My dress didn't have pockets."

"Christ." The word choked out of him, like he was drowning in reverse. "Take it out."

"Why? Does it bother you?"

"Yes," he ground out. "It's making me crazy. Take it out."

She didn't. Instead, she held his gaze, heavy-lidded and lovely in the blood-red light. "It was you in the water that day at Walden Pond." She was a dog with a bone, her determination inviolable. "I know it was. I just don't know why you won't admit it."

"Delaney—"

"Admit it."

His blood thundered in his ears. He couldn't deny her the truth if he tried. "It was me in the water."

"I knew it," she whispered, triumphant. "I *knew it*."

His only answer was to bend down and press his mouth to the place where her neck met her shoulder. Whatever else she might have said to him melted at her lips in a gasp. They moved together with an illicit slowness, neither of them meaning to do it, the stolen moment spooling away from them like thread.

"Delaney." Her skin pebbled beneath his breath. "Take it out."

"Why?"

"I can't stand it."

"You get it, then," she said.

Her words were an order. His heart was a jackhammer. Obedient, he rucked the velvet crush of fabric around her waist. The tone sounded again, flat and low, as he dragged his palm over the hard ridge of her hip. He was achingly aware, as ever, of the slipping time. It moved too fast for him to chase. He could feel it sharpening inside him—the understanding that this was the closest he'd ever been to her. The knowledge that it would never be enough.

He found the high-waisted hem of her stockings, tight against her torso. Slowly, fumbling, he fitted his fingers beneath the nylon. Slid his hand along her thigh. Her palms braced against the mirror, and the heat of her skin left streaks in the glass.

His hand closed around the shard and she swallowed a small, broken breath. The sound of it clouded his head. It made him drunk. Drawing it free, he slid her dress carefully back into place. His chest was a knot. His hands shook with need.

"Colton."

His name slipped out of her like a supplication. He wanted to tell her he was the last person to bear the weight of benediction. There was nothing inside him but death. But then she was tucking the broken shard into her bag and the moment was over, the impossible, maddening feel of her leaching out of his skin. She watched him in the glass as he came slowly back to himself, his breathing steadying.

"What are you?" she asked.

The light clicked on. The alarm tone cut out. A tired Brockton burr came in over the speaker. "Is everything all right in there?"

"Fine," Colton said, scooping up her coat and jabbing a thumb at the intercom in one swift motion. "Elbow caught the button."

"Yeah, okay." The intercom crackled out. The elevator lurched to life.

Colton turned to allow Lane the chance to gather herself, feeling his chest crack as he did. He shouldn't have done it. He shouldn't have yielded. He couldn't help it. Night after night of watching her sleep in his bed, in his clothes, in his arms. His resolve had splintered. It was the way she'd looked at him, her nose in the air, her eyes blazing.

"You're unknowable."

Behind him, he heard Lane's breathing level. He remained facing the doors, watching the numbers climb between floors. Tugging at his cuffs until they sat just right. The watch at his wrist said they were ten minutes late to the showcase. He didn't care.

Slowly, Lane crept up to stand beside him, readjusting her beret until it sat just so atop the sleek white of her bob. The air stretched thin and cold between them. The doors opened. Snatches of sound trickled into the elevator. The clatter of cutlery. The buzz of conversation. The tinkle of piano keys.

His heart was a riot in his throat. It beat so hard he thought maybe he'd choke on it.

Handing their coats to the waiting valet, he stepped out into the buzzing throng. Lane kept stride beside him, holding her bag tight against her stomach. Inside sat a fractured piece of a fractured boy, too cold and too unknowable. This time, when he offered her his arm, she took it. Her fingers felt impossibly small in the crook of his elbow. He knew, deep inside his chest, that he would spend the rest of his life yearning for this moment.

"Time for plan B," he said, and led her out onto the floor.

❦ 42 ❧

He'd taken her to an art gallery. Delaney didn't know what she'd been expecting, but it certainly hadn't been this. The parquet was a dazzling array of beautiful people dressed in beautiful things, but Delaney hardly noticed. She moved through the throng as if carried along on a sequin riptide, allowing herself to be led by Colton.

Colton, who had boxed her in against the glass. Colton, who had finally, *finally*, admitted the truth, his mouth pressed to her pulse. Colton, who'd taken her mittened hand twelve long years ago and begged her not to let go.

Her stomach swam, uneasy. Every part of her felt unsteady—like glass about to shatter. Her head was a hum, full of voices, full of haunts. She couldn't discern the dead from the living. Maybe she'd never been able to. The polite chatter of patrons and connoisseurs mingled with the dull ring between her ears, the murmuring pule of ghosts.

Ghosts.

For everything she'd seen, everything she'd experienced, she'd never believed in the dead. Not really. Ghosts were things for Ouija boards and séances, parlor tricks and horror movies and high school dares. They didn't exist the way they'd appeared to her tonight—gaunt faces trailing ether like smoke, struggling to retain form in her periphery. She felt hollowed out, more than a little shaken. Nothing made sense.

It makes perfect sense, actually, sang that voice in her head.

She staggered to a stop beside an empty table. She shut her eyes. It didn't shut out the flutter in her chest. It didn't stifle the truth. It

305

was the dead that spoke to her. It was the dead that clustered, restless in the shadows. It was the dead who descended upon her, kissing her awake, luring her into the dark.

Crawling at her feet.

Lane, they whispered. *Lane, Lane, Lane.*

Not friends, not allies, not the fanciful by-product of a little girl's whimsy, but souls, severed and wandering. They gathered at the doors, beckoning her through. They clung to her ankles like cats. They drew in close, like she was a light, incandescent. Like all they wanted was to be warm and seen. *Look at us. Look, look, look.*

How had she never understood?

You weren't looking, crooned that presence in her chest. *You didn't want to see.*

She opened her eyes to find herself alone. Colton watched her from a nearby bar top table, his mouth a ruinous, tapering line, his gaze assessing. She joined him, the tablecloth fluttering like a specter in her wake, white satin gleaming in the bold throw of grid lights.

The space was stark and white and open, the walls struck with shadows that stained the empty spaces around the spotlit art in inverse circles of dark. She set her clutch atop the table and watched a fat, beaded flame sputter inside its jeweled votive, feeling as though anyone passing by could see what she'd done just by looking. What she'd let him do, pressed together in the dark of the elevator. Her face was aflame. Her heart hadn't stopped racing.

Across from her, Colton was the picture of calm. Not a curl out of place, not a wrinkle in his suit. Smoothing his hand along his tie, he summoned a nearby waiter. Instantly, two glasses of champagne were set between them. She found herself staring into a flute of golden fizz, her face and the crowd reflected upside down along the brittle curve of the crystal.

Colton lifted his glass, the face of his watch flashing gold in the light. When she raised her eyes to his, it was to find his gaze a spectral dark, black as a sepulcher. His throat corded in a swallow. He didn't speak as he took a sip, his eyes never leaving hers.

The dead crawled at her feet.

A beast curled in her bones.

She was in a mirror world, under a mirror sky, with a boy who could walk through Hell. Nothing made sense anymore. She wasn't sure it ever had.

"Talk," she commanded. "It's unnerving when you're this quiet."

"We've always been quiet," he said, and she knew he meant the sleepy mornings in the lecture theater, the late nights studying in his living room, the endless midnights curled together in his bed.

"Yeah, well." She nudged a loose strand of white out of her eye. "You've always unnerved me."

He took another sip and regarded her carefully over the top of his glass. "What do you want me to say?"

"You said I'm not the only one you brought into Hell. Tell me who else."

He set down the glass, his fingers flexing along the tapered neck. "Schiller," he said. "Greg Kostopoulos. Julian Guzman. Ryan Peretti. Only, with them, we didn't come out the other side. I guided them in, and then I came back alone."

She thought of Nate in the meadow, the rusted penny woven into the grass. "You left them there?"

"It was part of the project," he said, and he didn't sound defensive.

He only sounded matter-of-fact. "They were supposed to find their way out on their own."

"But instead, they all ended up dead."

He swallowed hard. "Yes," he said. "They did."

"I don't get it. Why would anyone agree to do something so stupid?"

Colton frowned, scanning the sea of glittering people all around them. "Twenty years ago, and in our Boston, the Apostle's wife lost a hard-fought battle with a terminal illness." Drawing a breath, he gestured to a nearby painting. "This is her showcase."

Delaney followed his gaze, taking in the throngs of people in cocktail attire. They milled about the space, drinks in hand, studying the elaborately framed pieces lining the vast, well-lit walls. Muted watercolors and breathtaking acrylics, all featuring landscapes too lovely to be real. Tapering pines mirrored in a glassy lake, clusters of white poplars rising up from the snow, mountains and glades and broad, sun-swept pastures. There was something unsettlingly familiar about the pieces, though there was no way Delaney could have possibly seen them before.

"The Apostle has a theory," Colton said. "He thinks if something immortal can be harnessed and packed into the body of someone mortal, he can prevent the human body from ever suffering death."

At a nearby table, a cluster of women gathered around a lush painting of a wooded glade, the plays of light through the wind-whipped trees done by a patient, masterful hand. The artist—or the woman she assumed was the artist—stood among them, her hair a wisp of white atop her head, her smile quietly exuberant as she accepted their praise. Delaney gripped the edge of the table, unsteady.

"He wants his wife to live forever."

Over her shoulder, she heard Colton say, "Yes."

Understanding slow-crept over her. "She's no use to him here."

"No," he agreed. "No, she's not."

"That's— God." She turned back to him, horrified. "God, Colton. What are you telling me? You can't just traffic a person through realities. This woman has a life here. She has a mirror version of your advisor. What would that do to him? Whoever he is, he exists in this world, too."

"Except he doesn't." Colton's mouth twisted into a grimace. "Six years ago, he drank himself into a stupor at the local pub and then got behind the wheel of his car. Died on impact. He sees this as a reunification of two people who were rent apart too soon."

"Oh, is that how he sees it?" Delaney scoffed. "Because from where I'm standing, it's absolutely insane."

Something sharpened in Colton's stare. "Is it really so unbelievable? Look at you. You've done it. Radiant as ever, with something immortal in your bones."

"Look at Nate," she shot back, sickened. "Look at the others. What about them?"

She thought of Nate in the hospital, his eyes devoid of anything remotely human. He'd gone into Hell in search of a way to circumvent death, and when he found it, it ate him alive.

"They knew what they signed up for," Colton said. "Every single one of them had someone they'd do anything to keep alive. They pledged because they wanted to prove that death was optional. And it is. It only takes you if you let it."

"And how do you know?"

"Because," he said, proud and reaching and inaccessible. "I didn't let it take me."

She felt like she'd woken from a fever dream—or maybe like she was still inside it—the entire evening nothing more than a strange, lucid nightmare. "Do you hear yourself? You're reaching too far."

Colton slid a hand into his pocket. "'Ah, but a man's reach should extend his grasp, or what's a heaven for?'"

She frowned up at him. "What's that supposed to mean?"

"Robert Browning. 'I know both what I want and what might gain.'"

"Poetry. Of course it's poetry." She barked out a laugh, much too loud for the ambience of the posh gallery. The hum in her head was quickly rising to a crescendo, strident and infuriating. The sway of the crowd was dizzying. She needed space. She needed a minute to think. When she pushed away from the table, Colton came after her.

"Wednesday," he called. "*Delaney*, wait."

She kept on walking, her bag slung over her shoulder. She didn't make it far before his hand closed around her upper arm, rooting her in place.

"Don't leave" was all he said.

She rounded on him at once, teetering on the edge of tears. "You didn't bring me here to help me get this thing out of me. You brought me here to talk me into keeping it."

He didn't deny it. "Would it be so bad," he asked, "to outwit death?"

"Death is part of life," she bit back. "Nothing is permanent. Nothing stays. Everything comes to an end, that's just the way it goes. And if you don't figure that out, you'll end up permanently stalled. Lost and alone like the man from the museum, filling your house with cheap, meaningless snow globes."

His brows drew together. "I don't want to fight with you."

She wrenched her arm free of his grasp. "What did you expect? Because if you're trying to convince me that I should be happy to have this *thing* living in my head, you'll have to try a lot harder."

His jaw locked. For a moment, they stood like rocks in a stream, the crowd ebbing and flowing all around them. Music she couldn't place pulsed in the air, a different top forty for a different universe. She wondered, dully, if another copy of Delaney Meyers-Petrov and Colton Price were somewhere nearby. If they, too, were spending this night fighting. If they knew each other at all. The thought that they might not fractured through her, even as she wished to be anywhere but here, caught up in his shadow.

"I didn't bring you here to change your mind," he said, nearly too soft to hear. She was forced to read his lips in the quiet. "I brought you here to help me say goodbye."

He didn't speak. Not to answer her stream of questions, nor to fill the silence. He only walked on, tugging her in his wake with a relentlessness that left her breathless, jogging to keep up with him on the powdered white of the sidewalk. The streets outside the gallery were quiet as a grave, the dark held briefly at bay by the spangled lights of the matchstick city. It should have been a reprieve—the cool kiss of snow on her skin, the glittering elms on every corner. Instead, her skin stayed hot and fevered. Shadows throbbed at the edges of her vision.

Look at us.

Look at us.

She felt a little bit like a spindle, unraveling. As if she was moments away from coming all to pieces and spooling, ribbon-like, across the snow-laden lane.

"Price," she said, for the fourth time in as many minutes. He hadn't slowed, hadn't even glanced at her, driven on by the invisible spur of some unseen master, some wild notion that incited him to haste. Like the devil himself was breathing down their necks, great maw held open in a beatific grin. "*Colton.*"

She wouldn't go farther. Not until she knew where he was taking her.

Digging in her heels, she wormed her fingers out of his grasp. Her hand ached with the holding. Everything he did—every way he touched her—left little hurts along her bones. Left her stomach sick with wanting. It felt like something preternatural, this constant, unyielding pull to him. Like there was a cord threaded through both of them, tangling them into knots.

Close, crooned the voice. *So very close.*

"You're acting insane." Her words were swallowed up by the snow, by the dark, by the indefatigable presence in her head. "That's nothing new. But this, tonight—you're making me nervous."

He rounded on her, grim-faced in the light. For once, the arrogant spark had deadened in his eyes. The familiar way he held himself, all broad shoulders and pressed angles and ironed confidence, had winnowed away. He looked as if he'd been chiseled into a ghost of himself, his curls windblown, his tie rumpled.

"We're here," he said, his gaze affixed to a point somewhere just above her head.

They were in a residential neighborhood, the homes pressed neatly together in narrow town houses of grayed-out brick. The cheery lights from the tapered windows threw oblong squares of yellow gold over the needle-thin road. The snow fell and fell.

Colton drew a breath. "There."

She followed where he indicated, staring up the road, and saw nothing of note. Several snow-blanketed cars sat parked along the curb. A scarecrow stood lashed to a lamppost, his autumnal court laid to waste by the unseasonal squall. A faceless couple made their way down a nearby stoop, huddled close for warmth.

"Come on." Colton headed off after them, drawing Delaney's arm into his without tenderness or grace.

"We're following people now," she noted, wishing she'd worn more sensible shoes. Her feet were beginning to complain. A blister threatened to form on the back of her right heel. Colton didn't slow.

"Quiet."

"Don't shush me." She tried to wriggle out of his grasp and found herself rooted to him; his iron grip closed over her fingers. "Didn't anyone ever tell you it's socially unacceptable to follow strangers at night like this?"

"They're not strangers." They rounded first one corner and then another—tailing the couple toward the city proper. "Not to me."

They walked one block. Then another. Always hanging back, never getting close. Delaney felt distinctly like a voyeur, her heartbeat thudding in her ears. In her chest, the voice was silent, silent, silent. Only the dark murmured, jaded and ill at ease and huddled out of reach. As they idled at a crosswalk, she chanced a glance at Colton. He was quiet as the grave, his mouth soldered in a tight line, his jaw locked.

Softly, she asked, "Are we going to kill them?"

"No, Wednesday," he said, flat. "We're not going to kill anyone."

The next rounded corner brought them to a pop-up market. The night became emblazoned in streaks of vivid gold, the white-tented street vendors illuminated beneath rows and rows of tea lights strung between buildings. Scant crowds of people milled about, sipping cocoa by a central firepit, listening to the live band, walking hand in hand between artisanal shops.

The crisp petroleum smell of city winter faded away, replaced by the treacle scents of warm chocolate and freshly baked bread. Up ahead, the couple paused at a small shop and bent down to inspect the wares. At this new proximity, and with the aid of light, Delaney could see that the woman was pregnant. Every now and again, her hand ran absently over the prominent bulge beneath her coat.

Colton watched the couple without moving, every part of him threaded tight.

"Colton," she said, softer than before. "Who are those people?"

This time, he answered. This time, he offered up a truth, singular and raw. "That's my brother."

"Your—" Something in her sank impossibly low. "Oh."

Working her hand free of his, she turned back toward the vendor and the couple just in time to see the woman throw her head back and laugh. Her auburn hair caught gold in the lights. Next to her, the man grinned, tucking a newly wrapped parcel under his arm.

She could see it. The resemblance. It was there in the line of his shoulders, the sharp angle of his jaw, the crook of his smile. When they moved on, she watched them go, feeling a little like she'd felt while dreaming—as though she'd somehow stepped into Colton's nightmare instead of her own. She thought, without meaning to, of the boy's face half-buried in the earth, the little bones scattered in muddied furrows.

Look what he's done.

Look what he's done.

"Does he—"

But Colton was already speaking, his voice tight. "In every reality, it's the same. Either I'm dead, or he is. I've gone through a thousand doors, and I've yet to find any different."

She glanced up at him, surprised. "Colton—"

"I'm going to be an uncle." His breath came shredded. "They're expecting a baby in April." He tracked the movements of his brother and sister-in-law as they wound through the market, disappearing and then reappearing amid the throng. "I thought I could do it. I thought if I agreed to work with the Apostle, I could find a way to keep him. To make him whole again. But look at him, does that look like a man who isn't whole?"

Liam Price stood lit by the fire, his features thrown into stark relief, his arms around his wife. When she tilted her face up to his, he caught her, smiling, in a kiss.

"No," she admitted. "He looks happy."

"He moved on." There was nothing bitter in Colton's voice when he said it. Only sadness, deep and resolute. "He moved on, and I've been stuck chasing ghosts."

A truth. Here was a truth. Here was a piece of Colton Price he didn't give away, and he was giving it to her. Severing it from himself, here in this snowy Boston entire worlds away from home. She reached out without thinking and slipped her fingers back into his. His hand tightened instantly around hers. His throat bobbed in a swallow.

"I love you," he said, speaking suddenly and unexpectedly.

All the breath ran out of her on an exhale. "What?"

"God." The laugh that cracked out of him was caustic. "There it is. I love you. I've always loved you. And I don't—" His smile was bitter and not, she felt, entirely meant for her. "I don't want to do this anymore. I don't want to keep chasing things that are already gone."

Her entire body was a pulse, *bah-dum, bah-dum, bah-dum.*

Fingers flexing, he said, "I need you to give Liam something for me."

"Okay." Her heart raced much too fast. She was spinning out like a top.

I love you, he'd said. *I love you.*

Fishing in his coat, he drew out the small package she'd seen in his pocket. Instantly, understanding blossomed. It was the pale powder blue of newborns, of nursery walls and footie pajamas, of swaddles and snuggies. Of a little child in a mirror world who would never meet his uncle.

"It's just shoes," he said, dismissive—as if she'd judged him. "I didn't know what to get. I don't like babies."

"That's okay."

Carefully, he pressed the box into her hands. "Will you give it to them?"

She closed her fingers around the edges but didn't take it. "Why not you?"

"I can't." The look he gave her was packed full of grief. "Please, just help me with this one last thing. And then I'm done."

He'd never looked more wild, more desperate, more afraid. It made her afraid, too, to see him this way. Cold, calculated Colton Price, who always had an answer for everything. His tie was coming undone and there was snow in his lashes and he looked, for the first time ever, entirely too human.

"I want to be someone whole," he whispered.

"Okay," she said. "Okay, I'll do it."

She left him there at the edge of the market, caught beyond the reach of light like a lingering specter. Tangled up in shadow and haloed as he was by the dark, he looked the way the dead did—watchful and silent. Waiting for her to look back. The edges of him were winter dusted and cold, and he seemed to her like some pale, deathless king.

You are beginning to understand, sang the voice, crinkling through her like paper.

Her stomach was caught in an endless free fall. She pushed into the crowd, seeking out the couple they'd tailed all through the winter-bitten streets of Boston. She found them at a candle shop a few tents away, taking turns smelling the various bottled scents before setting them back atop their neatly stacked pyramids.

"Excuse me," she said, drawing close. She felt supremely ridiculous. But it was such a small ask, for such a big hurt. The couple turned to her, caught up in a private laugh, their eyes bright and their noses pinked from the cold. For an instant, they looked uncertain whether or not she'd meant to speak to them. She cleared her throat. "Are you Liam Price?"

Colton's brother frowned. "I am. Do I know you?"

"No." She could feel Colton's stare boring into her. "No, you don't. Look, I'm sorry to be so forward like this, but I have something for you." She held up the little box. "It's from a friend."

"A friend," Liam Price echoed. This close, she was further struck by his likeness. He had Colton's curls, Colton's jaw, Colton's nose. Only the eyes were different, a warm, honeyed brown where Colton's were perennially cold. Reaching out, he took the box between gloved fingers. "What friend is that, exactly?"

"I—" She faltered, wishing she'd rehearsed. "It's someone who means well." She drew back, feeling as though she ought to say more, unable to summon the words to navigate this scenario with grace. Casting about for something sensible to say, she managed to stammer out, "Congratulations to both of you."

And then she fled, plunging into the bundled throngs of customers without looking back to see if they'd follow.

When she reached the edge of the market, Colton was there. He looked different than when she'd left him. Gone was the disarray, the slight edge of panic. In its place was a quiet grit she didn't quite understand. He watched her approach him like a bridegroom, his lapels ornamented in fast-melting flakes that shone like diamonds in the light.

"I think I weirded them out," she said once she'd reached him. The cold was a wall. It bit through her tights. Colton only smiled.

"You did great."

"But—"

"Perfect," he insisted, drawing her into him. Leaning down, he pressed a champagne-stung kiss to her mouth. It swam through her in a dizzying swill, until she felt drunk on it.

Lacing her fingers over the nape of his neck, she rose up onto her toes until they collided in the golden-laced dark, the snow spiraling around them in fat, spotlit flurries. The sound he made at the impact was low and dark. It pooled deep in her belly. It wound around her bones.

It was a while before they came up for air. He smiled down at her, his eyes shining like ink.

"What now?" she asked, breathless.

"You tell me," he said. There was something regal in the lines of him. Something imperious in the way the dark gathered against his frame. It struck her again—as it often did—how not like a boy he seemed, but like a god, untouchable, unclaimable, unknowable.

You are not entirely wrong. The murmur stung her chest like smoke. It prickled all through her in a smolder. She found she didn't recoil from it, didn't shudder or cry out. Instead, the voice disseminated its message through her in purls of warmth. *The boy carved out much of himself years ago. Such is the price to pay to cross the endless, flowering fields.*

Tentatively, all packed with immortality like a vapor, Delaney ran a fingertip across the angry split of red at the corner of his mouth, the tight ridge of his scar. He captured her wrist, turning to press a kiss into the cradle of her palm.

The boy is as beholden to you as the keening dead, snaked that abysmal voice through her skull. *Command him. He will not refuse you.*

Her heart skipped a beat. It skipped several. In front of her, Colton's stare was black and unwavering. Rising onto her toes, she brushed a kiss to the broken blade of his smile.

"Let's go home," she said.

❧ 43 ❧

The world winnowed out. It winnowed in. A soundless cry. A snapping tether. Colton drowned, as he always did. He came up for air, lungs burning—as he always did. Chest pinched. Throat aflame. The crisp autumn night pulsed around him. The alleyway was black and cold. He was on dry ground and the dead were gone and his ghosts were gone and Delaney Meyers-Petrov was standing in front of him.

There was no singularity but her.

Everything he did was out of habit. By rote. He woke up. He fell asleep. He stomached the pin-and-needle prod of a curse he couldn't shake. He bore the silent dead and the silent feel of dying. The endless fall of nights spent alone. The taste of mud in his throat. The knowledge of what he was, like a too-heavy cross.

And now here was Lane.

Her eyes were moonlit, fringed in snow. The dark mauve of her mouth was smudged by his kisses. Her breath hung between them in serrated strips. His fingers were shackled around her wrists, silver nickels clutched in both her hands.

They would come for him.

Sooner or later, the Priory would learn what he'd done and they would come for him.

But for now, there was the world edged in tinsel and there was Lane.

Somewhere in the distance, a church bell was ringing. The midnight hour. That most liminal of spaces. And in front of him, a girl of in-betweens. One foot among the dead and one among the living. He'd seen the silent shades drop to their knees at her feet as he led her home. The deep carillon call pealed through him in a brassy knell. He was alive, alive, alive, and the minutes running through him felt suddenly euphoric. Like a drug for once, and not like a poison.

He tightened his grip. The bones of her wrist bit into his palm.

The bells sang into the sky.

"Stay the night with me," he said.

44

The house was sepulcher dark, black as a grave. Delaney could feel the dead crawling over and through it. Could feel them murmuring her name, clear enough now that she wondered how she'd never felt it before. It shivered through her head in a low chorale.

Yes, they whispered. *We are here, we are here.*

Look at us.

Look.

She didn't look. She was inextricably tangled in Colton, and he in her, the dark running over them in variances of deepest black and gold-threaded blue as they moved between street-lit windows and pale-papered walls, shedding coats and scarves and shoes as they went. His guidance was rough, unforgiving, and she found she liked it that way—liked the desperation in his touch, the way he backed her up the steps without a care for the way she stumbled, nylons slick against the finely lacquered wood.

Her fingers traveled over the slight stubble of his chin, down the strained cordage of his throat, to the strangled knot of his tie. She drew him closer, felt him stagger a step, and reveled in the slam of him against her. He was everywhere—his hands in her hair, tongue tangled in her mouth, his knee between her thighs.

And the dead followed.

They watched, murmuring and roiling, prostrate amid the shadows. She thought, suddenly, of how she'd spoken to them once, as a little girl. Tucked away in the shaded juniper trees, cast in dappled light, she'd felt the itch of dark along her skin, the bite of shadow like a frost. It had been too much, too much. Afraid, she'd climbed atop a lichen-kissed stone and bidden them obey.

"Stop that."

And they had.

She'd been left in silence and in sunlight, the forest empty, the windless afternoon streaming over her skin in streaks of gold. She'd felt a little like a proper queen then, buoyed atop her moss-plaited obelisk, the empty glade her court, the very dark at her command.

Just a peculiar little girl's peculiar little daydream.

She paused in the door to Colton's room, pulling back from him. His mouth was stained red from her kisses, his curls disheveled. He looked, in the low cast of streetlights from the window, like some black-eyed, beautiful thing. Like he wasn't even human.

His tie was gone, the buttons of his shirt undone. Breathless, he caught the doorframe in his hands, elbows crooked. Caging her in. The dead clung to him like a mantle. They chittered along the ground at his feet. They genuflected, going prone along the floor, and she wasn't entirely sure if their adulation was meant for him or for her.

Look at us.

Look.

And so she did.

"Be still," she snapped, refusing to feel foolish for it. The shadows fell. The streetlight framed in the window became a bright, burgeoning spot of gold. She blinked, stunned. Her heart was a wild, cantering creature beneath her bones.

Very good, crooned her odious passenger. *You are learning.*

In the door, Colton watched her with eyes that swallowed up the light. He didn't look surprised. Not unsettled, not alarmed. He only looked pleased.

He only smiled and said, "There you are."

❧ 45 ❧

The day Colton Price died, he'd only pulled himself up because Delaney Meyers-Petrov told him to.

"The water's too cold for swimming," she'd said. *"You need to get up."*

He'd been dead. He'd been dying. The cold had gone out of his bones and left something empty in its place. Something without any fight. At her command, the pain came rushing back. It slammed into him like an anvil, and suddenly his chest had been packed with mud, his mouth flavored like silt, his bones juddering hard enough to hurt. He'd never hurt so much. He'd never felt so alive.

Be still.

That's what she said, standing in his room. The dark a cold, beseeching specter. He couldn't see it. He couldn't hear it. But he'd walked through Hell often enough to know the feel of it. Sulfur and brimstone. The muddied brine of a slow-melting pond.

Be still, she said, and the dead listened.

The way he couldn't help but listen.

He fixed his gaze on hers. She'd never looked more like herself, eyes bright and chin upturned. The dark knew it. He knew it. They were in the presence of something regal. A gold-limned queen, the very depths of Hell at her beck and call.

"Come here," she said. An order, soft. He would have crawled across the floor to her, if she'd commanded it. He would have dragged himself, the way he'd torn through fire and through ice. The way he'd thrown himself at her feet, halfway dead and ice thawing in his lungs.

He surrendered a step into the room. In spite of her initial boldness, she drew back from his approach. Something primitive shot through him at the sight of her retreat.

"Malus navis," he said, without entirely meaning to.

Her breath caught. "What?"

"It's Latin."

"Meaning?"

He swallowed thickly. He couldn't look anywhere but at her. In his room. Under his thumb. The girl who could command the shades. He'd spent so long pretending this wasn't what he wanted that now it hurt to have her here. Like he'd spent years training his body to do one thing and now was asking it to do quite another.

"Colton," she chastised when he hesitated. "Tell me what it means."

"Beacon." The word fell out of him. "It means beacon."

He stepped again and she drew back again, until he was stalking her across the book-cluttered space of his room. His throat went dry. His blood heated. He liked this newest game a little too much. "It's a phrase the dead have," he explained, "for someone who draws them in like a moth to light."

He heard the very second her spine slammed into his bookshelf. Several tomes went toppling to the floor. It lit something in him, the way her fingers bit into wood, the way her knuckles went white against the shelving. The way he could see, even in darkness, her pulse hammering in her throat.

"Malus navis," she echoed.

He swore he felt the dark shift under their feet as he drew in close, bracing his hands against a shelf. Beneath him, her stare drilled into his.

"And what word do you have for me," she whispered.

He regarded her for a long moment before bringing a hand to his chest. Before tapping it against his sternum. Once. Twice. The sign for *mine*.

Her breath caught. Leaning in close, he pressed a kiss to the pulse beneath her ear. Her body arched instantly into his, like they were strung all together. Twin marionettes, their strings hopelessly twisted. A creature who walked with the dead and a woman who drew them close. He would never not be caught in her orbit.

"Mine," he said aloud. The word came out serrated.

"Mine." It felt so good to finally say it. His hands slid around her back, and then she was flush against him, her hands twisting in the curls at the nape of his neck, her mouth seeking his in the dark. They met in a collision of teeth and tongues, moving together until he thought he'd fall apart with the wanting.

"Colton." She spoke his name into his mouth. She spoke it into the core of him. She left careful kisses along the pinched stigmata of his smile. She undid him with a single word, the way she'd undone the pressing dead. "Please."

❧ 46 ❧

There were impressions of him everywhere. In the mattress, in the impossible knot of sheets, in the bruising way his fingers bit into her spine.

There was no sweetness in it. No careful ministrations, no whisper-quiet handling of blown-glass Delaney, liable to break. His grip was a vise, hard and grasping.

She'd commanded the dead with a word, commanded Colton Price with a word. Colton Price, who was something more than human, who answered to nothing and no one, who could peel back the edges of the sky like a god.

She'd been searching the shadows all her life, and now here he was, her name curling out of him in a whimper, and in this singular moment he felt like the answer to every question she'd ever had.

❧ 47 ❧

The horizon outside the window was a soft, burgeoning gray. For once, Colton had no sense of time. The minutes evaded him, abandoned him. Left him blissfully alone. He forgot, for a midnight, the speeding rush of seconds. The irreversible loss of moments. There was only Lane. There was only the feel of her curled into him, the room sinking into a whiteout haze. The sun rose and rose. In sheaves of bullion yellow and burnished gray. In pinpricks of gold that plumed, blister bright, over the tops of the neighboring buildings. He buried his face in the place where Lane's neck met her shoulder and shut his eyes.

Her fingers stayed twisted in his hair, nails scraping over his scalp in a way that made him impossibly tired. His limbs were weighted, his eyes heavy lidded.

Mine, rang the refrain in his head. *Mine, mine.*

He couldn't recall if it had stayed in his head or if he'd babbled it into her skin like an idiot.

He didn't care. He'd rendered himself untouchable, severing ties with Liam's mirror, giving Lane the shard of bone. He'd rid himself of collateral and in doing so made himself a target. The Apostle wouldn't want an errand boy he couldn't control.

The rising sun speared the room in swaths of too-bright gold, turning the lines of Lane indistinct. Like she was some strange, spectral thing. Like she might flicker out completely beneath the dawn.

"I love you," he said, half-asleep already.

He heard the intake of her breath. Felt the still of her finger against his clavicle. He didn't care. He didn't care if it scared her. She'd asked for truths. This was one of them. His most carefully guarded confession. And, anyway, he'd already given it to her. Caught up in the snow. Saying goodbye to his ghosts.

He was so close to unconsciousness that he barely heard her ask, "How did you do it?"

"Hmm?"

"How did you survive the ice?"

He was distinctly aware of her running a fingertip over the ink along his ribs. *Non omnis moriar.* Ink he'd never wanted. Ink he'd gotten in a dark room full of cloaked figures, lanterns igniting the artist's work in a bold slash of sickly yellow. Heralded by the rush of Latin, the chanting of the Priory. Promises made. Vows exchanged.

"Pledge, and you'll see your brother again."

"Pledge, and I'll teach you how to cheat death."

"Colton." Her hand was cool on his brow. He didn't understand how she was so cold when he was all fever. She smoothed his curls out of his eyes. "Don't sleep."

Another command, soft though it was. His lids fluttered, and he saw her sun-spangled before him, her hair falling around her face in a silvery curtain. And then there was black again. Black, and the slow-sinking into sleep.

"You're beautiful," he murmured.

"You're insufferable." She prodded him with an ice-cold toe. "Tell me. How did you survive?"

The creeping day was working its way through his lids in spikes of red. He pulled the sheets over his head. His voice was a muffle, half dreaming already.

"What makes you so sure I did?"

❧ 48 ❧

Get up, mayfly queen. There are things which need doing.

Delaney opened her eyes to find a red Matchbox car curving over the scarred roundabout of her knee. She lay perfectly still and watched as its brown-eyed driver steered the race car along her thigh, long fingers guiding it over the wrinkled hem of her shorts, the hard ridge of her hip. Beside her, Colton lay on his side, fully absorbed in his task.

"Good morning," she said when he'd reached her ribs. She rolled onto her back in a stretch and watched as the tires slipped over her T-shirt and toward her navel. "I'm glad you woke me. I need to get back to campus today."

He didn't appear to have heard her. Softly, he said, "Ask me for three things that are true."

"What, right now?"

"Yes."

"Okay." She tucked a hand beneath her cheek. "Three truths. Go."

"One." He drove the car lower. "I am deeply, sickeningly, alarmingly obsessed with you."

"I already knew that," she said, and wrested the car from his grasp. "So it's a waste of a truth."

He snatched it back, drawing her into him as he did. They rolled together until she was astride him, her knees pressed into the mattress. Slowly, she gathered the short crop of her hair into a stubby ponytail. He watched her do it, his jaw working.

331

"Two," he said. "I knew where you lived because sometimes I used to stand outside your house at night."

She stilled. Her hair fell loose from its tie, knifing around her jaw. "When?"

"When we were kids." His throat corded in a swallow. He tinkered with the car, his hands restless. "After the ice."

Wait. Don't run. I know you. I know you.

Her vision blurred. Her arms felt heavy. "Why did you stop?"

"Because," he said. "You kept following me and following me. You'd creep outside, half-asleep, like you could sense I was there. At first, it seemed harmless. I didn't know you'd get hurt."

She closed her eyes and remembered the high-beam brilliance of the Buick, the feel of screaming brakes jarring the sleepy dark awake. Her knees had been bloodied, her chest robbed of air. The boy she'd been chasing after was gone, swallowed up in the dark.

She rolled away from him, drawing her knees into her chest. "It was you."

"Yes." He sat up, repositioning himself so they came face-to-face in the tangled nest of his sheets.

"All that time, I thought I was going crazy. I thought I'd dreamt it all up. But it was you the whole time."

"It was." Then, "Are you angry with me?"

"Not anymore," she said.

"But you were?"

It was a simple question, but she found there was no simple answer. She recalled the implacable sadness of waking from a dreamless sleep, tucked safe in her bed with the dark empty beside her. The way she'd stare and stare into the woods and wish to see the face of a little shad-owed boy staring back. A prince of dark, a king of shades, a small, grieving boy with no one to go home to but her.

She felt suddenly and supremely ridiculous, for failing to recognize him right away. Absurd, that she hadn't known him from that very first moment in the elevator. Laughable, the way she'd spent years running, running after him in the dark only to slam straight into him in the light of day.

"I missed you," she said softly, "once you were gone. Isn't that stupid?"

"No." He didn't elaborate, and she didn't need him to. They'd both spent a lifetime yearning for something they didn't understand. And now here they were, and she had a hundred more questions for him. A thousand. They crowded in all at once. She ignored them.

"What's the third truth?"

He pulled his eyes shut. "I killed my brother."

"You didn't." She reached for him and thought better of it, fingers twisting in the hem of her T-shirt. "Colton, you didn't. He drowned."

"He did. But it was my fault. When I went through, he went in after me. He didn't even take the time to pull off all his gear." He opened his eyes, and his gaze was stricken with an old, dull grief. "Maybe if I'd been right there, just under the surface, he'd have been able to grab hold of me and pull me out."

"You couldn't have helped that," she said. "No one chooses to drown."

His smile didn't touch his eyes. "I was dying. I could feel it. The pain had stopped. Everything was dark. I couldn't even see the sun anymore. And then the water around me thinned. A door opened, and I went through it. I left my brother behind to die."

"Until I found you a week later," Delaney said, remembering.

"It wasn't a week for me." He braided his knuckles tight, as though kneading out an ache. "It was longer. It was endless. It was drowning, over and over, my lungs full of ice. It was dying on repeat, until time ceased to have any meaning. It drew to a standstill. For days. Years. Eons. Until one day, it stopped."

Her chest ached. "What happened? What changed?"

He peered up at her like he'd only just realized he hadn't been talking to himself.

"That's four truths," he pointed out.

"So give me four truths."

This time, the small curve of his smile was genuine. "I saw you," he said. "Standing in front of me with a pebble in your hand."

"Don't take this the wrong way," Adya said, once Delaney finally managed to put herself together and arrive at the campus's student center, "but you look different."

She slid into an empty chair beside Mackenzie, unwinding her scarf as she went. "Different, how?"

"It's the haircut." Mackenzie sipped a chocolate milk through a bendy straw and sized her up, one eye pinched shut. "It could be worse, I guess. At least you didn't give yourself bangs."

Across the table, Adya set down her fork, annoyed. "It's not the haircut. Lane, last time I saw you, you looked like you were prepping to play the part of 'starved Victorian widow' in the theater department's fall fete."

Delaney glowered as she pulled a stale croissant out of her bag. "That's kind of hurtful, actually."

"Maybe," Adya said. "But it's true. You were all pinched and pale and sweaty before—like you were coming down with a fever."

Delaney flaked away layers of her croissant, her appetite gone. "And now?"

"I don't know." Adya trilled her nails along the aluminum can of her drink. "Now it's like you're in high definition, and the rest of us are stuck in low resolution."

A slow creep of wings began to flutter through her veins. Then came the voice, low and slow. *A lepidoptera comes all apart in its chrysalis before emerging into its final form.*

She suppressed an unwelcome shudder, her croissant torn neatly in half.

"I think what Adya means to say," Mackenzie said, eyeballing the mess of bread on the table, "is that you look like you've been kissed. And honestly, thank God. It's been exhausting trying to pretend like you and Colton aren't dating."

"That's not at all what I mean, Mackenzie," Adya fired back, indignant, "and you know it. Look at her. *Look.*"

Mackenzie set down her drink and turned to peer at Delaney, inspecting her through a narrowed gaze. Delaney slid a buttery flake of croissant onto her tongue and let it sit there like a communion cracker. She felt a little bit like a glass doll on display.

Not glass, said the voice. *Diamond.*

"Stop," Delaney bit out, before she could stop herself.

"Fine," Mackenzie said, and looked away. "I was only doing what

Adya told me to do. Anyway, you look like regular-definition Laney to me. Although I did talk to my mom about your, uh, issue."

She said it like Delaney was experiencing a mild health inconvenience, and not like Delaney was being chewed up on the inside by something without a name.

"And?"

Mackenzie shrugged. "She didn't seem all that surprised. Apparently, you're not the first body-snatcher situation she's dealt with, which makes me wonder what else she hasn't told me."

"But what did she say? How do I get it out?"

You don't, skittered the voice. *We cannot be rent apart until I am good and ready to go.*

Next to her, Mackenzie spoke over the voice, unaware. "She said you should talk to Whitehall before you resort to any do-it-yourself–style exorcisms. Her words, not mine. Speaking of, are you going to Whitehall's Thanksgiving soiree on Sunday?"

"I don't know." She brushed crumbs off the thin pinstripe of her skirt. "I hadn't really thought about it."

"Come with us," Adya said, still eyeing Delaney with a skeptical, sideways stare. "You can pick his brain at the party. Plus, I want to keep an eye on you."

Delaney had been to Professor Whitehall's house before.

She stood on the gray-pavered walk, her grandmother's pelmeni cooling in her hands, and stared in rising horror at the whitewashed brick, the burlap-dotted garden. Her stomach was in upheaval. Her feet were leaden.

"Come on, ladies," Mackenzie called, already halfway up the walk.

Next to her, Haley looked startlingly normal in heeled boots and a red velvet dress, no animal onesie in sight. Mackenzie slid a hand in hers and called back, "We're not just fashionably late. We're late-late, *Adya*."

"I'm not sorry," Adya fired back, still retrieving her tray from the back of Haley's ancient purple Outback. "A mousse cake takes time to make. Is has *layers*. You can't just slap it in the oven and call it done."

"This is brownie slander," Mackenzie said, "and I won't stand for it."

The conversation faded into the trill between Delaney's ears. Her heart thudded into the wall of her chest. In the pocket of her pinafore, the bone shard sat tucked in a little velvet drawstring bag. It felt impossibly heavy. Weighted, like it knew it was back. Like it didn't want to be here.

"Lane?" Adya drew up next to her, tray in hand, cake dazzled in an assortment of bold-red berries. "Are you okay?"

"I don't think I can go in there," she whispered.

"Is it the crowds you're worried about? Because we can stick together. I'll cue you in if you look lost."

"That's not it." Her stomach swam. "It's just that this is where I took it from."

Adya frowned and peered up at the house. "No way. You mean—"

"The shard," Delaney finished for her. "Whitehall had it all along."

The door was open, and they let themselves in, toeing out of their shoes in the carpeted mudroom, with its glittering glass menagerie. The living room and kitchen were flooded already with students. They flocked around old and heavy furniture, the cushions well-loved, pillows mismatched and sagging.

"What are you going to do," Adya asked, sliding her cake tin onto a table of assorted desserts.

"I haven't decided yet."

"Will you call Colton?"

"I don't know." At the bottom of the stairs hung the painting of nyads, emerald loch glittering beneath a pastel sky. She guided Adya toward the bottom step, out of the current of incoming students. "Adya," she said in a whisper, low and urgent. "I brought it back."

Adya's face morphed into disgust. "You—what? You mean, you just have it in your pocket? Like a little rabbit's foot?"

"What was I supposed to do? He asked me to keep it safe."

"I don't think he meant carry it with you everywhere you go."

"Well, he definitely didn't mean bring it back here." She swallowed, her nerves coiling tight, and drew away from a rush of passing upperclassmen. "There's something else."

"What else?"

"There was someone upstairs, last time I came here. I think—I think they were locked in one of the rooms."

"Okay." Adya's mouth twisted at the corners. "That's a deeply terrifying thought."

"What if it's Nate? No one has seen him since he checked out of the hospital. What if Whitehall has been keeping him here all this time?"

Adya frowned. "Why?"

"I don't know, but I'm sure there's a reason."

"I'm not so sure," Adya said. "I've been casting out for Nate Schiller for days now. If he was here, I'd feel him."

Delaney didn't answer. Her attention had caught on the painting, several pieces clicking into place. The work was amateur—nothing at all like the professional pieces she'd seen in the lateral Boston gallery—but the feel of it was unmistakable.

Her stomach hooked. Somewhere in the kitchen, Dr. Whitehall was setting out platters of food, making small talk with his students. Whitehall, who'd threatened to expel her. Whitehall, who'd warned her away from Colton. Whitehall, who'd chastised her for interfering in Nate's case.

Whitehall, whose wife was a ghost.

"I'm going to go upstairs and look for Nate," she said.

Turning on her heel, she pushed out of the chuffing heat of the living room. Behind her, she heard the muffle of Adya's voice calling out her name, swallowed up in the inscrutable noise of chattering students.

Upstairs, the hall was the same carpeted hush. The walls were the same paneled dark. Everything smelled like an antiseptic clean. Bleach, strong enough to make her eyes water. And beneath it, something sour. Something dead.

She pushed her way into the very first room she found. The space was tight and small, the furniture covered with sheets. In the window the sun had begun to set, leaving the room disfigured in shadow, the remaining dregs of gold bleeding through the sheets until they turned sheer and pale, their innards skeletal against the dusk.

"Nate?"

"He's not here," sang a voice. She turned, startled, and saw no one. The door was still shut. The room was quiet. "He's not anywhere. Poor little dead boy, all gone, gone away."

Something moved through the space. Unseen, shuffling. It ruffled the sheets in its wake. The shadows climbed the walls, made oblong beneath the sinking sun, and she was given the distinct sense that the dead were doing their best to claw their way free of this room where she'd brought them.

Out.

Out.

We want out.

The smell of rot clung to the air. In the clutter, something laughed.

"So pretty, so neat," sang the voice, nearer now than before. "So good and sweet to eat."

"Who are you?" She inched her way backward, moving toward the door. In the bowels of the room, something clattered to the floor. A sheet fell away, revealing the paint-splattered wood of an artist's easel.

"Who," sang the voice. "Who? Who are we? We are you."

She reached behind her, fumbling for a doorknob. "That doesn't make any sense."

"Oh yes, it does. It makes perfect sense, little sweet, little flower, little pretty-itty Wednesday. We live together, he and I, like you live together, you and it. Tucked away inside. Nibbling like varmint." A giggle, shrill. "Only I am suckling on the teat of decay and you are going to live forever. My mad, forever kin. A girl made god. How the demon boy must worship at your feet."

Closer, closer. It dragged itself over the floor, pulling itself like a body clawing out of a grave.

And then it stood.

She clapped her hand over her mouth, stifling a scream.

It was a man, or what was left of a man. His head was concave, bashed in as if by a heavy object. His face was shrunken, skeletal, skin rotted to bone in places. His clothes were a shredded mess, arms pocked by road rash. Silver hair rose in broken clumps along his scalp.

Brethren, crooned the thing in her bones. *There you are.*

"What are you?"

"I am half-alive and all immortal." The lidless stare went wide. "Didn't they tell you? Isn't that their favorite thing to say? Non omnis moriar, we shall not wholly die." He laughed again, high and clear and cold. "What rot. What rubbish. Man is not made to last forever. This one has been dead for many years. He invited me inside and I whispered in his head. I sang in his skin. I told him all my secrets. He could have lived forever, but instead he died, crash, on the side of the road, and now I play him like a harpsichord."

Delaney slammed into the door. Her phone clattered hard against the floor and she left it, reaching for the knob, fumbling to get it open. The figure—the corpse—didn't run. It didn't move at all. It only watched her, teeth visible through a close-lipped smile.

"I would like," it said, regarding her oddly, "to speak with my kin."

Stay, ordered her haunt. *There are amends to be made.*

She didn't listen. She didn't have a chance. The door opened and she fell out into the hall, slamming into a figure as she went. This time, the scream that came out of her was full-bodied. She fell back, scrabbling away, and stumbled directly into the path of Richard Whitehall.

He was dressed for the holidays, in a collared shirt and festive vest, the wool stitched with fat dancing turkeys. His glasses sat pushed up on his head, and he regarded her through a cold, cold look.

"Interesting" was all he said.

"There's something—" She struggled to catch her breath, barely able to get the words out. Her heart hammered hard enough to hurt. "There's something in there. Something dead."

Whitehall only glanced over her shoulder, peering into the stuffy silence of the sheet-wrapped room. The easel lay shattered across the floor, wood splintered. His eye twitched.

"I'm looking for an old friend of mine," he said, pulling the door shut. "A man by the name of Mark Meeker. Do you know him?"

"No," Delaney lied. Her heart thundered against her chest.

With a sigh, Whitehall pulled his glasses into place. "His phone is off. Has been for days. But he sent a text, just before he went missing. Do you know what it said?"

For once, Delaney wished the voice within her had something clever to say. "No," she said again.

Whitehall's smile was small and cerebral. A professor's smile, carefully crafted. "'I found her.' *Her*. Now, isn't that interesting?" His smile waned. His hand lingered on the doorknob, holding shut the way to his wife's studio. Holding shut the way to that terrible, rotting thing.

"I meant what I said, Ms. Meyers-Petrov," he said. "You were an extraordinary student. A good girl, with a good head on your shoulders. You should have heeded my advice. You should have stayed far away from Colton Price. I'm afraid the cost of keeping his company will be far higher than you were willing to pay. I'm sorry it's come to this."

Something blunt collided with the crown of her head.

And then she saw only black.

❦ 49 ❧

Colton Price had a carefully curated routine. It looked like this: He woke up. He stretched. He went down into the basement and punished his muscles in a careful workout regimen. When it was done, he went to the kitchen and prepared himself a shake. He showered, listening to the rush of water, the masterful compositions of Handel. *Agrippina. Solomon.* Sometimes, if he was in the mood for it, *Judas Maccabeus.* In and out. Five minutes or less.

It was the same every day.

But not today.

Today he sat in a room he hadn't been inside in a very long time. In a dusty blue beanbag his mother had called "tacky" and "abominable" and his brother had called "comfortable" and "I'm getting it anyway."

He was much too large for it now. His knees stuck out at odd angles. The filling shifted, older and more tired than it had any right to be, and his tailbone rested flush against the hardwood beneath.

He didn't move. He looked at the bed. It was impeccably made. Not by Liam, but by the maid who had worked here once upon a time, before the house became a tomb. The bedspread was black-and-white checkered flannel. The cluster of fringed throw pillows were insisted on by their mother. Catalogue perfect. Home-and-garden pictorial. The headboard was gray oak. The flat top was lined with trophies.

They stared at him.

Colton stared back.

The light from the window was webbed in frost, the thick cover of ice magnifying the sun until it bathed the trophies in refracted gold. Set the dust alight on their etched marble columns. On shoulders of little metal sportsmen gilt in gleaming paints. His father had smashed a few of them after Liam died. Those were still on the floor. Shattered. Grotesque. Broken golden men for a buried golden boy. They sat at odd angles, arms akimbo or missing entirely. Time ran away and away from him, but here in this room it stood perfectly still.

"I came to say goodbye," he said into the quiet.

Downstairs, the doorbell rang. He ignored it. He wasn't even certain what time it was. For once, he hadn't thought to wear his watch. He'd woken to a sunrise. He'd woken to Lane. For the first time in a long time, he wasn't terrified by the thought of time careening to a stop.

The doorbell rang again.

"Just let yourselves in," he said. "I've been waiting."

They were late. He'd expected them sooner. He'd broken the Priory's cardinal rule. The Priory's only rule. Fed to him in a warning the day he'd accepted his initiate into Godbole's elusive chapter.

"One day soon, a girl named Delaney Meyers-Petrov will come to Godbole. You will stay away from her. Do you understand?"

A laugh built in his chest. Died in his throat. He couldn't believe he'd ever thought he could stay away. Whitehall knew, from the very moment he'd seen Colton's test results, that Colton was less a boy and more a creature. He knew, in the way Colton's mother had known, that Colton had come back different. That, in ripping himself from Hell, he'd carried a part of it home with him. That he'd nursed it, all this time, this tether to a world not meant for the living.

"*There is no good that can come of it*," Whitehall told him once. He'd been afraid of them. Of the possibility of their union, a boy half-dead and the girl who possessed the power to command him. He'd been terrified to think that quiet, obedient Colton might obey some-one other than him. He had, Colton thought, grown to like it a little too much—having sole dominion over something forged in hellfire.

"*There is an order that must be maintained here, Mr. Price. You and I are playing with something completely unprecedented, and I cannot do this without you. Focus on your brother. Stay away from the girl. Do not place yourself in a position where she might become a distraction.*"

The doorbell rang and rang and rang, as if someone was pushing the buttons a dozen times over. It heralded out a grating tune, ringing all through the house.

"Jesus Christ." He pulled himself up from the beanbag. He shut the door, whisper soft, on Liam's ghost. He headed down the stairs, still in gym shorts and an old T-shirt, assailed by the constant screech of the bell. "Jesus," he said again, wrenching open the door. "*What?*"

Adya Dawoud stood huddled on the stoop, her hijab the color of the sky, her boots melting the iced-over slush. The sound of the bell still reverberated through the foyer. Over her shoulder, Mackenzie Beckett idled on the sidewalk, her gaze thunderous. A sophomore whose name he couldn't quite recall hovered a few steps behind, shivering in a thin dress the color of blood.

"I don't recall inviting any of you over," Colton said.

"Lane is gone." The words were out of Dawoud before he'd finished speaking. At her news, he felt everything in him go resolutely still.

"What do you mean, gone?"

"We were all at Whitehall's Thanksgiving potluck and she just—"
Dawoud flared her fingers in a *poof* motion. "Left."

"You don't *look* like you've been in an accident," Beckett noted,
peering up at Colton through a stare like razor wire. Colton ignored
her, his focus trained on Dawoud.

"She went to Whitehall's," he repeated, a little dumbly. They'd
spoken on the phone just that morning, but she hadn't mentioned
Whitehall. He would have warned her against it. He would have told
her what waited for her there, locked upstairs in the empty studio. He
would have told her that she was walking into something she might
not walk away from.

"It's him," Dawoud said. "Isn't it? Whitehall is the reason all those
boys are dead."

"Yes," Colton said.

"What will he do to Lane?"

The question tore through him. Lane was his. She'd always been
his. And he was hers. They were painted the same shades. Threaded
with the same lines. He'd spent his whole life drawn to her, and she
to him. And Whitehall knew it. He knew it, and so he wouldn't be
careful with her.

He didn't answer Dawoud's question. Instead, he asked, "Have you
tried calling her?"

Dawoud's only response was to fish a phone out of the pocket of
her coat. The screen was black, glass splintered. He recognized the
case at once. Panic tightened his throat.

"Where did you find it?"

"Second floor," Dawoud said. "Outside one of the bedrooms."

"And where was Whitehall?"

"Gone."

"Shit." Colton speared his hand through his curls. "Fuck."

"Is it a demon?" Beckett asked, her stare unrelenting. "Inside of Lane? I talked to my mom, and she told me there are some malignant spirits who are capable of acting as hitchhikers. She called them skinwalkers."

"It's not a demon," said the sophomore in the red dress, speaking through chattering teeth. "I saw Lane in the library the other night. There's something looking out of her, but it's not demonic. Demons are made."

Adya looked annoyed. "And how do you know?"

The sophomore shrugged. "I read."

"She's right," Colton said. He knew enough of Hell to know that demons were made. Cobbled from the pleas of a small and begging boy. Packed with teeth and with tethers. Left crawling on all fours like an animal, drawn to the warmth of a little, living thing all clad in color.

Three sets of eyes found his as he fished in his pocket for his keys. He wasn't sure where Whitehall might have taken her. He wasn't sure, but he had a pretty good clue. "There's nothing demonic inside of Delaney," he said, pushing past them and heading for his car. "But you're not far from the truth."

"What else could it be?" Dawoud tailed him along the salted sidewalk, hugging her arms to herself in an effort to stave off the cold. Several spaces away, Colton's BMW chirped awake, headlights shelled in ice.

Behind him, he heard Beckett say, "Your car doesn't look like it's been in an accident, either."

"*Price.*" Dawoud was jogging to keep up now, her boots unwieldy against the cemented sleet. "What is it, if not a demon?"

He didn't look at her as he pulled open the driver's door. It gave with a protest, hinges frozen. Overhead, the sky was a flat November gray. His chest was a hollow.

"It doesn't have a name."

Out of the corner of his eye, he was faintly aware of a car turning the corner. He caught the flash of headlights, heard the careen of tires. Rubber on asphalt. Rubber on sleet. A black car, with blacked-out windows. Losing traction. Beckett's eyes met his over the glass-sheeted roof of his car.

"Oh," she said. "I had the time wrong."

And then he felt the impact.

❧ 50 ❧

Wake up, Delaney Meyers-Petrov. It is time to die.

Delaney woke to a splitting headache. She woke to the smell of decay. She was on the floor, her wrists and ankles bound in sleek, ceremonial rope. The room around her was dim, flooded with shadows that fussed and preened, worrying at her in cool fingers of dark.

Wake, they said.

Wake, wake, wake.

Miraculously, her implant hadn't run low on battery. Sound came to her in snatches, some more easily identifiable than others. Somewhere nearby, water drip, drip, dripped from a pipe. Distant trees rubbed their leathery branches. Color ran back into the room around her as her eyes adjusted to the low, low light.

She was in the Sanctum. In front of her was the wall of names, rising up in a formidable monolith of mottled blue black. The dead pool—the broad calligraphy of Nate's name visible from where she lay, her knees rammed into her stomach in a forced fetal position.

Several feet away, there lay a figure in the dark.

"Hello?" Her voice cast out of her. It shuddered the shadows. Sent them reeling. The figure on the ground didn't move. Again, she cried out, "Hello?"

All that rose up to meet her was the cold, cold dark and that chilly, irreducible voice inside her head. *There is no one home inside that one. All that lived there has gone away.*

The smell of rot mushroomed through the room in fermented, fruity notes. Rolling onto her knees, she propped her elbows on the floor. The door had been left open some time, and sticky yellow pine needles adhered to her forearms as she dragged herself inch by inch through the silver spill of coins.

The ambiguous form of the body took shape, solidifying into the slouching black of a hoodie, the coiled white wire of earbuds.

"Nate." His name rang through the room in a voice she didn't recognize. Her lungs ached. "Nate," she said again. "*Nate*, get up."

He didn't obey. He didn't move. A cloud of silvered motes hung suspended in the light over his frame, the air undisturbed. A sour taste crept up the back of her throat. Digging her elbows into his side, she dragged his considerable heft toward her until he rolled, arms sprawled, onto a bed of scattered pennies. The fetid smell of decomposition washed over her and she was very nearly ill. His face was bloated with several days' worth of decay. His mouth hung slack. His eyes were the same clean, clear blue as his mother's.

"This is in my head," she said, though she knew it wasn't. "It's happening in my head."

It is not, said that unwelcome voice. *I have already told you.*

She ignored it, staring down at Nate like she might catch his eye. Like he might suddenly shift and blink up at her, the way Colton did that day at the pond.

Her voice tumbled out of her in a whisper. "Where are you, really?"

"He's right here," came a voice. "Same as you or I."

A light flickered to life—a candle lit by an unseen hand. Another followed, setting the room and its contents ablaze. She blinked like a vole, drawing back from the stark shift in the room as if she, too, were made of shadow. Fleeing to the underneaths and the in-betweens, clawing up the walls. Only Nate stayed still, his skin waxen in the glow.

Run, whispered the dark, banished from her by flickering beads of fire. *Run away*.

Richard Whitehall appeared in her field of vision, dragging a chair behind him. The legs stuttered over stone in a brittle *tut-tut-tut*. Propping it a few feet from her, he lowered himself gingerly onto the edge of the seat.

For a long time, there was silence. Silence, save for the distant *plink* of water and the unsteady wheeze of Delaney's breathing. Expelling a huff, Whitehall pulled his glasses down to clean them, the way she'd watched him do all semester. Her mentor. Her teacher. Her captor. Everything he'd done had always seemed performative. This was no different.

"Remarkable" was all he said. He took his time polishing the lenses, holding the spectacles up for careful scrutiny before replacing them along the wide bridge of his nose. "You don't look any different. Right under my nose, seated in my lecture hall, and I didn't even see it. How do you feel? Strange, I'd imagine."

Her eyes pinched. Her throat was all sour. "What did you do to Nate?"

"I did nothing. I merely gave him the tools he needed to seek eternal life. He sought it, as did the others. He failed, as did the others."

"You killed him." The accusation spat out of her like poison.

The look Whitehall gave her was clinically sad. As though he were witnessing a tragedy from afar. As though she were a spectacle, and he the observer. Softly, he said, "Nathaniel Schiller went up against the gods and was deemed unworthy. But you? My god, look at you."

Delaney didn't answer. The shadows moaned, displeased. She could feel their fear. They wanted to leave this place. They wanted to stay wherever she was. The surety of it was so strong that she wasn't sure how she'd ignored it for so many years. She flexed her fingers, testing out the tightness of the rope. Too tight, too tight to wriggle free.

"I'd like to go home," she said when Whitehall continued to stare.

He let out a breath. "Spectacular. Your motor functions seem to be your own. Your speech patterns have remained the same. Home, you say. Home is—where? Can you confirm? Do you know a Mia Petrova and a Jace Meyers? Do you recognize those names?"

Her parents. *Her parents.* "My parents will be worried if I don't call to check in."

"Ah." He smiled a beatific smile. "Beautiful. Your cognitive functioning looks to be perfectly operative. We'll have to do a complete workup of course, but this—this is incredible. Beyond anything we've seen in past trials." He leaned forward, padded elbows resting on his knees. "How did you do it?"

She pulled at her binds again, a useless endeavor. Next to her, Nate stared and stared. "Do what?"

"How did you invite it inside you?"

"I don't know what you're talking about."

You do, crooned the voice. The being that was not her own. *We're fast friends, aren't we, Delaney Meyers-Petrov? Thick as thieves, you and me and we.*

Whitehall's smile flickered. He rose to his feet, circling around his chair to grip the spine between knuckles gone white.

"The others died," he said. "All of them. Schiller, Peretti, Guzman, Kostopoulos. I sent subject after subject into purgatory. Subject after subject was spat out on the mouth of Hell, babbling and strange, their skin coming loose. The plan was for them to look the depths of the underworld in the eye and carry a piece of it back out with them. A sliver of immortality. A slice of the afterlife. It never worked. The being inside them didn't need a soul, only a body. It ate away at the spirit until all that remained was a husk. And then it played mad puppeteer with the corpse."

Not us, said the voice. *Not we. I'm curled up along your bones like a happy cat.*

"Devan Godbole was the first," Whitehall continued. "He was my associate, my partner—the only man I'd ever met who could peel back the doors between worlds. In his case, it was an accident. We had no idea something else was living inside of him until he died. The greatest of scientific discoveries are often accidental. Do you know that?"

He glanced sidelong at her, waiting for an answer. When none came, he continued. "Sir Alexander Fleming discovered penicillin when he left petri dishes of staphylococcus stacked on a bench while he went on holiday. Charles Goodyear spilled rubber and sulfur on a hot stove and, in doing so, revolutionized the way tires were made. Men of legend. Men of change." His smile was rapturous. "Like them, I discovered immortality quite by chance. I hadn't meant to do it. But I did. I stumbled upon poor Devan dying on the side of a winding backroad and found, living within him, a malfeasance which could be neither killed nor exorcised."

The old man is a fool, sang the voice. *Tell him so.*

But Delaney didn't. She couldn't. She was thinking only of the terrible thing in Whitehall's upstairs bedroom, his head bashed in, his eyes wild, empty gulfs. She was thinking only of Nate, smiling that strange, inhuman smile, whispering secrets deep inside her head.

That was me, corrected the thing within her. It sounded annoyed. *Not the boy. The boy did nothing but cry. He was weak. He was small. He died almost instantly. They always do.*

"Why?" Delaney asked, because she wanted the voice in her head to go silent.

"Why do men seek immortality?" Whitehall boomed out a laugh. "Mankind has been seeking the elixir of life since the dawn of time. I'm merely the first to bottle it."

"If what you're saying is true, then you've knowingly killed multiple students."

"They knew the risks." He leaned over the back of his chair. "Every single one of them had someone they'd do anything to save. Every single one of them was terrified by the prospect of loss. It's a terrible thing, to say goodbye. I gave them an opportunity to circumvent death, and they took it. They, like me, saw the vast potential of a life without end. They were sworn into the Priory and branded loyal. They consented to share themselves with something immortal in order to live forever. The hope was, once perfected, they might share their discovery with their loved ones. Both on the edge of the grave and beyond. Most unfortunately, none of them succeeded."

The thing inside her giggled.

"Until me."

"Until you." His smile widened.

She closed her eyes. Opened them again. Her insides sang like a struck bell, shivering brass moving through her veins in a tintinnabu-lation. Nate peered up at her in an empty, plaintive stare. His eyes were blue, blue, blue. She'd never noticed.

"What about Colton?"

Whitehall made a soft, disappointed noise. "What about him?"

"The shard of bone. It was in your office."

"Ah," he breathed. "Was that you who broke into my house? Devan wouldn't say. He loves a riddle. Clever of Price, to have the sole person he's beholden to take possession of his token."

"Token?"

"Didn't he tell you? It's no ordinary thing, for someone dead to pull themselves out of the afterlife. But Colton Price is no ordinary boy. He carved pieces of himself away. He left them scattered about like Hansel in the wood. The way he tells it, he caught sight of a bright little light and followed it home." His eyes narrowed, and he peered down at Delaney through a steely gaze. "Do you know, Ms. Meyers-Petrov, the power of a True Name?"

She held her tongue. The thing inside of her rattled in anticipation.

"In Homer's *Odyssey*, Odysseus is captured by the giant Polyphemus. He is exceedingly careful not to reveal his name to the giant, to keep from being controlled. He instead gives a false name."

"Nobody," Delaney said, because she knew the tale.

Whitehall looked pleased. "A token is no true name, but it is iden-tical to Colton Price's true nature. And thus, through it, he can be controlled. As any demon might be controlled."

Her eyes jolted back to his. Her chest constricted. The edges of the room seemed to winnow in and out, the shadows shuddering in their keep. Her voice came out in a whisper, tremulous and so very afraid.

"What did you say?"

"This is news to you. It shouldn't be." Whitehall tutted his tongue. "Did you think he was human? All this time, did you think him wholly alive? You may be able to command the dead, Ms. Meyers-Petrov, but even you cannot order them back from beyond the grave."

Colton Price, who had always seemed so cold. Colton Price, who reminded her of something seraphic. Mars, god of war, resplendent and undying. Indomitable, impossible Colton.

"What do you mean?" Her voice was a scrape. "What do you mean, he's not human?"

"I mean," said Whitehall, pushing his glasses farther up on his nose, "that Colton Price drowned when he was nine years old, and he returned something *other*. One does not simply scrape himself free of death and come away whole. He walks like a boy, sure. Talks like a boy, yes. But there's sulfur in his bones and brimstone in his veins. He's a creature of Hades, and he's as bound to Hell as any haunt."

The boy carved out much of himself years ago. That was what the voice whispered to her, the night they'd been caught beneath the slow-falling snow. The night she'd looked at him all gilt in lamplight and thought him holy. In the pocket of her pinafore, the bone shard felt impossibly heavy.

"Forget Price." Whitehall's mouth was a grim line, his patience waning. "He's no longer willing to cooperate, and therefore he has outrun his usefulness to me. I won't waste another moment of my time. He'll be taken care of, and that's that."

"Taken care of." Her voice sounded as if it came from a hundred yards away. Behind her, the dark quavered, afraid. "You mean kill him?"

"We won't dwell on it," Whitehall said, brushing her off as if shooing away a fly. "The loss of Price is a disappointment, to be sure, but science is about moving forward. It's about progress. You're a success, Ms. Meyers-Petrov. That's something to celebrate. Something in you has allowed you to house an immortal spirit without consequence. We're going to find out what that is and harness it."

Harnessed, hissed that odious voice, audibly irate. *I cannot be harnessed. I, who have no name. I, who was here before the race of men. I, who will remain when they are dust.*

"Shut up," she said, without quite meaning to. "Shut *up*."

In front of her, Whitehall's energy shifted visibly, moving from frustration to curiosity, his eyes bright. "It speaks to you," he marveled. "Doesn't it?"

She clamped her mouth shut. It was taking everything in her not to scream. Not to thrash the way the dead thrashed, contorting over the dripping stone.

"Ms. Meyers-Petrov." Whitehall scooted his chair closer. "We are, you and I, on the brink of having dominion over death. I kindly ask you to indulge me. What is it saying?"

Tell him, slithered the voice, *we say, Die, you old pig.*

She bit her tongue. She willed the voice silent. She willed the tears dry. Throat hoarse, she asked, "What is it you want? Out of all of this."

The flames burgeoned bright in the flat lenses of Whitehall's glasses. He looked, for a moment, unbearably sad. "I want my wife back," he said.

"Your wife is dead." She didn't care if it was cruel. It was the truth.

"On this plane," Whitehall agreed. "Not the others. And until she's gone in every existence, there's a chance. Now, there's a reason you

357

haven't withered beneath the strain of playing host. We're going to find out why."

Delaney's chest felt stitched tight. It was difficult to draw breath. The ropes chafed her wrists bloody. Coins bit into her skin. As discreetly as she could, she scooped a penny into her hand, tucking it out of sight.

"Tell me," Whitehall ordered, "what the creature says when it speaks to you."

She didn't have a chance to formulate a response. All at once, the candles guttered out. Something shattered against stone. In the sudden onset of dark, the dead swarmed her like flies. She heard the buzz of them between her ears, their cries overlapping and strange. Shriveled and shrill, a tinnitus whistle through her skull.

And then, beneath it, a laugh like crinkling paper.

"My dear, my darling, my Dickie," came a voice she recognized— a voice she'd heard slithering through the twilit dark of Whitehall's second-story studio. A voice that belonged to a face mottled with decay, a skeleton's grin, a corpse's stare. "You left me home. You know how I despise being left at home."

Ah, murmured the thing in her veins. *My brethren.*

A mass shuffling moved through the room. It was the sound of shadows, shambling one into the other. It was the scrape of something unnatural dragging over stone.

"Get out," Delaney heard Whitehall command. "I did not invite you."

"I go where you go, old friend. You and I and we."

The candles flared to life all at once, flames climbing preternaturally high. It threw the room first into stark relief, and then into chaos.

Lit from beneath, Whitehall looked suddenly skeletal, the hollows of him engulfed in shadow, his mouth an open O of horror.

At the wall, the first of the names caught flame.

I believe, sang the beast in her bones, *it is time for us to bring this chapter to a close.*

⚜ 51 ⚜

ric Hayes had never been all that interested in immortality. He'd never had aspirations of cheating the afterlife. He had, for all intents and purposes, led a very normal life. There were no horror movies allowed in his house. No video games, no ghost stories. He'd been made to brush his teeth and go to bed at a reasonable hour. He said his prayers every night, the way his grandmother taught him. He received decent grades in school. He had a solid group of friends. He'd played fullback for his high school's football team until, in his junior year, he'd been in such a horrible collision midplay that it landed him in the hospital with a spinal injury that left him unable to walk for weeks.

"GiGi says you saw Jesus," his sister sang to him when he woke. She'd been perched on the edge of his bed, little legs kicking, her hair done in bows, the fat head of her favorite bear sagging onto its protruding stomach. *"I heard her telling your coach you're not allowed to play anymore."*

He'd had few encounters with the preternatural. Once, when he was eleven years old, his grandmother found him and his sister crouched around a Ouija board and she'd smacked him so hard across the back of the knuckles his hand stung for hours.

"That's evil," she'd said, in the soft, unflinching way she said everything. *"Out. I won't have it in my house."*

He'd grown up attending church. Not passionately, but obediently. Every Sunday found him trying fruitlessly to fit his fast-stretching limbs into a too-thin wooden pew. Head down, Bible open, the buttons on his checkered dress shirt done up so close to his throat he'd become convinced his grandmother meant to choke him with it. He'd mouth along with the rest of the congregation as they sang the hymns. With his grandmother's elbow in his side, he'd mumble the words of the doxology: *"Praise him, praise him, praise him, praise him, Jesus, blessed Savior, he's worthy to be praised."*

Sometimes—after his accident—when the congregation bowed their heads to pray, he thought he saw the great glass icons move behind the pulpit. A drip of blood. A rustle of robes. The crook of a finger. It was only ever out of the corner of his eye. It was only ever a trick of the light.

It chilled him all the same.

He'd never been tempted by the things that tempted Richard Whitehall. Fooling death, channeling things that had no name. *"Toying with the devil,"* his grandmother would say. She'd cross herself and make him say a penance. She'd heat him a bowl of soup and tell him, again, how Christ spent forty days and forty nights in the wilderness.

He'd staked everything he had on the promise of a football scholarship. But then the accident happened. The scouts stopped calling. His medical bills piled higher. His grandmother started forgetting little things. She left the burners lit on the stove. She let the house fill with smoke. And so he'd registered for the placement test the day he turned seventeen. If it hadn't been for his injury, his proctor said, they might have placed him in the pros.

He'd been a hell of a fullback.

Instead, his written submission, his cognitive exam all landed him at Godbole. Marvelous, Whitehall called him, delighted by his ability to see the doors move out of the corner of his eye. Only ever a glimpse. Only ever a shudder. When he stepped through a rift in time and space, he felt the impact all along his spinal cord. A crunch of bone. A grit of teeth. And then it was over.

It was only meant to be a free ride. He hadn't wanted to play around with the occult. But then his grandmother forgot his name at Thanksgiving dinner. Sometime after that, his sister called to say she'd found her standing down by the harbor in an early December snow, her feet bare, her nightgown unraveling.

The doctors told them it was incurable. Just a part of aging.

But Whitehall had a remedy.

Eric hadn't wanted to watch anyone die, he only wanted to stop death in its tracks.

He certainly hadn't wanted to smash into Colton Price's car. But he'd been speeding, driving as fast as he could, and the wheels lost traction as he took the corner onto the narrow street toward Price's family home. Skidding, he'd done his best to apply the brakes. He'd pumped and let go. Pumped and let go. He gave the wheel space to turn. He'd been raised on Boston winters, and he knew how to handle himself in inclement weather.

He still slammed into Colton's BMW anyway.

"She's gone, isn't she?" Price asked now, his breath fogging the front passenger window. They were on Storrow. They were racing through traffic. "Your grandmother."

Eric choked down the lump in his throat, taking the indicated turn-off. Something on the front of his car was rattling—the bumper, maybe—dragging along the road in sparks and hops. Flint against stone. "Yes," he said.

"When?"

"Yesterday morning."

Price stared into the middle distance, the blood draining out of his face. "We were so close."

"That's the thing," Eric said, changing lanes. "I don't think we were."

Between the seats, a flash of red curls appeared. "What's going to happen?" Mackenzie Beckett asked. "With Lane?"

"You should sit down, Mackenzie," Adya Dawoud chimed in from the back. "This car has been in one accident already today. It's barely road safe at this point."

"I don't die in a car accident." Mackenzie's bright eyes met Eric's in the rearview mirror. "*Lane*," she said, all emphasis. "*Talk*."

"Godbole is a cover," Eric explained. "All of it. The note-taking. The observations. All the work you've done and will do. It's just a straw man. A front."

"For what?" Adya asked. The row of trees outside ran past in cold, crystalline strips of dark. It reminded Eric of noisy Christmas mornings, falling over his sister to be the first down the stairs. Of sleepy car rides to church, the rear windows of the minivan still pebbled in ice.

The tattoo on his arm stung for weeks after he'd pledged. His grandmother hadn't been quiet about her disapproval. They'd moved her to the nursing home by then, and her memory was mostly in pieces. But she still remembered the foremost tenets of the faith she'd worked so hard to instill in her grandkids. She'd taken him by the ear, the calluses on her fingers hewn from decades of dish soaps and detergents. The force of her little frame bent him clean in half.

"That's the devil's Latin, Eric Carson Hayes. What did I tell you about the devil?"

"Whitehall is chasing immortality," Price said when Eric stayed quiet.

Mackenzie remained crushed between the two front seats, nails embedded in Eric's headrest. "What does he want with Lane?"

"Lane has managed to do what everyone else couldn't," Eric explained when Price seemed determined to say nothing. He'd tipped his head back against the headrest of his seat, his eyes squeezed shut. The wound along the edge of his mouth had pinked over in the days since Eric saw him last. Meeker had done that—pushing just a little bit too far. Hitting just a little bit too hard. Price had taken it without flinching, his eyes cold and black and other. Eric's stomach swam.

He tightened his grip on the wheel and said, "She's given Whitehall his cure."

"A cure?"

"Yeah, you know," he said. "For death."

"It's not a common cold." Adya sounded disgusted.

Price didn't open his eyes. "'And do not fear those who kill the body but cannot kill the soul. Rather fear him who can destroy both soul and body in Hell.'" Silence followed. Eric took the nearest exit, the blinker clicking through the car in a too-loud staccato. Flatly, Price added, "New Testament, Matthew, chapter ten, verse twenty-eight. Whitehall's fixation. He's been calling himself the Apostle for years."

"This is giving me the creeps," Adya said. "In case anyone was curious. What will Dr. Whitehall do with Lane?"

Eric braked, drawing to a stop as the light ahead clicked from yellow to red. The nurse on the phone told him his grandmother went in her sleep. Eyes closed, a smile on her face. His classmates went screaming.

Ripped limb to limb by whatever beast they'd clung to in the dark. He didn't see how that could possibly be the better alternative.

Voice cracking, he said, "He wants to find out how Lane has managed to successfully adapt to immortality when everyone else failed."

"Price," Mackenzie said suddenly, "roll down your window."

"You look like you're about to hurl," Adya added.

Price sat as if carved from stone, his jaw clenched, his stare dead ahead. When he didn't move, Eric did it for him, lowering the glass until the wind bit through the crack in a fanning chuff of bitter cold. It was the wrong thing to do.

The smell of smoke hit them first. It slipped into the car in spirals. It burned the air, fringed in still-smoldering strips of crumbling paper. Up ahead, the campus quad was thronged with people. Fire trucks lined the walkway, sirens flashing in orbs of red and blue, red and blue, red and blue.

"What the hell?" The question came from the back seat, from Mackenzie, but the sentiment was echoed in all of them. Price flung open the door, already halfway into a run. On the far side of the quad, smoke rose into the air in great columns of gray.

Deep within the woods, the Sanctum was on fire.

❧ 52 ❧

Delaney could see the dead.

That was the first thing she noticed. They stood like sentinels, for once silent and still instead of grasping and writhing, tearing at the ground where she walked. They stood posted at the edges of a ripped-open door, their faces gaunt and incorporeal, their eyes blazing hollows. They watched her and she watched them, and she had the distinct sense they were waiting for her.

They are, said the voice she'd come to expect. The voice she loathed, lamented. The voice she had, in the deepest, darkest parts of her, begun to trust. *They are always waiting for you, Delaney Meyers-Petrov. You are the warmth to which dying things cling.*

The room around her was aflame. To her right was a form. A figure, slumped and shuddering and afraid. His face was lined with tracks of red, gouges he'd put there by his own hand. His eyes were big and black. There was drool on his chin.

"Help," said Richard Whitehall, trying and failing to stand. "Help me."

She stepped away, out of his reach. Out of his direct line of sight. She was trying, as she had been for the past several minutes, to recall how she'd gotten here. Here, where she'd first run into Nate. Here, where she'd written her name on the wall. Here, at the end of all things.

She knew what it wanted her to do.

It wanted her to die.

It's not that I want you to die, contested that ever-present voice. *It's only that you will, before the end. You are strong, Delaney Meyers-Petrov, but mortal bones only bend so far before they break. And the work I must do will snap each and every one.*

"Why?" She asked the question aloud, turning the penny over and over in her hand. Clinging to it. "Why are you here? Why come at all?"

The doors have been open for too long. The path through Hell was not meant for living men to travel.

"What about Colton?" His name tasted acrid on her tongue. It twisted something up inside her. Colton Price, who she'd hated. Colton Price, who she'd loved. Colton Price, who had taken her hands and kissed her as the bowels of the afterlife thrashed all around them. Who had ferried her through Hell and back without batting an eye.

Colton Price, who was something other.

The boy is made of Hell, came the voice. *And it of him. He bargained away pieces of himself long ago. In doing so, he earned the right to cross our fields unharmed.*

Asphodel fields. Elysian fields. Her stomach was a stone. Her stories were coming true and coming true.

End this, whispered the dark.

End this, end this.

Across the screen of sputtering smoke, the figure of Richard Whitehall fell impossibly still. The feeble keen of his cries went quiet. Delaney probed herself, expecting to feel something. An ache. A terror. There was only the dull throb of emptiness in her chest. Only numb. Only a name, beating like a pulse.

Colton. Colton.

Colton, all full of secrets. Colton, who kept his true self shut away. Who'd carved pieces of himself out at her insistence. The dead took up her thoughts in an echo, the sound a fingerprint against their diaphanous pall. *Colton. Colton. Colton.* They gnashed their teeth. They tore at their scalps. They flickered in and out in wailing, winnowing blinks. She stayed resolutely still and stared at the body on the floor.

"Is he dead," she asked. "Whitehall?"

A laugh moved through her like a shiver. *My brother has slipped from his old body into this one. He is not acclimating as well as you. Already he has begun to wither. Already he has begun to waste. My brother is not a merciful sort. He has a hunger that cannot be sated. He loves playing games.*

Boots dragged against the floor. Fingernails scrabbled. Unfolding from his heap, Whitehall rose to his feet. In what little light emanated from the pulsing rift before them, she saw the slack lines of her professor's face, the unblinking dark of his eyes. His arms hung limp at his sides. His mouth opened and shut, opened and shut, as if the thing inside him was trying him on for size, testing out its new range of motion.

And now—now—a new voice joined the other. Where the presence within her felt like water bubbling over stone, this one was different, its edges serrated. Like a primordial snarl. Like something rising up from the deep. Something not meant to be heard by mortal ears.

But then, her ears had never worked.

"Kin," it said, in the same voice that had spoken to her in Whitehall's studio. "I am having a wonderful time among men. Have you really come to fetch me so soon?"

"Yes," she heard herself say, though she hadn't meant to. "It is time for us to go."

Then, reaching for the shard of bone in her pocket, she cried out, "Wait."

There is no time. The boy is coming.

"Wait," Delaney said again, more insistent this time than before. All around them, the shadows fell terribly, resolutely still. Only the crackle of flames remained, the smoke filling and filling her lungs. Sweat ran down her skin in slick, silvery tracks. In her left hand, the bone was a blade, digging sharp. In her right, the penny warmed against her skin. She shut her eyes. She hoped she wasn't making a mistake.

Softly, she said, "I need you to do something for me first."

❧ 53 ❧

They stood face-to-face. Whitehall and Lane. Lane and Whitehall. The rift in the ether hovered just behind them, a flat mirror opening thin enough to be invisible to the untrained eye. All around them was smoke, thick and bitter. Flames licked at the wall of names. Engulfed the salmon-colored couch in a fiery roar. Devoured the books, pages burning up into crisps that danced on the air.

And in the midst of it all, Whitehall and Lane were speaking in tongues.

In the doorway, Colton Price stood as still as Perseus and listened to the words spill out of Lane. Old words. Dead words. He could feel her fingerprints along the bend in his ribs. The soft prod of her touch. The delicate press of her thumb. Her hand was in her pocket, turning, turning, turning a piece of him like a talisman. The feel of it shuddered through him—a salve upon his soul, where in the wrong hands it had been a shame. A poultice, in place of a perversion.

In front of her, Whitehall looked halfway in the grave already. Colton had seen the dull pall of those eyes before. He recognized it at once. It was the same deathless thing that had burrowed a hole in Nate Schiller. In the others. Brothers of the Priory who thought Whitehall was going to teach them how to live forever.

Boys who'd died for a broken cause.

He wanted to run to Lane. To shake her awake. To summon every word and turn of phrase he knew. To banish the thing inside her and send it back where it belonged. Where he belonged. Among the dead. Away from the living.

Death had tried to claim him, once before. Maybe, if he'd let it, things would have been set right. Maybe, if he hadn't cheated Hell, Lane would have been left well enough alone.

Lane.

She looked like a saint, her hair spilling around her in spools of white, her face transcendent, her hands upturned. Weightless, as if she might levitate off the ground at any moment. A holy, hopeless thing. Everything that had happened to her was his fault, his doing.

All because he couldn't keep away.

"Lane," he said. He hadn't meant to. He couldn't help it. Once, he'd promised himself he would never say her name aloud again. Now it was the only shred of coherence he had remaining. "Lane," he called again, loud enough to be a shout. The sound came out muffled. Wind-snatched, though there was no wind.

Her head picked up.

Her eyes met his. Her stare was blown black and otherworldly.

"Demon," she said, and her voice was not hers, but something cold and slithering. Something he'd spent countless hours beseeching in the night. "She has already made her bargain."

"I don't care," he spat. "Unmake it."

The thing inside her blinked. A slow, inhuman shuttering of the eyes that chilled his blood. Tucked out of sight, the bone shard spun and spun against her palm. "She has left you a message."

"What message?" The room around him burned. His lungs were

stuffed with smoke. His skin was lit was cinders. He didn't care. "*What message?*"

The air thinned. The door drew closed. Half swallowed up in it, Delaney Meyers-Petrov glanced back at him. The voice that rang out of her was low and deep. "Find her where the asphodels grow."

❧ 54 ❧

I t was time. Time for goodbyes. Time for endings.

It would hate to leave the girl. It saw, after so many man-made weeks nestled in the ridges of her bones, why the dead followed her. Why the demon-boy clung to her. There was a warmth in her. A kindness that was overly sweet. The sort that soured the jaw to taste.

There was a quiet in her, too. Still as the mirror hush of a lake. Peaceful and strange. It was not used to such silence. To such repose. It looked to the man across the way—the man with eyes of the brethren. The man whose dead heart was held up only now by string. Still warm, but slowly fraying.

"You have remained too long among men, brother," it said.

"I had something to do. A lesson to teach."

"And have you seen it to its end?"

A smile spread, slowly unfurling. "I have. This man sought to yoke us for his purposes. I showed him that he could not."

"Then it is done. It is time to come home."

They kept the dominion of the dead, not the living. This girl would eventually tear beneath the strain of holding something infinite inside her. She'd rip like paper. It didn't want that.

It didn't want to make it slow. To prolong the inevitable.

It would, it had come to realize, feel something when Delaney Meyers-Petrov died.

And she would.

Die.

There was no other way.

Humans were not built to last forever. They were creatures made for entropy. Made to burn up and fizzle out like a flame. Dust to dust. At least it could make hers a peaceful sleep. No suffering. Not the way the others suffered.

And, anyway, she'd asked for this.

She held, in her hands, a piece of the underworld. An obol for the gods. The rules were rules, older than time and unchangeable. It would grant her passage. It would permit her one last request.

In the open door, the demon crept closer. The dead followed him like nervous dogs. Hiding behind him. It wondered if the boy knew he was something imperial. A half man, with Hell in his veins, fit for lording over the dead. One day, perhaps, he too would keep dominion alongside them.

Strange.

But it had seen stranger, in its eons on this stone.

The door was weakening. Withering. It was time. Time to shut the way to men. Time to leave the space between worlds in the keeping of the dead.

It took a breath—a supremely human thing to do, but the girl had worn on it. The breathing had become something sweet, the way the rest of her was sweet.

It closed its eyes.

It ripped the girl apart.

It felt very sorry to do so. But there was no other way.

The dead screamed.

And so, too, did the demon.

All the world winnowed to a still.

And then, at long last, there was quiet.

❦ 55 ❧

Delaney Meyers-Petrov was not made of glass. She was made from carbon and atoms. From skin and from bones. From something much too deep and much too quiet to name. She was pressed and pressed and pressed. She shone like adamant.

She was sitting on the edge of a pond. The air was cold, but she didn't feel it on her skin. She only glimmered, refracted like ice, like the polyhedral planes of a diamond cut to a sheen. Like something other. The water was flat and white, the surface frozen solid, save for a single dark pool atop a break in the ice. Fingers of blue bisected the rim in angry cracks, as if something had gone through and not resurfaced. A bubble rose. Another. The little muddy pool lapped at the ice.

Behind her, fat conifers rose up in sheaves of darkest green, branches bowed beneath thinning mantles of slow-melting snow. It drip-drop-dripped in crystalline flashes, like falling jewels in the ambiguous light. Overhead, the sky was the color of slate, the sun only a suggestion, an imprint, a memory, not quite correct.

It looked, some part of her realized, like the pond near her house, where her parents used to take her to skip stones. They'd spread out a blanket on the beach and her mother would set out an array of treats. Fat green grapes and baby carrots as long as her fingers, cucumber sandwiches cut into triangles, hefts of raisin-stuffed bread from the bakery, apple juice with a bendable straw. This memory, too, seemed like something faraway. Something she'd cobbled together.

And, anyway, this beach was not a beach at all, but a field. No sand, no mud, only flowers. White and brittle, the prettily spiked stalks bent under an unfelt wind. She knew their name, though she'd never seen them grown before. She could taste the word in her mouth.

Asphodels.

This was another memory, harder to reach. A mouth at her throat. A voice in her skin. A story—hers, or maybe someone else's—about a queen of the dead and a garland of white. The trees rustled, bending, whispering. Slowly, adamant fingers stiff, she fashioned herself a crown, lacing together the plucked stems in banded knots until they rested neatly end to end, the way she and her mother used to do with dandelions in the field behind their house.

She placed it upon her head.

Her mouth tasted like copper. She wondered, faintly, if perhaps she was dead.

Time passed. Time stood still. The trees whispered on without end.

She didn't know how long it was before she heard him.

"It was cold in the water." The voice came from all around her. From directly behind her. It eddied through the quiet of the field. She turned without standing, her waist girdled in blossoms of white, half buried in a grave of petals.

And there he stood. A boy she knew. Colton Price, as strong as the living. As bold as any memory. Behind her, that dark spot of water burbled again. She didn't look, and neither did he.

"It was even colder after," he said. "I sank like a stone to the muddy bottom, and then I woke up here. Trapped between worlds. Counting the minutes. Picking myself to pieces."

The dark line of trees stood still, like mourners beside a grave. The water lapped and murmured. She saw him swallow.

"Until you," he said.

The lines of him seemed supremely human, but there was something incongruous in the way the light was refracted off his features. Something that flickered just beyond the reach of her vision. His teeth seemed too sharp, the whites of his eyes swallowed in black. She felt as if maybe she should be afraid, but she was only buoyant. Only content. Armored in asphodels. Cradled in cold.

Colton surrendered a step, and the field of flowers shied away beneath him. "I begged," he said. "I crawled. I dragged myself through the dark until the dark gave way. And then I opened my eyes and you were there." His ankles were ringed in white. His laugh was the breath of wind through the trees. He opened up his hand to her and there, in the center of his palm, was a single flat pebble. "You were all done up in colors. You had braids in your hair."

"I remember." Her teeth clinked against something hard and round, tucked up into her cheek. Her voice slipped out from the trees, and not from her chest. As if she were already a part of this strange, unmoving place.

"You left me a message," he said. "You didn't need to." His veins traced through him in deep skeins of black. The snow dripped and dripped and dripped in radiant dazzles. "I will never not find you, Delaney. I can't help it. I follow where you lead."

He was in front of her, now. He was dropping to his knees. The flowers bowed low, as if before a king. He took her chin in his hand and pressed, drawing open her mouth. A penny slid out into his palm, the copper obol sparking in the light. His fist closed over the coin and he leaned in close, pressing his brow to hers. She stayed resolutely still, swallowing down his breaths.

"What are you," she asked, the way she had in the elevator, bathed in a well of dark the color of blood. Then, he hadn't answered her. This time, he smiled.

"Yours."

His incisors sharpened to points. At his brow were twin crests of severed bone. He'd never looked more like himself than in this singular moment.

"I brought you something," she said.

"Did you?"

She reached into the pocket of her skirt and withdrew the shard. Pale white and shell smooth; she cupped it between them like something coveted. The trees rustled, murmuring. The earth felt hungry.

Behind them, the struggle continued. Water lapped wetly at the ice. He didn't look. He didn't look, but there was turmoil in the bottomless brown of his gaze.

"There's a little boy in the water," she said.

His brows pinched together. "I know."

"Is that what you left behind?"

He didn't answer, and she didn't expect him to. He'd always been careful with the pieces of himself. Mindful not to let them show. She didn't need to see all of him to know that certain parts were out of reach, their shine rubbed off.

Leaning forward, she scooped a cupful of dirt into her hand. Another. Another. The trees rattled, branches bent. Colton watched her without moving, without breathing, his shoulders bowed, his hands in his lap. Listening to that ceaseless slap of water against the shore.

When she'd dug a sufficient furrow in the earth, she set the bone neatly into it. Carefully, she scooped the soil back over the top. A burial, for a boy who'd never been mourned. For a son who no one remembered. She'd learned, early on in life, that not all losses looked like death. Some losses were quiet. They made no sound. They slipped by unnoticed, impossible to grieve.

Gently, she patted the last of the sweet-smelling earth into place.

The rush of trees fell quiet. In the water, that horrible stirring went still. The pond's inky surface turned back to glass, reflecting the diamond-white sky in a dizzying palindrome. In front of her, something warm and bright swam into Colton's eyes. Raising his hand, he touched a finger to the petals at her brow.

"You look like a queen."

"Maybe I am."

His smile grew. "Get up, Delaney," he said, in a voice that quieted all the rest. "It's time to come back home."

❧ 56 ❧

D elaney woke to silence, as she usually did. She woke to sunlight,
as she usually did.

She woke in a hospital bed.

Her parents were there, Mia lost in a fitful sleep in the chair beside
the window, Jace in a chair by the narrow bed, a beanie crushed low
on his brow, his head resting on folded arms. His eyes lit up when he
felt her stir. His joy was a vibrant, silent thing, his words uncaught in
the stream. He kissed her hand, smoothed back her hair, roused her
mother. He spoke and signed and summoned for the doctors.

There was an endless flurry of doctors. Blood drawn and tests
done and sleep, so much sleep, medicated and heavy and inescapable.
The palms of her hands were burned, as if she'd stuck them into a
fire. She'd cracked her head on the cool concrete of the Sanctum and
suffered a concussion as a result. Her arm was broken in three different places. One side of her face was a scrape. It was, the doctors said,
as if she'd been dragged some great distance.

Richard Whitehall, she was told, was dead.

Godbole's experimental program was closed, pending an investigation, and the students had been put on leave until academic
reassignment was possible. She didn't know much else. The days went
and went and went and she dreamt and dreamt and dreamt. Of a
little frozen pond, of a dark-eyed prince, of a crown of asphodels.

Adya and Mackenzie came and went, sneaking in coffee, bringing by books, surfing through the limited channel selection on the

television until the sun sank low and the nurses stopped by to send them home.

Every day, she looked for him. For Colton Price, standing in her door. For the arrogant shrug of his shoulders, the gold flash of his watch, the careful knife of his smile. Each day, the sun rose and then fell without word.

"He's different," Mackenzie told her, peeling open the untouched cup of Delaney's applesauce. "Quieter."

On the television, a hospital drama played out in hues of blue. "How do you mean?"

"Whatever happened to the two of you in the Sanctum changed him somehow." On the tray between them sat three tarot cards, edged in gold. The high priestess, the lovers. A skeleton astride a white horse, bones robed in red. "It's like it took a piece of him. I can't even get a read on him anymore. There's no aura. There's no energy. There's nothing inside but silence."

Flowers arrived. One after the other, without cards and without comment and without end. They came in vases and in paper wrappings, in fat silken bows and glittering twine and explosions of colors. She was surrounded, daily, by great glass ewers of roses and crocks of lilies, carnations and gerbera daisies and sweet-smelling carnations.

And then, one day, a single asphodel.

She stared and stared at it, twisting it round in her fingers. She thought of a demon with the face of man, a boy turned god, a wide, flat field of asphodels. She closed her eyes and tended to the hollow in her chest until, unable to fight the trazodone lull of sleep, she finally dozed, white petals crushed in her palm.

For the first time in a long time, she slept without dreaming.

❧ 57 ❧

Nathaniel Schiller was laid to rest on a Thursday. The day was bright and cold. The earth was blanketed in a fresh-fallen snow. Delaney stood outside the columbarium where his family gathered and watched them say their goodbyes. His mother was a tiny spot of black against a green wall of arborvitae, her spine straight, her heart in her hands. Delaney couldn't hear the minister from her position, but then she'd never been one to draw much meaning from sound, and so she lingered through the silent service and said a silent goodbye, her heart threaded tight enough to hurt.

Once, out of the corner of her eye, she thought she saw a flash of dark beneath the snowy sheaves of a nearby elm. But when she looked there was nothing. Only a deep set of footprints, disappearing over the embankment.

When it was over, Delaney picked her way through the ankle-deep snow and back toward the shoveled walk, passing by winter-furred graves strewn with flowers. She didn't head toward her car. Instead, she continued on, her nylons wet and her toes numb with cold. She knew just where she was going—where she'd gone nearly every day since her doctor deemed her fit for discharge.

Liam Price's grave wasn't far. Around the bend. Along the crest of a hill. Beneath the fat, red berries of a dripping yew. Usually, she stood alone and listened to the winter trill of cardinals, the distant peal of a churchyard bell. Wrapped tight in her coat, leaving flowers in the snow. Alone.

Today, someone was else already there.

She saw him before he saw her, his collar pulled up around his throat, his overcoat caught in a gust of wind. From this distance, he looked every bit like the Colton she remembered, all flat planes and bladed edges and so perfectly human it hurt her chest.

He didn't look at her as she approached, though she could tell he sensed her. She kept her distance, heels clattering to a stop a few feet away. For several moments, they stood in total silence. Neither of them speaking, both of them watching. A perfect mirror of the way they began, buried in the sleepy quiet of the lecture hall, her heart in her throat and a coffee cooling on his desk.

She'd fallen in love with him in the quiet. Now, in silence, she loved him still.

She studied his profile. He studied the sky. His breathing looked strained, as though he were trying to remind himself to do it, the way Nate Schiller had once pretended to blink.

"Thank you for the flowers," she said when it was clear he didn't intend to speak. "All of them. Even the roses."

He stayed quiet.

"The asphodel was my favorite."

Again, he said nothing.

"I've been coming here every day, hoping maybe one day you'd be here." Her voice cast out between them, her echo muffled by the fallen snow. The wind picked up, ruffling his curls, and he shut his eyes. "I feel different," she said. "Ever since you brought me back. Like there's some small piece of me that's been scooped out."

He spoke then, and it felt like a mercy. "That feeling will ease in time."

"Has it eased for you?"

He glanced over at her, and she saw that black, interminable thing in his eyes. Slowly, he said, "Not this time."

She surrendered a step toward him, and he tensed. The sight of it drew her to a stop. Her fingertips felt impossibly cold, even in gloves. "That first night I came to your house," she said, desperate to hold him there with her. "I told you to let me in, and you opened the door so fast I thought it might splinter."

His throat worked in a swallow. "Yes."

"And then in the airport," she began, "with your watch—"

"Yes," he said again, before she'd finished.

"I didn't even say it yet."

"It doesn't matter," he said. "The answer to your question is yes. Yes, and yes, and yes."

She asked it anyway. "Do you have a choice? When I tell you to do something?"

Colton watched the sky, his head tipped back, his scarf unspooling. The sun was ringed in a corona of ice, the air thick with the promise of more snow. With no small amount of derision, he said, "Free will is a human trait."

"Oh." Delaney thought of the weight of bone in her hand. The way he'd told her Whitehall couldn't control him anymore. "But you're not beholden to just anyone. Only me."

"Only?" The sound that came out of him was a scoff. He still hadn't looked at her. "You have dominion over the dead, Delaney."

She bit back a smile, relieved by the small crest of his belligerence. By the feel of something familiar, surfacing through still waters. She drew nearer, willing him to look her way. "Mackenzie told me you paid Nate's funeral expenses."

Those black eyes shot to her, surprised. "Anonymously," he said, a touch too darkly.

"Don't be offended. Mackenzie knows everyone's business. She can't help herself."

He pushed out a single, solid breath. "Lane—"

She didn't let him finish. "I love you."

He stilled, every bit of him hewn from stone, and she pushed toward him. The way was uneven, and she scrabbled over slick patches of ice, waded through inches and inches of cold. Past the yew tree, with its fat berries cased in ice like glass, past the red, red cardinal fluffing its wings in the branches, past the fallen petals in the snow, until she reached him, solid as an effigy, quiet as the grave. Rising onto her toes, she slid her hands up over his chest and pressed a kiss to the pinched-white corner of his mouth.

"I'm in love with you, Colton Price," she said again, in case he needed reminding. "Not only that—I am deeply, sickeningly, alarmingly obsessed with you."

He didn't laugh. Instead, he caught her to him with the crook of an arm. His lips found her brow. His eyes fluttered shut. He didn't breathe.

"What did it cost you?" she asked. "Bringing me back like that?"

"Nothing," he lied. Beneath her gloves, his heart beat much too slow.

"Something. You feel different than before."

His eyes opened. His stare was dark as a void. "It aches," he admitted. "Staying here. I feel like I'm being pulled away a little bit at a time."

She thought of what he'd said to her, caught up in the flurrying dark of the pop-up market.

"I want to be someone whole."

Twice now, he'd carved himself all to pieces. Once, as a little boy, to save himself. The second time, to save her. Part of him would always be caught in the place between, one foot among the living and one among the dead. The way she was caught between silence and sound. Liminal places, both of them. Cleaved in two. Maybe there was solace to be found in their fractures. Maybe they'd fit together that way.

"And will you go where it's pulling you?" she asked.

His black stare held hers in thrall. "Do you want me to?"

"No," she said, and she'd never meant anything more. "But I'm not going to be the one to tell you to stay. I want you to do what you want. I want you to go where you feel drawn."

He touched his nose to hers. "I feel drawn to you."

The first flake fluttered between them, lancing downward in an elegant spiral. Another followed. Then five. Then ten. Then too many to count. The world was rendered white, the flat sun stifled beneath the wide canvas of a winter squall. Reaching for his free hand, Delaney laced their fingers all together.

"So then tell me," she said, "where should we go?"

The ruined line of his mouth sharpened into a smile. Stepping through the snow, he tugged her after him toward the little winding road. "Let's go home and see Gregor."

"I ruined Gregor," she said. "Remember?"

His smile didn't fade. His grip didn't falter. "That's okay," he said. "We'll just have to start again."

Unconscionable Love,
To what extremes will you not drive our hearts!
Virgil, *The Aeneid*

Acknowledgments

Growing up, I searched high and low for a fantasy with a main character who perceived the world the way I did. Because of that, this story feels a little bit like it's been a lifetime in the making. The list of people I have to thank would require an entire novel of their own, but I'll do my best to fit them all in here.

First and foremost, I want to thank my friends and family for their constant support over the years. I'm acutely aware of the fact that my inability to function is directly proportional to how close I've drawn to a deadline, and my community of friends are saints for continuing to put up with me and the generalized chaos that tends to follow in my wake.

To my husband—my partner in all things and my forever sounding board. A single paragraph isn't enough, so let me just say thank you for keeping me properly caffeinated and for always reminding me to do all the most basic things (like drink water and sleep and brush my hair) when I get too lost in the weeds of a story.

To my parents. Thank you for introducing me to books, and for all those nights spent reading aloud as I struggled to readjust to sound after five long years of silence. Most of all, thank for all that time you spent pretending you didn't hear the computer keys clicking away well past my bedtime. I learned how to write in those stolen hours, and I'm forever grateful.

To my brother. Thank you for being my movie buddy from day one. We've seen everything under the sun, and we've seen most of it together (even if I cried through all the scary bits). I don't think my head would be even half stuffed full of stories without you. You'll always be the first person I trust to read my ugly early drafts.

To my agent. Josh, thank you for taking a chance on Lane and Colton. I was so worried that this book might be too "out there," and you knew exactly what I was trying to do with it from the very first phone call. I am so grateful for all you've done to find my curious little story the perfect home.

To my editors. Mallory, thank you for all the hours spent letting me brainstorm at you over the phone, and for your masterful edit letters. Your guidance helped me shape the book into its final format. Rachel, thank you for believing in this story and for seeing its potential.

To Alex Kelleher-Nagorski and Daniela Escobar, thank you for all your enthusiasm and guidance every step of the way. To everyone on the sales, marketing, and publicity teams at both Scholastic and Gollancz, thank you for championing this book and helping it find its way into all the right hands. Jackie Dever, Emily Heddleson, Jessica White, Jackie Hornberger, and Janell Harris, thank you for your attention to detail and your patience in copy edits and proofreads. Maeve Norton and Sasha Vinogradova, thank you for the absolutely breathtaking cover. It is beyond anything I ever imagined.

To my found family. Bekah and Kevin, thank you for the hours of childcare and all the coffees in the midst of deadline stress. Amanda, thank you for loving books as much as me and for always helping me celebrate each milestone along the way.

To my village. I've been extremely fortunate over the years to stumble into a sincerely amazing community of writers, and there's hardly enough room to thank every brilliant soul I've met while on this journey, but I'll try.

Zoulfa Katouh and Meryn Lobb, words will never convey how grateful I am for every single conversation we've had, both the inane and the heartfelt. You've been the greatest debut crew a girl could ask for. I'm so honored to be on this journey with you both.

Lindsay Bilgram, I will always credit Peter Pan with bringing us together. This industry is tough, and there are truly days I would have quit if it wasn't for your infectious energy and love of all things bookish.

Reba Adler, thank you for letting me pepper you with out-of-context Lane and Colton snippets for two long years without end, and for always being willing to go on a buddy reading spree with the weirdest books, no questions asked.

Brittany Kelley, thank you for the phone calls, the laughter, the tears, and the hours of mutual commiserating. I could not have survived this pandemic without you and that's a fact.

Clementine Fraser, thank you for being the biggest source of positivity and light, and for always making the world seem a little less scary with your wisdom.

Hafsah Faizal, thank you for the endless laughs and the constant encouragement. It's not every day you get to pester your favorite author into a beautiful friendship, and I'm so infinitely grateful that we've become agent siblings.

Lyndall Clipstone, thank you for all the late-night mom/writer chats and for sharing my taste in all the top-tier tropes.

Hannah Whitten, thank you for always understanding that "vibes only" is the most critical part of the process. Your encouragement and advice got me through some of the biggest career shifts of the last year and a half.

Thank you to my earliest readers and to all the friends I've made along the way. Anna Munger, Ashley Reisinger, Allison Saft, Aiden Thomas, Emily Miner, Aliyah Fong, Ava Reid, Alina Khawaja, De Elizabeth, Gina Urso, Jen Elrod, Brittney Arena, Abigail Carlson, Ani Paoletti, Shannon Murphy, Tiffany White, Jordan Gray, Mato J Steger, Michael Roberts, and Robin Woodward. All of you have been so instrumental in giving me the courage to bring this story to life, and I'm so grateful to each and every one of you.

Last but not least, thank you for picking up this book. It means the world to me to know that *The Whispering Dark* is out there in the hands of readers. I hope you enjoyed the story.

ABOUT THE AUTHOR

Kelly Andrew lost her hearing when she was four years old. She's been telling stories ever since. Kelly lives in New England with her husband, two daughters, and a persnickety Boston terrier. You can find her online at @KayAyDrew.